The French & Indian War Novels: 3

The French & Indian War Novels: 3

The Lords of the Wild
A Story of the Old New York Border

•

The Sun of Quebec
A Story of a Great Crisis

Joseph A. Altsheler

LEONAUR

The French & Indian War Novels: 3
The Lords of the Wild & The Sun of Quebec
by Joseph A. Altsheler

FIRST EDITION

Leonaur is an imprint of Oakpast Ltd

ISBN: 978-1-84677-590-1 (hardcover)
ISBN: 978-1-84677-589-5 (softcover)

http://www.leonaur.com

Publisher's Note

The views expressed in this book are not necessarily
those of the publisher.

Contents

THE FRENCH & INDIAN WAR NOVELS

The Lords of the Wild

A Story of the Old
New York Border

Foreword

The Lords of the Wild tells a complete story, but it is also a part of the French and Indian War Series, of which the predecessors were *The Hunters of the Hills*, *The Shadow of the North*, *The Rulers of the Lakes* and *The Masters of the Peaks*. Robert Lennox, Tayoga, Willet, St. Luc, Tandakora and all the principal characters of the earlier volumes reappear.

Characters in the French and Indian War Series

Robert Lennox	A lad of unknown origin
Tayoga	A young Onondaga warrior
David Willet	A hunter
Raymond Louis De St. Luc	A brilliant French officer
Aguste De Courcelles	A French officer
François De Jumonville	A French officer
Louis De Galisonnière	A young French officer
Jean De Mézy	A corrupt Frenchman
Armand Glandelet	A young Frenchman
Pierre Boucher	A bully and bravo
Philibert Drouillard	A French priest
The Marquis Duquesne	Governor-General of Canada
Marquis De Vaudreuil	Governor-General of Canada
François Bigot	Intendant of Canada
Marquis De Montcalm	French commander-in-chief
De Levis	A French general
Bourlamaque	A French general
Bougainville	A French general
Armand Dubois	A follower of St. Luc
M. De Chatillard	An old French Seigneur
Charles Langlade	A French partisan
The Dove	The Indian wife of Langlade
Tandakora	An Ojibway chief
Daganoweda	A young Mohawk chief

11

Hendrick	An old Mohawk chief
Braddock.	A British General
Abercrombie	A British general
Wolfe	A British general
Col. William Johnson	Anglo-American leader
Molly Brant	Col. Wm. Johnson's Indian wife
Joseph Brant	Young brother of Molly Brant; afterward the great Mohawk Chief Thayendanegea
Robert Dinwiddie	Lieutenant-Governor of Virginia
William Shirley	Governor of Massachusetts
Benjamin Franklin	Famous American patriot
James Colden	A young Philadelphia captain
William Wilton	A young Philadelphia lieutenant
Hugh Carson	A young Philadelphia lieutenant
Jacobus Huysman	An Albany burgher
Caterina	Jacobus Huysman's cook
Alexander Mclean	An Albany schoolmaster
Benjamin Hardy	A New York merchant
Johnathan Pillsbury	Clerk to Benjamin Hardy
Adrian Van Zoon	A New York merchant
The Slaver	A nameless rover
Achille Garay	A French spy
Alfred Grosvenor	A young English officer
James Cabell	A young Virginian
Walter Stuart	A young Virginian
Black Rifle	A famous "Indian fighter"
Elihu Strong	A Massachusetts colonel
Alan Hervey	A New York financier
Stuart Whyte	Captain of the British sloop Hawk
John Latham	Lieutenant of the British sloop Hawk
Edward Charteris	A young officer of the Royal Americans
Zebedee Crane	A young scout and forest runner
Robert Rogers	Famous Captain of American Rangers

CHAPTER 1

The Blue Bird

The tall youth, turning to the right, went down a gentle slope until he came to a little stream, where he knelt and drank. Despite his weariness, his thirst and his danger he noticed the silvery colour of the water, and its soft sighing sound, as it flowed over its pebbly bed, made a pleasant murmur in his ear. Robert Lennox always had an eye for the beautiful, and the flashing brook, in its setting of deep, intense forest green, soothed his senses, speaking to him of comfort and hope.

He drank again and then sat back among the bushes, still breathing heavily, but with much more freedom. The sharp pain left his chest, new strength began to flow into his muscles, and, as the body was renewed, so the spirit soared up and became sanguine once more. He put his ear to the earth and listened long, but heard nothing, save sounds natural to the wilderness, the rustling of leaves before the light wind, the whisper of the tiny current, and the occasional sweet note of a bird in brilliant dress, pluming itself on a bough in its pride. He drew fresh courage from the peace of the woods, and resolved to remain longer there by the stream. Settling himself into the bushes and tall grass, until he was hidden from all but a trained gaze, he waited, body and soul alike growing steadily in vigour.

The forest was in its finest colours. Spring had never brought to it a more splendid robe, gorgeous and glowing, its green adorned with wild flowers, and the bloom of bush and tree like a gigantic stretch of tapestry. The great trunks of oak and elm and maple grew in endless rows and overhead the foliage gleamed, a veil of emerald lace before the sun.

Robert drank in the glory, eye and ear, but he never failed to watch the thickets, and to listen for hostile sounds. He knew full well that his life rested upon his vigilance and, often as he had been in danger in the great northern woods, he valued too much these precious days of his youth to risk their sudden end through any neglect of his own.

He looked now and then at the bird which still preened itself on a little bough. When the shadows from the waving foliage fell upon its feathers it showed a bright purple, but when the sunlight poured through, it glowed a glossy blue. He did not know its name, but it was a brave bird, a gay bird. Now and then it ceased its hopping back and forth, raised its head and sent forth a deep, sweet, thrilling note, amazing in volume to come from so small a body. Had he dared to make a sound Robert would have whistled a bar or two in reply. The bird was a friend to one alone and in need, and its dauntless melody made his own heart beat higher. If a creature so tiny was not afraid in the wilderness why should he be!

He had learned to take sharp notice of everything. On the border and in such times, man was compelled to observe with eye and ear, with all the five senses; and often too with a sixth sense, an intuition, an outgrowth of the other five, developed by long habit and training, which the best of the rangers possessed to a high degree, and in which the lad was not lacking. He knew that the minutest trifle must not escape his attention, or the forfeit might be his life.

While he relaxed his own care not at all, he felt that the bird was a wary sentinel for him. He knew that if an enemy came in haste through the undergrowth it would fly away before him. He had been warned in that manner in another crisis and he had full faith now in the caution of the valiant little singer. His trust, in truth, was so great that he rose from his covert and bent down for a third drink of the clear cool water. Then he stood up, his figure defiant, and took long, deep breaths, his heart now beating smoothly and easily, as if it had been put to no painful test. Still no sound of a foe, and he thought that perhaps the pursuit had died down, but he knew enough of the warriors of the woods to make sure, before he resumed a flight that would expose him in the open.

He crept back into the thicket, burying himself deep, and was careful not to break a twig or brush a leaf which to the unerring eyes of those who followed could mark where he was. Hidden well, but yet lying where he could see, he turned his gaze back to the bird. It was now pouring out an unbroken volume of song as it swayed on a twig, like a leaf shaken in the wind. Its voice was thrillingly sweet, and it seemed mad with joy, as its tiny throat swelled with the burden of its melody. Robert, in the thicket, smiled, because he too shared in so much gladness.

14

A faint sound out of the far west came to him. It was so slight that it was hard to tell it from the whisper of the wind. It barely registered on the drum of the ear, but when he listened again and with all his powers he was sure that it was a new and foreign note. Then he separated it from the breeze among the leaves, and it seemed to him to contain a quality like that of the human voice. If so, it might be hostile, because his friends, Willet, the hunter, and Tayoga, the Onondaga, were many miles away. He had left them on the shore of the lake, called by the whites, George, but more musically by the Indians, Andiatarocte, and there was nothing in their plans that would now bring them his way. However welcome they might be he could not hope for them; foes only were to be expected.

The faint cry, scarcely more than a variation of the wind, registered again though lightly on the drum of his ear, and now he knew that it came from the lungs of man, man the pursuer, man the slayer, and so, in this case, the red man, perhaps Tandakora, the fierce Ojibway chief himself. Doubtless it was a signal, one band calling to another, and he listened anxiously for the reply, but he did not hear it, the point from which it was sent being too remote, and he settled back into his bed of bushes and grass, resolved to keep quite still until he could make up his mind about the next step. On the border as well as elsewhere it was always wise, when one did not know what to do, to do nothing.

But the tall youth was keenly apprehensive. The signals indicated that the pursuing force had spread out, and it might enclose him in a fatal circle. His eager temperament, always sensitive to impressions, was kindled into fire, and his imagination painted the whole forest scene in the most vivid colours. A thought at first, it now became a conviction with him that Tandakora led the pursuit. The red leader had come upon his trail in some way, and, venomous from so many failures, would follow now for days in an effort to take him. He saw the huge Ojibway again with all the intensity of reality, his malignant face, his mighty body, naked to the waist and painted in hideous designs. He saw too the warriors who were with him, many of them, and they were fully as eager and fierce as their chief.

But his imagination which was so vital a part of him did not paint evil and danger alone; it drew the good in colours no less deep and glowing. It saw himself refreshed, stronger of body and keener of mind than ever, escaping every wile and snare laid for his ruin. It saw him making a victorious flight through the forest, his arrival at the shining lake, and his reunion with Willet and Tayoga, those faithful friends of many a peril.

He knew that if he waited long enough he would hear the Indian call once more, as the bands must talk to one another if they carried out a concerted pursuit, and he decided that when it came he would go. It would be his signal too. The only trouble lay in the fact that they might be too near when the cry was sent. Yet he must take the risk, and there was his sentinel bird still pluming itself in brilliant colours on its waving bough.

The bird sang anew, pouring forth a brilliant tune, and Robert from his covert smiled up at it again. It had a fine spirit, a gay spirit like his own and now it would surely warn him if danger crept too close. While the thought was fresh in his mind the third signal came, and now it was so clear and distinct that it indicated a rapid approach. But he was still unable to choose a way for his flight and he lingered for a sign from the bird. If the warriors were stealing through the bushes it would fly directly from them. At least he believed so, and fancy had so much power over him, especially in such a situation that belief became conviction.

The bird stopped singing suddenly, but kept his perch on the waving bough. Robert always insisted that it looked straight at him before it uttered two or three sharp notes, and then, rising in the air, hovered for a few minutes above the bough. It was obvious to him that his call had come. Steeped in Indian lore he had seen earth and air work miracles, and it was not less wonderful that a living creature should perform one now, and in his behalf.

For a breathless instant or two he forgot the warriors and watched the bird, a flash of blue flame against the green veil of the forest. It was perched there in order to be sure that he saw, and then it would show the way! With every pulse beating hard he stood up silently, his eyes still on the blue flash, confident that a new miracle was at hand.

The bird uttered three or four notes, not short or sharp now, but soft, long and beckoning, dying away in the gentlest of echoes. His imagination, as vivid as ever, translated it into a call to him to come, and he was not in the least surprised, when the blue flame like the pillow of cloud by day moved slowly to the northeast, and toward the lake. Stepping cautiously he followed his sign, thrilled at the doing of the miracle, his eyes on his flying guide, his ears attuned to warn him if any danger threatened from the forest so near.

It never occurred to Robert that he might not be led aright. His faith and confidence were supreme. He had lived too much with Tayoga not to share his belief that the hand of Manitou was stretched forth now to lead those who put their trust in him.

The blue flame that was a living bird flew slowly on, pausing an instant or two on a bough, turning for a short curve to right or left, but always coming back to the main course that pointed toward Andiatarocte.

He walked beside the little brook from which he had drunk, then across it and over a low hill, into a shallow valley, the forest everywhere, but the undergrowth not too dense for easy passage. His attentive ear brought no sound from either flank save those natural to the woods, though he was sure that a hostile call would come soon. It would be time for the bands to talk to one another. But he had no fear. The supreme intervention had been made in his favour, and he kept his eyes on his flying guide.

They crossed the valley and began the ascent of another and high hill, rough with rocky outcrops and a heavy growth of briars and vines. His pace became slower of necessity and once or twice he thought he had lost the blue flame, but it always reappeared, and, for the first time since its flight from the bough, it sang a few notes, a clear melodious treble, carrying far through the windy forest.

The lad believed that the song was meant for him. Clearly it said to him to follow, and, with equal clearness, it told him that safety lay only in the path he now travelled. He believed, with all the ardour of his soul, and there was no weariness in his body as he climbed the high hill. Near the summit, he heard on his right the long dying Indian cry so full of menace, its answer to the left, and then a third shout directly behind him. He understood. He was between the horns of a crescent, and they were not far away. He left faint traces only as he fled, but they had so much skill they could follow with speed, and he was quite sure they expected to take him. This belief did not keep his heart from beating high. They did not know how he was protected and led, and there was the blue flame before him always showing him the way. He reached the crest of the hill, and saw other hills, fold on fold, lying before him. He had hoped to catch a glimpse of the lake from the summit, but no glint of its waters came, and then he knew it must yet be miles away. His heart sank for a moment. Andiatarocte had appealed to him as a refuge. Just why he did not know, but he vaguely expected to find safety there. Perhaps he would meet Willet and Tayoga by its shore, and to him the three united always seemed invincible.

His courage was gone only an instant or two. Then it came back stronger than ever. The note of his guide, clear and uplifting, rose again, and he increased his speed, lest he be enclosed within those horns. The far slope was rocky and he leaped from one stony outcrop to another. Even if he could hide his trail only a few yards it would be so much time gained while they were compelled to seek it. He was forced to watch his steps here, but, when he was at the bottom and looked up, the blue flame was still before him. On it went over the next slope and he followed at speed, noticing with joy that the rocky nature of the ground continued, and the most skilful warrior who ever lived must spend many minutes hunting his traces. He had no doubt that he was gaining and he had proof of it in the fact that the pursuers now uttered no cry. Had they been closing in on him they would have called to one another in triumph.

Well for him that he was so strong and sound of heart and lung! Well for him too that he was borne up by a great spirit and by his belief that a supreme power was working in his behalf. He felt little weariness as he climbed a ridge. His breath was easy and regular and his steps were long and swift. His guide was before him. Whatever his pace, whether fast or slow, the distance between them never seemed to change. The bird would dart aside, perhaps to catch an insect, but it always returned promptly to its course.

His eyes caught a gleam of silver from the crest of the fourth ridge that he crossed, and he knew it was a ray of sunlight striking upon the waters of the lake. Now his coveted haven was not so far away, and the great pulses in his temples throbbed. He would reach the lake, and he would find refuge. Tandakora, in all his malice, would fail once more. The thought was so pleasant to him that he laughed aloud, and now feeling the need to use the strength he had saved with such care he began to run as fast as he could. It was his object to open up a wide gap between himself and the warriors, one so great that, if occasion came, he might double or turn without being seen.

The forest remained dense, a sea of trees with many bushes and cling-ing vines in which an ignorant or incautious runner would have tripped and fallen, but Robert was neither, and he did not forget, as he fled, to notice where his feet fell. His skill and presence of mind kept him from stumbling or from making any noise that would draw the attention of possible pursuers who might have crept up on his flank. While they had only his faint trail to guide them the pursuit was impeded, and, as long as they did not see him, his chance to hide was far greater.

He lost sight of his feathered guide two or three times, but the bird never failed to reappear, a brilliant blue flame against the green wall of the wilderness, his emblem of hope, leading him over the hills and valleys toward Andiatarocte. Now he saw the lake from a crest, not a mere band of silver showing through the trees, but a broad surface reflecting the sunlight in varied colours. It was a beacon to him, and, summoning the last ounce of his strength and will, he ran at amazing speed. Once more he heard the warriors behind him calling to one another, and they were much farther away. His mighty effort had not been in vain. His pulses beat hard with the throb of victory not yet won, but of which he felt sure, and he rejoiced too, because he had come again upon rocky ground, where his flight left so little trace that Tandakora himself would be baffled for a while.

He knew that the shores of the lake at the point he was nearing were comparatively low, and a vague plan to hide in the dense foliage at the water's edge came into his mind. He did not know just how he would do it, but he would be guided by events as they developed. The bird surely would not lead him on unless less to safety, and no doubt entered his mind. But it was highly important to widen yet more the distance between him and the warriors, and he still ran with all the speed at his command.

The last crest was reached and before him spread the splendid lake in its deep green setting, a glittering spectacle that he never failed to admire, and that he admired even now, when his life was in peril, and instants were precious. The bird perched suddenly on a bough, uttered a few thrilling notes, and was then gone, a last blue flash into the dense foliage. He did not see it again, and he did not expect to do so. Its work was done. Strong in the faith of the wilderness, he believed and always believed.

He crouched a few moments on a ledge and looked back. Tandakora and his men had not yet come in sight, nor could he hear them. Doubtless they had lost his trail, when he leaped from one stone to another, and were now looking for it. His time to hide, if he were to have one, was at hand, and he meant to make the most of the chance. He bent lower and remained there until his breathing became regular and easy after his mighty effort, all his five senses and the sixth that was instinct or divination, alert to every sound.

Two or three birds began to sing, but they were not his bird and he gave them no attention. A rabbit leaped from its nest under the bushes and ran. It went back on his trail and he considered it a sure sign that his pursuers were yet distant. He might steal another precious minute or two for his overworked lungs and heart. He knew the need of doing everything to gain a little more strength. It was his experience in border war and the stern training of Willet and Tayoga that made him able to do so, and he was ruler enough of himself to wait yet a little longer than he had planned. Then when he felt that Tandakora must be near, he straightened up, though not to his full height, and ran swiftly down the long slope to the lake.

He found at the bottom a narrow place between cliff and water, grown thickly with bushes, and he followed it at least half a mile, until the shores towered above him dark and steep, and the lake came up against them like a wall. He could go no farther and he waded into a dense growth of bushes and weeds, where he stood up to his waist in water and waited, hidden well.

He knew that if the warriors followed and saw him he would have little opportunity to escape, but the chances were a hundred to one against their finding him in such a covert. Rock and water had blotted out his trail and he felt safe. He secured his belt, containing his smaller weapons and ammunition, about his shoulders beyond touch of water, and put his rifle in the forks of two bushes, convenient to his hands.

It was a luxury to rest, even if one did stand half-sunken in a lake. The water was cold, but he did not yet feel the chill, and he listened for possible sounds of pursuit. He heard, after a while, the calls of warriors to one another and he laughed softly to himself. The shouts were faint and moreover they came from the crest of the cliff. They had not found his trail down the slope and they were hunting for him on the heights. He laughed again with sheer satisfaction. He had been right. Rock and water had come to his aid, and he was too well hidden even for the eager eyes of Tandakora and his warriors to follow him.

He waited a long time. He heard the cries nearer him, then farther away, and, at last, at such a great distance that they could barely be separated from the lap of the waters. He was growing cold now; the chill from the lake was rising in his body, but with infinite patience bred by long practice of the wilderness he did not stir. He knew that silence could be deceptive. Some of the warriors might come back, and might wait in a thicket, hoping that he would rise and disclose himself, thinking the danger past. More than one careless wanderer in the past had been caught in such a manner, and he was resolved to guard against the trick. Making the last call upon his patience, he stood motionless, while the chill crept steadily upward through his veins and muscles.

He could see the surface of the open lake through the veil of bushes and tall grass. The water broke in gentle waves under a light wind, and kept up a soft sighing that was musical and soothing. Had he been upon dry land he could have closed his eyes and gone to sleep, but, as it was, he did not complain, since he had found safety, if not comfort. He even found strength in himself, despite his situation, to admire the gleaming expanse of Andiatarocte with its shifting colours, and the far cliffs lofty and dim.

Much of Robert's life, much of its most eventful portion, was passing around this lake, and he had a peculiar affection for it. It always aroused in him a sense of beauty, of charm and of majesty, and he had grown too to look upon it as a friend and protector. He believed that it had brought him good luck, and he did not doubt that it would do so again.

He looked for a canoe, one perhaps that might contain Willet and Tayoga, seeking him and keeping well beyond the aim of a lurking marksman on the shore, but he saw no shadow on the water, nothing that could be persuaded into the likeness of a boat, only wild fowl circling and dipping, and, now and then, a gleam where a fish leaped up to fall swiftly back again. He was alone, and he must depend upon himself only.

He began to move a little, to lift one foot and then the other, careful to make no splash in the water, and the slight exercise checked the creeping chill. Encouraged, he increased it, stopping at intervals to listen for the approach of a foe. There was no sound and he walked back and forth a little. Presently his eyes, trained to observe all things, noticed a change in the air. A gray tint, so far a matter of quality rather than colour, was coming into it, and his heart leaped with joy. Absorbed in his vital struggle he had failed to reckon the passage of time. The day was closing and blessed, covering night was at hand. Robert loved the day and the sun, but darkness was always a friend of those who fled, and now he prayed that it would come thick and dark.

The sun still hung over the eastern shores, red and blazing, but before long it went down, seeming to sink into the lake, and the night that Robert had wished, heavy and black, swept over the earth. Then he left the water, and stood upon dry land, the narrow ledge between the cliff and the waves, where he took off his lower garments, wrung them as nearly dry as he could, and, hanging them on the bushes, waited for the wind to do the rest. His sense of triumph had never been so strong. Alone and relying only upon his own courage and skill, he had escaped the fierce Tandakora and his persistent warriors. He could even boast of it to Willet and Tayoga, when he found them again.

It was wonderful to feel safe, after great peril, and his bright imagination climbed the heights. As he had escaped them then, so he would slip always from the snares of his foes. It was this quality in him, the spirit of eternal hope, that appealed so strongly to all who knew him, and that made him so attractive.

After a while, he took venison and hominy from his knapsack and ate with content. Then he resumed his clothing, now dried completely by the wind, and felt that he had never been stronger or more fitted to cope with attack.

The darkness was intense and the surface of the lake showed through it, only a fitful gray. The cliff behind him was now a black bank, and its crest could not be seen at all. He was eager to go, but he still used the patience so necessary in the wilderness, knowing that the longer he waited the less likely he was to meet the band of Tandakora.

He lay down in a thicket of tall grass and bushes, resolved not to start before midnight, and he felt so much at peace that before he knew he was going to sleep he was sleeping. When he awoke he felt a little dismay at first, but it was soon gone. After all, he had passed the time of waiting in the easiest way, and no enemy had come. The moon and stars were not to be seen, but instinct told him that it was not beyond midnight.

He arose to go, but a slight sound came from the lake, and he stayed. It was merely the cry of the night bird, calling to its mate, one would have said, but Robert's attention was attracted by an odd inflection in it, a strain that seemed familiar. He listened with the utmost attention, and when it came a second time, he was so sure that his pulses beat very fast.

Willet and Tayoga, as he had hoped in the day, were out there on the lake. It had been foolish of him to think they would come in the full sunlight, exposed to every hostile eye. It was their natural course to approach in the dark and send a signal that he would know. He imitated the call, a soft, low note, but one that travelled far, and soon the answer came. No more was needed. The circle was complete. Willet and Tayoga were on the lake and they knew that he was at the foot of the cliff, waiting.

He took a long breath of intense relief and delight. Tandakora would resume the search for him in the morning, hunting along the crest, and he might even find his way to the narrow ledge on which Robert now stood, but the lad would be gone across the waters, where he left no trail.

He saw a stout young bush growing on the edge of the lake, and, leaning far out while he held on to it with one hand, he watched. He did not repeat the call. One less cautious would have done so, but he knew that his friends had located him already and he meant to run no risk of telling the warriors also where he stood. Meanwhile, he listened attentively for the sound of the paddles, but many long minutes passed before he heard the faint dip, dip that betokened the approach of Willet and Tayoga. He never doubted for an instant that it was their canoe and again his heart felt that triumphant feeling. Surely no man ever had more loyal or braver comrades! If he had malignant enemies he also had staunch friends who more than offset them.

He saw presently a faint shadow, a deeper dark in the darkness, and he uttered very low the soft note of the bird. In an instant came the answer, and then the shadow, turning, glided toward him. A canoe took form and shape and he saw in it two figures, which were unmistakably those of Willet and Tayoga, swinging their paddles with powerful hands. Again he felt a thrill of joy because these two trusty comrades had come. But it was absurd ever to doubt for an instant that they would come!

He leaned out from the tree to the last inch, and called in a penetrating whisper:

"Dave! Tayoga! This way!"

The canoe shifted its course a little, and entered the bushes by the side of Robert, the hunter and the Onondaga putting down their dripping paddles, and stepping out in the shallow water. In the dusk the great figure of Willet loomed up, more than ever a tower of strength, and the slender but muscular form of Tayoga, the very model of a young Indian warrior, seemed to be made of gleaming bronze. Had Robert needed any infusion of courage and will their appearance alone would have brought it with them.

"And we have found Dagaeoga again!" said the Onondaga, in a whimsical tone.

"No I have found you," said Robert. "You were lost from me, I was not lost from you."

"It is the same, and I think by your waiting here at midnight that you have been in great peril."

"So I have been, and I may be yet—and you too. I have been pursued by warriors, Tandakora at their head. I have not seen them, but I know from the venom and persistence of the pursuit that he leads them. I eluded them by coming down the cliff and hiding among the bushes here. I stood in the water all the afternoon."

"We thought you might be somewhere along the western shore. After we divided for our scout about the lake, the Great Bear and I met as we had arranged, but you did not come. We concluded that the enemy had got in the way, and so we took from its hiding place a canoe which had been left on a former journey, and began to cruise upon Andiatarocte, calling at far intervals for you."

He spoke in his usual precise school English and in a light playful tone, but Robert knew the depth of his feelings. The friendship of the white lad and the red was held by hooks of steel like that of Damon and Pythias of old.

"I think I heard your first call," said Robert. "It wasn't very loud,

23

but never was a sound more welcome, nor can I be too grateful for that habit you have of hiding canoes here and there in the wilderness. It's saved us all more than once."

"It is merely the custom of my people, forced upon us by need, and I but follow."

"It doesn't alter my gratitude. I see that the canoe is big enough for me too."

"So it is, Dagaeoga. You can enter it. Take my paddle and work."

The three adjusted their weight in the slender craft, and Robert, taking Willet's paddle instead of Tayoga's, they pushed out into the lake, while the great hunter sat with his long rifle across his knees, watching for the least sign that the warriors might be coming.

CHAPTER 2

The Live Canoe

Robert was fully aware that their peril was not yet over—the Indians, too, might have canoes upon the lake—but he considered that the bulk of it had passed. So his heart was light, and, as they shot out toward the middle of Andiatarocte, he talked of the pursuit and the manner in which he had escaped it.

"I was led the right way by a bird, one that sang," he said. "Your Manitou, Tayoga, sent that bird to save me."

"You don't really believe it came for that special purpose?" asked the hunter.

"Why not?" interrupted the Onondaga. "We do know that miracles are done often. My nation and all the nations of the Hodenosaunee have long known it. If Manitou wishes to stretch out his hand and snatch Dagaeoga from his foes it is not for us to ask his reason why."

Willet was silent. He would not say anything to disturb the belief of Tayoga, he was never one to attack anybody's religion, besides he was not sure that he did not believe, himself.

"We know too," continued Tayoga devoutly, "that Tododaho, the mighty Onondaga chief who went away to his star more than four hundred years ago, and who sits there watching over the Hodenosaunee has intervened more than once in our behalf. He is an arm of Manitou and acts for him."

He looked up. The sky was hidden by the thick darkness. No ray of silver or gray showed anywhere, but the Onondaga knew where lay the star upon which sat his patron saint with the wise snakes, coil on coil, in his hair. He felt that through the banks of mist and vapour Tododaho was watching over him, and, as long as he tried to live the right way taught to him by his fathers, the great Onondaga chieftain would lead him through all perils, even as the bird in brilliant blue plumage had shown Robert the path from the pursuit of Tandakora. The sublime faith of Tayoga never wavered for an instant.

The wind rose a little, a heavy swell stirred the lake and their light craft swayed with vigour, but the two youths were expert canoemen, none better in all the wilderness, and it shipped no water. The hunter, sitting with his hands on his rifle, did not stir, nor did he speak for a long time. Willet, at that moment, shared the faith of his two younger comrades. He was grateful too because once more they had found Robert, for whom he had all the affection of a father. The three reunited were far stronger than the three scattered, and he did not believe that any force on the lakes or in the mountains could trap them. But his questing eyes watched the vast oblong of the lake, looking continually for a sign, whether that of friend or foe.

"What did you find, Robert?" he asked at last.

"Nothing but the band of Tandakora," replied the lad, with a light laugh. "I took my way squarely into trouble, and then I had hard work taking it out again. I don't know what would have happened to me, if you two hadn't come in the canoe."

"It seems," said the Onondaga, in his whimsical precise manner, "that a large part of our lives, Great Bear, is spent in rescuing Dagaeoga. Do you think when we go into the Great Beyond and arrive at the feet of Manitou, and he asks us what we have done with our time on earth, he will put it to our credit when we reply that we consumed at least ten years saving Dagaeoga from his enemies?"

"Yes, Tayoga, we'll get white marks for it, because Robert has also saved us, and there is no nobler work than saving one's fellow creatures. Manitou knows also that it is hard to live in the wilderness and a man must spend a lot of time escaping death. Look to the east, Tayoga, lad, and tell me if you think that's a point of light on the mountain over there."

The Onondaga studied intently the dark wall of the east, and presently his eyes picked out a dot against its background, infinitesimal like the light of a firefly, but not to be ignored by expert woodsmen.

"Yes, Great Bear," he replied, "I see it is not larger than the littlest star, but it moves from side to side, and I think it is a signal."

"So do I, lad. The lake is narrow here, and the answer, if there be any, will come from the west shore. Now we'll look, all together. Three pairs of eyes are better than one."

The two lads ceased paddling, holding the canoe steady, with an occasional stroke, and began to search the western cliffs in methodical fashion, letting the eye travel from the farthest point in the north gradually toward the south, and neglecting no place in the dark expanse.

"There it is!" exclaimed Robert. "Almost opposite us! I believe it's in the very cliff at the point of which I lay!"

"See it, winking and blinking away."

"Yes, that's it," said Robert. "Now I wonder what those two lights are saying to each other across Lake George?"

"It might be worth one's while to know, for they're surely signalling. It may be about us, or it may be about the army in the south."

"I didn't find anything but trouble," said Robert. "Now what did you and Tayoga find?"

"Plenty traces of both white men and red," replied the hunter. "The forests were full of French and Indians. I think St. Luc with a powerful force is near the north end of Lake George, and the Marquis de Montcalm will soon be at Ticonderoga to meet us."

"But we'll sweep him away when our great army comes up from New York."

"So we should, lad, but the Marquis is an able general, wily and brave. He showed his quality at Fort William Henry and we mustn't underrate him, though I am afraid that's what we'll do; besides the forest fights for the defence."

"It's not like you to be despondent, Dave," said Robert.

"I'm not, lad. I've just a feeling that we should be mighty cautious. Some think the Marquis won't stand when our big army comes, but I do, and I look for a great battle on the shores of George or Champlain."

"And we'll win it," said Robert in sanguine tones.

"That rests on the knees of the gods," said Willet thoughtfully. "But we've got to deal with one thing at a time. It's our business now to escape from the people who are making those lights wink at each other, or the battle wherever it's fought or whoever wins won't include us because we'll be off on another star, maybe sitting at the feet of Tayoga's Tododaho."

"There's another light on the west shore toward the south," said the Onondaga.

"And a fourth on the eastern cliff also toward the south," added Robert. "All four of them are winking now. It seems to be a general conversation."

"And I wish we could understand their language," said the hunter earnestly. "I'm thinking, however, that they're talking about us. They must have found out in some manner that we're on the lake, and they want to take us."

"Then," said Robert, "it's time for Manitou to send a heavy mist that we may escape in it."

"Manitou can work miracles for those whom he favours," said Tayoga, "and now and then he sends them, but oftenest he withholds his hand, lest we become spoiled and rely upon him when we should rely upon ourselves."

"You never spoke a truer word, Tayoga," said the hunter. "It's the same as saying that heaven helps those who help themselves, and we've got to do a lot of work for ourselves this night. I think the Indian canoes are already on Andiatarocte looking for us."

Robert would have felt a chill had it not been for the presence of his comrades. The danger was unknown, mysterious, it might come from any point, and, while the foe prepared, they must wait until he disclosed himself. Waiting was the hardest thing to do.

"I think we'd better stay just where we are for a while," said the hunter. "It would be foolish to use our strength, until we know what we are using it for. It's certain that Manitou intends to let us fend for ourselves because the night is lightening, which is a hard thing for fugitives."

The clouds floated away toward the north, a star came out, then another, and then a cluster, the lofty shores on either side rose up clear and distinct, no longer vague black walls, the surface of the water turned to gray, but it was still swept by a heavy swell, in which the canoe rocked. Willet finally suggested that they pull to a small island lying on their right, and anchor in the heavy foliage overhanging the water.

"If it grows much lighter they'll be able to see us from the cliffs," he said, "and for us now situated as we are the most important of all things is to hide."

It was a tiny island, not more than a quarter of an acre in size, but it was covered with heavy forest, and they found refuge among the long boughs that touched the water, where they rested in silence, while more stars came out, throwing a silver radiance over the lake. The three were silent and Robert watched the western light that lay farthest south. It seemed to be about two miles away, and, as he looked he saw it grow, until he became convinced that it was no longer a light, but a fire.

"What is the meaning of it?" he asked, calling the attention of Willet.

The hunter looked for a while before replying. The fire still grew and soon a light on the eastern shore began to turn into a fire, increasing in the same manner.

"I take it that they intend to illuminate the lake, at least this portion of it," said Willet. "They'll have gigantic bonfires casting their light far over the water, and they think that we won't be able to hide then."

"Which proves that they are in great force on both shores," said Tayoga.

"How does it prove it?" asked Robert.

The Onondaga laughed softly.

"O Dagaeoga," he said, "you speak before you think. You are always thinking before you speak, but perhaps it is not your fault. Manitou gave you a tongue of gold, and it becomes a man to use that which he can use best. It is very simple. To drag up the fallen wood for such big fires takes many men. Nor would all of them be employed for such work. While some of them feed the flames others are seeking us. We can look for their canoes soon."

"Their plan isn't a bad one for what they want to do," said the hunter. "A master mind must be directing them. I am confirmed in my opinion that St. Luc is there."

"I've been sure of it all the time," said Robert; "it seems that fate intends us to be continually matching our wits against his."

"It's a fact, and it's strange how it's come about," said the hunter thoughtfully.

Robert looked at him, hoping he would say more, but he did not continue the subject. Instead he said:

"That they know what they're doing is shown by the fact that we must move. All the area of the lake about us will be lighted up soon."

The two bonfires were now lofty, blazing pyramids, and a third farther north began also to send its flames toward the sky.

The surface of the lake glowed with red light which crept steadily toward the little island, in the shadow of which the three scouts lay. It became apparent that they had no time to waste, if they intended to avoid being trapped.

"Push out," said Willet, and, with strong sweeps of the paddle, Robert and Tayoga sent the canoe from the shelter of the boughs. But they still kept close to the island and then made for another about a hundred yards south. The glow had not yet come near enough to disclose them, while they were in the open water, but Robert felt intense relief when they drew again into the shelter of trees.

The bonfire on the western shore was the largest, and, despite the distance, he saw passing before the flames tiny black figures which he knew to be warriors or French, if any white men were there. They were still feeding the fire and the pyramid of light rose to an extraordinary height, but Robert knew the peril was elsewhere. It would come on the surface of the lake and he shifted his gaze to the gray waters, searching everywhere for Indian canoes. He believed that they would appear first in the north and he scoured the horizon there from side to side, trying to detect the first black dot when it should show over the lake.

The waters where his eyes searched were wholly in darkness, an unbroken black line of the sky meeting a heaving surface. He looked back and forth over the whole extent, a half dozen times, and found nothing to break the continuity. Hope that the warriors of Tandakora were not coming sprang up in his breast, but he put it down again. Although imagination was so strong in him he was nevertheless, in moments of peril, a realist. Hard experience had taught him long since that when his life was in danger he must face facts.

"There's another island about a half mile away," he said to Willet. "Don't you think we'd better make for it now?"

"In a minute or two, lad, if nothing happens," replied the hunter. "I'd like to see what's coming here, if anything at all comes."

Robert turned his gaze back toward the north, passing his eyes once more to and fro along the line where the dusky sky met the dusky lake, and then he started a little. A dot detached itself from the centre of the line, followed quickly by another, another and others. They were points infinitely small, and one at that distance could have told nothing about them from their appearance only, but he knew they were Indian canoes. They could be nothing else. It was certain also that they were seeking the three.

"Do you see them?" asked Robert.

"Yes, and it's a fleet," replied Willet. "They are lighting up the lake with their bonfires, and their canoes are coming south to drive us into the open. There's generalship in this. I think St. Luc is surely in command."

The hunter expressed frank admiration. Often, in the long duel between them and the redoubtable French leader, he paid tribute to the valour and skill of St. Luc. Like Robert, he never felt any hostility toward him. There was nothing small about Willet, and he had abundant esteem for a gallant foe.

"It's time now to run for it again," he said, "and it's important to keep out of their sight."

"I think it will be better for us to swim," said Tayoga, "and let the canoe carry our weapons and ammunition."

"And for us to hide behind it as we've done before. You're right, lad. The canoe is low and does not make much of a blur upon the lake, but if we are sitting upright in it we can be much more easily seen. Now, quick's the word!"

They took off all their outer clothing and moccasins, putting the garments and their weapons into the little craft, and, sinking into the water behind it, pushed out from the overhanging boughs. It was a wise precaution. When they reached the long open stretch of water, Robert felt that the glow from the nearest bonfire was directly upon them, although he knew that his fancy made the light much stronger than it really was.

The canoe still merged with the colour of the waves which were now running freely, and, as the three swam with powerful strokes sending it swiftly ahead of them, Robert was hopeful that they would reach the next island, unseen.

The distance seemed to lengthen and grow interminable, and their pace, although rapid, was to Robert like that of a snail. Yet the longest journey must come to an end. The new island rose at last before them, larger than the others but like the rest covered throughout with heavy forest.

They were almost in its shelter, when a faint cry came from the lofty cliff on the west. It was a low, whining sound, very distant, but singularly penetrating, a sinister note with which Robert was familiar, the Indian war whoop. He recognized it, and understood its significance. Warriors had seen the canoe and knew that it marked the flight of the three.

"What do you think we'd better do?" he said.

"We'll stop for a moment or two at the island and take a look around us," replied Willet.

They moored the canoe, and waded to the shore. Far behind them was the Indian fleet, about twenty canoes, coming in the formation of an arrow, while the bonfires on the cliffs towered toward the sky. A rising wind swept the waves down and they crumbled one after another, as they broke upon the island.

"It looks like a trap with us inside of it," said the hunter. "That shout meant that they've seen our canoe, as you lads know. Warriors have already gone below to head us off, and maybe they've got another fleet, which, answering their signals, will come up from the south, shutting us between two forces."

"We are in their trap," admitted Robert, "but we can break out of it. We've been in traps before, but none of them ever held us."

"So we can, lad. I didn't mean to be discouraging. I was just stating the situation as it now is. We're a long way from being taken."

"The path has been opened to us," said the Onondaga.

"What do you mean?" asked Robert.

"Lo, Dagaeoga, the wind grows strong, and it sweeps toward the south the way we were going."

"I hear, Tayoga, but I don't understand."

"We will send the canoe with wind and waves, but we will stay here."

"Put 'em on a false scent!" exclaimed the hunter. "It's a big risk, but it's the only thing to be done. As the bird saved Robert so the wind may save us! The waves are running pretty fast toward the south now and the canoe will ride 'em like a thing of life. They're too far away to tell whether we are in it."

It was a daring thing to do but Robert too felt that it must be done, and they did not delay in the doing of it. They took out their clothing, weapons, and ammunition, Willet gave the canoe a mighty shove, and it sailed gallantly southward on the crest of the high waves.

"I feel as if I were saying good-by to a faithful friend," said Robert.

"It's more than a friend," said Willet. "It's an ally that will draw the enemy after it, and leave us here in safety."

"If Manitou so wills it," said Tayoga. "It is for him to say whether the men of Tandakora will pass us by. But the canoe is truly alive, Dagaeoga. It skims over the lake like a great bird. If it has a spirit in it, and I do not know that it has not, it guards us, and means to lead away our enemy in pursuit of it."

Quick to receive impressions, Robert also clothed the canoe with life and a soul, a soul wholly friendly to the three, who, now stooping down on the island, amid the foliage, watched the action of the little craft which seemed, in truth, to be guided by reason.

"Now it pauses a little," said Robert. "It's beckoning to the Indian fleet to follow."

"It is because it hangs on the top of a wave that is about to break," said Willet. "Often you see waves hesitate that way just before they crumble."

"I prefer to believe with Dagaeoga," said the Onondaga. "The canoe is our ally, and, knowing that we want the warriors to pass us, it lingers a bit to call them on."

"It may be as you say," said the hunter, "I'm not one to disturb the faith of anybody. If the canoe is alive, as you think, then—it is alive and all the better for us."

"Spirits go into the bodies of inanimate things," persisted the red youth, "and make them alive for a while. All the people of the Hodenosaunee have known that for centuries."

"The canoe hesitates and beckons again," said Robert, "and, as sure as we are here, the skies have turned somewhat darker. The warriors in the fleet or on the shore cannot possibly tell the canoe is empty."

"Again the hand of Manitou is stretched forth to protect us," said Tayoga devoutly. "It is he who sends the protecting veil, and we shall be saved."

"We'll have to wait and see whether the warriors stop and search our island or follow straight after the canoe. Then we'll know," said Willet.

"They will go on," said Tayoga, with great confidence. "Look at the canoe. It is not going so fast now. Why? Because it wishes to tantalize our enemies, to arouse in their minds a belief that they can overtake it. It behaves as if we were in it, and as if we were becoming exhausted by our great exertions with the paddles. Its conduct is just like that of a man who flees for his life. I know, although I cannot see their eyes, that the pursuing warriors think they have us now. They believe that our weakness will grow heavier and heavier upon us until it overpowers us. Tandakora reckons that our scalps are already hanging at his belt. Thus does Manitou make foolish those whom he intends to lead away from their dearest wish."

"I begin to think they're really going to leave us, but it's too early yet to tell definitely," said the hunter. "We shouldn't give them an earthly chance to see us, and, for that reason, we'd better retreat into the heart of the island. We mustn't leave all the work of deception to the canoe."

"The Great Bear is right," said Tayoga. "Manitou will not help those who sit still, relying wholly on him."

They drew back fifteen or twenty yards, and sat down on a hillock, covered with dense bushes, though from their place of hiding they could see the water on all sides. Unless the Indians landed on the island and made a thorough search they would not be found. Meanwhile the canoe was faithful to its trust. The strong wind out of the north carried it on with few moments of hesitation as it poised on breaking waves, its striking similitude to life never being lost for an instant. Robert began to believe with Tayoga that it was, in very fact and truth, alive and endowed with reason. Why not? The Iroquois believed that spirits could go into wood and who was he to argue that white men were right, and red men wrong? His life in the forest had proved to him often that red men were right and white men wrong.

Whoever might be right the canoe was still a tantalizing object to the pursuit. It may have been due to a slight shift of the wind, but it began suddenly to have the appearance of dancing upon the waves, swinging a little to and fro, teetering about, but in the main keeping its general course, straight ahead.

Tayoga laughed softly.

"The canoe is in a frolicsome mood," he said. "It has sport with the men of Tandakora. It dances, and it throws jests at them. It says, 'You think you can catch me, but you cannot. Why do you come so slowly? Why don't you hurry? I am here. See, I wait a little. I do not go as fast as I can, because I wish to give you a better chance.' Ah, here comes the fleet!'"

"And here comes our supreme test," said Willet gravely. "If they turn in toward the island then we are lost, and we'll know in five minutes."

Robert's heart missed a beat or two, and then settled back steadily. It was one thing to be captured by the French, and another to be taken by Tandakora. He resolved to fight to the last, rather than fall into the hands of the Ojibway chief who knew no mercy. Neither of the three spoke, not even in whispers, as they watched almost with suspended breath the progress of the fleet. The bonfires had never ceased to rise and expand. For a long distance the surface of the lake was lighted up brilliantly. The crests of the waves near them were tipped with red, as if with blood, and the strong wind moaned like the voice of evil. Robert felt a chill in his blood. He knew that the fate of his comrades and himself hung on a hair.

Nearer came the canoes, and, in the glare of the fires, they saw the occupants distinctly. In the first boat, a large one for those waters, containing six paddles, sat no less a person than the great Ojibway chief himself, bare as usual to the waist and painted in many a hideous design. Gigantic in reality, the gray night and the lurid light of the fires made him look larger, accentuating every wicked feature.

He seemed to Robert to be, in both spirit and body, the prince of darkness himself.

Just behind Tandakora sat two white men whom the three recognized as Auguste de Courcelles and François de Jumonville, the French officers with whom they had been compelled to reckon on other fields of battle and intrigue. There was no longer any doubt that the French were present in this great encircling movement, and Robert was stronger than ever in his belief that St. Luc had the supreme command.

"I could reach Tandakora from here with a bullet," whispered Willet, "and almost I am tempted to do it."

"But the Great Bear will not yield to his temptation," Tayoga whispered back. "There are two reasons. He knows that he could slay Tandakora, but it would mean the death of us all, and the price is too great. Then he remembers that the Ojibway chief is mine. It is for me to settle with him, in the last reckoning."

"Aye, lad, you're right. Either reason is good enough. We'll let him pass, if pass he means, and I hope devoutly that he does."

The fleet preserving its formation was now almost abreast of the island, and once Robert thought it was going to turn in toward them. The long boat of Tandakora wavered and the red giant looked at the island curiously, but, at the last moment the empty canoe, far ahead and dim in the dark, beckoned them on more insistently than ever.

"Now the die is cast," whispered the Onondaga tensely. "In twenty seconds we shall know our fate, and I think the good spirit that has gone into our canoe means to save us."

Tandakora said something to the French officers, and they too looked at the island, but the fleeing canoe danced on the crest of a high wave and its call was potent in the souls of white men and red alike. It was still too far away for them to tell that it was empty. Sudden fear assailed them in the darkness, that it would escape and with it the three who had eluded them so often, and whom they wanted most to take. Tandakora spoke sharply to the paddlers, who bent to their task with increased energy. The long canoe leaped forward, and with it the others.

"Manitou has stretched forth his hand once more, and he has stretched it between our enemies and us," said Tayoga, in a voice of deep emotion.

"It's so, lad," said the hunter, his own voice shaking a little. "I truly believe you're right when you say that as the bird was sent to save Robert so a good spirit was put into the canoe to save us all. Who am I and who is anybody to question the religion and beliefs of another man?"

"Nor will I question them," said Robert, with emphasis.

They were stalwart men in the Indian fleet, skilled and enduring with the paddle, and the fugitive canoe danced before them, a will o' the wisp that they must pursue without rest. Their own canoes leaped forward, and, as the arrow into which they were formed shot past the island, the three hidden in its heart drew the deep, long breaths of those who have suddenly passed from death to life.

"We won't stop 'em!" said Robert in a whimsical tone. "Speed ye, Tandakora, speed ye! Speed ye, De Courcelles and De Jumonville of treacherous memory! If you don't hasten, the flying canoe will yet escape you! More power to your arms, O ye paddlers! Bend to your strokes! The canoe that you pursue is light and it is carried in the heart of the wind! You have no time to lose, white men and red, if you would reach the precious prize! The faster you go the better you will like it! And the better we will, too! On! swift canoes, on!"

"The imagination of Dagaeoga has been kindled again," said Tayoga, "and the bird with a golden note has gone into his throat. Now he can talk, and talk much, without ever feeling weariness—as is his custom."

"At least I have something to talk about," laughed Robert. "I was never before so glad to see the backs of anybody, as I am now to look at the backs of those Indians and Frenchmen."

"We won't do anything to stop 'em," said the hunter.

From their hillock they saw the fleet sweep on at a great rate toward the south, while the fires in the north, no longer necessary to the Indian plan, began to die. The red tint on the water then faded, and the surface of the lake became a solemn gray.

"It's well for us those fires sank," said the hunter, "because while Tandakora has gone on we can't live all the rest of our lives on this little island. We've got to get to the mainland somehow without being seen."

"And darkness is our best friend," said Robert.

"So it is, and in their pursuit of the canoe our foes are likely to relax their vigilance on this part of the lake. Can you see our little boat now, Robert?"

"Just faintly, and I think it's a last glimpse. I hope the wind behind it will stay so strong that Tandakora will never overtake it. I should hate to think that a canoe that has been such a friend to us has been compelled to serve our enemies. There it goes, leading straight ahead, and now it's gone! Farewell, brave and loyal canoe! Now what do you intend to do, Dave?"

"Swim to the mainland as soon as those fires sink a little more. We have got to decide when the head of a swimming man won't show to chance warriors in the bushes, and then make a dash for it, because, if Tandakora overtakes the canoe, he'll be coming back."

"In a quarter of an hour it will be dark enough for us to risk it," said the Onondaga.

Again came the thick dusk so necessary to those who flee for life. Two fires on the high cliffs blazed far in the south, but the light from them did not reach the island where the three lay, where peril had grazed them before going on. The water all about them and the nearer shores lay in shadow.

"The time to go has come," said the hunter. "We'll swim to the western side and climb through that dip between the high cliffs."

"How far would you say it is?" asked Robert.

"About a half mile."

"Quite a swim even for as good swimmers as we are, when you consider we have to carry our equipment. Why not launch one of those fallen trees that lie near the water's edge and make it carry us?"

"A good idea, Robert! A happy thought does come now and then into that young head of yours."

"Dagaeoga is wiser than he looks," said the Onondaga.

"I wish I could say the same for you, Tayoga," retorted young Lennox.

"Oh, you'll both learn," laughed Willet.

As in the ancient wood everywhere, there were fallen trees on the island and they rolled a small one about six inches through at the stem into the lake. They chose it because it had not been down long and yet had many living branches, some with young leaves on them.

"There is enough foliage left to hide our heads and shoulders," said Willet. "The tree will serve a double purpose. It's our ship and also our refuge."

They took off all their clothing and fastened it and the arms, ammunition and knapsacks of food on the tree. Then, they pushed off, with a caution from the hunter that they must not allow their improvised raft to turn in the water, as the wetting of the ammunition could easily prove fatal.

With a prayer that fortune which had favoured them so much thus far would still prove kind, they struck out.

CHAPTER 3

In the Cliff

It was only a half mile to the promised land and Robert expected a quick and easy voyage, as they were powerful swimmers and could push the tree before them without trouble.

"When I reach the shore and get well back of the lake," he said to Tayoga, "I mean to lie down in a thicket and sleep forty-eight hours. I am entitled now to a rest that long."

"Dagaeoga will sleep when the spirits of earth and air decree it, and not before," replied the Onondaga gravely. "Can you see anything of our foes in the south?"

"Not a trace."

"Then your eyes are not as good as mine or you do not use them as well, because I see a speck on the water blacker than the surface of the lake, and it is moving."

"Where, Tayoga?"

"Look toward the eastern shore, where the cliff rises tall and almost straight."

"Ah, I see it now. It *is* a canoe, and it *is* moving."

"So it is, Dagaeoga, and it is coming our way. Did I not tell you that Manitou, no matter how much he favours us, will not help us all the time? Not even the great and pious Tododaho, when he was on earth, expected so much. Now I think that after saving you with the bird and all of us with the empty canoe he means to leave us to our own strength and courage, and see what we will do."

"And it will be strange, if after being protected so far by a power greater than our own we can't protect ourselves now," said Willet gravely.

"The canoe is coming fast," said Tayoga. "I can see it growing on the water."

"So it is, and I infer from its speed that it has at least four paddles in it. There's no doubt they are disappointed in not finding us farther down, and their boat has come back to look for us."

"This is not the only tree uprooted by the wind and afloat on the lake," said Tayoga, "and now it must be our purpose to make the warriors think it has come into the water naturally."

Long before the French word "camouflage" was brought into general use by a titanic war the art of concealment and illusion was practiced universally by the natives of the North American wilderness. It was in truth their favourite stratagem in their unending wars, and there was high praise for those who could use it best.

"Well spoken, Tayoga," said Willet. "Luckily these living branches hide us, and, as the wind still blows strongly toward the south, we must let the tree float in that direction."

"And not go toward the mainland!" said Robert.

"Aye, lad, for the present. It's stern necessity. If the warriors in that canoe saw the tree floating against the wind they'd know we're here. Trust 'em for that. I think we're about to run another gauntlet."

The trunk now drifted with the wind, though the three edged it ever so slightly, but steadily, toward the shore.

Meanwhile the canoe grew and grew, and they saw, as Willet had surmised, that it contained four paddles. It was evident too that they were on a quest, as the boat began to veer about, and the four Indians swept the lake with eager eyes.

The tree drifted on. Farther to the west and near the shore, another tree was floating in the same manner, and off to the east a third was beckoning in like fashion. There was nothing in the behaviour of the three trees to indicate that one of them was different from the other two.

The eyes of the savages passed over them, one after another, but they saw no human being hidden within their boughs. Yet Robert at least, when those four pairs of eyes rested on his tree, felt them burning into his back. It was a positive relief, when they moved on and began to hunt elsewhere.

"They will yet bring their canoe much closer," whispered Willet. "It's too much to expect that they will let us go so easily, and we've got to keep up the illusion quite a while longer. Don't push on the tree. The wind is dying a little, and our pace must be absolutely the pace of the breeze. They notice everything and if we were to go too fast they'd be sure to see it."

They no longer sought to control their floating support, and, as the wind suddenly sank very much, it hung lazily on the crests of little waves.

It was a hard test to endure, while the canoe with the four relentless warriors in it rowed about seeking them. Robert paid all the price of a vivid and extremely brilliant imagination. While those with such a temperament look far ahead and have a vision of triumphs to come out of the distant future, they also see far more clearly the troubles and dangers that confront them. So their nerves are much more severely tried than are those of the ordinary and apathetic. Great will power must come to their relief, and thus it was with Robert. His body quivered, though not with the cold of the water, but his soul was steady.

Although the wind sank, which was against them, the darkness increased, and the fact that two other trees were afloat within view, was greatly in their favour. It gave them comrades in that lazy drifting and diverted suspicion.

"If they conclude to make a close examination of our tree, what shall we do?" whispered Robert.

"We'll be at a great disadvantage in the water," the hunter whispered back, "but we'll have to get our rifles loose from their lashings and make a fight of it. I'm hoping it won't come to that."

The canoe approached the tree and then veered away again, as if the warriors were satisfied with its appearance. Certainly a tree more innocent in looks never floated on the waves of Lake George.

The three were masters of illusion and deception, and they did not do a single thing to turn the tree from its natural way of drifting. It obeyed absolutely the touch of the wind and not that of their hands, which rested as lightly as down upon the trunk. Once the wind stopped entirely and the tree had no motion save that of the swell. It wandered idly, a lone derelict upon a solitary lake.

Robert scarcely breathed when the canoe was sent their way. He was wholly unconscious of the water in which he was sunk to the shoulders, but every imaginative nerve was alive to the immense peril.

"If they return and come much nearer we must immerse to the eyes," whispered Willet. "Then they would have to be almost upon us before they saw us. It will make it much harder for us to get at our weapons, but we must take that risk too."

"They have turned," said Robert, "and here they come!"

It looked this time as if the savages had decided to make a close and careful inspection of the tree, bearing directly toward it, and coming so close that Robert could see their fierce, painted faces well and the muscles rising and falling on their powerful arms as they swept their paddles through the water. Now, he prayed that the foliage of the tree would hide them well and he sank his body so deep in the lake that a little water trickled into his mouth, while only the tips of his fingers rested on the trunk. The hunter and the Onondaga were submerged as deeply as he, the upper parts of their faces and their hair blending with the water. When he saw how little they were disclosed in the dusk his confidence returned.

The four savages brought the canoe within thirty feet, but the floating tree kept its secret. Its lazy drift was that of complete innocence and their eyes could not see the dark heads that merged so well with the dark trunk. They gazed for a half minute or so, then brought their canoe about in a half circle and paddled swiftly away toward the second tree.

"Now Tododaho on his star surely put it in their minds to go away," whispered the Onondaga, "and I do not think they will come back again."

"Even so, we can't yet make haste," said the hunter cautiously. "If this tree seems to act wrong they'll see it though at a long distance and come flying down on us."

"The Great Bear is right, as always, but the wind is blowing again, and we can begin to edge in toward the shore."

"So we can. Now we'll push the tree slowly toward the right. All together, but be very gentle. Robert, don't let your enthusiasm run away with you. If we depart much from the course of the wind they'll be after us again no matter how far away they are now."

"They have finished their examination of the second tree," said Tayoga in his precise school English, "and now they are going to the third, which will take them a yet greater distance from us."

"So they are. Fortune is with us."

They no longer felt it necessary to keep submerged to the mouth, but drew themselves up, resting their elbows on the trunk, floating easily in the buoyant water. They had carefully avoided turning the tree in any manner, and their arms, ammunition and packs were dry and safe. But they had been submerged so long that they were growing cold, and now that the immediate danger seemed to have been passed they realized it.

"I like Lake George," said Robert. "It's a glorious lake, a beautiful lake, a majestic lake, the finest lake I know; but that is no reason why I should want to live in its waters."

"Dagaeoga is never satisfied," said Tayoga. "He might have been sunk in some shallow, muddy lake in a flat country, but instead he is

41

put in this noble one with its beautiful cool waters, and the grand mountains are all about him."

"But this is the second time I've been immersed in a very short space, Tayoga, and just now I crave dry land. I can't recall a single hour or a single moment when I ever wanted it more than I do this instant."

"I'm of a mind with you in that matter, Robert," said the hunter, "and if all continues to go as well as it's now going, we'll set foot on it in fifteen minutes. That canoe is close to the third tree, and they've stopped to look at it. I think we can push a little faster toward the land. They can't notice our slant at that distance. Aye, that's right, lads! Now the cliffs are coming much nearer, and they look real friendly. I see a little cove in there where our good tree can land, and it won't be hard for us to find our way up the banks, though they do rise so high. Now, steady! In we go! It's a snug little cove, put here to receive us. Be cautious how you rise out of the water, lads! Those fellows see like owls in the dark, and they'd trace us outlined here against the shore. That's it, Tayoga, you always do the right thing. We'll crawl out of the lake behind this little screen of bushes. Now, have you lads got all your baggage loose from the tree?"

"Yes," replied Robert.

"Then we'll let it go."

"It's been a fine tree, a kind tree," said Robert, "and I've no doubt Tayoga is right when he thinks a good spirit friendly to us has gone into it."

They pushed it off and saw it float again on the lake, borne on by the wind. Then they dried their bodies as well as they could in their haste, and resumed their clothing. The hunter shook his gigantic frame, and he felt the strength pour back into his muscles and veins, when he grasped his rifle. It had been his powerful comrade for many years, and he now stood where he could use it with deadly effect, if the savages should come.

They rested several minutes, before beginning the climb of the cliff, and saw a second and then a third canoe coming out of the south, evidently seeking them.

"They're pretty sure now that we haven't escaped in that direction," said Willet, "and they'll be back in full force, looking for us. We got off the lake just in time."

The cliffs towered over them to a height of nearly two thousand feet, but they began the ascent up a slanting depression that they had seen from the lake, well covered with bushes, and they took it at ease, looking back occasionally to watch the futile hunt of the canoes for them.

"We're not out of their ring yet," said Willet. "They'll be carrying on another search for us on top of the cliffs."

"Don't discourage us, Dave," said Robert. "We feel happy now having escaped one danger, and we won't escape the other until we come to it."

"Perhaps you're right, lad. We'll enjoy our few minutes of safety while we can and the sight of those canoes scurrying around the lake, looking for their lost prey, will help along our merriment."

"That's true," said Robert, "and I think I'll take a glance at them now just to soothe my soul."

They were about three quarters of the way up the cliff, and the three, turning at the same time, gazed down at a great height upon the vast expanse of Lake George. The night had lightened again, a full moon coming out and hosts of stars sparkling in the heavens. The surface of the lake gleamed in silver and they distinctly saw the canoes cruising about in their search for the three. They also saw far in the south a part of the fleet returning, and Robert breathed a sigh of thankfulness that they had escaped at last from the water.

They turned back to the top, but the white lad felt a sudden faintness and had he not clung tightly to a stout young bush he would have gone crashing down the slope. He quickly recovered himself and sought to hide his momentary weakness, but the hunter had noticed his stumbling step and gave him a keen, questing glance. Then he too stopped.

"We've climbed enough," he said. "Robert, you've come to the end of your rope, for the present. It's a wonder your strength didn't give out long ago, after all you've been through."

"Oh, I can go on! I'm not tired at all!" exclaimed the youth valiantly.

"The Great Bear tells the truth, Dagaeoga," said the Onondaga, looking at him with sympathy, "and you cannot hide it from us. We will seek a covert here."

Robert knew that any further effort to conceal his sudden exhaustion would be in vain. The collapse was too complete, but he had nothing to be ashamed of, as he had gone through far more than Willet and Tayoga, and he had reached the limit of human endurance.

"Well, yes, I am tired," he admitted. "But as we're hanging on the side of a cliff about fifteen hundred feet above the water I don't see any nice comfortable inn, with big white beds in it, waiting for us."

"Stay where you are, Dagaeoga," said the Onondaga. "We will not try the summit to-night, but I may find some sort of an alcove in the cliff, a few feet of fairly level space, where we can rest."

Robert sank down by the friendly bush, with his back against a great uplift of stone, while Willet stood on a narrow shelf, supporting himself against a young evergreen. Tayoga disappeared silently upward.

The painful contraction in the chest of the lad grew easier, and black specks that had come before his eyes floated away. He returned to a firm land of reality, but he knew that his strength was not yet sufficient to permit of their going on. Tayoga came back in about ten minutes.

"I have found it," he said in his precise school English. "It is not much, but about three hundred feet from the top of the cliff is a slight hollow that will give support for our bodies. There we may lie down and Dagaeoga can sleep his weariness away."

"Camping securely between our enemies above and our enemies below," said Robert, his vivid imagination leaping up again. "It appeals to me to be so near them and yet well hidden, especially as we've left no trail on this rocky precipice that they can follow."

"It would help me a lot if they were not so close," laughed the hunter. "I don't need your contrasts, Robert, to make me rest. I'd like it better if they were a hundred miles away instead of only a few hundred yards. But lead on, Tayoga, and we'll say what we think of this inn of yours when we see it."

The hollow was not so bad, an indentation in the stone, extending back perhaps three feet, and almost hidden by dwarfed evergreens and climbing vines. It was not visible twenty feet above or below, and it would have escaped any eye less keen than that of the Onondaga.

"You've done well, Tayoga," said Willet. "There are better inns in Albany and New York, but it's a pretty good place to be found in the side of a cliff fifteen hundred feet above the water."

"We'll be snug enough here."

They crawled into the hollow, matted the vines carefully in front of them to guard against a slip or an incautious step, and then the three lay back against the wall, feeling an immense relief. While not so worn as Robert, the bones and muscles of Willet and Tayoga also were calling out for rest.

"I'm glad I'm here," said the hunter, and the others were forced to laugh at his intense earnestness.

Robert sank against the wall of the cliff, and he felt an immense peace. The arching stone over his head, and the dwarfed evergreens pushing themselves up where the least bit of soil was to be found, shut out the view before them, but it was as truly an inn to him at that moment as any he had ever entered. He closed his eyes in content and every nerve and muscle relaxed.

"Since you've shut down your lids, lad, keep 'em down," said the hunter. "Sleep will do you more good now than anything else."

But Robert quickly opened his eyes again.

"No," he said, "I think I'll eat first."

Willet laughed.

"I might have known that you would remember your appetite," he said. "But it's not a bad idea. We'll all have a late supper."

They had venison and cold hominy from their knapsacks, and they ate with sharp appetites.

Then Robert let his lids fall again and in a few minutes was off to slumberland.

"Now you follow him, Tayoga," said Willet, "and I'll watch."

"But remember to awake me for my turn," said the Onondaga.

"You can rely upon me," said the hunter.

The disciplined mind of Tayoga knew how to compel sleep, and on this occasion it was needful for him to exert his will. In an incredibly brief time he was pursuing Robert through the gates of sleep to the blessed land of slumber that lay beyond, and the hunter was left alone on watch.

Willet, despite his long life in the woods, was a man of cultivation and refinement. He knew and liked the culture of the cities in its highest sense. His youth had not been spent in the North American wilderness. He had tasted the life of London and Paris, and long use and practice had not blunted his mind to the extraordinary contrasts between forest and town.

He appreciated now to the full their singular situation, practically hanging on the side of a mighty cliff, with cruel enemies seeking them below and equally cruel enemies waiting for them above.

The crevice in which they lay was little more than a dent in the stone wall. If either of the lads moved a foot and the evergreens failed to hold him he would go spinning a quarter of a mile straight down to the lake. The hunter looked anxiously in the dusk at the slender barrier, but he judged that it would be sufficient to stop any unconscious movement. Then he glanced at Robert and Tayoga and he was reassured. They were so tired and sleep had claimed them so completely that they lay like the dead. Neither stirred a particle, but in the silence the hunter heard their regular breathing.

The years had not made Willet a sceptic. While he did not accept unquestioningly all the beliefs of Tayoga, neither did he wholly reject them. It might well be true that earth, air, trees and other objects were inhabited by spirits good or bad. At least it was a pleasing belief and he had no proof that it was not true. Certainly, it seemed as if some great protection had been given to his comrades and himself in the last day or two. He looked up through the evergreen veil at the peaceful stars, and gave thanks and gratitude.

The night continued to lighten. New constellations swam into the heavenly blue, and the surface of the lake as far as eye could range was a waving mass of molten silver. The portion of the Indian fleet that had come back from the south was passing. It was almost precisely opposite the covert now and not more than three hundred yards from the base of the cliff. The light was so good that Willet distinctly saw the paddlers at work and the other warriors sitting upright. It was not possible to read eyes at such a distance, but he imagined what they expressed and the thought pleased him. As Robert had predicted, the snugness of their hiding place with savages above and savages below heightened his feeling of comfort and safety. He was in sight and yet unseen. They would never think of the three hanging there in the side of the cliff. He laughed softly, under his breath, and he had never laughed with more satisfaction.

He tried to pick out Tandakora, judging that his immense size would disclose him, but the chief was not there. Evidently he was with the other part of the fleet and was continuing the vain search in the south. He laughed again and with the same satisfaction when he thought of the Ojibway's rage because the hated three had slipped once more through his fingers.

"An Ojibway has no business here in the province of New York, anyway," he murmured. "His place is out by the Great Lakes."

The canoes passed on, and, after a while, nothing was to be seen on the waves of Lake George. Even the drifting trees, including the one that had served them so well, had gone out of sight. The lake only expressed peace. It was as it might have been in the dawn of time with the passings of no human beings to vex its surface.

Something stirred in the bushes near the hunter. An eagle, with great spread of wing, rose from a nest and sailed far out over the silvery waters. Willet surmised that the nearness of the three had disturbed it, and he was sorry. He had a kindly feeling toward birds and beasts just then, and he did not wish to drive even an eagle from his home. He hoped that it would come back, and, after a while, it did so, settling upon its nest, which could not have been more than fifty yards away, where its mate had remained unmoving while the other went abroad to hunt.

There was no further sign of life from the people of the wilderness, and Willet sat silent a long time. Dawn came, intense and brilliant. He had hoped the day would be cloudy, and he would have welcomed rain, despite its discomfort, but the sun was in its greatest splendour, and the air was absolutely translucent. The lake and the mountains sprang out, sharp and clear. Far to the south the hunter saw a smudge upon the water which he knew to be Indian canoes. They were miles away, but it was evident that the French and Indians still held the lake, and there was no escape for the three by water. There had been some idea in Willet's mind of returning along the foot of the cliffs to their own little boat, but the brilliant day and the Indian presence compelled him to put it away.

The sun, huge, red and scintillating, swung clear of the mighty mountains, and the waters that had been silver in the first morning light turned to burning gold. In the shining day far came near and objects close by grew to twice their size. To attempt to pass the warriors in such a light would be like walking on an open plain, thought the hunter, and, always quick to decide, he took his resolution.

It was characteristic of David Willet that no matter what the situation he always made the best of it. His mind was a remarkable mingling of vigour, penetration and adaptability. If one had to wait, well, one had to wait and there was nothing else in it. He sank down in the little cove in the cliff and rested his back against the stony wall. He, Robert and Tayoga filled it, and his moccasined feet touched the dwarfed shrubs which made the thin green curtain before the opening. He realized more fully now in the intense light of a brilliant day what a slender shelf it was. Any one of them might have pitched from it to a sure death below. He was glad that the white lad and the red lad had been so tired that they lay like the dead. Their positions were exactly the same as when they sank to sleep. They had not stirred an inch in the night, and there was no sign now that they intended to awake any time soon. If they had gone to the land of dreams, they were finding it a pleasant country and they were in no hurry to return from it.

The giant hunter smiled. He had promised the Onondaga to awaken him at dawn, and he knew that Robert expected as much, but he would not keep his promise. He would let nature hold sway; when it chose to awaken them it could, and meanwhile he would do nothing. He moved just a little to make himself more comfortable and reclined patiently.

Willet was intensely grateful for the little curtain of evergreens. Without it the sharp eyes of the warriors could detect them even in the side of the lofty cliff. Only a few bushes stood between them and

47

torture and death, but they stood there just the same. Time passed slowly, and the morning remained as brilliant as ever. He paid little attention to what was passing on the lake, but he listened with all the power of his hearing for anything that might happen on the cliff above them. He knew that the warriors were far from giving up the chase, and he expected a sign there. About two hours after sunrise it came. He heard the cry of a wolf, and then a like cry replying, but he knew that the sounds came from the throats of warriors. He pressed himself a little harder against the stony wall, and looked at his two young comrades. Their souls still wandered in the pleasant land of dreams and their bodies took no interest in what was occurring here. They did not stir.

In four or five minutes the two cries were repeated much nearer and the hunter fairly concentrated all his powers into the organ of hearing. Faint voices, only whispers, floated down to him, and he knew that the warriors were ranging along the cliff just above them. Leaning forward cautiously, he peeped above the veil of evergreens, and saw two dark faces gazing over the edge of the precipice. A brief look was enough, then he drew back and waited.

CHAPTER 4

The Daring Attempt

Willet knew from their paint that the faces looking down were those of Huron warriors, but he was quite sure they had not seen anything, and that the men would soon pass on. It was impossible even for the sharpest eyes to pick out the three behind the evergreen screen. Nevertheless he put his rifle forward, ready for an instant shot, if needed, but remained absolutely still, waiting for them to make the next move.

His sensitive hearing brought down the faint voices again and once or twice the light crush of footsteps. Evidently, the warriors were moving slowly along the edge of the cliff, talking as they went, and the hunter surmised that the three were the subject of their attention. He imagined their chagrin at the way in which the chase had vanished, and he laughed softly to think that he and the lads lay so near their enemies, but invisible and so well hidden.

The voices became fainter and died away, the soft crush of footsteps came no more, and the world returned to all the seeming of peace, without any trace of cruelty in it; but Willet was not lured by such an easy promise into any rash act. He knew the savages would come again, and that unbroken vigilance was the price of life. Once more he settled himself into the easiest position and watched. He had all the patience of the Indians themselves, to whom time mattered little, and since sitting there was the best thing to be done he was content to sit there.

Robert and Tayoga slept on. The morning was far gone, but they still rambled happily in the land of dreams, and showed no signs of a wish to return to earth. Willet thought it better that they should sleep on, because youthful bodies demanded it, and because the delay which would be hard for Robert especially would thus pass more easily. He was willing for them to stay longer in the far, happy land that they were visiting.

The sun slowly climbed the eastern arch of the heavens. The day lost none of its intense, vivid quality. The waters of the lake glowed in wonderful changing colours, now gold, now silver, and then purple or blue. Willet even in those hours of anxiety did not forget to steep his soul in the beauty of Lake George. His life was cast amid great and continuous dangers, and he had no family that he could call his own. Yet he had those whom he loved, and if he were to choose over again the land in which to live he would choose this very majestic land in which he now sat. As human life went, the great hunter was happy.

The sound of a shot, and then of a second, came from the cliff above. He heard no cry following them, no note of the war whoop, and, thinking it over, he concluded that the shots were fired by Indians hunting. Since the war, game about the lake had increased greatly, and the warriors, whether attached to the French army or roving at their own will, relied chiefly upon the forest for food. But the reports were significant. The Indian ring about them was not broken, and he measured their own supplies of venison and hominy.

A little after noon Tayoga awoke, and he awoke in the Indian fashion, without the noise of incautious movements or sudden words, but stepping at once from complete sleep to complete consciousness. Every faculty in him was alive.

"I have slept long, Great Bear, and it is late," he said.

"But not too late, Tayoga. There's nothing for us to do."

"Then the warriors are still above!"

"I heard two shots a little while ago. I think they came from hunters."

"It is almost certainly so, Great Bear, since there is nothing in this region for them to shoot at save ourselves, and no bullets have landed near us."

"Yours has been a peaceful sleep. Robert too is now coming out of his great slumber."

The white lad stirred and murmured a little as he awoke. His re-entry into the world of fact was not quite as frictionless as that of his Indian comrade.

"Do not fall down the cliff while you stretch yourself, Dagaeoga," said the Onondaga.

"I won't, Tayoga. I've no wish to reach the lake in such fashion. I see by the sun that it's late. What happened while I slept?"

"Two great attacks by Tandakora and his men were beaten off by the Great Bear and myself. As we felt ourselves a match for them we did not consider it necessary to awaken you."

"But of course if you had been pushed a bit harder you would have called upon me. I'm glad you've concluded to use me for tipping the scales of a doubtful combat. To enter at the most strenuous moment is what I'm fitted for best."

"And if your weapons are not sufficient, Dagaeoga, you can make a speech to them and talk them to death."

The hunter smiled. He hoped the boys would always be willing to jest with each other in this manner. It was good to have high spirits in a crisis.

"Take a little venison and hominy, lads," he said, "because I think we're going to spend some time in this most spacious and hospitable inn of ours."

They ate and then were thirsty, but they had no water, although it floated peacefully in millions of gallons below.

"We're dry, but I think we're going to be much dryer," said Willet.

"We must go down one by one in the night for water," said Tayoga.

"We are to reckon on a long stay, then!" said Robert.

"Yes," said Willet, "and we might as well make ourselves at home. It's a great climb down, but we'll have to do it."

"If I could get up and walk about it would be easier," said Robert. "I think my muscles are growing a bit stiff from disuse."

"The descent for water to-night will loosen them up," said Willet philosophically.

It was a tremendously long afternoon, one of the longest that Robert ever spent, and his position grew cramped and difficult. He found some relief now and then in stretching his muscles, but there was nothing to assuage the intense thirst that assailed all three. Robert's throat and mouth were dry and burning, and he looked longingly at the lake that shimmered and gleamed below them. The waters, sparkling in their brilliant and changing colours, were cool and inviting. They bade him come, and his throat grew hotter and hotter, but he would make no complaint. He must endure it in silence all the afternoon, and all the next day too, if they should be held there.

Late in the afternoon they heard shots again, but they were quite sure that the reports, as before, were due to Indian hunters. Rogers with rangers might be somewhere in the region of the lakes, but they did not think he was anywhere near them. If a skirmish was occurring on the cliff they would hear the shouts of the combatants.

"The warriors will have a feast to-night," said Tayoga.

"And they will have plenty of water to drink," said Robert ruefully. "You remember that time when we were on the peak, and we found the spring in the slope?"

"But there is no spring here," said Tayoga. "We know that because we came up the cliff. There is no water for us this side of the lake."

The afternoon, long as it was, ended at last. The intense burning sunlight faded, and the cool, grateful shadows came. The three stirred in the niche, and Robert felt a little relief. But his throat and mouth were still dry and hard, and they pained him whenever he talked. Yet they forced themselves to eat a scant supper, although the food increased their thirst, but they knew that without it their strength would decrease, and they expected to obtain water in the dark.

The twilight passed, night came, but they waited with infinite patience refusing to move too soon, despite their great thirst. Instead, Tayoga suggested that he go to the crest of the cliff and see if there was a possible way out for them in that direction. Willet agreed, and the Onondaga crept up, without sound, disappearing in a few seconds among the short bushes that hung in the face of the cliff.

Tayoga was a trailer of surpassing skill, and he reached the top without rustling a bush or sending a single pebble rolling. Then he peered cautiously over the rim and beheld a great fire burning not more than a hundred yards away. Thirty or forty warriors were sitting around it, eating. He did not see Tandakora among them, but he surmised, that it was an allied band and that the Ojibway was not far off.

The feast that the three had expected was in full progress. The hunt had been successful, and the Indians, with their usual appetites, were enjoying the results. They broiled or roasted great pieces of deer over the coals, and then devoured them to the last shred. But Tayoga saw that while the majority were absorbed in their pleasant task, a half dozen sentinels, their line extending on either side of the camp, kept vigilant watch. It would be impossible for the three to pass there. They would have to go down to the lake for water, and then hide in their niche.

Tayoga was about to turn back from the cliff, when he heard a shout that he knew was full of significance. He understood the meaning of every cry and he translated it at once into a note of triumph. It sounded like the whoop over the taking of a scalp or the capture of a prisoner, and his curiosity was aroused. Something had happened, and he was resolved to see what it was.

Several of the warriors by the fire replied to the whoop, and then it came again, nearer but with exactly the same note, that of triumph. The Onondaga flattened his body against the earth, and drew himself a little higher. In the dusk, his black eyes glowed with interest, but he knew that his curiosity would soon be gratified. Those who had sent forth the cry were swiftly approaching the camp.

Four warriors came through the undergrowth and they were pushing a figure before them. It was that of a man in a bedraggled and torn red uniform, his hands tied behind him, and all the colour gone from his face. Powerful as was his self-control, Tayoga uttered a low cry of surprise. It was the young Englishman, Grosvenor, a prisoner of the hostile warriors, and in a most desperate case.

The Onondaga wondered how he had been taken, but whatever the way, he was in the hands of enemies who knew little mercy.

The warriors around the fire uttered a universal yell of triumph when they saw the captain, and many of them ran forward to meet Grosvenor, whirling their tomahawks and knives in his face, and dancing about as if mad with joy. It was a truly ferocious scene, the like of which was witnessed thousands of times in the great North American forests, and Tayoga, softened by long contact with high types of white men, felt pity. The light from the great fire fell directly on Grosvenor's face and showed its pallor. It was evident that he was weary through and through, but he tried to hold himself erect and he did not flinch when the sharp blades flashed close to his face. But Tayoga knew that his feelings had become blunted. Only the trained forest runner could keep steady in the face of such threats.

When they came near the fire, one of the warriors gave Grosvenor a push, and he fell amid cruel laughter. But he struggled to his feet again, stood a few minutes, and then sank down on a little hillock, where his captors left him alone for the present. Tayoga watched him thoughtfully. He knew that his presence in the Indian camp complicated their own situation. Robert would never hear of going away without an attempt at rescue and Tayoga's own good heart moved him to the same course. Yet it would be almost impossible to take the young Englishman from the centre of the Indian camp.

Tayoga knew too what grief his news would cause to young Lennox, between whom and Grosvenor a great friendship had been formed. For the matter of that, both the Onondaga and the hunter also were very partial to the Englishman.

The warriors presently untied Grosvenor's hands and gave him some food. The captive ate a little—he had no appetite for more—and then tried to smooth out his hair and his clothing and to make himself more presentable. He also straightened his worn figure, and sat more erect. Tayoga gave silent approval. Here was a man! He might be a prisoner, and be in a most desperate plight, but he would present the best possible face to his foes. It was exactly what an Onondaga or a Mohawk warrior would do, and the young Englishman, though he knew little of the forest, was living up to its traditions.

"If he has to die," reflected Tayoga, "he will die well. If his people hear that he has gone they will have no cause to be ashamed of the way in which he went. Here is the making of a great white warrior."

The Onondaga knew that Robert and Willet were now expecting him back, but his interest in Grosvenor kept him a while longer, watching at the cliff's rim. He thought it likely that Tandakora might come, and he had not long to wait. The huge Ojibway came striding through the bushes and into the circle of the firelight, his body bare as usual save for breech cloth, leggings and moccasins, and painted with the hideous devices so dear to the savage heart.

The warriors received him with deference, indicating clearly to Tayoga that they were under his authority, but without making any reply to their salutation he strode up to the prisoner, and, folding his arms across his mighty breast, regarded him, smiling cruelly. The Onondaga did not see the smile, but he knew it was there. The man would not be Tandakora if it were not. In that savage heart, the chivalry that so often marked the Indians of the higher type found no place.

Grosvenor, worn to the bone and dazed by the extraordinary and fearful situation in which he found himself, nevertheless straightened up anew, and gave back defiantly the stare of the gigantic and sinister figure that confronted him. Then Tayoga saw Tandakora raise his hand and strike the young Englishman a heavy blow in the face. Grosvenor fell, but sprang up instantly and rushed at the Ojibway, only to find himself before the point of a knife.

The young officer stood still a few minutes, then turned with dignity and sat down once more. Tayoga knew and appreciated his feelings. He had suffered exactly the same humiliation from Tandakora himself, and he meant, with all his soul, that some day the debt should be paid in full. Now in a vicarious way he took upon himself Grosvenor's debt also. The prisoner did not have experience in the woods, his great merits lay elsewhere, but he was the friend of Robert, therefore of Tayoga, and the Onondaga felt it only right that he should pay for both.

Tandakora sat down, a warrior handed him a huge piece of deer meat, and he began to eat. All the others, interrupted for a few minutes by the arrival of the chief, resumed the same pleasant occupation. Tayoga deciding that he had seen enough, began to climb down with great care. The descent was harder than the ascent, but he reached the niche, without noise, and the sight of him was very welcome to Robert and the hunter who had begun to worry over his absence, which was much longer than they had expected.

"Did you see the warriors, Tayoga?" asked young Lennox.

"I saw them, Dagaeoga. They are at the top of the cliff, only two or three hundred yards away; they have a good fire, and they are eating the game they killed in the day."

"And there is no chance for us to pass?"

"None to-night, Dagaeoga. Nor would we pass if we could."

"Why not? I see no reason for our staying here save that we have to do it."

"One is there, Dagaeoga, whom we cannot leave a prisoner in their hands."

"Who? It's not Black Rifle! Nor Rogers, the ranger! They would never let themselves be taken!"

"No, Dagaeoga, it is neither of those. But while I watched at the cliff's rim I saw the warriors bring in that young Englishman, Grosvenor, whom you know and like so well."

"What! Grosvenor! What could he have been doing in this forest!"

"That, I know not, Dagaeoga, save that he has been getting himself captured; how, I know not either, but I saw him brought in a prisoner. Tandakora came, while I watched, and smote the captive heavily in the face with his hand. That debt I take upon myself, in addition to my own."

"You will pay both, Tayoga, and with interest," said the hunter with conviction. "But you were right when you assumed that we could not go away and leave Grosvenor a prisoner in their hands. Because we're here, and because you saw him, your Manitou has laid upon us the duty of saving him."

Robert's face glowed in the dusk.

"We're bound to see it that way," he said. "We'd be disgraced forever with ourselves, if we went away and left him. Now, how are we to do it?"

"I don't know how yet," replied the Onondaga, "but we must first go down to the water. We've forgotten our thirst in the news I bring, but it will soon be on us again, fiercer and more burning than ever. And we must have all our strength for the great task before us."

"I think it's better for all three of us to go down to the lake at once," said Willet. "If anything happens we'll be together, and we are stronger against danger, united than separated. I'll lead the way."

It was a long and slow descent, every step taken with minute care, and as they approached the lake Robert found that his thirst was up and leaping.

"I feel that I could drink the whole lake dry," he said.

"Do not do that, Dagaeoga," said Tayoga in his precise way. "Lake George is too beautiful to be lost."

"We might swim across it," said Willet, looking at the silvery surface of the water unbroken by the dark line of any canoe. "A way has opened to us here, but we can't follow it now."

Robert knelt at the margin, and took a little drink first, letting the cool water moisten his mouth and throat before he swallowed it. How grateful it was! How wonderfully refreshing! One must almost perish with thirst before he knew the enormous value of water. And when it was found, one must know how to drink it right. He took a second and somewhat larger drink. Then, waiting a while, he drank freely and as much as he wanted. Strength, courage, optimism flowed back into his veins. As they came down the cliff he had not seen any way to rescue Grosvenor, nor did he see it now, but he knew that they would do it. His restored body and mind would not admit the possibility of failure.

They remained nearly an hour in the shadow of the bushes at the water's edge, and then began the slow and painful ascent to the niche, which they reached without mishap. Another half hour there, and, having examined well their arms, they climbed to the cliff's rim, where they looked over, and Robert obtained his first view of the Indian camp.

The feasting was over, the fires had sunk far down, and most of the warriors were asleep, but Tandakora himself sat with his arms across his chest, glowering into the coals, and a line of sentinels was set. A red gleam from his uniform showed where Grosvenor, leaning against a log, had fallen at last into a happy slumber, in which his desperate case was forgotten for the time.

"I confess that I don't know how to do it, still it must be done," whispered the hunter.

"Yes, it must be done," the Onondaga whispered back. "We must steal our friend out of the hands of his enemies. Neither do I know how to do it, but perhaps Tododaho will tell me. See, there is his star!"

He pointed to a great star dancing in the sky, a star with a light mist across its face, which he knew to be the wise snakes that lay coil on coil in the hair of the Onondaga sage who had gone away four hundred years ago to his place in the heavens, and prayed for a thought, a happy thought that would tell him the way. In a moment, his mind was in a state of high spiritual exaltation. An electric current seemed to pass from the remote star to him. He shut his eyes, and his face became rapt. In a few minutes, he opened them again and said quietly: "I think, Great Bear, that Tododaho has told us how to proceed. You and Dagaeoga must draw off the warriors, and then I will take Red Coat from those that may be left behind."

"It's mighty risky."

"Since when, Great Bear, have we been turned aside by risks! Besides, there is no other way."

"It seems that I can't think of any other."

Tayoga unfolded his plan. Robert and Willet must steal along the edge of the cliff and seek to pass to the north of the line of sentinels. If not detected, they would purposely cause an alarm, and, as a consequence, draw off the main portion of the band. Then it was their duty to see to it that they were not taken. Meanwhile Tayoga in the excitement and confusion was to secure the release of Grosvenor, and they would flee southward to the mouth of a small creek, in the lake, where Robert and Willet, after making a great turn, were to join them.

"It's complicated and it's a desperate chance," said Willet thoughtfully, "but I don't see anything else to do. Besides, we have got to act quickly. Being on the war-path, they won't hold him long, and you know the kind of death Tandakora will serve out to him."

Robert shuddered. He knew too well, and knowing so well he was ready to risk his life to save his friend.

"I think," said Tayoga, "that we had better wait until it is about two hours after midnight. Then the minds and bodies of the warriors will be at their dullest, and we will have the best chance."

"Right, Tayoga," said the hunter. "We'll have to use every trifle that's in our favour. Can you see Tandakora from here?"

"He is leaning against the big tree, asleep."

"I'm glad of that. He may be a bit confused when he awakes suddenly and rushes off after us, full tilt, with nearly all the warriors. If only two guards are left with the prisoner, Tayoga, you can dispose of 'em."

"Fortune may favour us."

"Provided we use our wits and strength to the utmost."

"That provision must always be made, Great Bear."

Using what patience they could, they remained at the edge of the cliff, crouched there, until they judged it was about two o'clock in the morning, the night being then at its darkest. Tandakora still slept against his tree, and the fires were almost out. The red gleam from the uniform of Grosvenor could no longer be seen, but Robert had

57

marked well the place where he sat, and he knew that the young Englishman was there, sleeping the sleep of utter exhaustion. Everything was still and peaceful.

"After all, we could escape through their lines, now," whispered Robert.

"So it turns out," said the hunter.

"But it looks as if we were held back in order that we might save Grosvenor."

"That too may be true."

"It is time to go," said Tayoga. "Farewell, Great Bear! Farewell, Dagaeoga! May we meet at the mouth of the creek as we have planned, and may we be four who meet there and not three!"

"May all the stars fight for us," said Robert with emotion, and then he and Willet moved away among the bushes, leaving Tayoga alone at the cliff's rim. Young Lennox knew that theirs was a most perilous venture. Had he given himself time to think about it he would have seen that the chances were about ten to one against its success, but he resolutely closed his mind against that phase of it and insisted upon hope. His was the spirit that leads to success in the face of overwhelming odds.

Willet was first, and Robert was close behind.

Neither looked back, but they knew that Tayoga would not move, until the alarm was given, and they could flee away with the pursuit hot upon their heels. Young Lennox saw again that they could now have slipped through the Indian lines, but the thought of deserting Grosvenor never entered his mind. It seemed though as if all the elements of nature were conspiring to facilitate the flight of the hunter and himself. The sentinels, whose dusky figures they were yet able to see, moved sleepily up and down. No dead wood that would break with a snap thrust itself before their feet. The wilderness opened a way for them.

"I think a warrior or two may be watching in the forest to the north of us," whispered Willet, "but we'll go through the line there. See that fellow standing under the tree, about a hundred yards to the south. He's the one to give the alarm."

But circumstances still favoured them. Nature was peaceful. When they wished for the first time in their lives that their flight should be detected, nothing happened, and the vigilance of the warriors who usually watched so well seemed to be relaxed. Robert was conscious that they were passing unseen and unheard between the sentinel on the north and the sentinel on the south.

Two hundred yards farther on, and the hunter brought his moccasin sharply down upon a dead stick which broke with a sharp snap, a sound that penetrated far in the still night. Robert, glancing back, saw the sentinel on the south stiffen to attention and then utter a cry of alarm, a shout sufficient to awaken any one of the sleeping Indians. It was given back in an instant by several voices from the camp, and then the hunter and the youth sprang to their task.

"Now we're to run as we've never run before," exclaimed Willet. "But we must let 'em think they're going to catch us."

First, sending back a tremendous shout of defiance that he knew would enrage Tandakora's men to the utmost, he raced with long swift steps through the forest, and Robert was always close on his heels. The yells of the Indians behind them, who pushed forward in pursuit, were succeeded by silence, and Robert knew they now were running for their lives. Luckily, they were coming into a country with which the hunter had some acquaintance, and, turning a little to the south, he led the way into a ravine down which they took a swift course. After a mile or so he stopped, and the two rested their lungs and muscles.

"They can't see our trail to-night," said the hunter, "and they'll have to depend on eye and ear, but they'll stick to the chase for a long time. I've no doubt they think all three of us are here, and that they may take us in one haul. Ready to start on again, Robert?"

"My breath is all right now, and I'll run a race with anybody. You don't think they've lost us, do you?"

"Not likely, but in case they have I'll tell 'em where we are."

He uttered a shout so piercing that it made Robert jump. Then he led again at a great pace down the ravine, and a single cry behind them showed that the pursuit was coming. As nearly as Robert could calculate, the warriors were about three hundred yards away. He could not see them, but he was sure they would hang on as long as the slightest chance was left to overtake Willet and himself.

They fled in silence at least another mile, and then, feeling their breath grow difficult again, they stopped a second time, still in the ravine and among thick bushes.

"Our flight may be a joke on them, as we intend to draw them after us," said Robert, "but constant running turns it into a joke on us too. I've done so much of this sort of thing in the last few days that I feel as if I were spending my life, dodging here and there in the forest, trying to escape warriors."

Willet laughed dryly.

"It's not the sort of life for a growing youth," he said, "but you'll have to live it for a while. Remember our task. If they lose our trail it's our business to make 'em find it again. Here's another challenge to 'em."

He shouted once more, a long, defiant war cry, much like that of the warriors themselves, and then he and Robert resumed their flight, leaving the ravine presently, and taking a sharper course toward the south.

"I think we'd have lost 'em back there if it hadn't been for that whoop of mine," said Willet.

"Perhaps it's about time to lose them," said Robert hopefully. "The sooner we do it the happier I'll feel."

"Not yet, Robert, my lad. We must give Tayoga all the time he needs for the work he's trying to do. After all, his task is the main one, and the most dangerous. I think we can slow up a bit here. We have to save our breath."

They dropped down to a walk, and took another deep curve toward the south, and now also to the east. Their present course, if persisted in, would bring them back to the lake. The night was still dark, but their trained eyes had grown so used to it that they could see very well in the dusk. Both were looking back and at the same time they saw a shadowy figure appear in the forest behind them. Robert knew that it was the vanguard of the pursuit which was drawing uncomfortably close, at least for him. A shout from the warriors was followed by a shot, and a bullet cut its way through the leaves near them.

"I think we ought to give 'em a hint that they come too close, at their peril," said Willet, and raising his own rifle he sent back an answering shot which did not go astray. The first warrior fell, and others who had come forward in the undergrowth gave back for the time.

"They'll take the hint," said the hunter, "and now we'll increase our speed."

He reloaded, as they ran, and a little later Robert sent a bullet that struck the mark. Once more the warriors shrank back for the time, and the hunter and lad, using their utmost speed, fled toward the southwest at such a great rate that the pursuit, at length, was left behind and finally was lost. Day found their foes out of sight, and two or three hours later they came to the mouth of the creek, where they were to meet Tayoga, in case he succeeded.

"And now the rest is in other hands than ours," said Willet.

Forcing themselves to assume a patience they could scarcely feel, they sat down to wait.

CHAPTER 5

Tayoga's Skill

They still had food left in their knapsacks, and they ate a portion, drinking afterward from the creek. Then they resumed their places in the dense undergrowth, where they could watch well and yet remain hidden. They could also see from where they lay the shimmering waters of Andiatarocte, and the lake seemed to be once more at peace. They felt satisfaction that they had completed their part of the great enterprise, but their anxiety nevertheless was intense. As Willet had truly said, Tayoga's share was the more dangerous and delicate by far.

"Do you think he will come?" Robert asked after a long silence.

"If any human being could come under such circumstances and bring Grosvenor with him, it is Tayoga," replied the hunter. "I think sometimes that the Onondaga is superhuman in the forest."

"Then he will come," said Robert hopefully.

"Best not place our hopes too high. The hours alone will tell. It's hard work waiting, but that's our task."

The morning drew on. Another beautiful day had dawned, but Robert scarcely noticed its character. He was thinking with all his soul of Tayoga and Grosvenor. Would they come? Willet was able to read his mind. He was intensely anxious himself, but he knew that the strain of waiting upon Robert, with his youthful and imaginative mind, was greater. He was bound to be suffering cruelly.

"We must give them time," he said. "Remember that Grosvenor is not used to the woods, and can't go through them as fast as we can. We must have confidence too. We both know what a wonder Tayoga is."

Robert sprang suddenly to his feet.

"What was that!" he exclaimed.

A sound had come out of the north, just a breath, but it was not the wind among the leaves, nor yet the distant song of a bird. It was the faint howl of a wolf, and yet Robert believed that it was not a wolf that made it.

"Did you hear it?" he repeated.

"Aye, lad, I heard it," replied the hunter. "'Tis a signal, and 'tis Tayoga too who comes. But whether he comes alone, or with a friend, I know not. To tell that we must bide here and see."

"Should not we send our answer?"

"Nay, lad. He knows where we are. This is the appointed place, and the fewer signals we give the less likely the enemy is to get a hint we're here. I don't think we will hear from Tayoga again until he shows in person."

Robert said no more, knowing full well the truth of the hunter's words, but his heart was beating hard, and he stirred nervously. He had been drawn strongly to Grosvenor, and he knew what a horrible fate awaited him at the hands of Tandakora, unless the Onondaga saved him. Nor would there be another chance for interruption by Tayoga or anybody else. But the minutes passed and he took courage. Tayoga had not yet come. If alone he would have arrived by this time. His slowness must be due to the fact that he had Grosvenor with him. More minutes passed and he heard steps in the undergrowth. Now he was sure. Tayoga was not alone. His moccasins never left any sound. He stood up expectant, and two figures appeared among the bushes. They were Tayoga, calm, his breath unhurried, a faint smile in his dark eyes, and Grosvenor, exhausted, reeling, his clothing worse torn than ever, but the light of hope on his face. Robert uttered a cry of joy and grasped the young Englishman's hand.

"Thank God, you are here!" he exclaimed.

"I thank God and I thank this wonderful young Indian too," panted Grosvenor. "It was a miracle! I had given up hope when he dropped from the skies and saved me!"

"Sit down and get your breath, man," said Willet. "Then you can tell us about it."

Grosvenor sank upon the ground, and did not speak again until the pain in his labouring chest was gone. Tayoga leaned against a tree, and Robert noticed then that he carried an extra rifle and ammunition. The Onondaga thought of everything. Willet filled his cap with water at the creek, and brought it to Grosvenor, who drank long and deeply.

"Tastes good!" said the hunter, smiling.

"Like nectar," said the Englishman, "but it's nectar to me too to see both of you, Mr. Willet and Mr. Lennox. I don't understand yet how it happened. It's really and truly a miracle."

"A miracle mostly of Tayoga's working," said the hunter.

"I thought the end of everything for me had come," said Grosvenor, "and I was only praying that it might not be harder for me than I could stand, when the alarm was heard in the forest, and nearly all the Indians ran off in pursuit of something or other. Only two were left with me. There was a shot from the woods, one of them fell, this wonderful friend of yours appeared from the forest, wounded the other, who took to his heels, then we started running in the other direction, and here we are. It's a marvel and I don't yet see how it was done."

"Tayoga's marvellous knowledge of the woods, his skill and his quickness made the greater part of the miracle," said the hunter, "and you see too, Lieutenant Grosvenor, that he even had the forethought to bring away with him the rifle and ammunition of the fallen warrior, that you might have arms now that you are strong enough to bear them again."

Tayoga without a word handed him the rifle and ammunition, and Grosvenor felt strength flowing back into his body when he took them.

"Could you eat a bite?" asked Willet.

"I think I could now," replied the Englishman, "although I'll confess I've had no appetite up to the present. My situation didn't permit hunger."

Willet handed him a piece of venison and he ate. Meanwhile Tayoga, who seemed to feel no weariness, and the others were watching. In a short time the hunter announced that it was time to go.

"We can't afford to delay here any longer and have 'em overtake us!" he said. "We're out of the ring now, and it's our affair to keep out. Lieutenant Grosvenor, you can tell us as we go along how you happened to be the prisoner of Tandakora."

"It needs only a few words," said the Englishman as they took their way southward through the woods. "I was at Albany with a body of troops, a vanguard for the force that we mean to march against the French at Ticonderoga. I was sent northward with ten men to scour the country, and in the woods we were set upon suddenly by savage warriors. My troopers were either killed or scattered, and I was taken. That was yesterday morning. Since then I have been hurried through the forest, I know not where, and I have had a most appalling experience. As I have said before, I'd long since given up hope for a miracle like the one that has saved me. What a horrible creature that giant Indian was!"

"Tandakora is all that you think him and more. He's been hunting us too, and when he comes back to his camp he'll be after us all four again. So, that's why we hurry."

63

"You're in no bigger hurry than I am," said Grosvenor with attempt at a smile. "If I could find the seven-league boots I'd put them on."

Tayoga once more led the way, and he examined the forest on all sides with eyes that saw everything.

Robert and Willet were greatly refreshed by their rest at the creek, and the promise of life that had been made again so wonderfully put new strength in Grosvenor's frame. So they were able to travel at a good pace, though the three listened continually for any sound that might indicate pursuit.

Yet as the morning progressed there was no hostile sign and their confidence rose.

Robert hoped most devoutly that they would soon come within the region of friends. While the French and Indians held the whole length of Lake Champlain and it was believed Montcalm would fortify somewhere near Ticonderoga, yet Lake George was debatable. It was generally considered within the British and American sphere, although they were having ample proof that fierce bands of the enemy roved about it at will.

Aside from the danger there was another reason why he wished so earnestly for escape from this tenacious pursuit. They were seeing the bottoms of their knapsacks. One could not live on air and mountain lakes alone, however splendid they might be, and, although the wilderness usually furnished food to three such capable hunters, they could not seek game while Tandakora and his savage warriors were seeking them. So, their problem was, in a sense, economic, and could not be fought with weapons only.

At a signal from Willet, who observed that Grosvenor was somewhat tired, they sank their pace to a slow walk, and in about three hours stopped entirely, sitting down on fallen timber which had been heaped in a windrow by a passing hurricane. They were still in dense forest and had borne away somewhat from Andiatarocte, but, through the foliage, they caught glimpses of the lake rippling peacefully in silver and blue and purple.

"Once more I want to thank you fellows for saving me," said Grosvenor.

"Don't mention it again," said the hunter. "In the wilderness we have to save one another now and then, or none of us would live. Your turn to rescue us may come before you think."

"I know nothing of the forest. I feel helpless here."

"Just the same, you don't know what weapon Tayoga's Manitou may place in your hands. The border brings strange and unexpected chances. But our present crisis is not over. We're not saved yet, and we can't afford to relax our efforts a particle. What is it, Tayoga?"

The Onondaga, rising from the fallen tree, had gone about twenty yards into the forest, where he was examining the ground, obviously with great concentration of both eye and mind. He waited at least a minute before replying. Then he said:

"Our friend, the lone ranger, Black Rifle, has passed here."

"How can you know that?" asked Grosvenor in surprise.

"Come and look at his traces," said Tayoga. "See where he has written his name in the earth; that is, he has left what you would call in Europe his visiting card."

Grosvenor looked attentively at the ground, but he saw only a very faint impression, and he never would have noticed that had not the Onondaga pointed it out to him.

"It might have been left by a deer," he objected.

"Impossible," said Tayoga. "The entire imprint is not made, but there is enough to indicate very clearly that a human foot and nothing else pressed there. Here is another trace, although lighter, and here another and another. The trail leads southward."

"But granting it to be that of a man," Grosvenor again objected, "it might be that of any one of the thousands who roam the wilderness."

The great red trailer who had inherited the forest lore of countless generations smiled.

"It is not any one of the thousands and it could not be," he said. "It is easy to tell that. The footsteps are those of a white man, because they turn out, and not in, as do ours of the red race. That is very easy; even Dagaeoga here, the great talker, knows it. The footsteps are far apart, so we are sure that they are those of a tall man; the imprints are deep, proving them to have been made by a heavy man, and at the outer edge of the heel the impression is deeper than on the inner edge. I noticed, when we last saw Black Rifle, which was not long ago, that he wore moccasins of moose hide, that he had turned them outward a little, through wear, and that a small strip of the hardest moose hide had been sewed on the right edge of each heel in order to keep them level. Those strips have made their marks here."

"Somebody else might have put strips of hide on his moccasin heels!"

"It is so, but Black Rifle is tall and large and heavy, and we know that the man who made this trail is tall, large and heavy. The chances are a hundred to one against the fact that any other man tall, large and heavy with moose hide strips to even the wear of his moccasin heels has passed here, especially as this is within the range of Black Rifle. I know that it is he as truly as I know that I am standing here."

"Of course," said Robert, who had never felt the slightest doubt of Tayoga's knowledge. "What was Black Rifle doing?"

"He was looking for St. Luc or Tandakora, because his trail does not lead straight on. See! here it comes, and here again. If Black Rifle had been on a journey he would have gone straight, but he is seeking something and so he turns about. Ah, he wishes to see if there are any canoes visible on the lake, for lo! the trail now leads toward the water! Here he found that none was to be seen and here he rested. Black Rifle had been long on his feet, two days and two nights perhaps, because it takes much to make him weary. He sat on this log. He left a strand from the fringe of his buckskin hunting shirt, caught on a splinter. Do you not see it, Lieutenant Grosvenor?"

"Now that you hold it up before my eyes I notice it But I should never have found it in the wilderness." "Minute observation is what every trailer has to learn," said Willet, "else you are no trailer at all, and you'll learn, Lieutenant, while you are with us, that Tayoga is probably the greatest trailer the world has ever produced."

"Peace, Great Bear! Peace!" protested the Onondaga.

"It's so, just the same. Now, what did Black Rifle do after he rested himself on the log?"

"He went back farther into the woods, turning away from the lake," replied Tayoga, "and he sat down again on another fallen log. Black Rifle was hungry, and he ate. Here is the small bone of a deer, picked quite clean, lying on the ground by the log. Black Rifle was a fortunate man. He had bread, too. See, here is a crumb in this crack in the log too deep down for any bird to reach with his bill. Black Rifle sat here quite a long time. He was thinking hard. He did not need so much time for resting. He remained sitting on the log while he was trying to decide what he would do. It is likely that Black Rifle thought a great force was behind him, and he turned back to see. Had he kept straight on toward the south, as he was going at first, he would not have needed so much time for thinking over his plans. Ah, he has turned! Lo! his trail goes almost directly back on his own course. It will lead to the top of the hillock there, because he wants to see far, and I think that after seeing he will turn again, and follow his original course."

"Why do you think that?" asked Grosvenor.

"Because, O Red Coat, it is likely that Black Rifle knew from the first which way he wanted to go and went that way. He has merely turned back, like a wise general, to scout a little, and see that no danger comes from the rear. Yes, he stood here on the hillock from which we can get a good view over the country, and walked to every side of the crest to find where the best view could be obtained. That, Red Coat, is the simplest of all things. Behold the traces of his moccasins as he walked from side to side. Nothing else could have made Black Rifle move about so much in the space of a few square yards. Now he leaves the hillock and goes down its side toward a low valley in which runs a brook. Black Rifle is thirsty and will drink deep."

"That you can't possibly know, Tayoga."

"But I do know it, Red Coat."

"You don't even know a brook is near."

"I know it, because I have seen it. My eyes are trained to the forest, and I caught the gleam of running water through the leaves to the west. Running water, of course, means a brook. Black Rifle's trail now leads toward it, and I assume that he was thirsty because he had just eaten well. We are nearly always thirsty after eating. But we shall see whether I am right. Here is the brook, and there are the faint traces made by Black Rifle's knees, when he knelt to reach the water. He started away, but found that he was still thirsty, so he came back and drank again. Here are his footprints about a yard from the others. This time, he will go back toward the south, and I think it is sure that he is looking for St. Luc, who must have gone in that direction with a strong force, Tandakora having stayed behind to take us. It is likely that Black Rifle went on, because a great British and American army is gathering below, which fact he knows well, and it is probable that Black Rifle follows St. Luc, because he will hunt the biggest game."

Grosvenor's eyes sparkled.

"I understand," he said. "It is a great art, that of trailing through the wilderness, and I can see how circumstances compel you to learn it."

"We have to learn it to live," said the hunter gravely, "but with Tayoga it is an art carried to the highest degree of perfection. He was born with a gift for it, a very great gift. He inherited all the learning accumulated by a thousand years of ancestors, and then he added to it by his own supreme efforts."

"Do not believe all that Great Bear tells you," said Tayoga modestly. "For unknown reasons he is partial to me, and enlarges my small merits."

"I think this would be a good place for all of you to wait, while I went back on the trail a piece," said the hunter. "If Black Rifle found it necessary to cover the rear, it's a much more urgent duty for us who know that we've been followed by Tandakora to do the same."

"The Great Bear is always wise," said Tayoga. "We will take our ease while we await him."

He flung himself down on the turf and relaxed his figure completely. He had learned long since to make the most of every passing minute, and, seeing Robert imitate him exactly, Grosvenor did likewise. The hunter had disappeared already in the bushes and the three lay in silence.

Grosvenor felt an immense peace. Brave as a young lion, he had been overwhelmed nevertheless by his appalling experiences, and his sudden rescue where rescue seemed impossible had taken him back to the heights. Now, it seemed to him that the three, and especially the Onondaga, could do everything. Tayoga's skill as a trailer and scout was so marvellous that no enemy could come anywhere near without his knowledge. The young Englishman felt that he was defended by impassable walls, and he was so free from apprehension that his nerves became absolutely quiet. Then worn nature took its toll, and his eyelids drooped. Before he was aware that he was sleepy he was asleep.

"You might do as Red Coat has done, Dagaeoga," said Tayoga. "I can watch for us all, and it is wise in the forest to take sleep when we can."

"I'll try," said Robert, and he tried so successfully that in a few minutes he too slumbered, with his figure outstretched, and his head on his arm. Tayoga made a circle about three hundred yards in diameter about them, but finding no hostile sign came back and lay on the turf near them. He relaxed his figure again and closed his eyes, which may have seemed strange but which was not so in the case of Tayoga. His hearing was extraordinarily acute, and, when his eyes were shut, it grew much stronger than ever. Now he knew that no warrior could come within rifle shot of them without his ears telling him of the savage approach. Every creeping footstep would be registered upon that delicate drum.

With eyes shut and brain rested, Tayoga nevertheless knew all that was going on near him. That eardrum of infinite delicacy told him that a woodpecker was tapping on a tree, well toward the north; that a little gray bird almost as far to the south was singing with great vigour and sweetness; that a rabbit was hopping about in the undergrowth, curious and yet fearful; that an eagle with a faint whirr of wings had alighted on a bough, and was looking at the three; that the eagle thinking they might be dangerous had unfolded his wings again and was flying away; that a deer passing to the west had caught a whiff of them on the wind and was running with all speed in the other direction; that a lynx had climbed a tree, and, after staring at them, had climbed down again, and had fled, his coward heart filled with terror.

Thus Tayoga, with his ears, watched his world. He too, his eyelids lowered, felt a peace that was soothing and almost dreamy, but, though his body relaxed, those wonderfully sensitive drums of his ears caught and registered everything. The record showed that for nearly two hours the life of the wilderness went on as usual, the ordinary work and play of animal and bird, and then the drums told him that man was coming. A footstep was registered very clearly, and then another and another, but Tayoga did not open his eyes. He knew who was coming as well as if he had seen him. The drums of his ears made signals that his mind recognized at once. He had long known the faint sound of those footsteps. Willet was coming back.

Tayoga, through the faculty of hearing, was aware of much more than the mere fact that the hunter was returning. He knew that Willet had found nothing, that the pursuit was still far away and that they were in no immediate danger. He knew it by his easy, regular walk, free from either haste or lagging delay. He knew it by the straight, direct line he took for the three young men, devoid of any stops or turnings aside to watch and listen. Willet's course was without care.

Tayoga opened his eyes, and lazily regarded the giant figure of his friend now in full view. Robert and Grosvenor slept on. "I am glad," said the Onondaga.

It was significant of the way in which they understood each other and the way they could read the signs of the forest that they could talk almost without words.

"So am I," said the hunter, "but I had hoped for it."

"Since it is so, we need not awaken them just yet."

"No, let them sleep another hour."

Tayoga meant that he was glad the enemy had not approached and Willet replied that he had hoped for such good luck. No further explanation was needed.

"You had the heaviest part of the burden to carry, last night," said the hunter, "so it would be wise for you to join them if you can, in the hour that's left. See if you can't follow them, at once."

"I think I can," said Tayoga. "At least I will try."

In five minutes he too had gone to the land of dreams and the hunter watched alone. Willet, although weary, was in high spirits. They had come marvellously through many perils, and Tayoga's achievement in rescuing Grosvenor, he repeated to himself, was well nigh miraculous. After such startling luck they could not fail, and an omen of continued good fortune was the fact they had encountered the trail of Black Rifle. He would be a powerful addition to their little force, when found, and Willet did not doubt that they would overtake him. The only problem that really worried him now was that of food. Small as was their army of four, it had to be provisioned, and, for the present, he did not see the way to do it.

He let the three sleep overtime, and when they awoke they were grateful to him for it.

"I am quite made over," said Grosvenor, "and I think that if I stay in the wilderness long enough I may learn to be a scout too. But as all my life has been spent in quite different kinds of country, I suppose it will take a hundred years to give me a good start."

Tayoga smiled.

"Not a hundred years," he said. "Red Coat has begun very well."

"And now with a lot of good solid food I'll feel equal to any march," continued Grosvenor. "Most Englishmen, you know, eat well."

Tayoga looked at Robert, who looked at Willet, who in his turn looked at the Onondaga.

"That's just what we'll have to do without," said the hunter gravely. "The bottoms of our knapsacks are looking up at us. We'll have a splendid chance to see how long we can do without food. One needs such a test now and then."

Grosvenor's face fell, but his was the true mettle. In an instant his countenance became cheerful again.

"I'm not hungry!" he exclaimed. "It was the delusion of a moment, and it passed as quickly as it came. I suffer from such brief spells."

The others laughed.

"That's the right spirit," said Willet, "and while we have nothing to eat we have lots of hope. I've been hungrier than this often, and, as you see, I've never starved to death a single time. There's always lots of food somewhere in the wilderness, if you only know how to put your hand on it."

"I think it is now best for us to follow on the trail of Black Rifle," said Tayoga.

"That's so," responded the hunter. "It's grown a lot colder, while you lads slept, though I think you can follow it without any trouble, Tayoga."

The red lad said nothing, but at once picked up the traces, which now led south, slanting back a little toward the lake.

"Black Rifle was going fast," he said. "His stride lengthens. He must have divined where St. Luc with his force lay, and he took a direct course for it. Ah, he turns suddenly aside and walks to and fro."

"That's curious," said the hunter. "I see the footprints all about. What did Black Rifle mean by moving about in such a manner?"

"It is not odd at all," said Tayoga. "Doubtless Black Rifle was suffering from the same lack that we are, and it was necessary for him to provision his army of one at once. He suddenly saw a chance to do so and he turned aside from his direct journey toward the south. So we shall soon see where Black Rifle shot his bear."

"And why not a deer?" said Grosvenor.

"Because his trail now leads toward that deep thicket on our right, a thicket made up of bushes and vines and briars. A deer could not have gone into it, but a bear could, and we know now it was a bear, because here are its tracks. Black Rifle killed the bear in the thicket."

"Are you sure of that, Tayoga?" asked Robert.

"Absolutely sure, Dagaeoga. It is in this case a matter of mind and not of eye. Black Rifle is too good a hunter to fire a useless shot, and too experienced to miss his game, when he needs it so badly. He would take every precaution for success. My mind tells me that it was impossible for him to miss."

"And he didn't miss," said Robert, as they entered the thicket. "See where the vines and briars were threshed about by the bear as he fell. Here are spots of blood, and here goes the path along which he dragged the body. All this is as plain as day."

"It was a fat bear too," said Tayoga. "Although it is early spring he had found so many good roots and berries that he had more than made up for the loss of weight in his long winter fast. We will soon find where Black Rifle cleaned his prize. A bear is too heavy to carry far. Ah, he did his work just beyond us in the little valley!"

"How do you know that?" asked Grosvenor. "We can't yet see into the valley."

The great red trailer smiled.

"This time, O Red Coat," he replied, "it is a combination of mind and eye. Mind tells me that Black Rifle could not clean and dress his bear unless he got it to water. Mind tells me that a brook is flowing in the valley just ahead of us, because there is scarcely a valley in the country that does not have its brook. Eye tells me that Black Rifle finished his task by the great oak there. Do you not see the huge buzzards flying above the tree? They are conclusive. Ah, the forest people gathered fast in numbers! They expected that Black Rifle would leave them a great feast."

They found a little brook of clear, cold water and, beside it, the place where Black Rifle had cleaned his bear, reserving afterward the choice portion for himself.

"When he went on," said Tayoga, "the forest people made a rush for what he did not want, which was much. Great birds came. We cannot see their trail through the air, but we can see where they hopped about here on the ground, tore at the flesh, and fought with one another for the spoil. A lynx came, and then another, and then wolves. The weasel and the mink too hung on the outskirts, waiting for what the bigger animals might leave. Among them they left nothing and they were not long in the task."

Only shining bones lay on the ground. They had been picked clean and all the forest people had gone after their brief banquet. The trails led away in different directions, but that of Black Rifle went on toward the south. The traces, however, were more distinct than they had been before he stopped for the bear.

"It is because he is carrying much weight," said Tayoga. "Black Rifle no longer skips along like a youth, as Red Coat here does."

"You can have all the sport with me you wish," said Grosvenor. "I don't forget that you saved my life, when by all the rules of logic it was lost beyond the hope of recovery."

"Black Rifle would not eat so much bear meat himself," said Tayoga, "nor would he carry such a burden, without good cause. It may be that he expects us. He has perhaps heard that we are in this region."

"It's possible," said the hunter.

Full of eagerness, they pressed forward on the trail.

CHAPTER 6

Black Rifle

They had been following the trail about half an hour, when Tayoga noticed that it was growing deeper.

"Ah," he said, "Black Rifle now walks much more slowly, so slow that he barely creeps, and his feet press down harder. I think he is going to make another stop."

"Maybe he intends to cook a part of that fat bear," said Grosvenor, struggling hard, though, to keep all trace of envy out of his voice. "You said a while back that he was going to kill the bear, because he was hungry, and it seems to me that he would be a very foolish man, if having got his bear, he didn't make use of any portion of it."

Tayoga laughed with sincere enjoyment.

"Red Coat reasons well," he said. "If a man is eager to eat, and he has that which he can eat, then he would be a silly man if he did not eat. Red Coat has all the makings of a trailer. In a few more yards, Black Rifle will stop and cook himself a splendid dinner. Here he put his bear meat upon this log. The red stains show it. Then he picked up dead and fallen wood, and broke it into the right length over the log. You can see where he broke places in the bark at the same time. Then he heaped them all in the little hollow, where he has left the pile of ashes. But, before he lighted a fire, with his flint and steel, he made a wide circle all about to see if any enemy might be near. We knew he would do that because Black Rifle is a very cautious man, but his trail proves it to any one who wishes to look. Then, satisfied, he came back, and started the flame. But he kept the blaze very low lest a prowling foe see it. When the bed of coals was fanned he cooked large portions of the bear and ate, because Black Rifle was hungry, ah, so hungry! and the bear was very savoury and pleasing to his palate!"

"Stop, Tayoga, stop!" exclaimed Grosvenor, "I can't stand such torture! You'll make me starve to death where I stand."

"But as you are about to become a warrior of the woods, Red Coat," said the Onondaga gravely, "you must learn to endure. Among us a warrior will purposely put the fire to his hand or his breast and hold it there until the flesh smokes. Nor will he utter a groan or even wince. And all his people will applaud him and call him brave."

Grosvenor shuddered. He did not see the lurking gleam of humour in the eye of Tayoga.

"I don't need to pretend for the sake of practice that I am starving," he said. "I'm starving in fact and I do it without the need of applause."

"But Black Rifle was enjoying himself greatly," continued the Onondaga, "and we can rejoice in the joys of a friend. If we have not a thing ourselves it is pleasant to know that somebody else had it. He used his opportunities to the utmost. Here are more bones which he threw away, with shreds of flesh yet on them, and which the forest people came to pick clean. Lo, their tracks are everywhere about Black Rifle's little camp. One of them became so persistent and bold—a wolf it was—that Black Rifle, not willing to shoot, seized a large stone, and threw it at him with great violence. There lies the stone at the edge of the wood, and as there is fresh earth on its under surface it was partly imbedded in the ground where Black Rifle snatched it up. There, just beyond your right foot, Red Coat, is a little depression, the place in the earth, from which he tore it. Black Rifle's aim was good too. He struck the wolf. At the foot of the bank there are red stains where several drops of blood fell. The wolf was full of mortification, pain and anger, when he ran away. He would never have been so bold and venturesome, if his hunger had not made him forget his prudence. He was as hungry as you are this minute, Red Coat."

"I suppose you are giving me preliminary practice in torture, Tayoga. Well, go on with it, old fellow. I'll try to stand it."

"No, that is enough as a beginning. We will follow the trail of Black Rifle again. After he had eaten so well he was so much refreshed that he will start again with a vigorous and strong step. Lo, it is as I said! He is taking a long stride, but I do not think he is walking fast. His pace is very slow. It may be that there is something in what Dagaeoga says. It is possible that Black Rifle is waiting for those who will not be unwelcome to him."

Robert was quite able to fathom what was passing in the brain of the Onondaga. He saw that the trail was growing quite fresh, and his spirits became buoyant.

"And Red Coat is hungry," said Tayoga, that lurking gleam of humour in his eye growing larger. "Let him remember that however he may suffer from lack of food he can suffer yet more. It is wonderful what the body can endure and yet live. Here Black Rifle stopped and rested on these stones, perhaps an hour. No, Red Coat, there are no signs to show it, but the trail on the other side is much fresher, which proves it. It is quite clear now that Black Rifle is waiting. He is not running away from anybody or anything. Ah! Red Coat, if we only had some of his precious bear steaks how welcome to us they would be!"

"Go on, Tayoga. As I told you, I'd try to stand it."

"That is well, Red Coat. But it is not enough merely to wish for Black Rifle's bear steaks. We will have a portion of them ourselves."

"Now, Tayoga, your talk sounds a little wild to me."

"But listen, Red Coat."

The Onondaga suddenly put his fingers to his lips, and blew a shrill whistle that penetrated far in the forest. In a few instants, the answer, another whistle, came back from a point a few hundred yards ahead, and Tayoga said quietly:

"Red Coat, Black Rifle is waiting for us. We will now go forward and he will give us our dinner."

They advanced without hesitation and the figure of the dark hunter rose up to meet them. His face showed pleasure, as he extended his hand first to Willet.

"Dave, old comrade," he said, "the sight of you in the forest is always a pleasure to the eye. I thought you'd be coming with the lads, and I've been making ready for you. I knew that Tayoga, the greatest trailer the world has ever known, would be sure to strike my traces, and that he'd read them like print. And here's Robert too, a fine boy, if I do say it to his face, and Lieutenant Grosvenor. You mayn't know me, Lieutenant, though I recall you, and I can tell you you're mighty lucky to fall into the hands of these three."

"I think so too," said Grosvenor earnestly.

"Red Coat is happy to see you," said Tayoga, "but he will be happier to see your bear."

"The Lieutenant is hungry," said Black Rifle. "Then come; there is enough for all."

"What made you wait for us?" asked Robert.

"You know how I roam the woods, doing as I please and under nobody's command. I found that Tandakora was by the lake with warriors and that St. Luc was not far away. Tandakora's men seemed to be trailing somebody, and hiding in the bushes, I spied on them. I was near enough to hear two warriors talking and I learned that it was you they were following. Then, coming on ahead, I left a trail for you to see. And I've got plenty of bear steaks already cooked for you."

"God bless you, Mr. Black Rifle," said Grosvenor fervently.

"Amen!" said Robert.

Black Rifle showed them his lair among dense bushes, and, after they had satisfied their hunger, the bear, divided in equal portions among all, was stored away in their knapsacks, Grosvenor luckily having retained his own as the Indians had not deprived him of it. They now had food enough for several days, and one great source of anxiety was removed.

"What had you found, Black Rifle?" asked Willet.

"St. Luc has a big force. He's throwing a sort of veil before Montcalm, while the Marquis fortifies to meet the attack of the British and Americans that all know is coming. Perhaps the Lieutenant can tell us most about that force!"

"It's to be a great one," said Grosvenor.

"And we'll go through to Quebec!" said Robert, his eyes flashing, his imagination at once alive. "We'll put out forever the fire that's always burning in the north and give our border peace."

"Easy, lads, easy!" said Willet. "A thing's never done until it's done. I feel pretty sure we'll do it, but we'll reckon with present difficulties first. It seems to me it's our duty now to follow St. Luc, and see what he means to do with his force. It's hard on you, Lieutenant, because you'll have to stay with us. You can't go back to Albany just yet."

Grosvenor glanced around at the unbroken forest. "I'm resigned," he said. "After that wonderful escape I'm ready for anything. I see that this is my great chance to become a scout, and I'll do the best I can."

"I take it," said Black Rifle, "that the main object of St. Luc is to clear the forest of all our scouts and skirmishers in order that we may be kept in complete ignorance of Montcalm's movements. We'll show him that he can't do it. You have not forgotten any of your skill, have you, Tayoga?"

"So far from forgetting any of it he's acquired more," said Willet, answering for the Onondaga. "When it comes to trailing that boy just breathes it in. He adds some new tricks every day. But I think we'd better lie by, the rest of today, and tonight, don't you, Black Rifle? We don't want to wear out our lads at the start."

"Well spoken, Dave," responded Black Rifle. "It's a camp in the enemy's country we'll have to make with the warriors all about us, but we must take the risk. We'd better go to the next brook and walk up it a long distance. It's the oldest of all tricks to hide your trail, but it is still the best."

They found the brook only a few hundred yards farther on, and extended their walk along its pebbly bed fully a mile and a half as a precaution, keeping to their wading until they could emerge on rocky ground, where they left no trail.

"It will be only chance now that will bring them down on us," said Willet. "Do you think, Lieutenant, that after such a long walk you could manage another bear steak?"

"If the company will join me!" replied Grosvenor. "I don't wish to show bad manners."

"I'll join you," said Willet, speaking for the others, "and I think we'll make a brief camp on that wooded hill there."

"Why on a hill, Mr. Willet? Why not in a hollow where it seems to me we would be better hidden?"

"Because, besides hiding ourselves, we want to see, and you can see better from a height than from a valley. In the bushes there we'll have a view all about us, and I don't think our enemies can come too near, unseen by us. When we get into the thicket on the hill, Lieutenant, you can resume that pleasant nap that you did not finish. Eight or ten hours more of sleep will be just the thing for you."

"All of you sleep a while," said Black Rifle. "I'll guard. I'm fresh. But be sure you walk on the stones. We must leave no trace."

They found a fairly comfortable place in the thicket and soon all were asleep except Black Rifle, who sat with his rifle between his knees, and from his covert scanned the forest on all sides.

Black Rifle felt satisfaction. He was pleased to be with the friends for whom he cared most. An historical figure, solitary, aloof, he was a vivid personality, yet scarcely anything was known about him. His right name even had disappeared, and, to the border, far and near he was just Black Rifle, or Black Jack, a great scout and a terror to the Indians. In his way, he was fond of Willet, Tayoga and young Lennox, and he felt also that he would like Grosvenor when he knew him better. So, while they slept, he watched with a vigilance that nobody save Tayoga could surpass.

Black Rifle saw the life of the forest go on undisturbed. The birds on the boughs went about their business, and the little animals worked or played as usual in the bushes. Everything said to him that no enemy was near, and his own five senses confirmed it. The afternoon passed, and, about twilight, Tayoga awoke, but the others slept on.

"Sleep now, Black Rifle," said the Onondaga. "I will take up the watch."

"I don't feel like closing my eyes just yet, Tayoga," replied the scout, "and I'll sit a while with you. Nothing has happened. Tandakora has not been able to find our trail."

"But he will hunt long for it, Black Rifle. When my race hates it hates well. Tandakora feels his grudge against us. He has tried to do us much harm and he is grieved because we have not fallen before him. He blames us for it."

"I know he does. Did you hear something walking in the thicket at the bottom of the hill?"

"It is only a bear. Perhaps he is looking for a good place in which to pass the night, but he will go much farther away."

"Why, Tayoga?"

"Because the wind is shifting about a little, and, in another minute, it will take him a whiff of the human odour. Then he will run away, and run fast. Now he is running."

"I don't hear him, Tayoga, but I take it that you know what you are saying is true."

"My ears are uncommonly keen, Black Rifle. It is no merit of mine that they are so. Why should a man talk about a gift from Manitou, when it really is the work of Manitou? Ah, the bear is going toward the south and he is well frightened because he never stops to look back, nor does he hesitate! Now he is gone and he will not come back again!"

Black Rifle glanced at the Onondaga in the dusk, and his eyes were full of admiration.

"You have wonderful gifts, Tayoga," he said. "I don't believe such eyes and ears as yours are to be found in the head of any other man."

"But, as I have just told you, Black Rifle, however good they may be the credit belongs to Manitou and not to me. I am but a poor instrument."

"Still you find 'em useful, and the exercise of such powers must yield a certain pleasure. They're particularly valuable just now, as I'm thinking we'll have an eventful night."

"I think so too, Black Rifle. With the warriors and the French so near us it is not likely that it could pass in peace."

"At any rate, Dave and the lads are not worrying about it. I never saw anybody sleep more soundly. I reckon they were pretty well worn out."

"So they were, and, unless danger comes very close, we will not awaken them. That it will be near us soon I do not doubt because Tododaho warns me that peril is at hand."

He was looking up at the star on which his patron saint sat and his face had that rapt expression which it always wore when his spirit leaped into the void to meet that of the great Onondaga chief who had gone away four hundred years ago. Black Rifle regarded him with respect. He too was steeped in Indian lore and belief, and, if Tayoga said he saw and heard what others could not hear or see, then he saw and heard them and that was all there was to it.

"What do you see, Tayoga?" he asked.

"Tododaho sits on his star with the wise snakes, coil on coil in his hair, and the great Mohawk, Hayowentha, who is inferior only to Tododaho, speaks to him from his own star across infinite space. They are talking of us, but it comes only as a whisper, like the dying voice of a distant wind, and I cannot understand their words. But both the great warriors look down warningly at us. They tell us to beware, that we are threatened by a great peril. I can read their faces. But a mist is passing in the heavens. The star of the Mohawk fades. Lo, it is gone! And now the vapours gather before the face of Tododaho too. Lo, he also has gone, and there are only clouds and mists in the far heavens! But the great chiefs, from their stars, have told us to watch and to watch well."

"I believe you! I believe every word you say, Tayoga," exclaimed Black Rifle, in a tone of awe. "The mist is coming down here too. I think it's floating in from the lake. It will be all over the thickets soon. I reckon that the danger threatening us is from the warriors, and if we are in a veil of fog we'll have to rely on our ears. I'm not bragging when I say that mine are pretty good, but yours are better."

Tayoga did not reply. He knew that the compliment was true, but, as before, he ascribed the credit to Manitou because he had made the gift and not to himself who was merely an involuntary agent. The mist and vapours were increasing, drifting toward them in clouds from the lake, a vanguard of shreds and patches, already floating over the bushes in which they lay. It was evident that soon they would not be able to see five yards from there.

In ten minutes the mist became a fog, white and thick. The sleeping three were almost hidden, although they were at the feet of the watchers, and the two saw each other but dimly. They seemed to be in a tiny island with a white ocean circling about them. The Onondaga lay flat and put his ear to the earth.

"What do you hear, Tayoga?" whispered the scout.

"Nothing yet, Black Rifle, but the usual whispers of the wilderness, a little wind among the trees and a distant and uneasy deer walking."

"Why should a deer be walking about at this time, and why should

79

he be uneasy, Tayoga? Any deer in his right mind ought to be taking his rest now in the forest."

"That is true, Black Rifle, but this deer is worried and when a deer is worried there is a cause. A deer is not like a man, full of fancies and creating danger when danger there is none. He is troubled because there are strange presences in the woods, presences that he dreads."

"Maybe he scents us."

"No, the wind does not blow from us toward him. Do not move! Do not stir in the least, Black Rifle! I think I catch another sound, almost as light as that made by a leaf when it falls! Ah, Manitou is good to me! He makes me hear to-night better than I ever heard before, because it is his purpose, I know not why, to make me do so! There comes the little sound again and it is real! It was a footstep far away, and then another and another and now many! It is the tread of marching men and they are white men!"

"How do you know they are white men, Tayoga?"

"Mingled with the sound of their footsteps is a little clank made by the hilts of swords and the butts of pistols striking against the metal on their belts. There is a slight creaking of leather, too, which could not possibly come from a band of warriors. I hear the echo of a voice! I think it is a command, a short, sharp word or two such as white officers give. The sounds of the footsteps merge now, Black Rifle, because the men are marching to the same step. I think there must be at least fifty of them. They are sure to be French, because we are certain our troops are not yet in this region, and because only the French are so active that they make these swift marches at night."

"Unfortunately that's so, Tayoga. Will they pass near us?"

"Very near us, but I do not think they will see us, as the fog is so thick."

"Should we wake the others and move?"

"No, at least not yet. Now they are going very slowly. It is not because they do not know the way, but because the fog troubles them. It is St. Luc who leads them."

"I don't see how your ear can tell you that, Tayoga."

"It is not my ear, it is my mind that tells me, Black Rifle. The French would not go through the forest to-night, unless they had warriors with them as guides, flankers and skirmishers. Only St. Luc could make them come, because we know that even the French have great trouble in inducing them to enter big battles. They like better ambush and foray. De Courcelles could not make them march on this journey nor could Jumonville. My reason tells me it could be only St. Luc. It must be!"

"Yes, I'm sure now it's St. Luc up to some trick that we ought to meet."

"But we do not know what the trick is, Black Rifle. Ah, they have stopped! All of them have stopped!"

"It is not possible that they have seen any traces of us, Tayoga! We left no trail. Besides, this fog is so thick and heavy; it's like a blanket hiding everything!"

"No, it is not that. We left no trail. They are so near that we could see them if there were no fog. Now I hear some one walking alone in front of the company. His step is quick, sharp and positive. It is St. Luc, because, being the leader, he is the only one who would walk that way at such a time. I think he wants to see for himself or rather feel just where they are. Now he too stops, and some one walks forward to join him. It is a Frenchman, because he has on boots. I can hear just the faintest creak of the leather. It must be De Courcelles."

"It may be his comrade Jumonville."

"No, it is De Courcelles, because he is tall while Jumonville is not, and the stride of this man who is going forward to join St. Luc is long. It is surely De Courcelles. St. Luc does not like him, but he has to use him, because the Frenchmen are not many, and a leader can only lead those who are at hand to be led. Now they talk together. Perhaps they are puzzled about the direction."

"Well, so would I be if I had to go anywhere in such a fog."

"They walk back together to the soldiers, and now there is no noise of footsteps."

"I take it that they're waiting for something."

"Aye, Black Rifle. They are waiting in the hope that the fog will rise. You know how suddenly a fog can lift and leave everything bright and clear."

"And they would see us at once. They'll be fairly on top of us."

"So they would be, if the fog should go quickly away."

"And do you think it will?" asked Black Rifle in alarm.

Tayoga laughed under his breath.

"I do not," he replied confidently. "There is no wind to take it away. The great bank of mist and vapour will be heavy upon the ground and will increase in thickness. It would not be wise for us to move, because there may be ears among them as keen as ours, and they might hear us. Then blinded by the fog we might walk directly into the hands of prowling warriors. Although we are not many yards from them we are safest where we are, motionless and still."

Black Rifle also lay down and put his ear to the earth.

"I hear very well myself, although not as well as you, Tayoga," he whispered, "and I want to notice what they're doing as far as I can. I make out the sound of a lot of footsteps, but I can't tell what they mean."

"They are sending groups in different directions, Black Rifle, looking for a way through the forest rather than for us. They are still uncertain where they are. Five or six men are going southward, about as many have turned toward the west, and two warriors and a Frenchman are coming toward us, the rest stay where they are."

"It's the three coming in our direction who are bothering me."

"But remember, Black Rifle, that we are hidden in the deep fog as a fish is hidden in the water, and it will be almost as hard to find us. They must step nearly upon us before they could see us."

Black Rifle, in his eventful life upon the border, had passed through many a crisis, but never any that tested his nerves more thoroughly than the one he now faced. He too heard the steps of the three warriors coming in their direction, cautiously feeling a way through the great bank of mist. It was true that they could pass near without seeing, but chance might bring them straight to the little group. He shifted his fingers to the lock and trigger of his rifle, and looked at the sleeping three whose figures were almost hidden, although they were not a yard away. He felt that they should be awake and ready but in waking, Grosvenor, at least, might make enough noise to draw the warriors upon them at once.

"They have shifted their course a little," whispered Tayoga, "and it leads to our right. Now they change back again, and now they keep turning toward the left. I think they will pass eight or ten yards from us, which will be as good as five hundred or a thousand."

The white man slowly raised his rifle, but did not cock it. That action would have made a clicking sound, sharp and clear in the fog, but the quick hands were ready for instant use. He knew, as Tayoga had said, that the chance of the warriors walking upon them in the blinding fog was small, but if the chance came it would have to be met with all their power and resource.

"I think they will come within about ten feet of us," continued Tayoga, in his soft whisper. "There are two tall warriors and one quite short. The tall ones take about three steps to the short one's four and even then the short man is always behind. They do not walk in single file as usual, but spread out that they may cover as much ground as possible. Now they are coming very near and I think it best, Black Rifle, that I talk no more for the present, but I will hold my rifle ready as you are doing, if unlucky chance should bring them upon us."

The footsteps approached and passed a little to the left, but came so near that Black Rifle almost fancied he could see the dim figures in the fog. When they went on he drew a mighty breath and wiped the perspiration from his face.

"We fairly grazed the edge of death," he whispered. "I'll sit up now and you can do the rest of the listening all by yourself, Tayoga."

"The three have rejoined the main body," said the Onondaga, "and the other parties that went out have also gone back. I think the one that went south probably found the way in which they wanted to go, and they will now move on, leaving us safe for the while. Yes, I can hear them marching and the clank of the French weapons and equipment."

He listened a few minutes longer, and then announced that they were quite beyond hearing.

"They are gone," he said, "and Great Bear, Dagaeoga, and Red Coat have not even known that they were here."

"In which they were lucky," said Black Rifle.

The scout awoke the three, who were much astonished to learn that such danger had passed so near them. Then they considered what was best for them to do next.

CHAPTER 7

The Forest Battle

"It is quite evident," said Robert, as they talked, "that we must follow on the trail of St. Luc. We've settled in our minds that he wants to keep our people busy along Lake George, while Montcalm fortifies higher up. Then it's our duty to find out what he's doing and stop it if we can."

All were in agreement upon the point, even Grosvenor, who did not yet feel at home in the woods.

"But we must wait until the fog lifts," said Willet. "If we moved now we might walk directly into the arms of the enemy, and we can afford to wait the night through, anyhow. Tayoga, we have got to keep you fresh, because your senses and faculties must be at their finest and most delicate pitch for trailing, so now you go to sleep. All the rest of you do the same, and I'll watch."

Soon four slumbered, and only the hunter was awake and on guard. But he was enough. His sight and hearing were almost as good as those of Tayoga himself and he too began to believe that the Onondaga's Manitou was a shield before them. Danger had come often and very near, but it had always passed, and, for the present, at least, he was not apprehensive. The fog might hang on all night if it chose. They could easily make up lost ground in the morning. Meanwhile they were accumulating fresh strength. The four were sleeping very placidly, and it was not likely that they would awake before dawn. Willet looked at their relaxed figures with genuine benevolence. There were the friends for whom he cared most, and he felt sure the young Englishman also would become an addition. Grosvenor was full of courage and he had already proved that he was adaptable. He would learn fast. The hunter had every reason to be satisfied with himself and the situation.

The fog did not go away. Instead, it thickened perceptibly, rolling up in new waves from the lake. The figures of the sleeping four were wrapped in it as in a white blanket, but Willet knew they were there. No air stirred, and, as he sat silent, he listened for sounds that might come through the white veil, hearing only the occasional stirring of some animal. Toward morning the inevitable change occurred. A wind arose in the south, gentle puffs in the beginning, then blowing steady and strong. The fog was torn away first at the top, where it was thinnest, floating off in shreds and patches, and then the whole wall of it yielded before the insistent breeze, driven toward the north like a mist, and leaving the woods and thickets free. Willet made a careful circle about the camp, at a range of several hundred yards, and found no sign of hostile presence. Then he resumed his silent vigil, and, an hour later, the sun rose in a shower of gold. Tayoga opened his eyes and Willet awakened the others.

"The fog is gone," said the hunter, "and eyes are useful once more. I've been around the camp and there is no immediate threat hanging over us. We can enjoy a good breakfast on Black Rifle's cold bear, and then we'll start on St. Luc's trail."

The path of the force that had marched past in the night was quite plain. Even Grosvenor, with his inexperience, could tell that many men had walked there. Most of the Frenchmen as well as the Indians had worn moccasins, but the imprints made by the boot heels of De Courcelles and Jumonville were clearly visible among the fainter traces.

"How many men would you say were in this force, Tayoga?" asked Willet.

"About fifty Frenchmen and maybe as many warriors," replied the Onondaga. "The Frenchmen stay together, but the warriors leave now and then in little parties, and the trail also shows where some of the parties came back. See, Red Coat, here is where two warriors returned. The French stay with St. Luc, not because they are not good scouts and trailers, but because the division of the work now allots this task to the Indians."

"You're right when you call the French good scouts and trailers," said Willet. "They seem to take naturally to forest life, and I know the Indians like them better than they do any other white people. As I often tell Robert, here, the French are enemies of whom anybody can be proud. There isn't a braver race in the world."

"I don't underrate 'em," said Grosvenor.

"It won't be long until we reach their camp," said Tayoga. "Sharp Sword is too great a leader to have carried his men very far in a blind fog. I do not think he went on more than a mile. It is likely that he stopped at the first brook, and the slope of the ground shows that we will come soon to a stream. More of the scouts that he sent out are returning to the main trail. They could not have gone far in the fog and of course they found nothing."

"We'll have, then, to beware lest we run into their camp before they've left it," said Willet.

"I don't think Sharp Sword would stay there after dawn," continued the Onondaga. "The fact that he marched at night in the fog shows that he is eager to get on, and I am quite sure we will find a cold camp. Here go the footsteps of St. Luc. I know they are his, because his foot is small and he wears moccasins. All the French soldiers have larger feet, and the other two Frenchmen, De Courcelles and De Jumonville, wear boots. Sharp Sword does not regard the two officers with favour. He does not associate with them more than is necessary. He keeps on the right side of the trail and they on the left. Here go his moccasins and there go their boots."

"And straight ahead is the brook by the side of which we'll find their camp," said Robert, who had caught the silver flash of water through the green foliage.

The trail, as he had said, led to the brook where the signs of an encampment were numerous.

"The fog was dense with them as it was with us," said Tayoga. "It is shown by the fact that they moved about a great deal, walking over all the ground, before they finally chose a place. If there had been no fog or even only a little they could have chosen at once what they wanted. Knowing that they had no enemy strong enough to be feared they kindled a fire here by this log, more for the sake of light than for warmth. Sharp Sword did not talk over anything with his lieutenants, De Courcelles and Jumonville. His trail leads to the north side of the camp, where he wrapped himself in his blanket and lay down. I imagine that the Canadian, Dubois, who goes with him, as an attendant, watched over him. De Courcelles and Jumonville slept on the other side of the camp. There go their boots. All the French soldiers but Dubois lay down to sleep, and only the warriors watched. They left at dawn, not stopping to eat breakfast. If they had eaten, birds would be here hunting shreds of flesh in the grass, but we do not see a single bird, nor has any wolf or other prowling animal been drawn by the odour of food. We were right in our surmise that Sharp Sword did not wish to delay. Perhaps there is some force of ours that he can catch in a trap, and he wishes to repeat his success against the Mountain Wolf."

"And it is our business to stop him," said Willet.

"If so, we must act promptly, Great Bear. When Sharp Sword makes up his mind to strike he strikes, quick and hard. After his brief camp here he continued his march toward the south. He threw out warriors as scouts and skirmishers. You can see their trail, leading off into the woods, and then his main force marched in a close and compact group. Just beyond the camp a little while after they made the new start he called De Courcelles and De Jumonville to him, and talked with them a little. Here is where his moccasins stood, and here is where their boots stood, facing him, while they received his orders. Then the boots walked back to the end of the line and St. Luc must have spoken to them very sharply."

"Why do you say that, Tayoga?" asked Grosvenor.

"You will notice that here where the trails of boots turn back the stems of grass in two or three places are broken off, not crushed down. De Courcelles and Jumonville kicked them in anger with the sharp toes of their boots, and they could have been angry only because Sharp Sword rebuked them."

"You must be right, Tayoga."

"It does not admit of any doubt, Red Coat. They took their places at the rear of the marching line, and Sharp Sword went on ahead. At no time does he permit them to walk beside him. He still regards the two Frenchmen with much disfavour, and he will continue to do so though he must use them in his expedition."

Tayoga spoke in his precise school English, in which he never omitted or abbreviated a word, but he was very positive. It did not occur to any of the others to doubt him. They had seen too many evidences of his surpassing skill on the trail. They swung along and Grosvenor noticed that many birds now appeared, hopping about in the path, as if searching among the bushes and in the grass for something.

"It looks as if they were seeking food dropped by our foes," he said.

"Did we not say that Red Coat would learn and learn fast!" exclaimed Tayoga. "He has in him the spirit of the forester, and, in time, he will make a great trailer. I have observed the birds, Red Coat, and your conclusion is correct. Sharp Sword's force did not pause to cook breakfast or even to eat it at the camp, but they took it as they walked along swiftly, dropping shreds of flesh or grains of hominy or bones picked clean as they walked. The birds have come to feast on their leavings. Doubtless, they have eaten all already and are merely hunting for more that does not exist. It is strange that no prowling wolf has come. Ah, I see the nose of one now in the thicket! Sharp Sword and his force cannot be very far ahead, and we shall have to be very cautious how we proceed."

"I think it likely," said Willet, "that Tandakora and his band will join him soon. If he is intending an attack upon us somewhere he will want to mass his full strength for it."

"Tandakora will join him before he makes his next camp," said Tayoga, in the most positive manner. "Great Bear reasons well. I expect to see the trail of the Ojibway chief, within an hour."

They went forward slowly, lest they walk into an ambush set by the foe, and, before they had gone two miles, the Onondaga pointed to a new trail coming out of the forest and merging into that of St. Luc.

"Dagaeoga knows who has walked here!" he said.

"Yes," replied Robert. "It's easy to tell where the great feet of Tandakora have passed. I suppose he leaves bigger footprints than any other man now in the province of New York. His warriors were with him too when he joined St. Luc. We were right in supposing that the French leader meditates an attack upon us somewhere."

"Tandakora talked a while with St. Luc," said Tayoga, when they had gone a hundred yards farther. "The big moccasins and the small moccasins stood together beside the trail. The earth was dampened much by the fog last night and it leaves the impressions. I think he talked longer with the Ojibway than he did with De Courcelles and Jumonville. Tandakora is an evil man but perhaps St. Luc feels less dislike for him than he does for the two white men. The Ojibway is only a savage from the region of the Great Lakes, but the Frenchmen should know that the straight way of life is the right way. You do not forget, Dagaeoga, how De Courcelles planned with the others that time we were in Quebec, to have you killed by the bully, Boucher!"

"I don't forget it," said Robert. "I can never forget it, nor do I forget how Dave took my place and sent the bully to a land where he can never more do murder. Much as I hate Tandakora, I don't blame St. Luc for hating him less than he does De Courcelles and Jumonville."

"After the talk they went on together to the head of the line," said Tayoga. "Now they increase their speed. The stride of St. Luc lengthens and as it lengthens so must those of all the rest. We are not now in any danger of running into them, but we may incur it before night."

They did not abate their own speed, but continued in the path without pause, until nearly noon. The broad trail led straight on, over hills, across valleys and always through deep forest, cut here and there by clear streams. The sun came out, and it was warm under the trees. Grosvenor, unused to such severe exertion of this kind, began to breathe with difficulty. But Tayoga called a halt in time at the edge of a brook, and all knelt to drink.

"St. Luc's men were tired and thirsty too, Red Coat," said the Onondaga. "All of them drank. You can see the prints of their knees and feet as they bent over the water. It is a good brook. Manitou has filled the wilderness with its like, that man and beast may enjoy them. We will rest here a while, if Great Bear and Black Rifle say so."

"We do," said the two men together.

They remained fully an hour by the little stream. Robert himself, used as he was to the wilderness, was glad of the rest, and Grosvenor fairly revelled in it, feeling that his nerves and muscles were being created anew. They also made further inroads on their bear and Grosvenor was glad to see the birds coming for the shreds they dropped. He had quite a kindly feeling for the little winged creatures.

"I don't want to think that everything in the woods is an enemy," he said.

When they resumed the pursuit they found another new trail merging into that of the main force. It was a mixed band, red and white as the character of the footprints showed, and numbered about twenty men.

"It is clear," said Tayoga, "that as we supposed, Sharp Sword is planning a heavy stroke. All the detached forces are coming in, under instructions, to join him. We know that Montcalm drew back into the north after his great blow at Fort William Henry, and we think he is going to fortify on Champlain or between the two lakes. Some of our people must be along the shores of Andiatarocte and Sharp Sword does not want them to find out too much about Montcalm."

"At any rate I think our own enterprise will culminate before night," said Willet. "We should overtake them by dusk if we try."

"Sharp Sword's men will make a new camp before long," said Tayoga, "and from that they will launch their attack upon whatever point or force of ours they intend to attack. They are not going so fast now, and the trail is growing very warm. Sharp Sword's stride is shortening and so, of course, is the stride of all the others. I think he now feels that the need of hurrying is over, and he is likely to become much more deliberate."

"And the ground is beginning to slope down toward a deep valley," said Willet. "Water and wood will be plentiful there, and I think that's where St. Luc will make his camp to-night."

"I think so too," said Tayoga. "And since the dusk is not far away maybe they have lighted the fire already. Suppose, Great Bear, we climb the hill on our right and see if our eyes can reach their smoke."

The crest of the hill was about three hundred feet above them, but when they reached it they could see a great distance on all sides, the lake a vast glittering bowl on their left and the mighty green wilderness of hills, mountains and woods on their right. Directly ahead of them was a faint dark line against the dazzling blue of the sky.

"Smoke!" said Tayoga.

"St. Luc's smoke," said Willet.

"The very smoke of the camp for which we were looking and which we were expecting!" said Black Rifle.

Robert's pulses beat hard, as they always did when he knew the great French Chevalier to be near. But that emotion soon passed and in its place came the thought of the enemy's presence. However much he admired St. Luc he was an official foe, to be met upon the battlefield.

"We must look into their camp," he said.

"So we must," said Willet, "and to do that we shall have to go much nearer. The risk is too great now, but it will soon be night, and then we can approach. We can see them well, then, because they'll build all the fires they like, since they think they have nothing to fear."

Then the five waited in silence among the thick woods on the crest of the hill, and Grosvenor prepared his mind for his first stalk. Full of courage, ambitious, eager to excel, he resolved to acquit himself with credit. But this was war, far different from that on the open fields of Europe for which his early training had fitted him. One must lie in the deep forest and depend upon the delicacy of eye and ear and an exceeding quickness of hand. It had not been long since he would have considered his present situation incredible, and, even now, it required some effort to convince himself that it was true.

But there beside him were the comrades whom he liked so well, Robert, Tayoga and the hunter whom he had known before and the strange dark figure of Black Rifle, that man of mystery and terror. Around him was the wilderness now in the glow of advancing twilight, and before him he knew well lay St. Luc and the formidable French and Indian force. Time and place were enough to try the soul of an inexperienced youth and yet Grosvenor was not afraid. His own spirit and willingness to dare peril made a shield for him. His comrades were only four in number, but Grosvenor felt that, in fact, they were twenty. He did not know what strange pass into which they would lead him, but he felt sure they would succeed.

He saw the red rim of the sun sink behind the western crests, and then the last twilight died into the night. Heavy darkness trailed over the forest, but soon moon and stars sprang out, and the sky became silver, the spire of smoke reappearing across its southern face. But Willet, who was in reality the leader of the little party, gave no sign. Grosvenor knew that they were waiting for the majority of St. Luc's force to go to sleep, leaving only the sentinels before they approached, but it was hard to sit there so long. His nerves were on edge and his muscles ached, but his spirit put a powerful rein over the flesh and he said never a word, until far in the night Willet gave the order to advance.

"Be careful, lads," he said, "and now is your chance, Lieutenant, to show how well you can keep up the start you've made as a trailer. That smoke over there which merges from several camp fires is our beacon." They crept through the thickets. Grosvenor saw the dark gray tower against the sky grow larger and larger, and at last a luminous glow that came from the camp fires, rose under the horizon.

"To the edge of this last hill," whispered Willet, "and I think we can see them."

They redoubled their care as they advanced, and then, thrusting their heads through the bushes, looked down into the little valley in which the camp of St. Luc was pitched.

Several fires were burning, and Robert distinctly saw the French leader standing before one of them, not in forest green, but in his splendid officer's uniform of white and silver. A gallant and romantic figure he looked, outlined by the blaze, young, lithe and strong. Again the heart of the lad throbbed, and he was drawn powerfully toward St. Luc. What was it that caused this feeling and why had the Chevalier on more than one occasion and at risk shown himself to be his friend?

Not as many in the camp as they had expected had yet gone to sleep. Tandakora, sombre and gigantic, gnawed the flesh from the big bone of a deer and then, throwing the bone into the fire, approached St. Luc. Robert saw them talking and presently De Courcelles and Jumonville came also. The four talked a little while and now and then the Chevalier pointed toward the south.

"That is where they intend their blow to fall," whispered Tayoga.

"Beyond a doubt, lad," the hunter whispered back, "but we may be able to anticipate 'em."

The wild scene, the like of which he had never looked upon before, cast a strange spell over Grosvenor. He too recognized, even at the distance, the power of St. Luc's personality, and Tandakora, looming, immense, in the firelight, was like some monster out of an earlier, primordial world. Warriors and soldiers asleep were scattered before the fires, and, at the edge of the forest, walked the sentinels. It was an alert and formidable camp, and the young Englishman felt that he and his comrades were grazing the extreme edge of danger.

De Courcelles and Jumonville presently left St. Luc and went to another fire, where they lay down and fell asleep, their military cloaks spread over them. Then the short, dark Canadian Dubois appeared and St. Luc spoke to him also. Dubois bowed respectfully and brought a blanket, which he spread before the fire. St. Luc lay down on it, and he too was soon asleep.

"It's time for us to go," whispered Willet, "but I'd feel safer if Tandakora also went to sleep. That savage is likely to send out scouts."

"Tandakora does not mean to sleep to-night," said Tayoga. "He suspects that we are somewhere near and he is troubled. If he were not uneasy he would take his rest, which is what a chief always does when the opportunity presents itself. But he has thrown his second bone into the fire, and he walks about, looking now at the sleepers and now at the forest. I think he will soon send two or three runners toward the south. See, he is speaking to them now, and two are starting."

Two Indians left the camp and glided silently into the woods. Then Tandakora stopped his restless pacing, and lay down on the ground. His face was in the shadow, but he seemed to be asleep.

The four on the hill crept away as cautiously as they had come, and they agreed that they would make a curve around St. Luc's camp, travelling all night toward the south. Willet was anxious about the two warriors whom Tandakora had sent out, and he felt that they might possibly encounter them on the way. He led his little group first toward the lake and then bore south, being quite sure that before noon the next day they would reach a British or American detachment of some kind. Everything indicated such proximity and they were agreed that they would find their friends on the shores of the lake. It was not likely that either colonials or regulars would leave the open water and go far into woods which furnished so many perils.

They were refreshed by sleep and plenty of food and they made good time. They walked in single file, Willet leading with Tayoga last and Grosvenor in front of him. The young Englishman's ambition, encouraged by success, was rising higher than ever, and he was resolved that this night trail which he was treading should be a good one, so far as he was concerned. Robert walked in front of him and he was careful to step exactly where young Lennox did, knowing that if he did so he would break no sticks and make no undue noise. The test was severe, but he succeeded. By and by his breath grew short once more. Nevertheless he was glad when Willet halted, and asked Tayoga if he heard any unusual sound in the forest. Before replying the Onondaga lay down and put his ear to the ground.

"I do hear a sound which is not that of the trees nor of an animal," he replied. "It is made by men walking, and I think they are the two warriors whom Tandakora sent out from the camp."

"And if you can hear them walking they must be very near. That is sure."

"It is true, Great Bear. These two warriors are sent south to spy upon whatever force of ours St. Luc means to attack, and it may be that they will strike our trail, although they are not looking for it. There is light enough now to show our traces to good trailers."

"Aye, Tayoga, you speak truly. Lie down, lads, we must not show ourselves. It's possible that they'll pass on and not dream of our presence here."

"It is in the hands of Manitou," said the Onondaga gravely. "They are still walking toward the south at an even pace, which shows that they have seen nothing. I can hear their footfalls, only a whisper against the earth, but unmistakable. Now, they are just behind us, and their course is the same as ours. Ah, the footfalls cease! They have stopped. They have seen our trail, Great Bear. Manitou has given his decree against us, and who are we to complain? He has done so much for us that now he would put us to the test, and see whether we are worthy of his favour. We shall have to fight the messengers."

"It should be easy enough for us who are five to beat two warriors," said Robert.

"We can surely beat two," said Tayoga, "but they will try to hold us while they call help. It will not be long before you hear the cry of a night bird, doubtless an owl."

"Have they begun to move again?" asked Robert.

"I cannot hear a sound. Perhaps they are stirring, but they creep so cautiously that they make no noise at all. It would be their object to make their own position uncertain and then we would go on at great peril from their bullets. It will be best for us to stay a while where we are."

Tayoga's words were accepted at once as wise by the others. It was impossible to tell where the two warriors now lay, and, if they undertook to go on, their figures would be disclosed at once by the brilliant moonshine. So they flattened themselves against the ground in the shadow of the bushes and waited patiently. The time seemed to Grosvenor to be forever, but he thrilled with the belief in coming combat. He still felt that he was in the best of all company for forest and midnight battle, and he did not fear the issue.

Willet was hopeful that the skies would darken, but they did not do so. The persistent moon and a host of stars continued to shine down, flooding the forest with light, and he knew that if any one of them stood up a bullet would be his instant welcome. At last came the cry of the night bird, the note of the owl, as Tayoga had predicted, rising from a point to their right and somewhat behind them, but too far away for rifle shot. It was a singular note, wild, desolate and full of menace.

"There may have been another band of warriors in this direction," whispered Tayoga, "perhaps a group of hunters who had not yet returned to St. Luc, and he is calling to them."

"No earthly doubt of it," said Black Rifle. "Can you hear the reply, Tayoga?"

"Now I hear it, though it is very faint. It is from the south and the warriors will soon be here. We shall have a band to fight."

"Then we'd better bear off toward the west," said Willet. "Come, lads, we have to creep for it."

They made their way very slowly on hands and knees away from the lake, Willet leading and Tayoga bringing up the rear. It was hard and painful work for Grosvenor, but again he succeeded in advancing without noise, and he began to think they would elude the vigilance of the savage scouts, when a sibilant whisper from Willet warned them to fall flat again. His command was just in time as a rifle cracked in the bushes ahead of them, and Grosvenor distinctly heard the bullet as it hissed over their heads. Willet threw his rifle to his shoulder but quickly took it down again. The Indian who had fired was gone and a little puff of smoke rising above the bushes told where he had been. Then the five crept away toward the right and drew into a slight hollow, rimmed around with bushes, where they lay hugging the earth.

"Our course took us almost directly into the path of that fellow," said Willet, "and of course he saw us. I'm sorry I didn't get a shot at him."

"Do not worry, Great Bear," said Tayoga. "You will find plenty of use for your bullets. The band has come. Hark to the war whoop!"

The long, piercing yell, so full of menace and most sinister in its dying note, swelled through the forest. Grosvenor, despite his courage and confidence in his comrades, shivered. He had heard that same yell many a time, when Braddock's army was cut down in the deep forest by an invisible foe. He could never forget its import. But he grasped his rifle firmly, and strove to see the enemy, who, he knew, was approaching. His four comrades lay in silence, but the muzzle of every weapon was thrust forward.

"It's fortunate we found this little hollow," said Willet. "It will give us shelter for a while."

"And we'll need it," said Black Rifle. "They know where we are, of course, but they'll take their time about attacking."

"Keep your heads down, lads," said Willet. "Don't be too eager to see. If they're too far away for us to shoot at we are too far away for them too."

Five minutes later and a flash came from a thicket on their left. Willet pulled trigger at the flash and a death cry came back.

"That's one out of the way," said Black Rifle calmly, "and they're mad clean through. Hear 'em yell!"

The fierce war whoop died in many echoes, and bullets spattered the rocks about them. The five made no further reply as yet, but the forest battle was now on.

CHAPTER 8

The Boat Builders

Robert and Grosvenor lay, side by side, propped up partly on their elbows, their rifles thrust well forward, and watching toward the north. They were not able to see anything, save the dark outline of the forest, and a little puff of smoke rising where an Indian had fired. The wilderness itself was absolutely still but Robert's vivid imagination as usual peopled it thickly. Although his eye did not reach any human figure his mind pictured them everywhere, waiting patiently for a chance at his comrades and himself. He, more than any other of the five, realized the full extent of the danger. His extraordinary fancy pictured to him every possibility, and so his courage was all the greater, because he had the strength to face them with a tranquil mind.

A flash in the thicket and a bullet struck on a rock near Robert, glanced off and buried itself in a tree beyond them. He shivered a little. Fancy pictured the bullet not as missing, but as hitting him. Then he steadied himself, and was as ready as Willet or Black Rifle for whatever might come.

"I think that shot was fired by a sharpshooter who has crept forward ahead of the others," whispered the hunter. "He's lying behind that low bush to the west."

"I'm of your mind about it," said Black Rifle. "As soon as he reloads he'll chance another shot at where he thinks we're lying, and that will be his last."

Robert heard the low words, and he shivered again a little. He could never grow used to the taking of human life, even in dire necessity. He knew that Willet had spoken the truth, and that the red sharpshooter would fire only one more shot. Soon he had the proof. The second flash came from the same point. Again the bullet glanced among the rocks, but, before the report of the rifle died, another answered. It was that of the hunter and he found his mark. A cry came from the bush, followed by a fierce yell of anger from those farther back, and then the sinister stillness settled again over the wilderness.

"The Indian has gone!" whispered Grosvenor in an awed tone to Robert.

"Yes, Dave fired at the flash, and he never misses. The cry showed it. But it will make the warriors all the more eager to take us."

The silence lasted about a quarter of an hour, and then fire was opened upon them from three sides, bullets singing over their heads, or spattering upon the rocks.

"Lie flat, lads," commanded Willet. "This is random lead, and if we keep close to the earth 'twill all pass us by. The warriors are seldom good marksmen."

But one of the bullets, glancing from a rock, nipped Black Rifle in the shoulder. It was a very slight wound, though, and its only effect was to make him more eager to reach his enemy. In a few minutes his chance came as he caught a glimpse of a dusky but incautious figure among the trees, and, quick as a flash, drew trigger on it. There was no cry, but he saw the shadowy figure go down, not to rise again, and the fierce soul of Black Rifle was satisfied.

Scattered shots were fired, after another silence, and a bullet grazed the back of Grosvenor's hand, drawing a drop or two of blood. It stung for a few moments, but, on the whole, he was proud of the little hurt. It was a badge of honour, and made him truly a member of this great forest band. It also stimulated his zeal, and he became eager for a shot of his own. He watched intently and when the warriors fired again he sent his bullet at the flash, as he had seen Willet and Black Rifle do. He did not know whether he had hit anything, but he hoped. Tayoga, who fired for the first time presently brought down a warrior, and Robert wounded another. But Willet and Black Rifle talked together in whispers and they were anxious.

"They won't try to rush us so long as we keep among the rocks," said the hunter. "They know now that we're good shots, but they'll hold us here until day when their main force will come up and then we'll be finished."

"It seems pretty certain that's their plan now," said the scout, "and between you and me, Dave, we've got to get away from here some-how. The moon has faded a bit, and that will help us a little. What do you think, Tayoga?"

"We did not escape other traps to remain here in this," replied the Onondaga. "We must take the chance and go."

97

"In half an hour, perhaps. When the clouds floating up there get well before the moon."

Robert heard them distinctly and he glanced at the moon which was steadily growing paler, while the shadows were deepening over the forest. Yet it was obvious that it would not become very dark, and the half hour of which Willet had spoken would probably measure the limit of the increase.

"Can you hear them moving in the bush, Tayoga?" asked Willet.

The Onondaga put his ear to the ground.

"Only a light sound toward the north reaches me," he replied. "Warriors there seem to be moving about. It may be that they have received more help. I think, Great Bear, that the time for us to go, if we go at all, is coming fast."

Willet decided in a few minutes that it would not be any darker than it was then; and, choosing a southern direction, he crept from the rocks, the others following him in line, Tayoga as usual bringing up the rear. They made a hundred yards in silence, and, then, at a low signal from the hunter, they sank down, almost flat, every one listening for a sound from the besiegers. Only Tayoga was able to hear faint noises to right and left.

"They do not know yet that we have left the rocks," he whispered, "and they are still watching that point. Manitou may carry us in safety between them."

They were about to resume their painful creeping, when a half dozen rifles on their right flashed, and they dropped down again. But the bullets did not come their way, instead they rang among the rocks which they had just left. Tayoga laughed softly.

"They think we are still there," he whispered, "and they send much lead against the inoffensive stone. The more the better for us."

"I'm devoutly glad the rocks catch what is intended for us," said Grosvenor, feeling intense relief. "How long do you think it will be, Tayoga, before I can stand up and walk like a man again?"

"No one can answer that question," replied the Onondaga. "But remember, Red Coat, that you are getting splendid practice in the art of going silently along a trail on a dark night. It is what every forest runner must learn."

Grosvenor in the dusk could not see the twinkle in Tayoga's eye, but, drawing upon fresh founts of courage and resolution, he settled himself anew to his task. His elbows and knees ached and it was difficult to carry his rifle as he crawled along, but his ambition was as high as ever, and he would not complain. The lone hoot of an owl came from the point on the right, where one of the Indian groups lay, and it was promptly answered by a like sound from the left where another group was hidden.

"I think they're beginning to suspect that we may have slipped away," said Willet, "and they're talking to one another about it. Now they'll stalk the rocks to see, but that will take time, which we can use handily. Come on, lads, we'll go as fast as possible."

Curving around a small hill, Willet rose to his feet and the others, with intense relief, did likewise. Robert's and Grosvenor's joints were young and elastic, and the stiffness quickly left them, but both had done enough creeping and crawling for one night. All stood listening for a minute or two. They heard no more shots fired at the rocks, but the two owls began to call again to each other.

"Do you understand them, Tayoga?" asked Willet.

"They talk the Huron language," replied the Onondaga, in his precise fashion, "that is, their signals are those used by the Hurons. They are asking each other what has happened at the rocks, and neither can tell. Their expression is that of doubt, impatience and worry. They say to each other: 'Those whom we believed we held in a trap may have broken out of it. It will take time to see and also much peril if they are still in the trap, because they can use their rifles well.' We annoy them much, Great Bear."

The big hunter chuckled.

"I don't mind that," he said. "Their worries are not my worries. Ah, there they go again! What are they saying now, Tayoga?"

"Their tone grows more anxious. You can tell what they feel by the expression of the owl. Their fear that we may have stolen out of the trap is increasing, but they cannot know unless they go and see, and then they may be creeping into the muzzles of our rifles. It is a difficult problem that we have given them to solve, Great Bear."

"We'll leave it for 'em, lads. Now that we're on our feet we'll go at speed."

They walked very rapidly, but they stopped when they heard once more the faint cries of the owls, now almost lost in the distance. Tayoga interpreted them.

"They are cries of anger," he said. "They have discovered that we are not in the rocks, and now they will look around for our trail, which will be hard to find in the darkness of the night."

"And the thing for us to do is to keep on toward the south as hard as we can."

"So it would be, Great Bear, but others are coming up from the south, and we would go directly into their arms."

"What do you mean, Tayoga?"

"A number of men are advancing, and I think they are warriors."

"Then we have merely slipped out of one trap to fall into another."

"It is possible, Great Bear. It is also possible that those who come are friends. Let me put my ear to the earth, which is the bringer of sound. It is clear to me that those who walk toward us are warriors. White men would not tread so lightly. I do not think, Great Bear, that any force of the Indians who are allied with the French would be coming up from the south, and the chances are that these be friends."

He sent forth the call of a bird, a beautiful, clear note, and it was answered instantly with a note as clear and as beautiful.

"They are friends!" said Tayoga joyfully. "These be the Ganeagaono!"

"Ganeagaono?" exclaimed Grosvenor.

"Mohawks," explained Robert. "The Keepers of the Eastern Gate. The leading warriors of the Six Nations and friends of ours. We are, in truth, in luck."

Ten dusky figures came forward to meet them, and with great joy Robert recognized in the leader the fierce young Mohawk chief, Daganoweda, who once before had come to their help in a crisis. But it was Tayoga who welcomed him first.

"Daganoweda, of the clan of the Turtle, of the nation, Ganeagaono, of the great League of the Hodenosaunee, the sight of you is very pleasant to our eyes," he said.

"Tayoga, of the clan of the Bear, of the Nation, Onondaga, of the great League of the Hodenosaunee, you are my brother and we are well met," the chief rejoined.

They saluted each other and then Daganoweda greeted the others, all of whom were known to him of old save Grosvenor, but who was presented duly in the ceremonious style loved by the Iroquois.

"We are pursued by men of Tandakora," said Willet. "They are not far away now. We do not wish to fight them because we would hasten below with a warning."

The black eyes of the fierce Mohawk flashed.

"Will the Great Bear give us his battle?" he said.

He asked for it as if for a favour.

"We usually fight our own quarrels through," replied Willet, "but as I said, duty calls us from here in haste. Then, since you wish it, Daganoweda, we pass the fight to you. But have you enough men?"

"Ten Mohawks are enough to meet any wandering band of our enemies that may be in the woods," replied the young chief, proudly. "Let Great Bear and his friends go in peace. This fight is ours."

Despite the dusk, Robert saw Daganoweda's eyes glisten. He thoroughly understood the fierce soul of the young Mohawk chief, who would not let such a brilliant opportunity for battle pass him.

"Then farewell, Daganoweda," said Willet. "You have been a friend at the right moment."

He led again in the flight toward the south and the five saw the chief and his warriors passing the other way sink into the dusk. Soon they heard shots behind them and they knew that the Mohawks were engaged in battle with the Hurons and their friends. They sped on for a long time, and when they stopped they were close to the shores of the lake, the water showing dimly through the trees.

"I think we may rest easy for a while now," said Willet. "I'm certain not one of those warriors was able to get by the Mohawks, and it's not likely that an enemy is within several miles of us. Can you hear anything, Tayoga?"

"Nothing," replied the Onondaga. "Tododaho, on his star, tells me that we have this part of the forest to ourselves."

"That being so, we'll stay here a long time. Lads, you might unroll your blankets and make the best of things."

Grosvenor's blanket had not been taken from him when he was a prisoner, and it was still strapped on his back. He and Robert found the rest most welcome and they were not slow in wrapping the blankets around their bodies and making themselves comfortable. Without willing it, they fell asleep, but were awakened shortly after dawn.

"See!" said Willet, pointing toward the south.

A filmy trail of blue smoke rose across the clear, blue sky.

"That, whatever it is," said the hunter, "is what St. Luc is advancing against, but in spite of all the risks we've run we'll be there in time to give warning."

Robert looked with the deepest interest at the smoke, which was a long way off, but it seemed to rise from the lake's edge and he thought it must be a British or American post. It was at a most exposed and dangerous point, but his heart thrilled at Willet's words. Yes, in spite of every danger that had been thrown across their path, they would be able to carry word in time.

"We'll be there in half an hour, and we'll know what's going forward," said Willet.

"We'll know before then," said Grosvenor confidently. "Our marvellous Indian friend here will tell us when we're half way."

Tayoga smiled, but said nothing, and they started again, Willet, as usual, leading, and the Onondaga bringing up the rear. The spire of smoke thickened and darkened, and, to Robert and Grosvenor, it seemed most friendly and alluring. It appeared to rise from a little point of land thrust into the lake but they could not yet see its base, owing to an intervening hill. Just before they reached the crest of the hill Tayoga said:

"Wait a moment, Great Bear. I think I hear a sound from the place where the smoke rises, and we may be able to tell what it means."

They stopped promptly, and the Onondaga put his ear to the earth.

"I hear the sounds very distinctly now," he said. "They are of a kind not often occurring on these shores."

"What are they?" asked Robert eagerly.

"They are made by axes biting into wood. Many men are cutting down trees."

"They're building a fort, and they're in a hurry about it or they would not be felling trees so early in the morning."

"Your reasoning about the hurry is good, Dagaeoga. The white man will not go into the forest with his axe at daybreak, unless the need of haste is great, but it is not a fort they build. Mingled with the fall of the axes I hear another note. It is a humming and a buzzing. It is heard in these forests much less often than the thud of the axe. Ah! I was in doubt at first, but I know it now! It is the sound made by a great saw as it eats into the wood."

"A saw mill, Tayoga!"

"Yes, Dagaeoga, that is what it is, and now mind will tell us why it is here. The logs that the axes cut down are sawed in the mill. The saw would not be needed if the logs were to be used for building a fort. The axe would do it all. The logs are being turned into planks and boards."

"Which shows that they're being used for some purpose requiring much finer finish than the mere building of a fort."

"Now the mind of Dagaeoga is working well. Great Bear and I have been on the point where the new saw mill stands."

"And the timber there is fine," interrupted Willet.

"Just the kind that white men use when they build long boats for travelling on the lakes, boats that will carry many men and armband supplies. We know that a great army of red coats is advancing. It expects to come up George and then probably to Champlain to meet Montcalm and to invade Canada. It is an army that will need hundreds of boats for such a purpose, and they must be built."

"And they're building some of 'em right here on this point, before us!" exclaimed Robert.

Tayoga smiled.

"It is so," he said precisely. "There cannot be any doubt of it. A saw mill could not be here for any other purpose. But if we had not come it would be destroyed or captured before night by St. Luc."

"Come on, lads, and we'll soon be among 'em," said Willet.

From the crest of a hill they looked down upon a scene of great activity. The sun was scarcely risen but more than fifty men were at work on the forest with axes, and, at the very edge of the water, a saw mill was in active operation. Along the shore, where as many more toiled, were boats finished and others in all stages of progress. Soldiers in uniform, rifles on shoulder, walked about.

It was a pleasant sight, refreshing to the eyes of Robert and Grosvenor. Here were many men of their own race, and here were many activities, telling of great energy in the war. After so much peril in the forest they would be glad to be in the open and with their own kind again.

"Look, Robert," said Willet, "don't you know them?"

"Know whom?" asked young Lennox.

"The officers of this camp. The lads in the brave uniforms. If my eyes make no mistake, and they don't make any, the fine, tall young fellow standing at the edge of the water is our Philadelphia friend, Captain Colden."

"Beyond a doubt it is, Dave, and right glad am I to see him, and there too is Wilton, the fighting Quaker, and Carson also. Why this is to be, in truth, a reunion!"

Willet put his hands to his mouth trumpet fashion, and uttered a long, piercing shout. Then the five advanced and marched into the camp of their friends, where they received a welcome, amazed but full of warmth, Grosvenor, too, being made to feel at home.

"Have you dropped from the skies?" asked Colden.

"Scarcely that," replied Robert, laughing with pleasure, "but we've been shot out of the forest, and very glad we are to be here. We've come to tell you also that we've been pursued by a strong French and Indian force, led by St. Luc himself, and that it will be upon you before nightfall."

"And I, trained in my boyhood not to fight, will have to fight again," said Wilton.

"I know that none will do it better," said Robert.

"But we will give you breakfast," said Colden, "and while you are eating I will put the camp in a posture of defence. We are here building boats to be used by the army in its advance against Montcalm, and we didn't know that the enemy in force was south of Crown Point."

There were several sheds and in one of these a most abundant breakfast was served to them, including coffee and white bread, neither of which they had seen in a long time, and which were most welcome. While they ate, they saw the young Pennsylvania officers arranging their forces with skill and rapidity.

"They've learned a lot since we were with 'em that time at Fort Refuge," said Robert.

"They've had to learn," said Willet. "The forests in these times are a hard teacher, but they're bright and good boys, just the same. Nobody would learn faster."

"Even as Red Coat has learned to be a scout and to know the trail," said Tayoga, "but he is not sorry to come among white men and to have good food once more."

"No, I'm not," said Grosvenor emphatically. "My ambition to be a fine trailer was high last night, and it's still with me, but I had enough of creeping and crawling to last me a long time, and if we have to fight again I think I can fight better standing up."

"We will have to fight again. Be sure of that," said Tayoga decisively.

Before breakfast was over Colden came to them, and Robert told, in detail and with great vividness, all they had seen. The young Philadelphia captain's face became very grave.

"It was you who warned us before Fort Refuge," he said, "and now you come again. You helped us to success then, and you'll help us now. Even if your coming does bring news of danger I'll consider it a good omen."

"We'll be proud to stand in line with you once more," said Robert, although he felt that, with St. Luc in command, the attack of the French and Indians would be formidable. Colden would have available for battle between one hundred and fifty and two hundred men, about fifty of whom were soldiers. But all the others, the boat builders and the rest, were capable fighters too. They could certainly make a powerful resistance even to the daring and skilful French Chevalier, and, with a certain number of boats finished, the lake also was open to them, in case retreat became necessary. Luckily, too, St. Luc had no cannon. Courageous Captain Colden considered their situation far from desperate. There was hope too that Daganoweda and his Mohawks might come, not only those he had with him in the night battle, but others as well. The Mohawks, loving a combat, would not let go by such a one as that now threatening.

Willet rose from his breakfast and surveyed the position. There were no real buildings, only sheds, the largest covering the saw mill, and the others used for the protection of tools and of the men, when they slept, against the weather. All the trees for a distance well beyond rifle shot had been cut away for timber, a lucky fact, as the hostile Indians could not now use them for ambush. Stout arms were throwing the fallen trees into a long line of breastworks, and the place already began to look like a fortified point. Willet's eyes glistened.

"Although St. Luc beat us when we were with Rogers," he said, "I think we'll hold him here. We've certain advantages that will help us mightily."

"Thanks to you and your comrades for bringing us such timely warning," repeated Colden. "I'll confess that I did not suspect any enemy was nearer than Champlain, and neither we nor our superiors at Albany have feared an attack here."

"It's sure to come," said Willet.

Grosvenor, refreshed and reinvigorated, was taking an active share in the preparations. He had smoothed and brushed his uniform with scrupulous care, and despite the great hardships through which he had passed, looked once more neat and trim. He had returned to his incarnation as a trim young British officer. Adaptable and liking the Americans, equipped moreover with a certain experience of the border, he was at once on the best of terms with Colden, Wilton, Carson and the others, and was, in truth, one of them. Wilton found him a belt and a small sword, which he buckled on, and which as a badge of office gave him a certain moral strength, making him in fact a thoroughly happy man that morning.

Black Rifle, after food, had slid quietly into the forest to spy out the enemy. Robert, flexible, vivid, his imagination always alive, was with Tayoga, helping him with the breastworks, and keeping an eye at the same time on the forest. The lake behind him stretched away, vast, peaceful and beautiful, but he seldom looked at it now. He did not anticipate danger that way. It would come through the woods.

A gradual slope, hemmed in on either side by high cliffs and only a few hundred yards wide, led to the point on which the saw mill stood. St. Luc must approach by the slope. The cliffs were impossible, and, the longer he looked at it, the better Robert liked the position. Daring men such as Colden had could hold it against a much larger force. Let St. Luc come, he would find a brave and ready defence.

"Dagaeoga thinks we can hold the saw mill even against Sharp Sword," said Tayoga.

"How do you know I think it?"

"Because it is printed on Dagaeoga's face. When Dagaeoga's fancy is alive, which is nearly all the time, his eyes speak and they tell one very clearly what he thinks. His eyes say that the slope is narrow; St. Luc can come that way only; we have here more than one hundred and fifty good rifles; and in face of the storm of lead that we can send against him he cannot rush us. That is what the eyes and face of Dagaeoga say."

"You're right, Tayoga, that is what my brain thinks, though I didn't know it was printed on my face. But it's all the easier for you to read it, because you're probably thinking the same that I do."

"I do, Dagaeoga. Since St. Luc is not able to effect a surprise, he has a great task before him, though he will persist in it, because he wants to destroy our force and our boats also."

But the morning passed without any demonstration from the forest. Many of the boat builders began to believe it was a false alarm, and murmured at the continuous and hard labour on the breastworks, but Colden, knowing that Willet and his friends were to be trusted implicitly, held them to their tasks. The hunter also looked into the question of food supply and found it ample. They had brought much food with them from Albany and the forest had furnished much more. There was no occasion for alarm on that point, since the siege could not be a long one. Noon came and no sign of the enemy. Willet began to think the attack would be postponed until night, as St. Luc doubtless had learned already that he could not carry the place by surprise. But he relied most upon the word of Black Rifle who had not yet returned from the forest. The dark scout came back about the middle of the afternoon, and he told Colden and Willet that he had seen nothing of Daganoweda and his Mohawks, though there were indications in the forest that they had defeated the Hurons the night before. But St. Luc Was at hand, not much more than a mile away, where he had pitched a camp. More French and Canadians had arrived and he now led a force of at least five hundred men, the great majority of whom were warriors. He thought an attack would be made after dark, but in what form it was impossible to say.

"Which means," said Colden, "that I must have sentinels who will never relax their vigilance."

"Particularly as the night is going to be dark," said Willet. "There's a haze over the lake now, and the sun will set in a mist."

The twilight was heavy as he had predicted, and it was soon black on the mountains and the lake. But within the camp fires were burning, throwing a cheerful light, and many guards were posted. Crude but effective fortifications stretched all along the forest side of the camp, and Willet, Black Rifle and Tayoga were among the stumps in front of them. No enemy would be able to hide there even in the night. Wagons in which they had brought their supplies were drawn up in a circle, and would form an inner line of defence. Robert was with Grosvenor and Wilton near the centre of the camp.

"Knowing the French and Indians as I now do," said Wilton, "I never doubt for an instant that an attack will come before morning. My experience at Fort Refuge is sufficient indication. It is strange that I, who was reared not to believe in fighting, should now be compelled to do it all the time."

"And while my profession is fighting," said Grosvenor, "I always expected to fight in the open fields of Europe and now I'm learning my trade in the deep forests of North America, where it's quite another sort of business. How long do you think it will be, Lennox, before we hear the owls hoot and the wolves bark?"

Robert laughed.

"We've had a lot of such signals in the last few days," he replied, "but in this country battles are not always opened with 'em. Still, I dare say we'll hear 'em."

Out of the forest in front of them came a long, lonely hoot.

"Speak of the owl and you hear his voice," said Wilton.

"If Tayoga were here he could tell us exactly what that owl, who is no owl but an Indian, meant," said Grosvenor, "also the tribe of the Indian, his age, his complexion, what he had for supper, how he is feeling and whether he is married or single. Oh, I assure you, Wilton, you needn't smile! I've seen the Onondaga do things much more marvellous. Nothing short of trailing a bird through the air would really test his wilderness powers."

"I wasn't smiling at your belief, Grosvenor," said the young Quaker, "I was merely smiling at your earnestness. When you tell me anything about Tayoga's skill on the trail I shall believe it, I don't care what it is. I saw him do marvellous things when we were at Fort Refuge."

The owl ceased its melancholy cry, and no other sound came from the forest, while the camp waited, with as much patience as it could muster, for the attack.

CHAPTER 9

The Masked Attack

Light clouds floated before the moon, and the surface of the lake was ruffled by a southern wind. As no attack was anticipated from the south, the guard in that quarter was comparatively small, but it was composed, nevertheless, of good men, the boat builders mostly, but all experienced with the rifle and under the direct command of Carson. But the main force was always kept facing the forest, and, there, behind the logs, Colden stood with the four—Black Rifle again being outside. The hooting of the owls had not been repeated and the long wait had become hard upon the nerves of the young Philadelphia captain.

"Do you feel sure that they will attack to-night?" he asked Willet. "Perhaps St. Luc, seeing the strength of our position, will draw off or send to Montcalm for cannon, which doubtless would take a week."

The hunter shook his head.

"St. Luc will not go away," he said, "nor will he send for cannon, which would take too long. He will not use his strength alone, he will depend also upon wile and stratagem, against which we must guard every minute. I think I'll take my own men and go outside. We can be of more service there."

"I suppose you're right, but don't walk into danger. I depend a lot on you."

Willet climbed over the logs. Tayoga, Robert and Grosvenor followed.

"Red Coat buckled on a sword, and I did not think he would go on a trail again," said Tayoga.

"One instance in which you didn't read my mind right," rejoined the Englishman. "I know that swords don't belong on the trail, but this is only a little blade, and you fellows can't leave me behind."

"I did read your mind right," said Tayoga, laughing softly. "I merely spoke of your sword to see what you would say. I knew all the time that you would come with us."

The stumps, where the forest had been cut away, stretched for a distance of several hundred yards up the slope, and, a little distance from the breastwork, the dark shadow of Black Rifle came forward to meet them.

"Nothing yet?" asked the hunter.

"Nothing so far. Three or four good men are with me among the stumps, but not a warrior has yet appeared. I suppose they know we'll be on watch here, and it's not worth while taking so great a risk."

They advanced to the far edge of the stump region and crouched there. The night was now quite dark, the moon almost hidden, the stars but few, and the forest a solid black line before them.

"Why can't Tayoga use his ears?" said Grosvenor. "He'll hear them, though a mile away."

"A little farther on and he will," replied Willet, "but we, in our turn, don't dare to go deep into the forest."

A hundred yards more and the Onondaga put ear to earth, but it was a long time before he announced anything.

"I hear footsteps fairly near to us," he said at last, "and I think they are those of warriors. They would be more cautious, but they do not believe we are outside the line of logs. Yes, they are warriors, all warriors, there is no jingle of metal such as the French have on their coats or belts, and they are going to take a look at our position. They are about to pass now to our right. I also hear steps, but farther away, on our left, and I think they are those of Frenchmen."

"Likely De Courcelles and Jumonville wanting also to look us over," said Willet.

"There is another and larger force coming directly toward us," continued the Onondaga, "and I think it includes both French and warriors. This may be the attack and perhaps it would be better for us to fall back."

They withdrew a little, but remained among the stumps, though hidden carefully. Robert himself could now hear the advance of the large force in front of them, and he wondered what could be St. Luc's plan of battle. Surely he would not try to take the sawmill by storm in face of so many deadly rifles!

Black Rifle suddenly left the others and crept toward the right. Robert's eyes followed him, and his mind was held by a curious sort of fascination. He knew that the scout had heard something and he almost divined what was about to occur. Black Rifle stopped a moment or two at a stump, and then curved swiftly about it. A dusky figure sprang up, but the war cry was choked in the throat of the Huron, and then the knife, wielded by a powerful arm, flashed. Robert quickly turned his eyes away, because he did not wish to see the fall of the blade, and he knew that the end was certain. Black Rifle came back in a few moments. His dark eyes glittered, but he had wiped the knife, and it was in his belt again.

"His comrades will find him in a few minutes," said Willet, "and we'd better not linger here."

"They went back toward the sawmill and presently they heard a terrible cry of rage, a cry given for the fallen warrior.

"I don't think I shall ever grow used to such yells," said Grosvenor, shuddering.

"I've never grown used to 'em yet," said Robert.

The shout was followed by a half dozen shots, and a bullet or two whistled overhead, but it was clear that all of them had been fired at random. The warriors, aware that the chance of surprise had passed, were venting their wrath in noise. Willet suddenly raised his own rifle and pulled the trigger. Another dusky figure sprang up and then fell prone.

"They were coming too close," he said. "That'll be a warning. Now back, lads, to the breastwork!"

As they retreated the shots and yells increased, the forest ringing with the whoops, while bullets pattered on the stumps. Both Grosvenor and Robert were glad when they were inside the logs once more, and Colden was glad to see them.

"For all I knew you had fallen," he said, "and I can't spare you."

"We left our mark on 'em," said the saturnine Black Rifle. "They know we're waiting for 'em."

The demonstration increased in volume, the whole forest ringing with the fierce whoops. Stout nerves even had good excuse for being shaken, and Colden paled a little, but his soul was high.

"Sound and fury but no attack," he said.

Willet looked at him approvingly.

"You've become a true forest leader, Captain Colden," he said. "You've learned to tell the real rush from the pretended one. They won't try anything yet a while, but they're madder than hornets, and they're sure to move on us later. You just watch."

Yet Colden, Wilton and the others were compelled to argue with the men, especially with the boat builders and wood choppers. Stern military discipline was unknown then in the forest; the private often considered himself a better man than his officer, and frequently told him so. Troops from the towns or the older settled regions seemed never to grow used to Indian methods of warfare. They walked again and again into the same sort of ambush. Now, they felt sure, because the Indian fire had evaporated in scattered shots, that the French and the warriors had gone away, and that they might as well be asleep, save for the guards. But Colden repressed them with a stern hand.

"If it hadn't been for our experience at Fort Refuge I might feel that way myself," he said. "The silence is certainly consoling, and makes one feel that all danger has passed."

"The silence is what I dread most," said Robert. "Is anything stirring on the lake?"

"Not a thing," replied Wilton, who had been watching in that quarter. "I never saw George look more peaceful."

Robert suggested that they go down to the shore again, and Wilton, Grosvenor and he walked through the camp, not stopping until they stood at the water's edge.

"You surely don't anticipate anything here," said Wilton.

"I don't know," replied Robert, thoughtfully, "but our enemies, both French and Indians, are full of craft. We must guard against wile and stratagem."

Wilton looked out over the lake, where the gentle wind still blew and the rippling waters made a slight sighing sound almost like a lullaby. The opposite cliffs rose steep and lofty, showing dimly through the dusk, but there was no threat in their dark wall. To south and north the surface melted in the darkness, but it too seemed friendly and protecting. Wilton shook his head. No peril could come by that road, but he held his peace. He had his opinion, but he would not utter it aloud against those who had so much more experience than he.

The darkness made a further gain. The pallid moon went wholly out, and the last of the stars left. But they had ample wood inside the camp and they built the fires higher, the flames lighting up the tanned eager faces of the men and gleaming along the polished barrels of their long rifles. Willet had inspected the supply of ammunition and he considered it ample. That fear was removed from his mind.

Tayoga went to the edge of the forest again, and reported no apparent movement in the force of St. Luc. But they had built a great fire of their own, and did not mean to go away. The attack would come some time or other, but when or how no man could tell.

Robert, who could do as he pleased, concluded to stay with Wilton on the shore of the lake, where the darkness was continually creeping closer to the shore. The high cliffs on the far side were lost to sight and only a little of Andiatarocte's surface could now be seen. The wind began to moan. Wilton shivered.

"The lake don't look as friendly as it did an hour ago," he said.

A crash of shots from the slope followed his words. The war whoop rose and fell and rose again. Bullets rattled among the stumps and on the crude stockade.

"The real attack!" said Wilton.

"Perhaps," said Robert.

He was about to turn away and join in the defence, but an impulse from some unknown source made him stay. Wilton's duty kept him there, though he chafed to be on the active side of the camp. The sharp crack of rifles showed that the defenders were replying and they sent forth a defiant cheer.

"They may creep down to the edge of the stumps and try to pick off our men," said Robert, "but they won't make a rush. St. Luc would never allow it. I don't understand this demonstration. It must be a cover for something else."

He looked thoughtfully into the darkness, and listened to the moan of the lake. Had the foe a fleet he might have expected an attack that way, but he knew that for the present the British and Americans controlled Andiatarocte.

The darkness was still gathering on the water. He could not see twenty yards from the land, but behind him everything was brightness. The fires had been replenished, the men lined the stockade and were firing fast. Cheers replied to whoops. Smoke of battle overhung the camp, and drifted off into the forest. Robert looked toward the stockade. Again it was his impulse to go, and again he stayed. There was a slight gurgling in the water almost at his feet, and a dark figure rose from the waves, followed in an instant by another, and then by many more. Robert, his imagination up and leaping, thrilled with horror. He understood at once. They were attacked by swimming savages. While the great shouting and turmoil in their front was going on a line of warriors had reached the lake somewhere in the darkness, and were now in the camp itself.

He was palsied only for a moment. Then his faculties were alive and he saw the imminent need. Leaping back, he uttered a piercing shout, and, drawing his pistol, he fired point blank at the first of the warriors. Wilton, who had felt the same horror at sight of the dark faces, fired also, and there was a rush of feet as men came to their help.

The warriors were armed only with tomahawk and knife, and

they had expected a surprise which they might have effected if it had not been for Robert's keenness, but more of them came continually and they made a formidable attack. Sending forth yell after yell as a signal to their comrades in front that they had landed, they rushed forward.

Neither Robert nor Wilton ever had any clear idea of that fierce combat in the dark. The defenders fired their rifles and pistols, if they had time, and then closed in with cold steel. Meanwhile the attack on the front redoubled. But here at the water's edge it was fiercest. Borderer met warrior, and now and then, locked in the arms of one another, they fell and rolled together into the lake. Grosvenor came too, and, after firing his pistols, he drew his small sword, plunging into the thick of the combat, thrusting with deadly effect.

The savages were hurled back, but more swimming warriors came to their aid. Dark heads were continually rising from the lake, and stalwart figures, almost naked, sprang to the shore. Tomahawks and knives gleamed, and the air echoed with fierce whoop of Indian and shout of borderer. And on the other side of the camp, too, the attack was now pressed with unrelenting vigour. The shrill call of a whistle showed that St. Luc himself was near, and Frenchmen, Canadians and Indians, at the edge of the cleared ground and in the first line of stumps, poured a storm of bullets against the breastwork and into the camp.

Many of the defenders were hit, some mortally. The gallant Colden had his fine three cornered hat, of which he was very proud, shot away, but, bare-headed, calm and resolute, he strode about among his men, handling his forces like the veteran that he had become, strengthening the weak points, applauding the daring and encouraging the faltering. Willet, who was crouched behind the logs, firing his rifle with deadly effect, glanced at him more than once with approval.

"Do you think we can hold 'em off, Tayoga?" the hunter said to the Onondaga, who was by his side.

"Aye, Great Bear, we can," replied Tayoga. "They will not be able to enter our camp here, but this is not their spearhead. They expect to thrust through on the side of the water, where they have come swimming. Hark to the shouts behind us!"

"And the two lads, Robert and the young Englishman, have gone there. I think you judge aright about that being their spearhead. We'll go there too!"

Choosing a moment when they were not observed by the others, lest it might be construed as a withdrawal in the face of force, they slipped away from the logs. It was easy to find such an opportunity as the camp was now full of smoke from the firing, drifting over every-thing and often hiding the faces of the combatants from their com-rades only a few yards away.

But the battle raged most fiercely along the water's edge. There it was hand to hand, and for a while it looked as if the dusky warriors would make good their footing. To the defenders it seemed that the lake spewed them forth continually, and that they would overwhelm with weight of numbers. Yet the gallant borderers would not give back, and encouraging one another with resounding cheers they held the doubtful shore. Into this confused and terrible struggle Willet and Tayoga hurled themselves, and their arrival was most opportune.

"Push 'em back, lads! Push 'em back! Into the water with 'em!" shouted the stalwart hunter, and emptying rifle and pistol he clubbed the former, striking terrific blows. Tayoga, tomahawk in hand, went up and down like a deadly flame. Soldiers and borderers came to the danger point, and the savages were borne back. Not one of them coming from the water was able to enter the camp. The terrible line of lead and steel that faced them was impassable, and all the time the tremendous shouts of Willet poured fresh courage and zeal into the young troops and the borderers.

"At 'em, lads! At 'em!" he cried. "Push 'em back! Throw 'em into the water! Show 'em they can't enter our camp, that the back door, like the front door, is closed! That's the way! Good for you, Grosvenor! A sword is a deadly weapon when one knows how to use it! A wonderful blow for you, Tayoga! But you always deal wonderful ones! Careful, Robert! 'Ware the tomahawk! Now, lads, drive 'em! Drive 'em hard!"

The men united in one mighty rush that the warriors could not withstand. They were hurled back from the land, and, after their fash-ion when a blow had failed, they quit in sudden and utter fashion. Springing into the water, and swimming with all their power, they disappeared in the heavy darkness which now hovered close to shore. Many of the young soldiers, carried away by the heat of combat, were about to leap into the lake and follow them, but Willet, running up and down, restrained their eager spirits.

"No! No!" he cried. "Don't do that. They'll be more'n a match for you in the water. We've won, and we'll keep what we've won!"

All the warriors who had landed, save the dead, were now gone, evidently swimming for some point near by, and the battle in front, as if by a preconcerted signal, also sank down suddenly. Then St. Luc's silver whistle was heard, and French and Indians alike drew off.

Robert stood dazed by the abrupt end of the combat. His blood was hot, and millions of black specks danced before his eyes. The sudden silence, after so much shouting and firing, made his pulses beat like the sound of drums in his ears. He held an empty pistol in his right hand, but he passed his left palm over his hot face, and wiped away the mingled reek of perspiration and burned gunpowder. Grosvenor stood near him, staring at the red edge of his own sword.

"Put up your weapon, Red Coat," said Tayoga, calmly. "The battle is over—for the time."

"And we've won!" exclaimed Grosvenor. "I could hardly believe it was real when I saw all those dark figures coming out of the water!"

Then he shuddered violently, and in sudden excess of emotion flung his sword from him. But he went a moment later and picked it up again.

The attack had been repulsed on every side, but the price paid was large. Fifteen men were dead and many others were wounded. The bodies of seventeen Indians who had fallen in the water attack were found and were consigned to the waves. Others, with their French allies, had gone down on the side of the forest, but most of the fallen had been taken away by their comrades.

It was a victory for Colden and his men, but it left serious alarm for the future. St. Luc was still in the forest, and he might attack again in yet greater force. Besides, they would have to guard against many a cunning and dangerous device from that master of forest warfare. Colden called a council, at which Willet and Black Rifle were central figures, and they agreed that there was nothing to be done but to strengthen their log outworks and to practice eternal vigilance. Then they began to toil anew on the breastworks, strengthening them with fresh timber, of which, fortunately, they had a vast supply, as so much had been cut to be turned into boats. A double guard was placed at the water's edge, lest the warriors come back for a new attack, and the wounded were made as comfortable as the circumstances would admit. Luckily Willet and many others were well acquainted with the rude but effective border surgery, much of it learned from the Indians, and they were able to give timely help.

The hurt endured in silence. Their frontier stoicism did not allow them to give voice to pain. Blankets were spread for them under the sheds or in the sawmill, and some, despite their injuries, fell asleep from exhaustion. Soldiers and borderers walked behind the palisades, others continually moulded bullets, while some were deep in slumber, waiting their turn to be called for the watch.

It began to rain by and by, not heavily, but a slow, dull, seeping fall that was inexpressibly dreary, and the thick, clammy darkness, shot with mists and vapours from the lake, rolled up to the very edge of the fires. Robert might have joined the sleepers, as he was detached from immediate duty, but his brain was still too much heated to admit it. Despite his experience and his knowledge that it could not be so, his vivid fancy filled forest and water with enemies coming forward to a new attack. He saw St. Luc, sword in hand, leading them, and, shaking his body violently, he laughed at himself. This would never do.

"What does Dagaeoga see that is so amusing?" asked Tayoga.

"Nothing, Tayoga. I was merely ridiculing myself for looking into the blackness and seeing foes who are not there."

"And yet we all do it. If our enemies are not there they are at least not far away. I have been outside with Black Rifle, and we have been into the edge of the forest. Sharp Sword makes a big camp, and shows all the signs of intending to stay long. We may yet lose the sawmill. It is best to understand the full danger. What does Dagaeoga mean to do now?"

"I think I'll go back to the water's edge, and help keep the watch there. That seems to be my place."

He found Wilton still in command of the lake guard, and Grosvenor with him. The young Quaker had been shocked by the grim battle, but he showed a brave front nevertheless. He had put on his military cloak to protect himself from the rain, and Robert and Grosvenor had borrowed others for the same purpose.

"We've won a victory," said Wilton, "but, as I gather, it's not final. That St. Luc, whose name seems to inspire so much terror, will come again. Am I not right, Lennox?"

"You're right, Wilton. St. Luc will come not a second time only, but a third, and a fourth, if necessary."

"And can't we expect any help? We're supposed to have command of this lake for the present."

"I know of none."

The three walked up and down, listening to the mournful lapping of the waves on the beach, and the sigh of the dripping rain. The stimulus of excited action had passed and they felt heavy and depressed. They could see only a few yards over the lake, and must depend there upon ear to warn them of a new attack that way. The fact added to their worries, but luckily Tayoga, with his amazing powers of hearing, joined them, establishing at once what was in effect a listening post, although it was not called then by that name. Wilton drew much strength from the presence of the Onondaga, while it made the confidence of Grosvenor supreme.

"Now we'll surely know if they come," he said.

A long while passed without a sign, but they did not relax their vigilance a particle, and Tayoga interpreted the darkness for them.

"There was a little wind," he said, after a while, "but it is almost dead now. The waves are running no longer. I hear a slight sound to the south which was not there before."

"I hear nothing, Tayoga," said Robert.

"Perhaps not, Dagaeoga, but I hear it, which is enough. The sound is quite faint, but it is regular like the beating of a pulse. Now I can tell what it is. It is the stroke of a paddle. There is a canoe upon the lake, passing in front of us. It is not the canoe of a friend, or it would come at once to the land. It contains only one man. How do I know, Red Coat? Because the canoe is so small. The stroke of the paddle is light and yet the canoe moves swiftly. A canoe heavy enough to hold two men could not be moved so fast without a stroke also heavy. How do I know it is going fast, Dagaeoga? Do not ask such simple questions. Because the sound of the paddle stroke moving rapidly toward the north shows it. Doubtless some of Sharp Sword's warriors brought with them a canoe overland, and they are now using it to spy upon us."

"What can we do about it, Tayoga?"

"Nothing, Red Coat. Ah, the canoe has turned and is now going back toward the south, but more slowly. The man in it could locate our camp easily by the glow of the fires through the mist and vapours. Perhaps he can see a dim outline of our figures."

"And one of us may get a bullet while we stand here watching."

"No, Red Coat, it is not at all likely. His aim would be extremely uncertain in the darkness. The warrior is not usually a good marksman, nor is it his purpose here to shoot. He would rather spy upon us, without giving an alarm. Ah, the man has now stopped his southward journey, and is veering about uncertainly! He dips in the paddle only now and then. That is strange. All his actions express doubt, uncertainty and even alarm."

"What do you think has happened, Tayoga?"

"Manitou yet has the secret in his keeping, Dagaeoga, but if we wait in patience a little it may be revealed to me. The canoe is barely moving and the man in it watches. Now his paddle makes a little splash as he turns slightly to the right. It is certain that he has been alarmed. The spy thinks he is being spied upon, and doubtless he is right. He grows more and more uneasy. He moves again, he moves twice in an aimless fashion. Although we do not see him in the flesh, it is easy to tell that he is trying to pierce the darkness with his eyes,

117

not to make out us, but to discern something very near the canoe. His alarm grows and probably with good cause. Ah, he has made a sudden powerful stroke, with the paddle, shooting the canoe many feet to the left, but it is too late!"

"Too late for what, Tayoga?" exclaimed Robert.

The Onondaga did not reply for a moment or two, but stood tense and strained. His eyes, his whole attitude showed excitement, a rare thing with him.

"It was too late," he repeated. "Whatever threatened the man in the canoe, whatever the danger was, it has struck. I heard a little splash. It was made by the man falling into the water. He has gone. Now, what has become of the canoe? Perhaps the warrior when he fell dropped the paddle into the water, and the canoe is drifting slowly away. No, I think some one is swimming to it. Ah, he is in the canoe now, and he has recovered the paddle! I hear the strokes, which are different from those made by the man who was in it before. They have a longer sweep. The new man is stronger. He is very powerful, and he does not take the canoe back and forth. He is coming toward the land. Stand here, and we will welcome Daganoweda of the Ganeagaono. It might be some other, but I do not think it possible. It is surely Daganoweda."

A canoe shot from the mists and vapours. The fierce young Mohawk chief put down the paddle, and, stepping from the light craft into the shallow water, raised his hand in a proud salute. He was truly a striking figure. The dusk enlarged him until he appeared gigantic. He was naked except for belt and breech cloth, and water ran from his shining bronze body. A tomahawk and knife in the belt were his only weapons, but Robert knew instinctively that one of them had been wielded well.

"Welcome, Daganoweda," he said. "We were not looking for you, but if we had taken thought about it we might have known that you would come."

The dark eyes of the Mohawk flashed and his figure seemed to grow in stature.

"There has been a battle," he said, "and Sharp Sword with a great force is pressing hard upon the white brothers of the Ganeagaono. It was not possible for Daganoweda to stay away."

"That is true. You are a great chief. You scent the conflict afar, and you always come to it. Our people could have no truer, no braver ally. The arrival of Daganoweda alone is as the coming of ten men."

The nostrils of the chief dilated. Obviously he was pleased at Robert's round and swelling sentences.

"I come in the canoe of a foe," he said. "The warrior who was in it has gone into the lake."

"We know that. Tayoga, who is a wonder for hearing, and a still greater wonder at interpreting what he hears, followed your marvellous achievement and told us every step in its progress. He even knew that it was you, and announced your coming through the mists and vapours."

"Tayoga of the clan of the Bear, of the nation Onondaga, of the great League of the Hodenosaunee, is a great warrior, and the greatest trailer in the world, even though he be so young."

Tayoga said nothing, and his face did not move, but his eyes gleamed.

"Do you come alone?" asked Robert.

"The warriors who were with me when you met us in the woods are at hand," replied the chief, "and they await my signal. They have crept past the line of Sharp Sword, though Tandakora and many men watched, and are not far away. I will call them."

He sent forth twice the harsh cry of a water fowl. There was no answer, but he did not seem to expect any, standing at attention, every line of his figure expressing supreme confidence. The others shared his belief.

"I hear them. They come," said Tayoga at length.

Presently a slight sound as of long, easy strokes reached them all, and in a few moments a line of dark heads appeared through the mists and vapours. Then the Mohawks swam to land, carrying their rifles and ammunition, Daganoweda's too, on their heads, and stood up in a silent and dripping line before their chief.

"It is well," said Daganoweda, looking them over with an approving eye. "You are all here, and we fight in the next battle beside our white brothers."

"A battle that you would be loath to miss and right glad we are to welcome such sturdy help," said the voice of Willet behind them. "I'll tell Captain Colden that you're here."

The young captain came at once, and welcomed Daganoweda in proper dignified fashion. Blankets and food were given to the Mohawks, and they ate and warmed themselves by the fire. They were not many, but Robert knew they were a great addition. The fiery spirit of Daganoweda alone was worth twenty men.

"I think that we'd better seek sleep now," said young Lennox to Grosvenor. "I admit one is tempted to stay awake that he may see and hear everything, but sooner or later you've got to rest."

They found a good place under one of the sheds, and, wrapped in blankets, soon sank to slumber. The day after such a momentous night came dark and gloomy, with the rain still dripping. A north wind had arisen, and high waves chased one another over the lake. There was still much fog on the land side, and, under its cover, the French and Indians were stalking the camp, firing at every incautious head.

"Most of those bullets are French," said Tayoga, "because the warriors are not good sharpshooters, and they are aimed well. I think that Sharp Sword has selected all the best French and Canadian marksmen and has sent them down to the edge of the woods to harass us. As long as the fog hangs there we may expect their bullets."

The fire of these hidden sharpshooters soon became terribly harassing. From points of vantage they sent their bullets even into the very heart of the camp. Not a head or a shoulder, not an arm could be exposed. Three men were killed, a dozen more were wounded, and the spirit of the garrison was visibly affected. At the suggestion of Willet, Colden selected thirty sharpshooters of his own and sent them among the stumps to meet the French and Canadian riflemen.

Robert and Tayoga were in this band, and Willet himself led it. Daganoweda and three of his warriors who were good shots also went along. Black Rifle was already outside on one of his usual solitary but fierce man-hunts. All the men as soon as they left the breastworks lay almost flat on the wet ground, and crept forward with the utmost care. It was a service of extreme danger, none could be more so, and it was certain that not all of them would come back.

CHAPTER 10

In the Fog

When Robert went into the fog and began to creep from stump to stump, his imagination leaped up at once and put a foe at every point in front of him. Perhaps he deserved more credit for courage and daring than any of the others, because his vivid fancy foresaw all the dangers and more. Tayoga was on his right and Willet on his left. Daganoweda, who had all the eagerness of Black Rifle himself, was farther down the line. Flashes of fire appeared now and then in the fog ahead of them, and bullets hummed over their heads.

Robert, essentially humane, began to share, nevertheless, the zeal of these hunters of men around him. The French and Canadians were seeking their lives and they must strike back. He peered through the fog, looking for a chance to fire, forgetting the wet ground, and the rain which was fast soaking him through and through. He was concerned only to keep his rifle and powder dry. Two flashes on his right showed that the defenders were already replying.

"We cannot go much farther, Dagaeoga," whispered Tayoga, "or we will be among them. I shall take this stump just ahead."

"And I the one beside it. I don't mind admitting that a thick stump between you and your enemy is a good thing."

He sank down behind his chosen bulwark, and stared through the fog. The flashes of fire continued, but they were on his right and left, and nothing appeared directly in front of him. A cry came from a point farther down the line. One of the defenders had been hit and presently another fell. Robert again saw all the dangers and more, but his mind was in complete command of his body and he watched with unfailing vigilance. He saw Willet suddenly level his rifle across his protecting stump and fire. No cry came in response, but he believed that the hunter's bullet had found its target. Tayoga also pulled trigger, but Robert did not yet see anything at which to aim, although the sound of shots from the two hostile fronts was now almost continuous.

The combat in the dim mists had a certain weird quality and Robert's imaginative mind heightened its effect. It was almost like the blind shooting at the blind. A pink dot would appear in the fog, expand a little, and then go out. There would be a sharp report, the whistling of a bullet, perhaps, and that was all. The white men fought in silence, and, if there were any Indians with the French and Canadians they imitated them.

Robert, at last, caught a glimpse of a dusky figure about thirty yards in front of him, and, aiming his rifle, quickly fired. He had no way of knowing that he had hit, save that no shot came in reply, but Tayoga, who was once again ear to the ground, said that their foes were drawing back a little.

"They find our fire hotter than they had expected," he said. "If they can shoot in the fog so can we, and the Great Bear is more than a match for them in such a contest."

The whole line crept forward and paused again behind another row of stumps. A general volley met them and they found protection none too soon. Bullets chipped little pieces off the stumps or struck in the ground about them. But Robert knew that they had been fired largely at random, or had been drawn perhaps by a slight noise. There was a strong temptation to return the fire in a like manner, but he had the strength of mind to withhold his aim for the present, and not shoot until he had a sure target.

Yet the dim battle in the fog increased in volume. More skirmishers from the forces of St. Luc came up, and the line of fire spread to both left and right. A yell was heard now and then, and it was evident that the Indians in large numbers were coming into the combat. Willet's band was reinforced also from the camp, and his line extended to meet that of the foe. Rifles cracked incessantly, the white fog was sprinkled with pink dots, and, above the heads of the men, it was darkened by the smoke that rose from the firing. At rare intervals a deep cheer from a borderer replied to the savage war whoop.

A man four stumps from Robert was hit in the head and died without a sound, but Willet, firing at the flash of the rifle that slew him, avenged his loss. A bullet grazed Robert's head, cutting off two locks of hair very neatly. Its passage took his breath for a moment or two, and gave him a shock, but he recovered quickly, and, still controlling his impulse to pull trigger in haste, looked for something at which to aim.

The fog had not lifted at all, but by gazing into its heart a long time, Robert was able to see a little distance. Now and then the figure of an enemy, as he leaped from the shelter of one stump to another, was outlined dimly, but invariably there was not enough time for a shot. Soon he made out a large stump not very far ahead of him, and he saw the flash of a rifle from it. He caught a glimpse only of the hands that held the weapon, but he believed them to be a white man's hands and he believed also that the man behind the stump was one of the best French sharpshooters.

Robert resolved to bring down the Frenchman, who presently, when firing once more, might then expose enough of himself for a target. He waited patiently and the second shot came. He saw the hands again, the arms, part of one shoulder and the side of the head, and taking quick aim he pulled the trigger, though he was satisfied that his bullet had missed.

But the flame of battle was lighted in Robert's soul. Hating nobody and wishing good to all, he nevertheless sought to kill, because some one was seeking to kill him, and because killing was the business of those about him. What came to be known later as mass psychology took hold of him. All his mental and physical powers were concentrated on the single task of slaying an enemy. The affair now resolved itself into a duel between single foes.

Deciding to await a third shot from his enemy, he made his position behind the stump a little easier, poised, as it were, ready to throw every faculty, physical and mental, into his reply to that expected third shot. He was quite sure, too, that he would have a chance, because the man had exposed so much more of himself at the second shot than at the first, and his escape from the bullets would make him expose yet more at the third. His heart began to throb hard, and his pulses were beating fast. The battle was still going on about him, but he forgot all the rest of it, the shots, the shouts, the flashes, and remembered only his own part. He judged that in another minute the man would show himself. So believing, he laid his rifle across his stump, cocked it, and was ready to take aim and fire in a few seconds.

His foe's head appeared, after just about the delay that he had expected, and Robert's hand sprang to the trigger at the very moment the man pulled his own. The bullet hummed by his cheek. His finger contracted and then it loosened. A sudden acuteness of vision, or a chance thinning of the fog at that point, enabled him to see the man's face, and he recognized the French partisan, Charles Langlade, known also to the Indians as the Owl, who, with his wife, the Dove, had once held him in a captivity by no means unkind.

His humane instincts, his gratitude, his feeling for another flared up even in that moment of battle and passion, when the man-hunting impulse was so strong. His aim, quick as it was, had been sure and deadly, but, deflecting the muzzle of the rifle a shade, his finger contracted again. The spurt of fire leaped forth and the bullet sang by the ear of Langlade, singing to him a little song of caution as it passed, telling such a wary partisan as he that his stump was a very exposed stump, dangerous to the last degree, and that it would be better for him to find one somewhere else.

Robert did not see the Owl go away, but he was quite sure that he had gone, because it was just the sort of thing that such a skilled forest fighter would do. The fog thickened again, and, in a few more minutes, both lines shifted somewhat. Then he had to watch new stumps at new points, and his thoughts were once more in tune with those about him, concentrated on the battle and the man-hunt.

A bullet tipped his ear, and he saw that it came from a stump hardly visible in the fog. The sharpshooter was not likely to be Langlade again, and, at once, it became Robert's ambition to put him out of action. No consideration of mercy or humanity would restrain him now, if he obtained a chance of a good shot, and he waited patiently for it. Evidently this new sharpshooter had detected his presence also, and the second duel was on.

The man fired again in a minute or two, and the bullet chipped very close. He was so quick, too, that Robert did not get an opportunity to return his fire, but he recognized the face and to his great surprise saw that it was De Courcelles who had taken a place in line with the skirmishers. Rage seized him at once. This was the man who had tried to trick him to his death in that affair with the bully, Boucher, at Quebec. He was shaken with righteous anger. All the kindliness and mercy that he had felt toward Langlade disappeared. He was sure, too, that De Courcelles knew him and was trying his best to kill him.

Robert peered over his stump and sought eagerly for a shot. He could play at that game as well as De Courcelles, but his enemy was cautious. It was some time before he risked another bullet, and then Robert's, in reply, missed, though he also had been untouched. His anger increased. Although he had little hate in his composition he could not forget that this man De Courcelles had been a party to an infamous attempt upon his life, and even now, in what amounted to a duel, was seeking to kill him. His own impulses, under such a spur, and for the moment, were those of the slayer. He used all the skill that he had learned in the forest to secure an opportunity for the taking of his foe's life.

Robert sought to draw De Courcelles' fire again, meanwhile having reloaded his own rifle, and he raised his cap a little above the edge of the stump. But the trick was too old for the Frenchman and he did not yield to it. Taking the chance, he thrust up his face, dropping back immediately as De Courcelles' bullet sang over his head. Then he sprang up and was in time to pull trigger at his enemy, who fell back.

Robert was able to tell in the single glimpse through the fog that De Courcelles was not killed. The bullet had struck him in the shoulder, inflicting a wound, certainly painful but probably not dangerous, although it was likely to feed the man's hate of Robert. Even so, young Lennox was glad now that he had not killed him, that his death was not upon his hands; it was enough to disable him and to drive him out of the battle.

The fighting grew once more in volume and fury. Rifles cracked continuously up and down the line. The war whoop of the Indians was incessant, and the deep cheer of the borderers replied to it. But Robert saw that the end of the combat was near; not that the rage of man was abated, but because nature, as if tired of so much strife, was putting in between a veil that would hide the hostile forces from each other. The fog suddenly began to thicken rapidly, rolling up from the lake in great, white waves that made figures dim and shadowy, even a few paces away.

If the fighting went on it would be impossible to tell friend from foe, and Willet at once sent forth a sharp call which was repeated up and down the line. The French leaders took like action, and, by mutual consent, the two forces fell apart. The firing and the shouts ceased abruptly and a slow withdrawal was begun. The fog had conquered.

"Is Dagaeoga hurt?" asked Tayoga.

"Untouched," replied Robert.

"I saw that you and the Frenchman, De Courcelles, were engaged in a battle of your own. I might have helped you, but if I know you, you did not wish my aid."

"No, Tayoga. It was man to man. I confess that while our duel was on I was filled with rage against him, and tried my best to kill, but now I'm glad I gave him only a wound."

"Your hate flows away as De Courcelles' blood flows out."

"If you want to put it that way. But do you hear anything of the enemy, Tayoga? Fog seems to be a conductor of sound now and then."

"Nothing except the light noises of withdrawal. The retreating

125

footsteps become fainter and fainter, and I think we shall have peace for to-day. They might fire bullets at random against the camp, but St. Luc will not let them waste lead in such a manner. No, Dagaeoga, we will lie quiet now and dress our wounds."

He was right, as the firing was not renewed, though the pickets, stationed at short intervals, kept as sharp a watch as they could in the fog, while the others lay by the fires which were now built higher than usual. Colden was hopeful that St. Luc would draw off, but Tayoga and Black Rifle, who went out again into the fog, reported no sign of it. Beyond a doubt, he was prepared to maintain a long siege.

"We must get help," said Willet. "We're supposed to control Lake George and we know that forces of ours are at the south end, where they've advanced since the taking of Fort William Henry. We'll have to send messengers."

"Who are they to be?" asked Colden.

"Robert and Tayoga are most fit. You have plenty of boats. They can take a light one and leave at once, while the fog holds."

Colden agreed. Young Lennox and the Onondaga were more than willing, and, in a half hour, everything was ready for the start. A strong canoe with paddles for two was chosen and they put in it their rifles, plenty of ammunition and some food.

"A year from now, if the war is still going on, I'll be going with you on such errands," said Grosvenor confidently.

"Red Coat speaks the truth. He learns fast," said Tayoga.

"I won't tell you lads to be careful, because you don't need any advice," said Willet.

Many were at the water's edge, when they pushed off, and Robert knew that they were followed by the best of wishes, not only for their success but for themselves also. A few strokes of the paddles and the whole camp, save a luminous glow through the fog, was gone. A few more strokes and the luminous glow too departed. The two were alone once more in the wilderness, and they had little but instinct to guide them in their perilous journey upon the waters. But they were not afraid. Robert, instead, felt a curious exaltation of the spirit. He was supremely confident that he and Tayoga would carry out their mission, in spite of everything.

"It is odd how quickly the camp sank from sight," he said.

"It is because we are in the heart of a great fog," said Tayoga. "Since it was thick enough to hide the battle it is thick enough also to hide the camp and us from each other. But, Dagaeoga, it is a friendly fog, as it conceals us from our enemies also."

"That's so, Tayoga, but I'm thinking this fog will hold dangers for us too. St. Luc is not likely to neglect the lake, and he'll surmise that we'll send for help. We've had experience on the water in fogs before, and you'll have to use your ears as you did then."

"So I will, Dagaeoga. Suppose we stop now, and listen."

But nothing of a hostile nature came to them through the mists and vapours, and, resuming the paddles again, they bore more toward the centre of the lake, where they thought they would be likely to escape the cruising canoes of the enemy, if any should be sent out by St. Luc. They expected too that the fog would thin there, but it did not do so, seeming to spread over the full extent of Andiatarocte.

"How long do you think the fog will last?" asked Robert.

"All day, I fear," replied Tayoga.

"That's bad. If any of our friends should be on the shore we won't be able to see 'em."

"But we have to make the best of it, Dagaeoga. We may be able to hear them."

The fog was the greatest they had ever seen on Andiatarocte, seeming to ooze up from the depths of the waters, and to spread over everything. The keenest eyes, like those of Robert and Tayoga, could penetrate it only a few yards, and it hung in heavy, wet folds over their faces. It was difficult even to tell direction and they paddled very slowly in a direction that they surmised led to the south. After a while they stopped again that Tayoga might establish a new listening post upon the water, though nothing alarming yet came to those marvellous ears of his. But it was evident that he expected peril, and Robert also anticipated it.

"A force as large as St. Luc's is sure to have brought canoes overland," said young Lennox, "and in a fog like this he'll have them launched on the lake."

"It is so," said Tayoga, using his favourite expression, "and I think they will come soon."

They moved on once more a few hundred yards, and then, when the Onondaga listened a long time, he announced that the hostile canoes were on the lake, cruising about in the fog.

"I hear one to the right of us, another to the left, and several directly ahead," he said. "Sharp Sword brought plenty of canoes with him and he is using them. I think they have formed a line across the lake, surmising that we would send a message to the south. Sharp Sword is a great leader, and he forgets nothing."

"They can't draw a line that we won't pass."

Now they began to use their paddles very slowly and gently, the canoe barely creeping along, and Tayoga listening with all his powers. But the Onondaga was aware that his were not the only keen ears on the lake, and that, gentle as was the movement of the paddies that he and Robert held, it might be heard.

"The canoe on our right is coming in a little closer to us," he whispered. "It is a very large canoe, because it holds four paddles. I can trace the four separate sounds. They try to soften their strokes lest the hidden messenger whom they want to catch may hear them, but they cannot destroy the sound altogether. Now, the one on the left is bearing in toward us also. I think they have made a chain across the lake, and hope to keep anything from passing."

"Can you hear those ahead of us?"

"Very slightly, and only now and then, but it is enough to tell us that they are still there. But, Dagaeoga, we must go ahead even if they are before us; we cannot think of turning back."

"No such thought entered my head, Tayoga. We'll run this gauntlet."

"That was what I knew you would say. The canoes from both right and left still approach. I think they carry on a patrol in the fog, and move back and forth, always keeping in touch. Now, we must go forward a little, or they will be upon us, but be ever so gentle with the paddle, Dagaeoga. That is it! We make so little sound that it is no sound at all, and they cannot hear us. Now, we are well beyond them, and the two canoes are meeting in the fog. The men in them talk together. You hear them very well yourself, Dagaeoga. Their exact words do not come to our ears, but we know they are telling one another that no messenger from the beleaguered camp has yet passed. Now, they part and go back on their beat. We can afford to forget them, Dagaeoga, and think of those ahead. We still have the real gauntlet to run. Be very gentle with the paddle again.

"I hear the canoes ahead of us very clearly now. One of them is large also with four paddles in it, and two of the men are Frenchmen. I cannot understand what they say, but I hear the French accent; the sound is not at all like that the warriors make. One of the Frenchmen is giving instructions, as I can tell by his tone of command, and I think the canoes are going to spread out more. Yes, they are moving away to both right and left. They must feel sure that we are here somewhere in the fog, trying to get by them, but the big canoe with the Frenchmen in it keeps its place. Bear a little to the left, Dagaeoga, and we can pass it unseen."

It was the most delicate of tasks to paddle the canoe, and cause scarcely a ripple in the water, but they were so skilful they were able to do it, and make no sound that Robert himself could hear. Although his nerves were steady his excitement was intense. A situation so extraordinary put every power of his imagination into play. His fancy fairly peopled the water with hostile canoes; they were in a triple ring about him and Tayoga. All his pulses were beating hard, yet his will, as usual, was master of his nerves, and the hand that held the paddle never shook.

"A canoe on the outer line, and from the left, is now bearing in toward us," whispered Tayoga. "There are two men in it, as the strokes of the paddles show. They are coming toward us. Some evil spirit must have whispered to them that we are here. Ah, they have stopped! What does it mean, Dagaeoga? Listen! Did you not hear a little splash? They think to surprise us! They keep the paddles silent and try a new trick! Hold the canoe here, Dagaeoga, and I will meet the warrior who comes!"

The Onondaga dropped his rifle, hunting shirt and belt with his pistol in it, into the bottom of the canoe, and then, his knife in his teeth, he was over the side so quickly that Robert did not have time to protest. In an instant he was gone in the fog, and the youth in the canoe could do nothing but wait, a prey to the most terrible apprehensions.

Robert, with an occasional motion of the paddle, held the canoe steady on the water, and tried to pierce the fog with his eyes. He knew that he must stay just where he was, or Tayoga, when he came back, might never find him. If he came back! If—He listened with all his ears for some sound, however slight, that might tell him what was happening.

Out of the fog came a faint splash, and then a sigh that was almost a groan. Young Lennox shuddered, and the hair on his head stood up a little. He knew that sound was made by a soul passing, but whose soul? Once more he realized to the full that his lot was cast in wild and perilous places.

A swimming face appeared in the fog, close to the canoe, and then his heart fell from his throat to its usual place. Tayoga climbed lightly into the canoe, no easy feat in such a situation, put on his belt and replaced the knife in the sheath. Robert asked him nothing, he had no need to do so. The sigh that was almost a groan had told the full tale.

"Now we will bear to the right again, Dagaeoga," said Tayoga, calmly, as the water dripped from him. Robert shivered once more. His fertile fancy reproduced that brief, fierce struggle in the water, but he said nothing, promptly following the suggestion of Tayoga, and sending the canoe to the right. The position was too perilous, though, for them to continue on one course long, and at the end of forty or fifty yards they stopped, both listening intently.

"Some of them are talking with one another now," whispered Tayoga. "The warrior who swam does not come back to his canoe, and they wonder why he stays in the water so long. Soon they will know that he is never coming out of the water. Now I hear a voice raised somewhat above the others. It is a French voice. It is not that of St. Luc, because he must remain on shore to direct his army. It is not that of De Courcelles, because you wounded him, and he must be lying in camp nursing his hurts. So I conclude that it is Jumonville, who is next in rank and who therefore would be likely to command on this important service. I am sure it is Jumonville, and his raised voice indicates that he is giving orders. He realizes that the swimmer will not return and that we must be near. Perhaps he knows or guesses that the messengers are you and I, because he has learned long since that we are fitted for just such service, and that we have done such deeds. For instance, our journey to Quebec, on which we first met him."

"Then he'll think Dave is here too, because he was with us then."

"No, he will be quite sure the Great Bear is not here. He knows that he is too important in the defence of the camp, that, while Captain Colden commands, it is the Great Bear who suggests and really directs everything. His sharp orders signify some sudden, new plan. They have a fleet of canoes, and I think they are making a chain, with the links connected so closely that we cannot pass. It is a real gauntlet for us to run, Dagaeoga."

"And how are we to run it?"

"We must pass as warriors, as men of their own."

"I do not look like a warrior."

"But you can make yourself look like one, in the fog at least, enough, perhaps, to go by. Your hair is a little long; take off your hunting shirt, and the other shirt beneath it, bare yourself to the waist, and in such a fog as this it would take the keenest of eyes, only a few yards away, to tell that you are white. Quick, Dagaeoga! Lay the garments on the bottom of the canoe. Bend well upon your paddle and appear to be searching the water everywhere for the messengers who try to escape. I will do the same. Ah, that is well. You look and act so much like a warrior of the woods, Dagaeoga, that even I, in the same canoe, could well take you for a Huron. Now we will whisper no more for a while, because they come, and they will soon be upon us."

Robert bent over his paddle. His upper clothing lay in the bottom of the canoe, with his rifle and Tayoga's upon the garments, ready to be snatched up in an instant, if need should come. The cold, wet fog beat upon his bare shoulders and chest, but he did not feel it. Instead his blood was hot in every vein, and the great pulses in his temples beat so hard that they made a roaring in his ears.

Distinct sounds now came from both left and right, the swish of paddles, the ripple of water against the side of a canoe, men talking. They were coming to the chain that had been stretched in front of them, and their fate would soon be decided. Now, they must be not only brave to the uttermost, but they must be consummate actors too.

Figures began to form themselves in the fog, the outline of a canoe with two men in it appeared on their right, another showed just ahead, and two more on the left. Robert from his lowered eyes, bent over the paddle, caught a glimpse of the one ahead, a great canoe, or rather boat, containing five men, one of whom wielded no paddle, but who sat in its centre, issuing orders. Through the fog came a slight gleam of metal from his epaulets and belt, and, although the face was indistinct, Robert knew that it was Jumonville.

The officer was telling the canoes to keep close watch, not to let the chain be broken, that the messengers were close at hand, that they would soon be taken, and that their comrade who did not come back would be avenged. Robert bent a little lower over his paddle. His whole body prickled, and the roaring in his ears increased.

Tayoga suddenly struck him a smart blow across his bowed back, and spoke to him fiercely in harsh, guttural Huron. Robert did not understand the words, but they sounded like a stern rebuke for poor work with the paddle. The blow and the words stimulated him, keyed him to a supreme effort as an actor. All his histrionic temperament flared up at once. He made a poor stroke with the paddle, threw up much surplus water, and, as he cowered away from Tayoga, he corrected himself hastily. Tayoga uttered a sharp rebuke again, but did not strike a second time. That would have been too much. Robert's next stroke was fine and sweeping, and he heard Jumonville say in French which many of the Indians understood:

"Go more toward the centre of the lake and take a place in the line."

Tayoga and Robert obeyed dumbly, passing Jumonville's boat at a range of five or six yards, going a little beyond the line, and, turning about as if to make a curve that would keep them from striking any other canoe. Again Robert made a false stroke with the paddle, causing the canoe to rock dangerously, and now, Tayoga, fully justified by the fierce code of the forest in striking him again, snatched his own paddle out of the water and gave him a smart rap with the flat of it across the back, at the same time upbraiding him fiercely in Huron.

"Dolt! Fool!" he exclaimed. "Will you never learn how to hold your paddle? Will you never know the stroke? Will you tip us both into the water at such a time, when the messengers of the enemy are seeking to steal through? Do better with the paddle or you shall stay at home with the old women, and work for the warriors!"

Robert snarled in reply, but he did not repay the blow. He made another awkward sweep that sent them farther on the outward curve, and he heard Jumonville's harsh laugh. He was still the superb actor. His excitement was real, and he counterfeited a nervousness and jerkiness that appeared real also. One more wild stroke, and they shot farther out. Jumonville angrily ordered them to return, but Robert seemed to be possessed by a spell of awkwardness, and Tayoga craftily aided him.

"Come back!" roared Jumonville.

Robert and Tayoga were fifteen yards away, and the great blanket of fog was enclosing them.

"Now! Now, Dagaeoga!" whispered the Onondaga tensely. "We paddle with all our might straight toward the south!"

Two paddles wielded by skilful and powerful arms flashed in the water, and the canoe sped on its way. A shout of anger rose behind them, and Robert distinctly heard Jumonville say in French:

"After them! After them! It was the messengers who stole by! They have tricked us!"

Those words were sweet in the ears of young Lennox. He had played the actor, and the reward, the saving of their lives, had been paid. It was one of their greatest triumphs and the savour of it would endure long. The very thought gave fresh power to his arm and back, and he swept his paddle with a strength that he had never known before. The canoe skimmed the water like a bird and fairly flew in their chosen course.

Robert's own faculties became marvellously acute. He heard behind them the repeated and angry orders of Jumonville, the hurried strokes of many paddles, the splashing of canoes turned quickly about, a hum of excited voices, and then he felt a great swell of confidence. The roaring in his ears was gone, his nerves became amazingly steady, and every stroke with his paddle was long and finished, a work of art.

Four or five minutes of such toil, and Tayoga rested on his paddle. Robert imitated him.

"Now we will take our ease and listen," said the Onondaga. "The fog is still our friend, and they will think we have turned to one side in it, because that is the natural thing to do. But you and I, Dagaeoga, will not turn just yet."

"I can't hear anything, Tayoga, can you?"

"I cannot, Dagaeoga, but we will not have long to wait. Now, I catch the light swish of a paddle. They are feeling about in the fog. There goes another paddle—and more. They come closer, but we still bide here a little. I hear the voice of Jumonville. He is very angry. But why should he be more angry at any other than at himself? He saw us with his own eyes. He shouts many sharp orders, and some of them are foolish. They must be so, because no man could shout orders so fast, and in such a confused way, and have them all good. He sends more canoes to both right and left to seek us. You and I can afford to laugh, Dagaeoga."

Sitting at rest in their canoe they laughed. With Robert it was not so much a laugh of amusement as a laugh of relief after such tremendous tension. He felt that they were now sure to escape, and with Tayoga he waited calmly.

Chapter 11

The Happy Escape

The spirits of young Lennox rose to the zenith. Although they were still grazing the edge of peril, he had supreme confidence in Tayoga and also in the fog. It was a great fog, a thick fog, a kindly fog, and it had made possible their escape and the achievement of their mission. Having held so long it would hold until they needed it no longer.

"Have they come any nearer, Tayoga?" he asked.

"Jumonville is still giving orders, and sending the canoes somewhat at random. He is not the leader Sharp Sword would be in an emergency, nor anything like it. He is having his own boat paddled about uncertainly. I can hear the paddles of the four men in it. Now and then he speaks angrily, too. He is upbraiding those who are not to blame. How are you feeling now, Dagaeoga? Has Manitou already filled you with new strength?"

"I'm feeling as well as I ever did in my life. I'm ready to swing the paddle again."

"Then we go. The fog will not wait for us forever. We must use it while we have it."

They swept their paddles through the water in long and vigorous strokes, and the canoe shot forward once more. They were confident now that no enemy was ahead of them, and that none of those behind could overtake them. The wet, cold fog still enclosed them like a heavy, damp blanket, but their vigorous exercise and their high spirits kept them warm. After ten minutes they made another stop, but as Tayoga could hear nothing of Jumonville's party they pushed on again at speed. By and by the Onondaga said:

"I feel the fog thinning, Dagaeoga. A wind out of the west has risen, and soon it will take it all away."

"But it has served its purpose. I shall always feel well toward fogs.

Yes, here it goes! The wind is rising fast, and it is taking away the mists and vapours in great folds."

The water began to roughen under the stiff breeze. The fog was split asunder, the pieces were torn to fragments and shreds, and then everything was swept away, leaving the surface of the lake a silver mirror, and the mountains high and green on either shore. Far behind them hovered the Indian canoes, and four or five miles ahead a tower of smoke rose from the west bank.

"Certainly our people," said Robert, looking at the smoke.

"There is no doubt of it," said the Onondaga, "and that is where we will go."

"And those behind us know now that we tricked them in the fog and have escaped. They give forth a shout of anger and disappointment. Now they turn back."

They eased their strokes a little as the pursuit had been abandoned, but curved more toward the centre of the lake, lest some hidden sharpshooter on shore might reach them, and made fair speed toward the smoke, which Robert surmised might be made by a vanguard of troops.

"We ought to have help for Colden and Willet very soon," he said.

"It will not be long," said Tayoga; "but Dagaeoga has forgotten something. Can he not think what it is?"

"No, Tayoga, I can't recall anything."

"Dagaeoga's body is bare from the waist up. It is well for an Indian to go thus into a white camp, but it is not the custom of the people to whom Lennox belongs."

"You're right. I've had so much excitement that I'd forgotten all about my clothes. I must be true to my race, when I meet my brethren."

He reclothed himself, resumed his paddle, and they pushed on steadily for the smoke. No trace of the fog was left. The lake glistened in the sun, the ranges showed green from base to summit, and the tower of smoke deepened and broadened.

"Can you make out what lies at the foot of it, Tayoga?" asked Robert.

"I think I can see a gleam of the sun on an epaulet. It is certainly a camp of your people. The lake is supposed to be under their command, and if the French should make a new incursion here upon its shores they would not build their fires so boldly. Now, I see another gleam, and I hear the ring of axes. They are not boat builders, because no boats, either finished or unfinished, show at the water's edge. They are probably cutting wood for their fires. I hear, too, the crack of a whip, which means that they have wagons, and the presence of wagons indicates a large force. They may be coming ahead with supplies for our great army when it advances. I can now see men in uniform, and there are some red coats among them. Hold your paddle as high as you can, Dagaeoga, as a sign that we are friends, and I will send the canoe in toward the shore. Ah, they see us now, and men are coming down to the lake's edge to meet us! It is a large camp, and it should hold enough men to make St. Luc give up the siege of Colden."

The two sent the canoe swiftly toward the land, where soldiers and others in hunter's dress were already gathered to meet them. Robert saw a tall, thin officer in a Colonial uniform, standing on the narrow beach, and, assuming him to be in command, he said as the canoe swept in:

"We are messengers, sir, from the force of Captain Colden, which is besieged at the sawmill ten or twelve miles farther north."

"Besieged, did you say?" said the officer, speaking in a sharp, dry voice. "It's one of those French tricks they're always playing on us, rushing in under our very noses, and trying to cut out our forces."

"That's it, sir. The French and Indian host, in this case, is led by St. Luc, the ablest and most daring of all their partisans, and, unless you give help, they'll have to escape as best they can in what boats they have."

"As I'm a good Massachusetts man, I expected something of this kind. I sent word to Pownall, our Governor, that we must be extremely cautious in respect to the French, but he thinks the army of General Abercrombie will overwhelm everything. Forest fighting is very different from that of the open fields, a fact which the French seem to have mastered better than we have. My name, young sir, is Elihu Strong. I'm a colonel of the Massachusetts militia, and I command the force that you see posted here."

"And mine, sir, is Robert Lennox, a free lance, and this is Tayoga, of the clan of the Bear, of the great Onondaga nation, a devoted friend of ours and the finest trailer the world has ever produced."

"Ah, I heard something of you both when I was at Albany from one Jacobus Huysman, a stout and worthy burgher, who spoke well of you, and who hazarded a surmise that I might meet you somewhere in the neighbourhood of the lakes."

"We lived in the house of Mynheer Jacobus when we went to school in Albany. We owe him much."

"There was a third who was generally with you, a famous hunter, David Willet, was there not?"

"He is with Captain Colden, sir, assisting in the defence."

"I'm glad he's there. Judging from what I've heard of him, he's a tower of strength. But come into the camp. Doubtless, both of you need food and rest. The times be dark, and we must get out of each day whatever it has to offer."

Robert looked at him with interest. He was the forerunner of a type that was to develop markedly in New England, tall, thin, dry-lipped, critical, shrewd and tenacious to the last degree. He and his kind were destined to make a great impress upon the New World. He gave to the two the best the camp had, and ordered that they be treated with every courtesy.

"I've a strong force here," he said, "although it might have been stronger if our Governor and Legislature had done their full duty. Still, we must make the best of everything. My men reported Indians in the forest to the north of us, and that, perhaps, is the reason why we have not come into contact with Captain Colden, but I did not suspect that he was besieged."

Robert, as he ate the good food set before him, looked over the camp, which had been pitched well, with far-flung pickets to guard against ambush, and his eyes glistened, as they fell upon two brass cannon, standing side by side upon a slight rise in the centre of the camp. The big guns, when well handled, were always effective against forest warriors. Colonel Strong's eyes followed his.

"I see that you are taking notice of my cannon," he said. "They're good pieces, but if our governor and legislature had done their duty they'd be four instead of two. Still, we have to make the best of what we have. I told Shirley that we must prepare for a great war, and I tell Pownall the same. Those who don't know him always underrate our French foe."

"I never do, sir," said Robert. "I've seen too much of him to do that."

"Well, well, we'll do the best we can. I've four hundred men here, though if the Governor and the Legislature of Massachusetts had done their full duty they'd be eight hundred, not to say a thousand. I'll advance as soon as possible to the relief of Colden. He can surely hold out until the morrow."

"Not a doubt of it, sir, and, if you'll pardon me for making a suggestion, I wouldn't begin any advance until the morning. Not much of the day is left. If we started this afternoon, night would overtake us in the woods and the Chevalier de St. Luc is sure to plant an ambush for us."

"Sensibly spoken, young sir. We're an eternally rash people. We're always walking into traps. I've in my force about twenty good scouts, though if the Governor and Legislature of Massachusetts had done their full duty they'd be forty, not to say fifty, and I don't want to risk their loss in night fighting in the forest."

He went away and Robert saw him moving among his men, giving orders. Elihu Strong, a merchant, nevertheless had made himself a strenuous soldier at his province's call, and he was not unwilling to learn even from those not more than half his age.

"Open Eyes will do well," said Tayoga.

"Open Eyes?"

"Aye, Dagaeoga. The colonel who is named Strong I will call Open Eyes, because he is willing to look and see. He will look when you tell him to look, and many who come from the cities will not do that. And because his eyes are open he will not stick his head into an ambush. Yet he will always complain of others."

"And sometimes of himself, too," laughed Robert. "I think he'll be fair in that respect. Now, Tayoga, we'll rest here, and be easy with ourselves until to-morrow morning, when we advance."

"We will stay, Dagaeoga, but I do not know whether it will be so easy. Since Jumonville saw us escape he will tell St. Luc of it, and Sharp Sword will send a force here to harry Open Eyes, and to make him think the forest is full of warriors. But Open Eyes, though he may complain, will not be afraid."

It was even as the Onondaga predicted. The foe came with the twilight. The dark wilderness about them gave back whoops and yells, and furtive bands skirmished with Strong's scouts. Then the shouts of the warriors increased greatly in number, and seemed to come from all points about the camp. It was obvious to Robert that the enemy was trying to make Strong's men believe that a great force was confronting them, and some of them, unused to the woods, showed apprehension lest such an unseen and elusive danger overwhelm them. But Elihu Strong never flinched. The forest was almost as much of a mystery to him as it was to his troops, but he was there to dare its perils and he dared them.

"I shall keep my men in camp and await attack, if they make it," he said to Robert, to whom he seemed to have taken a great fancy, "and whatever happens I shall move forward in the morning to the relief of Colden."

He shut his thin lips tightly together and his pale blue eyes flashed. The merchant, turned soldier, had the stoutest of hearts, and a stout heart was what was needed in his camp that night. The warriors gave his men no rest. They circled about continually, firing and whooping, and trying to create panic, or at least a fear that would hold Strong where he was.

Robert went to sleep early, and, when he awakened far in the night, the turmoil was still going on. But he saw Elihu Strong walking back and forth near one of the fires, and in the glow his thin face still reflected an iron resolution. Satisfied that the camp was in no danger of being frightened, young Lennox went back to sleep.

A gray, chilly morning came, and soon after dawn Elihu Strong began to prepare his men for their perilous progress, serving first an ample hot breakfast with plenty of tea and coffee.

"Open Eyes not only watches but he knows much," said Tayoga. "He has learned that an army marches better on a full stomach."

Strong then asked Robert and Tayoga to serve in a way as guides, and he made his dispositions, sending his scouts in advance, putting his most experienced soldiers on the flanks and heading his main column with the two brass cannon. The strictest injunctions that nobody straggle were given, and then the force took up its march.

They had not been molested while at breakfast, and when making the preparations, but as soon as they left the fire and entered the deep forest, the terrifying turmoil burst forth again, fierce whoops resounding on every side and bullets pattering on the leaves or bark. Colonel Strong left his scouts and flankers to deal with the ambushed warriors, and the main column, face to the front, marched steadily toward Colden's camp. It was to be a trial of nerves, and Robert was quite confident that the stern New England leader would win.

"The savages make a tremendous tumult," he said to young Lennox, "but their bullets are not reaching us. We're not to be shaken by mere noise."

"When they find that out, as they soon will," said Robert, "they'll make an attack. Some French officers and troops must be with them. Perhaps Jumonville came in the night to lead them."

He and Tayoga then went a short distance into the forest ahead of the scouts, and Tayoga saw ample evidence that the French were present with the Indians.

"You are right in your surmise that Jumonville came in the night," he said. "He wore boots, and here are the imprints of his heels. I think he is not far away now. Watch well, Dagaeoga, while I lie on the earth and listen."

Ear to the ground, the Onondaga announced that he could hear men on both sides of them moving.

"There is the light step of the warriors," he said, "and also the heavier tread of the French. I think I can hear Jumonville himself. It sounds like the crush of boots. Perhaps they are now seeking to lay an ambush."

"Then it's time for us to fall back, Tayoga, both for our own sakes and for the sake of Colonel Strong's force."

The two retreated quickly lest they be caught in an ambush, and gave warning to Elihu Strong that an attack was now probable, a belief in which they were confirmed by the report the scouts brought in presently that a creek was just ahead, a crossing always being a favourite place for an Indian trap.

"So be it," said Colonel Strong, calmly. "We are ready. If the Governor and Legislature of Massachusetts had done their full duty, we'd be twice as strong, but even as we are we'll force the passage of the creek."

"You will find a body of the warriors on this side of the stream," said Tayoga. "They will give way after a little firing, tempting you to think you have won an easy victory. Then when about half of your men are across they will attack with all their might, hoping to cut you down."

"I thank you for telling me," said Colonel Strong. "I've no doubt you know what you're talking about. Your manner indicates it. We might be much better equipped than we are if those in authority in my province had done their full duty, but we will make way, nevertheless. I'll cover the passage of the creek with the guns."

The firing in front already showed that Tayoga's prediction was coming true, and it was accompanied by a tremendous volume of yelling, as if the whole Indian force were gathered on the near side of the creek.

Robert from the crest of a hill saw the stream, narrow and deep, though not too deep for fording as he was to learn later, fringed on either side with a dense growth of low bushes, from the shelter of which warriors were sending their bullets toward the white force. The men were eager to go against them at once, but the scouts were sent forward through the undergrowth to open up a flanking fire, and then the main column marched on at a steady pace.

The crash of the rifles grew fast. The warriors on the near side of the creek leaped from the bushes as Strong's men drew near, waded the stream and disappeared in the forest on the other bank, giving forth howls of disappointment as they fled. The soldiers, uttering a shout of triumph, undertook to rush forward in pursuit, but Strong restrained them.

"It's the ambush against which the Onondaga warned us," he said to his lieutenants, "and we won't run into it. Bring forward the cannon."

The two brass guns, fine twelve pounders, were moved up within close range of the creek, and they swept the forest on the other side with balls and grape shot. It was probably the first time cannon were ever heard in those woods, and the reports came back in many echoes. Boughs and twigs rained down.

"It is a great sound," said Tayoga admiringly, "and the warriors who are trying to plant an ambush will not like it."

"But you'll remember Braddock's fate," said Robert. "The cannon didn't do much then."

"But this is different, Dagaeoga. Open Eyes has his eyes open. He is merely using the cannon as a cover for his advance. They will be backed up by the rifles. You will see."

The soldiers approached the creek cautiously, and, when the first ranks were in the water, the cannon raked the woods ahead to right and left, and to left and right. The best of the riflemen were also pushed forward, and, when the warriors opened fire, they were quickly driven away. Then the whole force, carrying the cannon with them, crossed, and stood in triumph on the other side.

"Did I not tell you that Open Eyes knew what he was doing?" said Tayoga.

"It seems that he does," Robert replied, "but we haven't yet arrived at Colden's station. An attack in force is sure to come."

"Dagaeoga speaks truth. I think it will occur a mile or two farther on. They will make it before Captain Colden's men can learn that we are on the march."

"Then they won't wait long. Anywhere will do, as the forest is dense everywhere."

Since they had carried the ford with but little loss, the cannon that had blazed the way ceased to fire, but the gunners regarded them proudly and Robert did not withhold admiration. They were pioneers, fine brass creatures, and when handled right they were a wonderful help in the forest. He did not blame the gunners for patting the barrels, for scraping the mud of the creek's crossing from the wheels, and for speaking to them affectionately. Massive and polished they gleamed in the sun and inspired confidence.

Tayoga went ahead in the forest, but came back soon and reported a low ridge not more than half a mile farther on, a likely place for an attack, which he judged would come there. It would be made by the united force of the French and Indians and would be severe.

"So be it," said Elihu Strong, whose iron calm nothing disturbed. "We are ready for the foe, though St. Luc himself should come. It is true that instead of two cannon we might have had four or even six, or twice as many men, if the Governor and Legislature of Massachusetts had done their full duty, but we'll let that pass. Will you, Lennox, and you, Tayoga, advance with the scouts and be my eyes?"

Robert appreciated the compliment to the full, and promptly

replied in the affirmative for them both. Then he and Tayoga at once plunged into the forest with the borderers who were there to provide against ambush, all of them approaching the menacing ridge with great care. It was a long projection, rising about a hundred feet, and grown densely with trees and bushes. It looked very quiet and peaceful and birds even were singing there among the boughs. The leader of the scouts, a bronzed man of middle age named Adams, turned to Tayoga.

"I see nothing there," he said, "but I've heard of you and your power to find things where others can't. Do you think they're on that ridge waiting for us?"

"It is certain," replied the Onondaga. "It is the place best fitted for them, and they will not neglect it. Let me go forward a little, with my friend, Dagaeoga, and we will unveil them."

"We'll wait here, and if they're on it I believe you'll soon know it," said Adams confidently.

Tayoga slid forward among the bushes and Robert followed. Neither made the slightest noise, and they drew much nearer to the ridge, which still basked in the sun, peaceful and innocent in looks. Not a warrior or a Frenchman appeared there, the bushes gave back no glint of weapons, nothing was disclosed.

"They may be hidden in that jungle, but they won't stir until we're under the muzzles of their rifles. What do you propose to do?" asked Robert.

"I will tempt them, Dagaeoga."

"Tempt them? I don't understand you."

"Tododaho on his great star which we cannot see in the day, but which, nevertheless, is there, whispers to me that Tandakora himself is among the bushes on the ridge. It is just such an ambush as he loves. As you know, Dagaeoga, he hates us all, but he hates me most. If he sees a good opportunity for a shot at me he will not be able to forego it."

"For Heaven's sake, Tayoga, don't make a martyr of yourself merely to draw the enemy's fire!"

"No such thought was in my mind. I am not yet ready to leave the world, which I find bright and full of interest. Moreover, I wish to see the end of this war and what will happen afterward. Risks are a part of our life, Dagaeoga, but I will take none that is undue."

Tayoga spoke in his usual precise, book English, explaining everything fully, and Robert said nothing more. But he awaited the actions of the Onondaga with intense interest. Tayoga crept forward five or six yards more, and then he stumbled, striking against a bush and shaking it violently. Robert was amazed. It was incredible that the Onondaga should be so awkward, and then he remembered. Tayoga was going to draw the enemy's fire.

Tayoga struck against another bush, and then stood upright and visible. Those hidden on the ridge, if such there were, could see him clearly. The response was immediate. A gigantic figure stood up among the bushes, levelled a rifle and fired at him point blank. But the Onondaga, quick as lightning, dropped back and the bullet whistled over his head. Robert fired at the great painted figure of Tandakora, but he too missed, and in a moment the Ojibway chief sank down in the undergrowth. A shout came from the hidden Indians about him.

"They are there," said Tayoga, "and we know just where many of them lie. We will suggest to Open Eyes that he fire the cannon at that point."

They rejoined Adams.

"You were right, as I knew you'd be," said the scout. "You've located 'em."

"Yes, because Tandakora could not resist his hate of me," said the Onondaga.

They withdrew to the main force, and once more the brave brass guns were brought up, sending solid shot and grape into the bushes on the ridge, then moving forward and repeating the fire. Many rifles opened upon them from the thickets, and several men fell, but Elihu Strong held his people in hand, and the scouts drove back the sharpshooters. Meanwhile the whole force advanced and began to climb the ridge, the cannon being turned on the flanks, where the attack was now heaviest. A fierce battle ensued, and the guns, served with great skill and effectiveness, kept the Indians at bay. More of Strong's men were slain and many were hit, but their own rifles backed up the guns with a deadly fire. Thus the combat was waged in the thickets a full two hours, when they heard a great shout toward the north, and Willet, at the head of a hundred men, broke his way through to their relief. Then French and Indians drew off, and the united forces proceeded to the point, where Colden, Wilton, Carson and Grosvenor gave them a great welcome.

"We are here," said Elihu Strong. "If the Governor and Legislature of Massachusetts had done their full duty we might have been here sooner, but here we are."

"I knew that you would come back and bring help with you," said Grosvenor to Robert. "I felt sure that Tayoga would guide the canoe through every peril."

"Your confidence was not misplaced," said Robert. "He did some wonderful work. He was as great a trailer on the water as he is on land. Now that we are so much stronger, I wonder what St. Luc is going to do."

But Black Rifle came in the next morning with the news that the Chevalier and his whole force were gone.

They had stolen away silently in the night, and were now marching northward, probably to join Montcalm.

"I'm not surprised," said Willet. "We're now too strong for him and St. Luc is not the man to waste his time and strength in vain endeavours. I suspect that we will next hear of him near Champlain, somewhere in the neighbourhood of Ticonderoga. I think we'd better follow his trail a little distance."

Willet himself led the band that pursued St. Luc, and it included Tayoga, Robert, Grosvenor, Black Rifle and Adams, Daganoweda and his Mohawks having left shortly before on an expedition of their own. It was an easy enough task, as the trail necessarily was wide and deep, and the Onondaga could read it almost with his eyes shut.

"Here went Sharp Sword," he said after looking about a while. "I find traces of his moccasins, which I would know anywhere because I have seen them so many times before. Here another Frenchman joined him and walked beside him for a while. It was Jumonville, whose imprints I also know. They talked together. Perhaps Jumonville was narrating the details of his encounter with us. Now he leaves St. Luc, who is joined by another Frenchman wearing moccasins. But the man is heavy and walked with a heavy step. It is the Canadian, Dubois, who attends upon Sharp Sword, and who is devoted to him. Perhaps Sharp Sword is giving him instructions about the camp that they will make when the day is over. Now Dubois also goes, and here come the great moccasins of Tandakora. I have seen none other so large in the woods, and a child would know them. He too talks with Sharp Sword, but Sharp Sword does not stop for him. They walk on together, because the stride continues steady and even, just the length that a man of Sharp Sword's height would make when walking. Tandakora is very angry, not at Sharp Sword—he would not dare to show anger against him—but at the will of Manitou who would not let him win a victory over us. He did not get much satisfaction from Sharp Sword, because he stayed with him only a very short time. Here his trail leads away again, and Sharp Sword once more walks on alone.

"Perhaps Sharp Sword prefers to be alone. Most men do after a disappointment, and he knows that his attack upon the boat builders

144

has been a failure. Sharp Sword does not like failures any more than other people do, and he wants to think. He is planning how to win a great success, and to atone for his failure here. I do not see anything of De Courcelles. I do not find his trail anywhere, which shows that the wound you gave him, Dagaeoga, was severe. He is being carried either by warriors or French soldiers on a litter. It is far more likely to be soldiers, and here I find them, the trail of four men who walk exactly even, two by two all the time. The rage of De Courcelles will mount very high against you, Dagaeoga, and you will have to beware of him."

"I am ready for him," said Robert, proudly.

The broad trail led steadily on toward the north, but Willet, after a while, spread out his own little force, taking no chances with forest ambush. He considered it highly probable that before long Tandakora would curve aside with some of his warriors, hoping to trap the unwary. He was confirmed in his opinion by the Onondaga's reading of the trail.

"I find the footprints of the Ojibway chief again," said Tayoga. "Here they go at the edge of the trail. Now he has stopped. His stride has ceased, and he stands with his moccasins close together. He is probably talking with his warriors and he meditates something. The rage of Tandakora is as great as that of De Courcelles, but Tandakora is not hurt, and he is able to strike. He moves on again, and, ah! here he goes into the woods. Beyond question he is now engaged in planting an ambush for those who would follow St. Luc. Shall we go back, Great Bear, or shall we meet the Ojibway's ambush with an ambush of our own?"

The black eyes of the Onondaga sparkled.

"We ought to turn back," replied Willet, "but I can't resist playing Tandakora's own game with him. It may give us a chance to rid the border of that scourge. We'll leave the trail, and go into the deep bush."

Led by the hunter the little band plunged into the forest and began a careful circle, intending to come back to the trail some distance ahead, and to post themselves behind Tandakora in case that wily savage was planning an ambush, as they felt sure he was. They redoubled their precautions, ceasing all talk for the while, and allowing no bushes to rustle as they passed. Willet led the line, and Tayoga brought up the rear. Grosvenor was just behind Robert. He, too, was now able to bring down his feet in soundless fashion, and to avoid every stick or twig that might break with a crack beneath his weight. While he was aware of the perils before them, his heart beat high. He felt that he was making further progress, and that he was becoming a worthy forest runner.

After two careful hours of travel, they came back again to the broad trail which showed that St. Luc was still maintaining steady progress toward the north. But both the hunter and the Onondaga felt sure that Tandakora and a chosen band were now to the south, waiting in ambush for those who would come in pursuit.

"We'd better draw 'em if we can," said Willet. "Let 'em know we're here, but make 'em believe we're friends."

"I think I can do it," said Tayoga. "I know Huron and St. Regis signals. It is likely that some of the warriors with Tandakora are Hurons, and, in any event, the Ojibway will understand the signals."

He imitated the cawing of a crow, and presently the answer came from the forest about a quarter of a mile to the south. The cry was repeated, and the answer came duly a second time. No one in the little band now doubted that Tandakora and his men were there.

"Shall we attack?" asked Robert.

"I think we can sting them a little," replied Willet. "Our numbers are few, but the force of the Ojibway is not likely to be large. It was his purpose to strike and get away, and that's what we'll do. Now, Tayoga, we're relying upon you to get us into a good position on his flank."

The Onondaga led them in another but much smaller circle toward the forest, from which the answering caws of the crow had come. The way went through dense thickets but, before he reached his chosen spot, he stopped.

"Look," he said, pointing to the earth, where there were faint traces that Robert could scarcely see and over which he would have passed, unnoticing. "Here is where Tandakora went on his way to the ambush. It is a little trail, and it was to be only a little ambush. He has only about ten warriors with him. The Ojibway has come back for revenge. He could not bear to leave without striking at least one blow. Perhaps he slipped away from Sharp Sword to try the ambush on his own account."

"They can't be far ahead," said the hunter.

"No," said the Onondaga. "They will be coming back in response to my call, and I think we would better await them here."

They disposed themselves in good order for battle, and then sank to the earth. Light waves of air registered delicately but clearly on those wonderful eardrums of Tayoga's. Faint though the sound was, he understood it. It was the careful tread of men. Tandakora and his warriors were on the way, called by the crow. He knew when they came within a hundred yards of where he and his companions lay, and he knew when they spread out in cautious fashion, to see what manner of friends these were who came. He knew, too, that Tandakora would not walk into a trap, and he had not expected at any time that he would, it having been merely his purpose when he cawed like a crow to call him back to fair and honourable combat, ambush against ambush. He noted when the thin line of detached warriors began to advance again, he was even able to trace the step of Tandakora, heavier than the others, and to discern when the Ojibway chief stopped a second time, trying to pierce the thickets with his eyes.

"Tandakora is in doubt," he whispered to Robert. "The call of the crow which at first seemed so friendly has another meaning now. He is not so sure that friends are here after all, but he does not understand how an enemy happens to be behind him. He is angry, too, that his own pretty ambush, in which he was sitting so cunningly waiting for us, is broken up. Tandakora's humour is far from good, but, because of it, mine is excellent."

"You certainly learned the dictionary well when you were in our schools," Robert whispered back, but as full as ever of admiration for Tayoga's powers. "Has all sound ceased now?"

"They are not stirring. They have become quite sure that we are enemies and they wait for us to act first."

"Then I'll give 'em a lead," said Willet, who lay on Tayoga's right.

He thrust out a foot, bringing it down on a dead stick so hard that it broke with a sharp snap, but instantly drew away to the shelter of another bush. A rifle cracked in front of them and a bullet cut the air over the broken stick. Before the warrior who fired the bullet could sink back Black Rifle pulled the trigger at a certain target, and the man fell without a sound.

"A fine shot, Captain Jack," said Willet, and a few minutes later the hunter himself made another just as good. For a half hour the combat was waged in the deep thickets, mere glimpses serving for aim, but the combatants were as fierce and tenacious as if the issue were joined by great armies. Four warriors fell, Willet's band suffered only a few scratches, and then, at a signal from him, they melted away into the woods, curved about again, and took up the return journey toward their own force.

"We did enough," said Willet, when he was sure they were not pursued by Tandakora. "All we wanted to do was to sting the Ojibway and not to let him forget that those who ambush may be ambushed. He'll be fairly burning with anger."

"How are you feeling, Red Coat?" asked Tayoga.

"As well as could be expected after such an experience," replied Grosvenor with pride. But the young Englishman was very sober, too. A warrior had fallen before his rifle, and, with the heat of battle over, he was very thoughtful.

CHAPTER 12

The French Camp

They returned to the camp without further event. Colden and Strong were gratified to learn that the retreat of St. Luc was real, and that he was certainly going toward Champlain, with the obvious intention of joining Montcalm.

"We owe you a great debt of gratitude, Colonel," said the young officer, frankly, to Elihu Strong. "If you had not come I don't think we could have held out against St. Luc."

"We did the best we could," replied Elihu Strong. "If the Governor and Legislature of Massachusetts had done their full duty we'd have been here earlier, with twice as many men and guns, but as it is we did our best, and man can do no more."

They decided that they would hold the point and await the coming of the great army under Abercrombie which was to crush Montcalm. The outworks were built higher and stronger and the brass cannon were mounted upon them at points, where they could sweep the forest. These fine twelve-pounders were sources of much moral courage and added greatly to the spirits of the troops. They had shown their power at the forcing of the ford and at the taking of the ridge, and their brazen mouths, menacing the forest, looked well.

Willet and his comrades considered it their duty to stay there also, and wait for Abercrombie, and, the third day after the retreat of St. Luc, Robert and Tayoga went into the woods to see whether Tandakora had turned back again with his warriors. They reckoned that the Ojibway chief's anger was so strong that he would make another attempt at revenge upon those who had defeated him. There was a rumour that the Indians with the French were becoming much dissatisfied, that they were awed by the reports of the mighty British and American force advancing under Abercrombie, and might leave the French to meet it alone.

"Do you think there is much in these rumours?" asked Robert, as he and the Onondaga went into the forest.

"I do," replied Tayoga. "The warriors with the French do not like the cannon, and they say the force that is coming against Montcalm is very vast. A great battle may be fought, but Tandakora and his men are not likely to be there. They will go away and await a better day."

"Then I'm glad they'll desert for a while. They're the eyes and ears of the French. That will leave our own scouts and forest runners the lords of the wild, though it seems to me, Tayoga, that you're the true and veritable lord of the wild."

"Then if that were so, though you praise my skill too much, Dagaeoga, you and the Great Bear and Black Rifle also are lords of the wild."

"Lords of the wild! I like the term. It is something to be that at this time and in this region. We're mainly a wilderness people, Tayoga, and our wars are waged in the woods. We're not more than two miles from the camp now, and yet we're completely lost in the forest. There's not a trace of man. I don't even see any smoke soiling the sky."

"It is so, Dagaeoga, and we are again in the shadow of peril. Dangers in the forest are as thick as leaves on the trees. Here is an old trail of our enemies."

"I'm not interested in old trails. What we're looking for is new ones."

"If we keep going toward the north it may be that we will find them, Dagaeoga."

Several miles farther on they came to other trails which the Onondaga examined with great interest and care. Two or three he pronounced quite recent, but he did not read any particular purpose in them.

"It is likely that they were made by hunters," he said. "While the armies are gathering, the warriors are sure to seek game. Here two of them passed, and here they stood behind a tree. It is sure now that those two were hunting. I think they stood behind a tree to ambush a deer. The deer was to the west of them. The traces they left in the soft earth under the tree show that the toes of their moccasins pointed toward the west and so they were looking that way, at the deer, which probably stood in the thicket over there nibbling at its food. They must have had an easy shot. Now, we'll enter the thicket. Lo, Dagaeoga, here is where the deer fell! Look at the little bushes broken and at the dark stain on the ground where its life flowed out. They dragged the body to the other side of the thicket, and cut it up there. Nothing could be plainer, the traces are so numerous. They were casual hunters, and it is not worth our while to follow them."

Northward they still pursued their course, and struck another and larger trail which made Tayoga look grave.

"This is the path of seven or eight warriors," he said, "and it is likely that they are a scouting party. They have come back, as we expected, to spy upon us and to cut off stragglers from our camp. We will follow it a little while."

It led south by west and seemed to go on with a definite purpose, but, after a mile or so, it divided, four warriors, as Tayoga said, going in one direction and three in the other.

"Suppose I follow those on the north a short distance while you take those on the south," suggested Robert.

"We will do so," said Tayoga, "and in an hour come back to this point."

The three warriors were on the north, and, as the earth was soft, Robert saw their trail quite clearly leading steadily west by north. His own ambition to excel as a trailer was aroused and he followed it with great energy. Two or three times when the ground became hard and rocky he lost it, but a little search always disclosed it again, and he renewed the pursuit with increased zeal. He went on over a hill and then into a wide valley, well grown with thickets. Pushing his way through the bushes he sought the traces and was startled by a sound almost at his shoulder. Keyed to the dangers of the forest he whirled instantly, but it was too late. A powerful warrior threw himself upon him, and though Robert, by a great effort, threw him off he sprang back and another on the other side also seized him. He was borne to the earth and a third Indian coming up, he was quickly secured.

Robert at first was so sick with chagrin that he did not think about his life. In nine cases out of ten the warriors would have tomahawked him, and this he soon realized, thankful at the same time that he had been spared, for the present, at least. Yet his mortification endured. What would Tayoga say when he saw by the trail that he had been caught so easily? He had fairly walked into the trap, and he was now a prisoner the second time. Yet he showed the stoicism that he had learned in a forest life. While the Indians bound his wrists tightly with rawhide thongs he stood up and looked them squarely in the face.

One of the warriors took his rifle and examined it with a pleased eye. Another appropriated his pistol and a third helped himself to his knife and hatchet.

"I've four shillings in an inside pocket," said Robert. "If you want 'em, take 'em."

But the warriors did not understand English and shook their heads. Evidently they were satisfied with the spoil they had taken already.

"Which way?" asked Robert.

They replied by leading him to the northwest. He was hopeful at first that Tayoga might rescue him as he had done once before, but the warriors were wary and powerful, and three, too, were too many for the Onondaga alone to attack. The thought passed and by an effort of the will he resigned himself to his immediate captivity. They did not mean to take his life, and while there was no hope for the present there was plenty of it for the future. He could be in a far worse case. His unfailing optimism broke through the shell of mortification, and he became resolutely cheerful.

"Which way, my friends?" he said to the warriors.

But again they understood no English and shook their heads.

"Don't plume yourself too much on that rifle," he said, speaking to the warrior who had taken his favourite weapon. "You have it for the present, but when I escape for the second time I mean to take it with me. I give you fair warning."

The warrior, who seemed to be good natured, shook his head once more, and grinned, not abating at all his air of proprietorship so far as the rifle was concerned.

"And you with the pistol," continued the prisoner, "I beg to tell you it's mine, not yours, and I shall claim it again. What, you don't understand? Well, I'll have to find some way to make you comprehend later on."

The three warriors walked briskly and Robert, of course, had no choice but to keep pace with them. They indicated very conclusively that they knew where they meant to go, and so he assumed that a hostile camp was not very far away. Resolved to show no sign of discouragement, he held his head erect and stepped springily. About three miles, and he saw a gleam of uniforms through the trees, a few steps more and his heart gave a leap. He beheld a group of Indians, and several Frenchmen, and one of them, tall, young, distinguished, was St. Luc.

The Chevalier was in a white uniform, trimmed with silver, a silver hilted small sword by his side, and his smile was not unpleasant when he said to Robert:

"I sent out these three warriors to find me a prisoner and bring him in, but I little suspected that it would be you."

"I suspected as little that it was you to whom I was being taken," said Robert. "But since I had to be a prisoner I'm glad I'm yours instead of De Courcelles' or Jumonville's, as those two soldiers of France have as little cause to love me as I have to love them."

"Monsieur De Courcelles is suffering from a bullet wound."

"It was my bullet."

"You say that rather proudly, but perhaps I'd better not tell it to him. It seems, Mr. Lennox, that you have a certain facility in getting yourself captured, as this is the second time within a year."

"I was treated so well by the French that I thought I could risk it again," said Robert jauntily.

The Chevalier smiled. Robert felt again that current of understanding and sympathy, that, so it seemed to him, had passed so often between them.

"I see," said St. Luc, "that you are willing to give credit to France, the evergreen nation, the nation of light and eternal life. We may lose at times, we may be defeated at times, but we always rise anew. You British and Americans will realize that some day."

"I do not hate France."

"I don't think you do. But this is scarcely a time for me to give you a lecture on French qualities. Sit down on this log. I trust that my warriors did not treat you with undue harshness."

"I've nothing to complain of. They took my weapons, but that is the law of war. I'd have done the same in their place. As I see it, they're not particularly bad Indians. But if you don't mind, I'd like you to cut these rawhide thongs that bind my wrists. They're beginning to sting."

The Chevalier drew a knife and with one sweep of its keen edge severed the rawhide. Robert's wrists flew apart and the blood once more flowed freely through his veins. Though the stinging did not cease he felt great relief.

"I thank you," he said politely, "but, as I told you before, I do not hold it against your warriors, because they bound me. I'd have escaped had they given me any chance at all, and I warn you now, as I warned them, that I intend to escape later on."

St. Luc smiled. "I'll accept the challenge," he said, "and I'll see that you don't make good your boast. I can assure you, too, if by any possibility you should escape, it certainly will not be before the great battle."

"Great battle! What great battle? You don't mean that Montcalm will dare to meet Abercrombie?"

"Such an idea was in my mind."

"Why, we'll come with four or five to one! The Marquis de Montcalm cannot stand against such a powerful force as ours. We've definite information that he won't be able to muster more than three or four thousand men. We hear, too, that the Indians, frightened by our power, are leaving him, for the time, at least."

"Some of your surmises may be correct, but your facts don't follow from them. The Marquis de Montcalm, our great leader, will await your Abercrombie, no matter what your force may be. I violate no military secret when I tell you that, and I tell you also that you are very far from being assured of any victory."

The Chevalier suddenly dropped his light manner, and became intensely earnest. His eyes gleamed for an instant with blue fire, but it was only a passing moment of emotion. He was in an instant his old, easy self again.

"We talk like the debaters of the schools," he said, "when we are at war. I am to march in a few minutes. I suggest that in return for certain liberties you give me your pledge to attempt no escape until we arrive at the camp of the Marquis de Montcalm."

"I can't do it. Since I've promised you that I will escape I must neglect no chance."

"So be it. Then I must guard you well, but I will not have your wrists bound again. Here comes an expert rover of the forest who will be your immediate jailer."

A white man at the head of several warriors was approaching through the woods. He was young, lean, with a fierce, hooked Roman nose, and a bold, aggressive face, tanned to the colour of mahogany. Robert recognized him at once, and since he had to be a prisoner a second time, he took a certain pleasure in the meeting.

"How do you do, Monsieur Langlade?" he said. "You see, I've come back. I forgot to tell you good-by, and I'm here to make amends for my lack of politeness. And how is the patient and watchful spouse, the Dove?"

Robert spoke in good French and the partisan stared in astonishment. Then a pleased look of recognition came into his eyes.

"Ah, it's young Mr. Lennox," he exclaimed. "Young Mr. Lennox come back to us. It's not mere politeness that makes me tell you I'm glad to see you. You did make a very clever escape with the aid of that Indian friend of yours. I hope to capture Tayoga some day, and, if I do, it will be an achievement of which I shall boast all the rest of my life. But we'll take good care that you don't leave us again."

"He has just warned me that he intends to escape a second time," said St. Luc.

"Then it will be a pretty test of mettle," said the Owl, appreciation showing in his tone, "and we welcome it. Have you any commands for me, sir?"

He spoke with great respect when he addressed the query to St.

Luc, and the Chevalier replied that they would march in a half hour. Then Langlade gave Robert food, and took a little himself, sitting with the prisoner and informing him that the Dove had worried greatly over his escape. Although she was not to blame, she considered that in some indirect manner it was a reflection upon her vigilance, and it was many months before she was fully consoled.

"I must send word to her by one of our runners that you have been retaken," said the Owl, "and I wish to tell you, Mr. Lennox, that the Dove's younger sister, who is so much like her in looks and character, is still unmarried and perhaps it may come into the mind of the Chevalier de St. Luc or the Marquis de Montcalm to send you back to our village."

"You're once more most polite," laughed Robert, "but I'm far too young, yet, to think of marriage."

"It's not an offer that I'd make to many young men," said Langlade regretfully. "In truth, I know of none other to whom I'd have mentioned it."

When they took up the march the force numbered about fifty men, and Robert walked between Langlade and a stalwart Indian. St. Luc was further on. They did not seem to fear any ambush and Langlade chattered after his fashion. He made the most of the French resources. He spoke as if the Marquis de Montcalm had ten or fifteen thousand veteran French regulars, and half as many Indian warriors.

"Don't consider me contentious, Monsieur Langlade," said Robert, at last, "but I know full well that your general has not half that many troops, no, not a third, and that nearly all his Indians are about to leave him."

"And how do you know that?" exclaimed the Owl. "Well, one Frenchman equals two of the English or the Bostonnais, and that doubles our numbers. You don't see any chance to escape, do you?"

"Not at present," laughed Robert.

"Not now, nor at any other time. No man ever escapes twice from the French."

The talk of Langlade, his frank egotism and boastfulness for himself personally and for the French collectively, beguiled the journey which soon became strenuous, the force advancing at a great pace through the forest. At night a fire was built in the deep woods, the knapsacks furnished plenty of food, and Robert slept soundly on a blanket until dawn. He had seen before closing his eyes that a strict guard was set, and he knew that it was not worth while to keep awake in the hope of escape. Like a wise man he dismissed the hope of the impossible at once, and waited calmly for another time. He knew too that St. Luc had originally sent out his warriors to capture a prisoner from whom they might drag information, but that the Chevalier would not try to cross-examine him, knowing its futility.

They travelled northward by east all the next day, through very rough country, slept another night in the forest, and on the third day approached a great camp, which held the main French force. Robert's heart thrilled. Here was the centre of the French power in North America. Vaudreuil and Bigot at Quebec might plan and plot and weave their webs, but in the end the mighty struggle between French and English and their colonies must be decided by the armies.

He knew that this was the outlet of Lake George and he knew also that the army of Abercrombie was gathering at the head of the same lake. His interest grew keener as they drew nearer. He saw clusters of tents, cannon parked, and many fires. There were no earthworks or other fortifications, and he inferred from their absence that Montcalm was undecided whether to go or stay. But Robert thought proudly that he would surely go, when the invincible Anglo-American army advanced from its base at the head of the lake. The whole camp lay under his eye, and he had enough military experience now to judge the French numbers by its size. He did not think they were much in excess of three thousand, and as Abercrombie would come four or five to one, Montcalm must surely retreat.

"I take it that this is Ticonderoga," he said to St. Luc.

"Aye," replied the Chevalier.

"And in effect you have Champlain on one side of you and George on the other. But you can't hold the place against our great force. I'm here in time to join you in your retreat."

"We don't seem to be retreating, as you'll notice, Mr. Lennox, and I don't know that we will. Still, that rests on the knees of the gods. I think you'll find here some old friends and enemies of yours, and though your people have made a great outcry against the Marquis de Montcalm because of the affair at Fort William Henry, I am sure you will find that the French know how to treat a prisoner. I shall put you for the present in the care of Monsieur Langlade, with whom you appear to have no quarrel. He has his instructions."

It was the second time that Robert had entered the camp of Montcalm and his keen interest drove away for the present all thought of himself. He noted anew the uniforms, mostly white faced with blue or violet or red or yellow, and with black, three-cornered hats. There were the battalions of Guienne, La Reine, Béarn, La Sarre, Langue-doc, Berry and Royal Roussillon. The Canadians, swarthy, thick and strong, wore white with black facings. Some Indians were about, but fewer than Robert had expected. It was true then that they had become alarmed at Abercrombie's advancing might, and were leaving the French to their fate.

"You are to stay in a tent with me," said Langlade, "and you will be so thoroughly surrounded by the army, that you will have no earthly chance of escape. So I think it better that you pledge your word not to attempt it for a while, and I can make things easier for you."

"No, I decline again to give such a pledge," said Robert firmly. "I warn you, as I've warned the Chevalier de St. Luc, that I'm going to escape."

Langlade looked at him searchingly, and then the face of the partisan kindled.

"I believe you mean it!" he exclaimed. "You rely on yourself and you think, too, that clever Onondaga, Tayoga, will come again to your aid. I acknowledge that he's a great trailer, that he's master of some things that even I, Charles Langlade, the Owl, do not know, but he cannot steal you away a second time."

"I admit that I've been thinking of Tayoga. He may be here now close to us."

The Owl gave a startled look at the empty air, as if he expected Tayoga to be hovering there, formidable but invisible.

"I see you do fear him," laughed Robert.

"I do, but we shall be a match for him this time, though I never underrate his powers."

A young officer in a captain's uniform stopped suddenly and looked at Robert. Then he advanced and extended his hand.

"It is evident that you like the French," he said, "since you are continually coming back to them."

"De Galissonnière!" exclaimed Robert, as he warmly shook the extended hand. "Yes, here I am, and I do like many of the French. I'm sorry we're official enemies."

"I know that our people will treat you well," jested De Galissonnière, "and then, when we take New York, you can tell the inhabitants of that city what good masters we are and teach them to be reconciled."

Young Lennox made a reply in like spirit, and De Galissonnière passed on. But a man walking near with his shoulder well bound greeted him in no such friendly manner. Instead a heavy frown came over his face and his eyes flashed cruelly. It was De Courcelles, nursing the wound Robert had given him, and at the same time increasing his anger. The youth returned his gaze defiantly.

"Colonel De Courcelles does not like you," said Langlade, who had noticed the brief exchange.

"He does not," replied Robert. "It was my bullet that hurt his shoulder, but I gave him the wound in fair combat."

"And he hates you because of it?"

"That and other things."

"What a strange man! A wound received in fair and honourable battle should be a tie that binds. If you had given it to me in a combat on equal terms I'd have considered it an honour conferred upon me by you. It would have wiped away all grievance and have made us friends."

"Then, Monsieur Langlade, I'm afraid I missed my opportunity to make our friendship warmer than it is."

"How is that?"

"I held you also under the muzzle of my rifle in that battle in the forest, but when I recognized you I could not send the bullet. I turned the weapon aside."

"Ah, that was in truth a most worthy and chivalrous act! Embrace me, my friend!"

"No! No! We American men never embrace or kiss one another!"

"I should have remembered. A cold people! But never mind! You are my brother, and I esteem you so highly that I shall let nothing on earth take you away from us. Can you not reconsider your decision about the sister of the Dove? She would make you a most admirable wife, and after the war we could become the greatest rangers, you and I, that the forest has ever known. And the life in the woods is marvellous in its freedom and variety!"

But Robert plead extreme youth once more, and the Owl was forced to be resigned. The small tent in which guard and prisoner were to sleep was almost in the centre of the camp and Robert truly would have needed wings and the power of invisibility to escape then. Instead of it he let the thought pass for a while and went to sleep on a blanket.

★ ★ ★ ★ ★ ★ ★ ★

While young Lennox slept St. Luc was in the tent of Montcalm talking with his leader. The Marquis was in much perplexity. His spies had brought him word of the great force that was mustering in the south, and he did not know whether to await the attack at Ticonderoga or to retreat to the powerful fortifications at Crown Point on

Lake Champlain. His own ardent soul, flushed by the successes he had already won, told him to stay, but prudence bade him go. Now he wanted to hear what St. Luc had to say and wanting it he knew also that the Chevalier was the most valiant and daring of his captains. He wished to hear from the dauntless leader just what he wished to hear and nothing else.

"Your observations, then, confirm what the spies have reported?" he said. "The enemy can easily control Lake George!"

"He has only to make an effort to do so, my general," replied St. Luc. "I could have captured the boat builders on the point or have compelled their retirement, but large forces came to their relief. The numbers of the foe are even greater than we had feared."

"How many men do you think General Abercrombie will have when he advances against us?"

"Not less than fifteen thousand, sir, perhaps more."

The face of Montcalm fell.

"As many as that!" he exclaimed. "It is more than four to one!"

"He cannot have less, sir," repeated St. Luc positively.

Montcalm's brow clouded and he paced back and forth.

"And the Indians who have been so powerful an ally," he said at last. "They are frightened by the reports concerning the Anglo-American army. After their fashion they wish to run away before superior force, and fight when the odds are not so great. It is most embarrassing to lose their help, at such a critical time. Can you do nothing with this sullen giant, Tandakora, who has such influence over them?"

"I fear not, sir. He was with me on the expedition from which I have just returned, and he fared ill. He is in a most savage humour. He is like a bear that will hide in the woods and lick its hurts until the sting has passed. I think we may consider it certain, sir, that they will desert us, for the time."

"And we shall have but little more than three thousand French and Canadians to defend the honour of France and His Majesty's great colony in North America. We might retreat to the fortifications at Crown Point, and make an advantageous stand there, but it goes ill with me to withdraw. Still, prudence cries upon me to do so. I have talked with Bourlamaque, Trepezec, Lotbiniére, the engineer, Langy, the partisan, and other of my lieutenants whom you know. They express varying opinions. Now, Colonel de St. Luc, I want yours, an opinion that is absolutely your own."

St. Luc drew himself up and his warrior soul flashed through his blue eyes.

"Sir," he said, "it goes as ill with me as it does with you to retreat. My heart is here at Ticonderoga. Nor does prudence suggest to me that we retreat to Crown Point. My head agreeing with my heart says that we should stand here."

"And that is your conviction?"

"It is, sir. Ticonderoga is ours and we can keep it."

"Upon what do you base this opinion? In such a crisis as this we must be influenced by sound military reasons and not by sentiment."

"My reasons, sir, are military. That is why my heart goes with my head. It is true that the Anglo-American army will come in overwhelming numbers, but they may be overwhelming numbers that will not overwhelm. As we know, the British commanders have not adapted themselves as well as the French to wilderness, campaigning. Their tactics and strategy are the same as those they practice in the open fields of Europe, and it puts them at a great disadvantage. We have been willing to learn from the Indians, who have practiced forest warfare for centuries. And the British Colonials, the Bostonnais, fall into the faults of the parent country. In spite of all experience they, continue to despise wilderness wile and stratagem, and in a manner that is amazing. They walk continually into ambush, and are cut up before they can get out of it. I am not one to cheapen the valour of British and British Colonials. It has been proved too often on desperate fields, but in the kind of war we must wage here deep in the wilds of North America, valour is often unavailing, and I think, sir, that we can rely upon one fact. The enemy will take us too lightly. He is sure to do something that will keep him from using his whole force at the right moment against us. Our forest knowledge will work all the time in our behalf. I entreat you, sir, to keep the army here at Ticonderoga and await the attack."

St. Luc spoke with intense earnestness, and his words had all the ring of conviction. Montcalm's dark face was illumined. Again he walked back and forth, in deep thought.

"The engineer, Lotbiniére, a man whose opinion I respect, is of your mind," he said at last. "He says that whether Crown Point or Ticonderoga, it's merely either horn of the dilemma, and naturally, if the dangers of the two places are even, we prefer Ticonderoga and no retreat. The Marquis de Vaudreuil had a plan to save Ticonderoga by means of a diversion with a heavy force under Bourlamaque, De Levis and Longueuil into the Mohawk Valley. But some American rangers taken near Lake George by Langy told him that Abercrombie already had thirty thousand men at the head of George and the Marquis at once abandoned the scheme. It was lucky for us the rangers exaggerated so much that the plan was destined to failure, as we needed here the men who were sent on it. We save or lose Ticonderoga by fighting at Ticonderoga itself and by nothing else. I thank you, Colonel de St. Luc, for your gallant and timely words, I have been wavering and they have decided me. We stay here and await the Anglo-American army."

"And the star of France will not fail us," said St Luc, with intense conviction.

"I trust not. I feel more confidence since I have decided, and I do know this: the young men who are my lieutenants are as brave and skilful leaders as any chief could desire. And the troops will fight even ten to one, if I ask it of them. It is a pleasure and a glory to command troops of such incomparable bravery as the French. But we must try to keep the Indians with us. I confess that I know little about dealing with them. Has this savage chief, Tandakora, come back to Ticonderoga?"

"I think he is here, sir. Do you wish me to talk with him?"

"I do. I wish it very much."

"He is very sullen, sir. He holds that the Indians have received no rewards for their services."

"We have given them blankets and food and muskets and ammunition."

"He takes those as a matter of course. But he means something else. To tell you the truth, sir, the savages want us to give prisoners to them."

Montcalm's face clouded again.

"To burn at the stake, or to torture to death otherwise!" he exclaimed. "My reputation and what is more, the reputation of France, suffers already from the massacre at William Henry, though God knows I would have prevented it if I could. It happened so suddenly and so unexpectedly that I could not stop it, until the harm was done. But never, St. Luc, never will I give up a prisoner to them for their tortures, though every savage in our armies desert us!"

"I hold with you, sir, that we cannot surrender prisoners to them, even though the cause of France should suffer."

"Then talk to this savage chief. Make him see reason. Promise him and his people what you wish in muskets, ammunition, blankets and such things, but no prisoners, not one."

St. Luc, with a respectful salute, left the tent. He was torn by conflicting emotions. He was depressed over the smallness of the French numbers, and yet he was elated by Montcalm's decision to stay at Ticonderoga and await Abercrombie. He was confident, as he had said, that some lucky chance would happen, and that the overwhelming superiority of the Anglo-American army would be nullified.

The Chevalier cast a discriminating eye over the French position. The staunch battalion of Berry lay near the foot of Lake George, but the greater part of the army under the direct command of Montcalm was in camp near a saw mill. The valiant Bourlamaque was at the head of the portage, and another force held the point of embarkation on Lake George. But he knew that Montcalm would change these dispositions when the day of battle came.

On the westward side of the camp several fires burned and dark figures lay near them. St. Luc marked one of these, a gigantic savage, stretched at his ease, and he walked toward him. He pretended, at first, that his errand had nothing to do with Tandakora, but stood thoughtfully by the fire, for a minute or two. Nor did the Ojibway chief take any notice. He lay at ease, and it was impossible to tell what thoughts were hidden behind his sullen face.

"Does Tandakora know what the commander of the French army has decided to do?" said St. Luc, at last.

"Tandakora is not thinking much about it," replied the chief.

"Montcalm is a brave general. He shows that he is not afraid of the great army the English and the Bostonnais have gathered. He will not retreat to Crown Point or anywhere else, but will stay at Ticonderoga and defeat his foes."

The black eyes of the Ojibway flickered.

"Tandakora does not undertake to tell Montcalm what he must do," he said, "nor must Montcalm undertake to tell Tandakora what he should do. What Montcalm may do will not now keep Tandakora awake."

St. Luc's heart filled with hot anger, but he was used to dealing with Indians. He understood their minds from the inside, and he had a superb self-control of his own.

"We know that Tandakora is a great chief," he said evenly. "We know too that he and his men are as free as the winds. As they blow where they please so the warriors of Tandakora go where they wish. But Onontio and Tandakora have long been friends. They have been allies, they have fought side by side in many a battle. If Onontio falls, Tandakora falls with him. If the British and Bostonnais are victorious, there will be room for none of the tribes save the League of the Hodenosaunee, and them Tandakora hates. Onontio will not be able to protect them any more, and they will be driven from all their hunting grounds."

He paused to watch his words take effect and they obviously stirred the soul of the savage chief who moved uneasily.

"It is true," he said. "Sharp Sword never tells a falsehood. If

161

Onontio is struck down then the British, the Bostonnais and the Hodenosaunee triumph, but my warriors bring me word that our enemies have gathered the greatest force the world has ever seen at the head of Andiatarocte. They come thicker than the leaves of the forest. They have more guns than we can count. They will trample Montcalm and his soldiers under their feet. So, according to our custom, Tandakora and his warriors would go away into the forest, until the British and the Bostonnais scatter, unable to find us. Then, when they are not looking, we will strike them and take many scalps."

Tandakora spoke in his most impressive manner, and, when he ceased, his eyes met St. Luc's defiantly. Again the blood of the Chevalier burned with wrath, but as before he restrained himself, and his smooth voice gave no hint of anger as he replied:

"Odds are of no avail against Montcalm. The children of Onontio are used to dealing with them. Remember, Tandakora, the great victories Montcalm won at Oswego and William Henry. He has the soul of a mighty chief. He has decided to stay here at Ticonderoga and await the enemy, confident that he will win the victory. Tandakora is a great warrior, is he willing to have no share in such a triumph?"

The cruel eyes of the Ojibway glistened.

"The heart of Tandakora is heavy within him," he said. "He and his warriors are not afraid of the British and the Bostonnais. They have fought by the side of Montcalm, but they do not receive all the rewards that Onontio owes them."

"Onontio has given to them freely of his muskets and powder and bullets, and of his blankets and food."

"But he takes from them the prisoners. We have no scalps to carry home."

"It is against the custom of the French to put prisoners to death or torture. Moreover, we have no prisoners here. The rangers taken by Langy have already been sent to Canada."

"There is one in the camp now. He was captured by three of my warriors, those you sent out, and by the law of war he belongs to me. Yet Sharp Sword and Montcalm hold him. I speak of the youth Lennox, the comrade of the Onondaga, Tayoga, who is my bitterest enemy. I hate Lennox too because he has stood so often in my way and I demand him, to do with as I please, because it is my right."

The Ojibway moved close to St. Luc and the fierce black eyes glared into those of stern blue. The Chevalier did not change his smooth, placatory tone as he replied: "I cannot give up Lennox. It is true that he was taken by your warriors, but they were then in my service, so he is my prisoner. But he is only a single captive, a lad. Ask for some other and greater reward, Tandakora, and it shall be yours."

"Give me the prisoner, Lennox, and I and my warriors stay and fight with you at Ticonderoga. Refuse him and we go."

The chief's words were sharp and decisive and St. Luc understood him. He knew that the savage Ojibway hated young Lennox intensely, and would put him to the torture. He never hesitated an instant.

"I cannot yield the prisoner to you," he said. "The custom of the French will not permit it."

"The warriors are a great help in battle, and the reward I ask is but small. St. Luc knows that Montcalm needs men here. What is this boy to St. Luc that he refuses so great a price for him?"

"It cannot be done, Tandakora. I keep the prisoner, Lennox, and later I will send him to Canada to be held there until the war is over."

"Then the forest to-morrow will swallow up Tandakora and his warriors."

The chief returned to the fire and lay at ease in his blanket. St. Luc walked thoughtfully back toward the tent of Montcalm. He knew that it was his duty to report the offer of Tandakora to his chief, but he did so reluctantly.

"You have refused it already?" said the Marquis.

"I have, sir," replied St. Luc.

"Then you have done well. I confirm you in the refusal."

St. Luc saluted with great respect, and again retired from the tent.

CHAPTER 13

Eve of Battle

Robert awoke the next morning, well physically, but depressed mentally. He believed that a great battle—and a great victory for the Anglo-American army—was coming, and he would have no part in it. The losses of Braddock's defeat and the taking of Fort William Henry by Montcalm would be repaired, once more the flag of his native land and of his ancestral land, would be triumphant, but he would be merely a spectator, even if he were as much as that. It was a bitter reflection, and again he thought of escape. But no plan seemed possible. He was held as firmly in the centre of an army, as if he were in the jaws of a powerful vice. Nor was it possible for Tayoga, however great his skill and daring, to reach him there. He strove to be philosophical, but it is hard for youth to reconcile itself at first, though it may soon forget.

Breakfast was given to him, and he was permitted to go outside the tent into a small open space, though not beyond. On all sides of him stretched the impassable lines of the French army. There were several other prisoners within the enclosure, a ranger, a hunter, and three or four farmers who had been taken in forays farther south.

The fresh air and the brilliant sunshine revived Robert's spirits. He looked eagerly about him, striving to divine the French intentions, but he could make nothing of them. He knew, however, upon reflection, that this would be so. The French would not put any prisoners in a position to obtain information that would be of great value in the possible event of escape.

He undertook to talk with the other prisoners, but they were a melancholy lot, not to be cheered. They were all thinking of a long, in truth, an indefinite, imprisonment in Canada, and they mourned. Many people had been taken into Canada by French and Indians in former forays and had been lost forever.

Robert turned away from his comrades and sat down on a stone, where he speculated idly on what was passing about him. He believed that the French would withdraw to Crown Point, at least, and might retreat all the way to Canada, leaving Lake Champlain, as well as Lake George, to the complete control of the Anglo-American forces. He expected to see preparations to that effect, and, when he saw none, he concluded that they were merely postponed for a day or two. So far as he could judge, the aspect of the French army was leisurely. He did not observe any signs of trepidation, but then, withdrawal was always easy in the great North American wilderness. There was yet plenty of time for it.

He noticed a complete absence of Indians, and the fact struck him with great surprise. While he was advancing various theories to account for it, young Captain Louis de Galissonnière came, and greeted him cordially.

"I hope you understand that we French know how to treat a prisoner," he said.

"I've nothing of which to complain," replied Robert. "This is the second time that I've been with you, and on this occasion, as on the first, I seem to be more of a guest than a captive."

"You're the special prisoner of Colonel de St. Luc, who stands extremely high with the Marquis de Montcalm. The colonel wishes you to be treated well and seems to favour you. Why is it?"

"Frankly, I don't know, but I learned long since that he was a most chivalrous foe. I suppose I am to be sent into Canada along with the other prisoners?"

"I suppose so, but there is no way for you to go just now."

"Why can't I go with your army?"

"With our army?"

"It retreats, of course, before our overwhelming force."

De Galissonnière laughed.

"You are disposed to be facetious," he said. "You will observe that we are not retreating. You see no preparations to do so, but that's all I will tell you. More would be valuable information for the enemy, should you escape."

"I've warned Colonel de St. Luc that I mean to escape in due time. I don't like to reject such noble hospitality as you're showing me, but my duty to my country demands it."

Robert was now in a most excellent humour. His sanguine temperament was asserting itself to the full. What he wished to see he saw. He was slipping away from the French; and he was advancing with the

English and Americans to a great and brilliant victory. His face was flushed and his eyes sparkled. De Galissonnière looked at him curiously, but said nothing.

"I observe one very significant fact," continued Robert.

"What is that?"

"I see no Indians, who are usually so numerous about your camps. You needn't tell me what has happened, but I've been among Indians a great deal. I know their ways, and I'll tell you. They see that yours is a lost cause, and they've deserted you. Now, isn't that so?"

The young Frenchman was silent, but it was the turn of his face to flush.

"I didn't expect you to answer me in words," continued Robert, triumphantly, "but I can see. The Indians never fight in a battle that they consider lost before it's joined, and you know as well as I do, Captain de Galissonnière, that if the Marquis de Montcalm awaits our attack his army will be destroyed."

"I do not know it at all."

Then Robert felt ashamed because he had been led away by his enthusiasm, and apologized for a speech that might have seemed boastful to the young Frenchman, who had been so kind to him. But De Galissonnière, with his accustomed courtesy, said it was nothing, and when he left, presently, both were in the best of humours.

Robert, convinced that he had been right about the Indians, watched for them as the morning went on, but he never saw a single warrior. There could be no doubt now that they had gone, and while he could not consider them chivalric they were at least wise.

The next familiar face that he beheld was one far from welcome to him. It was that of a man who happened to pass near the enclosure and who stopped suddenly when he caught sight of Robert. He was in civilian dress, but he was none other than Achille Garay, that spy whose secret message had been wrested from him in the forest by Robert and Tayoga.

The gaze that Garay bent upon Robert was baleful. His capture by the three and the manner in which he had been compelled to disclose the letter had been humiliating, and Robert did not doubt that the man would seek revenge. He shivered a little, feeling that as a prisoner he was in a measure helpless. Then his back stiffened.

"I'm glad to see, Garay, that you're where you belong—with the French," he called out. "I hope you didn't suffer any more from hunger in the woods when Willet, the Onondaga and I let you go."

The spy came closer, and his look was so full of venom that young Lennox, despite himself, shuddered.

"Time makes all things even," he said. "I don't forget how you and your friends held me in your power in the forest, but here you are a prisoner. I have a good chance to make the score even."

Robert remembered also how this man had attempted his life in Albany, for some reason that he could not yet fathom, and he felt that he was now, and, in very truth, a most dangerous enemy. Nevertheless, he replied, quietly:

"That was an act of war. You were carrying a message for the enemy. We were wholly within our rights when we forced you to disclose the paper."

"It makes no difference," said Garay. "I owe you and your comrades a debt and I shall pay it."

Robert turned his back on him and walked to the other side of the enclosure. When he turned around, five minutes later, Garay was gone. But Robert felt uncomfortable. Here was a man who did not have the gallantry and chivalry that marked so many of the French. If he could he would strike some great blow.

He strove to dismiss Garay from his mind, and, in his interest in what was going on about him, he finally succeeded. He saw Frenchmen and Canadians leaving the camp and others returning. His knowledge of war made him believe that those coming had been messengers sent forth to watch the Anglo-American army, and those going were dispatched on the same service. Their alarm must be great, he reflected pleasantly, and none could bring to Montcalm any reassuring news. Once he saw Montcalm, and once St. Luc, but neither spoke to him.

He and his comrades, the other prisoners, slept that night in the open, the weather being warm. A blanket was allotted to every one by their captors, and Robert, long used to unlimited fresh air, preferred the outside to the inside of a tent. Nothing disturbed his slumbers, but he expected that the French retreat would begin the next day. On the contrary, Montcalm stayed in his camp, nor was there any sign of withdrawal on the second and third days, or on others that came. He inferred then that the advance of Abercrombie had been delayed, and the French were merely hanging on until their retreat became compulsory.

He had been in the camp about a week, and as he saw no more of Garay he concluded that the man had been sent away on some errand. It was highly probable that he was now in the south spying upon the Anglo-American army. It was for just such duties that he was fitted. Then he began to think of him less and less.

His old impatience and keen disappointment because he was a prisoner when such great days were coming, returned with doubled vigour.

He chafed greatly and looked around again for an opportunity to escape, but did not see the remotest possibility of it. After all, he must reconcile himself. His situation could be far worse. He was well treated, and some of the French leaders, while official enemies, were personal friends.

His mind also dwelled upon the singular fact that the French army did not retreat. He tried to glean something from De Galissonnière, who talked with him several times, but the young captain would not depart from generalities. He invariably shut up, tight, when they approached any detail of the present military situation.

A dark night came with much wind and threat of rain. Robert thought that he and his fellow captives would have to ask the shelter of tents, but the rain passed farther to the west, though the heavy darkness remained. He was glad, as the weather was now oppressively warm, and he greatly preferred to sleep on a blanket in the open air.

The night was somewhat advanced when he lay down. The other prisoners were asleep already. He had not found any kindred minds among them, and, as they were apathetic, he had not talked with them much. Now, he did not miss them at all as he lay on his blanket and watched the wavering lights of the camp. It was still quite dark, with a moaning wind, but his experience of weather told him that the chance of rain was gone. Far in the west, lightning flickered and low thunder grumbled there now and then, but in the camp everything was dry. Owing to the warmth, the fires used for cooking had been permitted to burn out, and the whole army seemed at peace.

Robert himself shared this feeling of rest. The storm, passing so far away, soothed and lulled him. It was pleasant to lie there, unharmed, and witness its course at a far point. He dozed a while, fell asleep, and awoke again in half an hour. Nothing had changed. There was still an occasional flicker of lightning and mutter of thunder and the darkness remained heavy. He could dimly see the forms of his comrades lying on their blankets. Not one of them stirred. They slept heavily and he rather envied them. They had little imagination, and, when one was in bad case, he was lucky to be without it.

The figure lying nearest him he took to be that of the hunter, a taciturn man who talked least of them all, and again Robert felt envy because he could lose all care so thoroughly and so easily in sleep. The man was as still and unconcerned as one of the mountain peaks that looked down upon them. He would imitate him, and although sleep might be unwilling, he would conquer it. A resolute mind could triumph over anything.

He shut his eyes and his will was so strong that he held them shut a full ten minutes, although sleep did not come. When he opened them again he thought that the hunter had moved a little. After all, the man was mortal, and had human emotions. He was not an absolute log.

"Tilden!" he called—Tilden was the hunter's name.

But Tilden did not stir, nor did he respond in any way when he called a second time. He had been mistaken. He had given the man too much credit. He was really a log, a dull, apathetic fellow to whom the extraordinary conditions around them made no appeal. He would not speak to him again as long as they were prisoners together, and, closing his eyes anew, he resolutely wooed slumber once more.

Robert's hearing was not so wonderfully keen as Tayoga's, but it was very keen, nevertheless, and as he lay, eyes shut, something impinged upon the drums of his ears. It was faint, but it did not seem to be a part of the usual sounds of the night. His ear at once registered an alarm on his brain.

His eyes opened. The man whom he had taken to be the hunter was bending over him, and, dark though it was, he distinctly saw the gleam of a knife in his hand. His first feeling, passing in a flash, was one of vague wonderment that anybody should menace him in such a manner, and then he saw the lowering face of Garay. He had been a fool to forget him. With a convulsive and powerful effort he threw his body to one side, and, when the knife fell, the blade missed him by an inch.

Then Robert sprang to his feet, but Garay, uttering an angry exclamation at his missed stroke, did not attempt another. Instead, agile as a cat, he ran lightly away, and disappeared in the darkness of the camp. Robert sat down, somewhat dazed. It had all been an affair of a minute, and it was hard for him to persuade himself that it was real. His comrades still slept soundly, and the camp seemed as peaceful as ever.

For a time Robert could not decide what to do. He knew that he had been threatened by a formidable danger, and that instinct, more than anything else, had saved him. He was almost prepared to believe that Tayoga's Tododaho, looking down from his remote star, had intervened in his behalf.

The question solved itself. Although he knew that Garay had made a foul attempt upon his life he had no proof. His story would seem highly improbable. Moreover, he was a prisoner, while Garay was one of the French. Nobody would believe his tale. He must keep quiet and watch. He was glad to see that the night was now lightening. Garay would not come back then, at least. But Robert was sure that he would repeat the attack some time or other. Revenge was a powerful motive, and he undoubtedly had another as strong. He must guard against Garay with all his five senses.

The night continued to brighten. The lightning ceased to flicker, the storm had blown itself out in the distance, and a fine moon and a myriad of stars came out. Things in the camp became clearly visible, and, feeling that Garay would attempt nothing more at such a time, Robert closed his eyes again. He soon slept, and did not awaken until all the other prisoners were up.

"Mr. Tilden," he said to the hunter, "I offer you my sincere apologies."

"Apologies," said the hunter in surprise. "What for?"

"Because I mistook a much worse man for you. You didn't know anything about it at the time, but I did it, and I'm sorry I wronged you so much, even in thought."

The hunter touched his forehead. Clearly the misfortunes of the young prisoner were weighing too heavily upon him. One must endure captivity better than that.

"Don't take it so hard, Mr. Lennox," he said. "It's not like being in the hands of the Indians, and there is always the chance of escape."

De Galissonnière visited him again that morning, and Robert, true to his resolution, said nothing of Garay. The captain did not speak of the Anglo-American army, but Robert judged from his manner that he was highly expectant. Surely, Abercrombie was about to advance, and the retreat of Montcalm could not be more than a day away. De Galissonnière stayed only ten minutes, and then Robert was left to his own devices. He tried to talk to Tilden, but the hunter lapsed again into an apathetic state, and, having little success, he fell back on his own thoughts and what his eyes might behold.

In the afternoon he saw Montcalm at some distance, talking with St. Luc and Bourlamaque, and then he saw a man whose appearance betokened haste and anxiety approach them. Robert did not know it then, but it was the able and daring French partisan, Langy, and he came out of the forest with vital news.

* * * * * * * *

Meanwhile Langy saluted Montcalm with the great respect that his successes had won from all the French. When the Marquis turned his keen eye upon him he knew at once that his message, whatever it might be, was of supreme importance.

"What is it, Monsieur Langy?"

"A report on the movements of the enemy."

"Come to my tent and tell me of it fully, and do you, St. Luc and Bourlamaque, come with me also. You should hear everything."

They went into the tent and all sat down. St. Luc's eyes never left the partisan, Langy. He saw that the man was full of his news, eager to tell it, and was impressed with its importance. He knew Langy even better than Montcalm did. Few were more skilful in the forest, and he had a true sense of proportion that did not desert him under stress. His eyes travelled over the partisan's attire, and there his own great skill as a ranger told him much. His garments were disarranged. Burrs and one or two little twigs were clinging to them. Obviously he had come far and in haste. The thoughts of St. Luc, and, in truth, the thoughts of all of them, went to the Anglo-American army.

"Speak, Monsieur Langy," said Montcalm. "I can see that you have come swiftly, and you would not come so without due cause."

"I wish to report to you, sir," said Langy, "that the entire army of the enemy is now embarked on the Lake of the Holy Sacrament, and is advancing against us."

Montcalm's eyes sparkled. His warlike soul leaped up at the thought of speedy battle that was being offered. A flame was lighted also in St. Luc's blood, and Bourlamaque was as eager. It was no lack of valour and enterprise that caused the French to lose their colonies in North America.

"You know this positively?" asked the commander-in-chief.

"I have seen it with my own eyes."

"Tell it as you saw it."

"I lay in the woods above the lake with my men, and I saw the British and Americans go into their boats, a vast flock of them. They are all afloat on the lake at this moment, and are coming against us."

"Could you make a fair estimate of their numbers?"

"I obtained the figures with much exactitude from one or two stragglers that we captured on the land. My eyes confirm these figures. There are about seven thousand of the English regulars, and about nine thousand of the American colonials."

"So many as that! Five to one!"

"You tell us they are all in boats," said St. Luc. "How many of these boats contain their artillery?"

"They have not yet embarked the cannon. As nearly as we can gather, the guns will not come until the army is at Ticonderoga."

"What?"

"It is as I tell you," replied Langy to St. Luc. "The guns cannot come up the lake until a day or two after the army is landed. Their force is so great that they do not seem to think they will need the artillery."

St. Luc, his face glowing, turned to Montcalm.

"Sir," he said, "I made to you the prophecy that some chance, some glorious chance, would yet help us, and that chance has come. Their very strength has betrayed them into an error that may prove fatal. Despising us, they give us our opportunity. No matter how great the odds, we can hold earthworks and abattis against them, unless they bring cannon, or, at least we may make a great attempt at it."

The swarthy face of Montcalm was illumined by the light from his eyes.

"I verily believe that your gallant soul speaks truth, Chevalier de St. Luc!" he exclaimed. "I said once that we would stand and I say it again. We'll put all to the hazard. Since they come without cannon we do have our chance. Go, Langy, and take your needed rest. You have served us well. And now we'll have the others here and talk over our preparations."

The engineers Lotbiniére and Le Mercier were, as before, zealous for battle at Ticonderoga, and their opinion counted for much with Montcalm. De Levis, held back by the vacillating Vaudreuil, had not yet come from Montreal, and the swiftest of the Canadian paddlers was sent down Lake Ticonderoga in a canoe to hurry him on. Then the entire battalion of Berry went to work at once with spade and pick and axe to prepare a breastwork and abattis, stretching a line of defence in front of the fort, and not using the fort itself.

★ ★ ★ ★ ★ ★ ★ ★

Robert saw the Frenchmen attack the trees with their axes and the earth with their spades, and he divined at once the news that Langy had brought. The Anglo-American army was advancing. His heart throbbed. Victory and rescue were at hand.

"Mr. Tilden," he said to the hunter, "listen to the ring of the axe and the thud of the spade!"

"Aye, I hear 'em," was the apathetic reply; "but they don't interest me. I'm a prisoner."

"But it may mean that you won't be a prisoner much longer. The French are fortifying, and they've gone to work with so much haste and energy that it shows an imminent need. There's only one conclusion to be drawn from it. They're expecting our army and a prompt attack."

Tilden began to show interest.

"On my life, I think you're right," he said.

And yet Montcalm changed his mind again at the last moment. Two veteran officers, Montguy and Bernès, pointed out to him that his present position was dominated by the adjacent heights, and in order to escape that danger he resolved to retreat a little. He broke up his camp late in the afternoon of the next day, part of the army fell back through the woods more than a mile, and the rest of it withdrew in boats on the lake to the same point.

Robert and his comrades were carried with the army on land to the fort. There he became separated from the others, and remained in the rear, but luckily for his wishes, on a mount where he could see most that was passing, though his chance of escape was as remote as ever.

He stood on the rocky peninsula of Ticonderoga. Behind him the great lake, Champlain, stretched far into north and south. To the west the ground sloped gently upward a half mile and then sank again. On each side of the ridge formed thus was low ground, and the ridge presented itself at once to the military eye as a line of defence. Hugues, one of his officers, had already recommended it to Montcalm, and men under two of his engineers, Desandrouin and Pontleroy, were now at work there.

The final line of defence was begun at dawn, and Robert, whom no one disturbed, witnessed a scene of prodigious energy. The whole French army threw itself heart and soul into the task. The men, hot under the July sun, threw aside their coats, and the officers, putting their own hands to the work, did likewise. There was a continuous ring of axes, and the air resounded with the crash of trees falling in hundreds and thousands.

The tops and ends of the boughs were cut off the trees, the ends left thus were sharpened and the trees were piled upon one another with the sharp ends facing the enemy who was to come.

Robert watched as these bristling rows grew to a height of at least nine feet, and then he saw the men build on the inner side platforms on which they could stand and fire over the crest, without exposing anything except their heads. In front of the abattis more trees with sharpened boughs were spread for a wide space, the whole field with its stumps and trees, looking as if a mighty hurricane had swept over it.

Robert was soldier enough to see what a formidable obstruction was being raised, but he thought the powerful artillery of the attacking army would sweep it away or level it. He did not know that the big guns were being left behind. In truth, Langy's first news that the cannon would not be embarked upon the lake was partly wrong. The loading of the cannon was delayed, but after the British and Americans reached their landing and began the march across country for the attack, the guns, although brought down the lake, were left behind as not needed. But the French knew all these movements, and whether the cannon were left at one point or another, it was just the same to them, so long as they were not used in the assault.

Robert's intense mortification that he should be compelled to lie idle and witness the efforts of his enemies returned, but no matter how he chafed he could see no way out of it. Then his absorption in what was going on about him made him forget his personal fortunes.

The setting for the great drama was wild and picturesque in the extreme. On one side stretched the long, gleaming lake, a lake of wildness and beauty associated with so much of romance and peril in American story. Over them towered the crest of the peak later known as Defiance. To the south and west was Lake George, the Iroquois Andiatarocte, that gem of the east, and, on all sides, save Champlain, circled the forest, just beginning to wither under the fierce summer sun.

The energy of the French did not diminish. Stronger and stronger grew abattis and breastwork, the whole becoming a formidable field over which men might charge to death. But Robert only smiled to himself. Abercrombie's mighty array of cannon would smash everything and then the brave infantry, charging through the gaps, would destroy the French army. The French, he knew, were brave and skilful, but their doom was sure. Once St. Luc spoke to him. The chevalier had thrown off his coat also, and he had swung an axe with the best.

"I am sorry, Mr. Lennox," he said, "that we have not had time to send you away, but as you can see, our operations are somewhat hurried. Chance put you here, and here you will have to stay until all is over."

"I see that you are expecting an army," said Robert, "and I infer from all these preparations that it will soon be upon you."

"It is betraying no military secret to admit that it is even so. Abercrombie will soon be at hand."

"And I am surprised that you should await him. I judge that he has sufficient force to overwhelm you."

"We are never beaten before battle. The Marquis de Montcalm would not stay, unless he had a fair chance of success."

Robert was silent and St. Luc quickly went back to his work. All day the men toiled, and when the sun went down, they were still at their task. The ring of axes and the crash of falling trees resounded through the dark. Part of the soldiers put their kettles and pots on the fires, but the others laboured on. In the night came the valiant De Levis with his men, and Montcalm gave him a heartfelt welcome. De Levis was a host in himself, and Montcalm felt that he was just in time. He expected the battle on the morrow. His scouts told him that Abercrombie would be at hand, but without his artillery. The Marquis looked at the formidable abattis, the rows and rows of trees, presenting their myriad of spiked ends, and hope was alive in his heart. He regretted once more the absence of the Indians who had been led away by the sulky Tandakora, but victory, won with their help, demanded a fearful price, as he had learned at William Henry.

Montcalm, St. Luc, De Levis, Bourlamaque, Lotbiniére and other trusted officers held a consultation far in the night. An important event had occurred already. A scouting force of French and Canadians under Trepezec and Langy had been trapped by rangers under Rogers and troops under Fitch and Lyman. The French and Canadians were cut to pieces, but in the battle the gallant young Lord Howe, the real leader of the Anglo-American army, had been killed. He had gone forward with the vanguard, exposing himself rashly, perhaps, and his life was the forfeit. Immediate confusion in the Anglo-American councils followed, and Montcalm and his lieutenants had noticed the lack of precision and directness.

Robert did not see the French officers going to the council, but he knew that the French army meant to stay. Even while the men were cutting down the trees he could not persuade himself wholly that Montcalm would fight there at Ticonderoga, but as the night advanced his last faint doubt disappeared. He would certainly witness a great battle on the morrow.

He could not sleep. Every nerve in him seemed to be alive. One vivid picture after another floated before his mind. The lake behind him grew dim. Before him were the camp fires of the French, the wooden wall, the dark line of the forest and hills, and the crest of Defiance looking solemnly down on them. Although held firmly there, within lines which one could not pass, nobody seemed to take any notice of him. He could rest or watch as he chose, and he had no choice but to watch.

He saw the French lie down on their arms, save for the numerous sentinels posted everywhere, and after a while, though most of the night was gone, the ring of axes and the fall of trees ceased. There was a hum of voices but that too died in time, and long after midnight, with his back against a tree, he dozed a little while.

He was awakened by a premonition, a warning out of the dark,

CHAPTER 14

Ticonderoga

The French army rose with the sun, the drums beating the call to battle. Montcalm stationed the battalions of Languedoc and La Sarre on the left with Bourlamaque to command them, on the right De Levis led the battalions of Béarn, Guienne and La Reine. Montcalm himself stood with the battalion of Royal Roussillon in the centre, and St. Luc was by his side. Volunteers held the sunken ground between the breastwork and the outlet of Lake George, a strong force of regulars and Canadians was on the side of Lake Champlain under the guns of the fort there. Then, having taken their places, all the parts of the army went to work again, strengthening the defences with axe and spade, improving every moment that might be left.

All thought of escape left Robert's mind in the mighty and thrilling drama that was about to be played before him. Once more he stared at the long line of the lake, and then his whole attention was for the circling forest, and the hills. That was where the army of his country lay. Nothing was to be expected from the lake. Victory would come from the woods, and he looked so long at the trees that they blurred together into one mass. He knew that the English and Americans were near, but just how near he could not gather from those around him.

He brushed his eyes to clear them, and continued to study the forest. The sun, great and brilliant, was flooding it with light, gilding the slopes and crests of Defiance, and tingeing the green of the leaves with gold. Nothing stirred there. The wilderness seemed silent, as if men never fought in its depths. Time went slowly on. After all, the army might not advance to the attack that day. If so, his disappointment would be bitter. He wanted a great victory, and he wanted it at once.

His eyes suddenly caught a gleam on the crest of Defiance. A bit of red flashed among the trees. He thought it was the uniform of a British soldier, and his heart beat hard. The army was surely advancing, the attack would be made, and the victory would be won that day, not on the morrow nor next week, but before the sun set.

The blood pounded in his temples. He looked at the French. They, too, had seen the scarlet gleam on Defiance and they were watching. Montcalm and St. Luc began to talk together earnestly. De Levis and Bourlamaque walked back and forth among their troops, but their gaze was upon the crest. The men lay down axe and spade for the time, and reached for their arms. Robert saw the sunlight glittering on musket and bayonet, and once more he thrilled at the thought of the great drama on which the curtain was now rising.

Another scarlet patch appeared on the crest and then more. He knew that the scouts and skirmishers were there, doubtless in strong force. It was likely that the rangers, who would be in forest green, were more numerous than the English, and the attack could not now be far away. A sharp crack, a puff of white smoke on the hill, and the first shot of Ticonderoga was fired. Then came a volley, but the French made no reply. None of the bullets had reached them. Robert did not know it then, but the gleam came from the red blankets of Iroquois Indians, the allies of the English, and not from English uniforms. They kept up a vigorous but harmless fire for a short while, and then drew off.

Silence descended once more on the forest, and Robert was puzzled. It could not be possible that this was to be the only attack. The smoke of the rifles was already drifting away from the crest, gone like summer vapour. The French were returning to their work with axe and spade. The forest covered and enclosed everything. No sound came from it. Montcalm and St. Luc, walking up and down, began to talk together again. They looked no longer toward the crest of Defiance, but watched the southern wilderness.

The work with the axe increased. Montcalm had no mind to lose the precious hours. More trees fell fast, and they were added to the formidable works. The sun grew hotter and poured down sheaves of fiery rays, but the toilers disregarded it, swinging the axes with muscles that took no note of weariness. Robert thought the morning would last forever. An hour before noon De Galissonnière was passing, and, noticing him sitting on a low mound, he said:

"I did not know what had become of you, Mr. Lennox, but I see that you, like ourselves, await the battle."

"So I do," said Robert as lightly as he could, "but it seems to me that it's somewhat delayed."

"Not our fault, I assure you. Perhaps you didn't think so earlier, but you see we're willing to fight, no matter how great the odds."

"I admit it. The Marquis de Montcalm has his courage—perhaps too much."

De Galissonnière glanced at the strong works, and his smile was confident, but he merely said:

"It is for the future to tell."

Then he went on, and Robert hoped that whatever happened the battle would spare the young Frenchman.

Up went the sun toward the zenith. A light wind rustled the foliage. Noon was near, and he began to wonder anew what had become of the advancing army. Suddenly, the echo of a crash came out of the forest in front. He stood erect, listening intently, and the sound rose again, but it was not an echo now. It was real, and he knew that the battle was at hand.

The crashes became continuous. Mingled with them were shouts, and a cloud of smoke began to float above the trees. The French fired a cannon as a signal, and, before the echoes of its report rolled away, every man dropped axe or spade, and was in his place, weapon in hand. The noise of the firing in front grew fast. Montcalm's scouts and pickets were driven in, and the soldiers of the advancing army began to show among the trees. The French batteries opened. The roar in Robert's ear was terrific, but he stood at his utmost height in order that he might see the assault. His eyes caught the gleam of uniforms and the flash of sunlight on bayonet and rifle. He knew now that his own people, dauntless and tenacious, were coming. He did not know that they had left their artillery behind, and that they expected to destroy the French army with bayonet and rifle and musket.

The fire from the French barrier increased in volume. Its crash beat heavily and continuously on the drums of Robert's ears. A deadly sleet was beating upon the advancing English and Americans. Already their dead were heaping up in rows. Montcalm's men showed their heads only above their works, their bodies were sheltered by the logs and they fired and fired into the charging masses until the barrels of rifles and muskets grew too hot for them to hold. Meanwhile they shouted with all their might: *"Vive la France! Vive notre General! Vive le Roi!"* and St. Luc, who stood always with Montcalm, hummed softly and under his breath: *"Hier, sur le pont d'Avignon, j'ai oui chanter la belle."*

"It goes well," he said to Montcalm.

"Aye, a fair beginning," replied the Marquis.

Fire ran through French veins. No cannon balls were coming from the enemy to sweep down their defences. Bullets from rifle and musket were beating in vain on their wooden wall, and before them came the foe, a vast, converging mass, a target that no one could miss. They were far from their own land, deep in the great North American wilderness, but as they saw it, they fought for the honour and glory of France, and to keep what was hers. They redoubled their shouts and fired faster and faster. A great cloud of smoke rose over the clearing and the forest, but through it the attacking army always advanced, a hedge of bayonets leading.

Robert saw everything clearly. His heart sank for a moment, and then leaped up again. Many of his own had fallen, but a great red curve was advancing. It was the British regulars, the best troops in the charge that Europe could furnish, and they would surely carry the wooden wall. As far as he could see, in front and to left and right, their bayonets flashed in the sun, and a cry of admiration sprang to his lips. Forward they came, their line even and beautiful, and then the tempest beat upon them. The entire French fire was concentrated upon the concave red lines. The batteries poured grape shot upon them and a sleet of lead cut through flesh and bone. Gaps were torn in their ranks, but the others closed up, and came on, the American Colonials on their flanks charging as bravely.

Robert suddenly remembered a vision of his, vague and fleeting then, but very real now. He was standing here at Ticonderoga, looking at the battle as it passed before him, and now it was no vision, but the truth. Had Tayoga's Manitou opened the future to him for a moment? Then the memory was gone and the terrific drama of the present claimed his whole mind.

The red lines were not stopped. In the face of awful losses they were still coming. They were among the trees where the men were entangled with the boughs or ran upon the wooden spikes. Often they tripped and fell, but rising they returned to the charge, offering their breasts to the deadly storm that never diminished for an instant.

Robert walked back and forth in his little space. Every nerve was on edge. The smoke of the firing was in eye, throat and nostril, and his brain was hot. But confidence was again supreme. "They'll come! They'll come! Nothing can stop them!" he kept repeating to himself.

Now the Colonials on the flank pressed forward, and they also advanced through the lines of the regulars in front and charged with them. Together British and Americans climbed over the mass of fallen trees in face of the terrible fire, and reached the wooden wall itself, where the sleet beat directly upon their faces. For a long distance behind them, their dead and wounded lay in hundreds and hundreds.

Many of them tried to scale the barrier, but were beaten back. Now Montcalm, St. Luc, De Levis, Bourlamaque and all the French leaders made their mightiest efforts. The eye of the French commander swept the field. He neglected nothing. Never was a man better served by his lieutenants. St. Luc was at every threatened point, encouraging with voice and example. Bourlamaque received a dangerous wound, but refused to quit the field. Bougainville was hit, but his hurt was less severe, and he took no notice of it, two bullets pierced the hat of De Levis, St. Luc took a half dozen through his clothes and his body was grazed three times, but his gay and warlike spirit mounted steadily, and he hummed his little French air over and over again.

More British and Americans pressed to the wooden wall. The new Black Watch, stalwart Scotchmen, bagpipes playing, charged over everything. Two British columns made a powerful and tremendous attack upon the French right, where stood the valiant battalions of Béarn and Guienne. It seemed, for a while, that they might overwhelm everything. They were against the barrier itself, and were firing into the defence. Montcalm rushed to the spot with all the reserves he could muster. St. Luc sprang among the men and shouted to them to increase their fire. This point became the centre of the battle, and its full fury was concentrated there. A mass of Highlanders, tearing at the wooden wall, refused to give back. Though they fell fast, a captain climbed up the barrier. Officers and men followed him. They stood a moment on the crest as if to poise themselves, and then leaped down among the French, where they were killed. Those who stood on the other side were swept by a hurricane of fire, and at last they yielded slowly.

Robert saw all, and he was seized with a great horror. The army was not crashing over everything. Those who entered the French works died there. The wooden wall held. Nowhere was the line of defence broken. Boats loaded with troops coming down the outlet of Lake George to turn the French left were repelled by the muskets of the Canadian volunteers. Some of the boats were sunk, and the soldiers struggled in the water, as cannon balls and bullets beat upon them.

His view of the field was blurred, for a while, by the smoke from so much firing, which floated in thickening clouds over all the open spaces and the edges of the forest. It produced curious optical illusions. The French loomed through it, increased fourfold in numbers, every individual man magnified in size. He saw them lurid and gigantic, pulling the triggers of their rifles or muskets, or working the batteries. The cannon also grew from twelve-pounders or eighteen-pounders into guns three or four times as large, and many stood where none had stood before.

The smoke continued to inflame his brain also, and it made him pass through great alternations of hope and fear. Now the army was going to sweep over the wooden wall in spite of everything. With sheer weight and bravery it would crush the French and take Ticonderoga. It must be. Because he wanted it to be, it was going to be. Then he passed to the other extreme. When one of the charges spent itself at the barrier, sending perhaps a few men over it, like foam from a wave that has reached its crest, his heart sank to the depths, and he was sure the British and Americans could not come again. Mortal men would not offer themselves so often to slaughter. If the firing died for a little space he was in deep despair, but his soul leaped up again as the charge came anew. It was certainly victory this time. Hope could not be crushed in him. His vivid fancy made him hear above the triumphant shouts of the French the deep cheers of the advancing army, the beating of drums and the playing of invisible bands.

All the time, whether in attack or retreat, the smoke continued to increase and to inflame and excite. It was like a gas, its taste was acrid and bitter as death. Robert coughed and tried to blow it away, but it returned in waves heavier than ever, and then he ceased to fight against it.

The British and American troops came again and again to the attack, their officers leading them on. Never had they shown greater courage or more willingness to die. When the first lines were cut down at the barrier, others took their places. They charged into the vast mass of fallen trees and against the spikes. Blinded by the smoke of so much firing, they nevertheless kept their faces toward the enemy and sought to see him. The fierce cheering of the French merely encouraged them to new attempts.

The battle went on for hours. It seemed days to Robert. Mass after mass of British and Colonials continued to charge upon the wooden wall, always to be broken down by the French fire, leaving heaps of their dead among those logs and boughs and on that bristling array of spikes. At last they advanced no more, twilight came over the field, the terrible fire that had raged since noon died, and the sun set upon the greatest military triumph ever won by France in the New World.

Twilight gathered over the most sanguinary field America had yet seen. In the east the dark was already at hand, but in the west the light from the sunken sun yet lingered, casting a scarlet glow alike over the fallen and the triumphant faces of the victors. Within the works where the French had stood fires were lighted, and everything there was brilliant, but outside, where so much valour had been wasted, the shadows that seemed to creep out of the illimitable forest grew thicker and thicker.

182

The wind moaned incessantly among the leaves, and the persistent smoke that had been so bitter in the throat and nostrils of Robert still hung in great clouds that the wind moved but little. From the woods came long, fierce howls. The wolves, no longer frightened by the crash of cannon and muskets, were coming, and under cover of bushes and floating smoke, they crept nearer and nearer.

Robert sat a long time, bewildered, stunned. The incredible had happened. He had seen it with his own eyes, and yet it was hard to believe that it was true. The great Anglo-American army had been beaten by a French force far less in numbers. Rather, it had beaten itself. That neglect to bring up the cannon had proved fatal, and the finest force yet gathered on the soil of North America had been cut to pieces. A prodigious opportunity had been lost by a commander who stayed a mile and a half in the rear, while his valiant men charged to certain death.

Young Lennox walked stiffly a few steps. No one paid any attention to him. In the dark, and amid the joyous excitement of the defenders, he might have been taken for a Frenchman. But he made no attempt, then, to escape. No such thought was in his mind for the moment. His amazement gave way to horror. He wanted to see what was beyond the wooden wall where he knew the dead and wounded lay, piled deep among the logs and sharpened boughs. Unbelievable it was, but it was true. His own eyes had seen and his own ears had heard. He listened to the triumphant shouts of the French, and his soul sank within him.

A few shots came from the forest now and then, but the great army had vanished, save for its fallen. Montcalm, still cautious, relaxing no vigilance, fearing that the enemy would yet come back with his cannon, walked among his troops and gave them thanks in person. Beer and wine in abundance, and food were served to them. Fires were lighted and the field that they had defended was to be their camp. Many scouts were sent into the forest to see what had become of the opposing army. Most of the soldiers, after eating and drinking, threw themselves upon the ground and slept, but it was long before the leader and any of his lieutenants closed their eyes. Although he felt a mighty joy over his great victory of the day, Montcalm was still a prey to anxieties. His own force, triumphant though it might be, was small. The enemy might come again on the morrow with nearly four to one, and, if he brought his cannon with him, he could take Ticonderoga, despite the great losses he had suffered already. Once more he talked with St. Luc, whom he trusted implicitly.

The Chevalier did not believe a second attack would be made, and his belief was so strong it amounted to a conviction.

"The same mind," he said, "that sent their army against us without artillery, will now go to the other extreme. Having deemed us negligible it will think us invincible."

St. Luc's logic was correct. The French passed the night in peace, and the next morning, when De Levis went out with a strong party to look for the enemy he found that he was gone, and that in his haste he had left behind vast quantities of food and other supplies which the French eagerly seized. Montcalm that day, full of pride, caused a great cross to be erected on his victorious field of battle and upon it he wrote in Latin: *Quid dux? quid miles? quid strata ingentia ligna? En Signum! en victor! Deus hic, Deus ipse triumphat.*

Which a great American writer has translated into:

Soldier and chief and ramparts' strength are nought;
Behold the conquering cross! 'Tis God the triumph wrought.

But for Robert the night that closed down was the blackest he had ever known. It had never occurred to him that Abercrombie's army could be defeated. Confident in its overwhelming numbers, he had believed that it would easily sweep away the French and take Ticonderoga. The skill and valour of Montcalm, St. Luc, De Levis and the others, no matter how skilful and valiant they might be, could avail nothing, and, after Ticonderoga, it would be a mere question of time until Crown Point fell too. And after that would come Quebec and the conquest of Canada.

Now, when his spirits had soared so high, the fall was correspondingly low. His sensitive mind, upon which events always painted themselves with such vividness, reflected only the darkest pictures. He saw the triumphant advance of the French, the Indians laying waste the whole of New York Province, and the enemy at the gates of New York itself.

The night itself was a perfect reproduction of his own mind. He saw through his spirits as through a glass. The dusk was thick, heavy, it was noisome, it had a quality that was almost ponderable, it was unpleasant to eye and nostril, he tasted and breathed the smoke that was shot through it, and he felt a sickening of the soul. He heard a wind moaning through the forest, and it was to him a dirge, the lament of those who had fallen.

He knew there had been no lack of bravery on the part of his own. After a while he took some consolation in that fact. British and Americans had come to the attack long after hope of success was gone. They had not known how to win, but never had men known better how to die. Such valour would march to triumph in the end.

He lay awake almost the whole night, and he did not expect Abercrombie to advance again. Somehow he had the feeling that the play, so far as this particular drama was concerned, was played out. The blow was so heavy that he was in a dull and apathetic state from which he was stirred only once in the evening, and that was when two Frenchmen passed near him, escorting a prisoner of whose face he caught a glimpse in the firelight. He started forward, exclaiming:

"Charteris!"

The young man, tall, handsome and firm of feature, although a captive, turned.

"Who called me?" he asked.

"It is I, Robert Lennox," said Robert. "I knew you in New York!"

"Aye, Mr. Lennox. I recognize you now. We meet again, after so long a time. I could have preferred the meeting to be elsewhere and under other circumstances, but it is something to know that you are alive."

They shook hands with great friendliness and the Frenchmen, who were guarding Charteris, waited patiently.

"May our next meeting be under brighter omens," said Robert.

"I think it will be," said Charteris confidently.

Then he went on. It was a long time before they were to see each other again, and the drama that was to bring them face to face once more was destined to be as thrilling as that at Ticonderoga.

The next night came heavy and dark, and Robert, who continued to be treated with singular forbearance, wandered toward Lake Champlain, which lay pale and shadowy under the thick dusk. No one stopped him. The sentinels seemed to have business elsewhere, and suddenly he remembered his old threat to escape. Hope returned to a mind that had been stunned for a time, and it came back vivid and strong. Then hope sank down again, when a figure issued from the dusk, and stood before him. It was St. Luc.

"Mr. Lennox," said the Chevalier, "what are you doing here?"

"Merely wandering about," replied Robert. "I'm a prisoner, as you know, but no one is bothering about me, which I take to be natural when the echoes of so great a battle have scarcely yet died."

St. Luc looked at him keenly and Robert met his gaze. He could not read the eye of the Chevalier.

"You have been a prisoner of ours once before, but you escaped," said the Chevalier. "It seems that you are a hard lad to hold."

"But then I had the help of the greatest trailer and forest runner in the world, my staunch friend, Tayoga, the Onondaga."

"If he rescued you once he will probably try to do it again, and the great hunter, Willet, is likely to be with him. I suppose you were planning a few moments ago to escape along the shore of the lake."

"I might have been, but I see now that it is too late."

"Too late is a phrase that should be seldom used by youth."

Robert tried once again to read the Chevalier's eye, but St. Luc's look contained the old enigma.

"I admit," said young Lennox, "that I thought I might find an open place in your line. It was only a possible chance."

St. Luc shrugged his shoulders, and looked at the darkness that lay before them like a great black blanket.

"There is much yet to be done by us at Ticonderoga," he said. "Perhaps it is true that a possible chance for you to escape does exist, but my duties are too important for me to concern myself about guarding a single prisoner."

His figure vanished. He was gone without noise, and Robert stared at the place where he had been. Then the hope of escape came back, more vivid and more powerful than ever. "Too late," was a phrase that should not be known to youth. St. Luc was right. He walked straight ahead. No sentinel barred the way. Presently the lake, still and luminous, stretched across his path, and, darting into the bushes along its edge, he ran for a long time. Then he sank down and looked back. He saw dimly the lights of the camp, but he heard no sound of pursuit.

Rising, he began a great curve about Ticonderoga, intending to seek his own army, which he knew could not yet be far away. Once he heard light footsteps and hid deep in the bush. From his covert he saw a band of warriors at least twenty in number go by, their lean, sinewy figures showing faintly in the dusk. Their faces were turned toward the south and he shuddered. Already they were beginning to raid the border. He knew that they had taken little or no part in the battle at Ticonderoga, but now the great success of the French would bring them flocking back to Montcalm's banner, and they would rush like wolves upon those whom they thought defenceless, hoping for more slaughters like that of William Henry.

Tandakora would not neglect such a glowing opportunity for scalps. His savage spirit would incite the warriors to attempts yet greater, and Robert looked closely at the dusky line, thinking for a moment that he might be there. But he did not see his gigantic figure and the warriors flitted on, gone like shadows in the darkness. Then the fugitive youth resumed his own flight.

Far in the night Robert sank down in a state of exhaustion. It was a physical and mental collapse, coming with great suddenness, but he recognized it for what it was, the natural consequence flowing from a period of such excessive strain. His emotions throughout the great battle had been tense and violent, and they had been hardly less so in the time that followed and in the course of the events that led to his escape. And knowing, he forced himself to do what was necessary.

He lay down in the shelter of dense bushes, and kept himself perfectly quiet for a long time. He would not allow hand or foot to move. His weary heart at last began to beat with regularity, the blood ceased to pound in his temples, and his nerves grew steadier. He dozed a little, or at least passed into a state that was midway between wakefulness and oblivion. Then the terrible battle was fought once more before him. Again he heard the crash and roar of the French fire, again he saw British and Americans coming forward in indomitable masses, offering themselves to death, once again he saw them tangled among the logs and sharpened boughs, and then mowed down at the wooden wall.

He roused himself and passed his hands over his eyes to shut away that vision of the stricken field and the vivid reminder of his terrible disappointment. The picture was still as fresh as the reality and it sent shudders through him every time he saw it. He would keep it from his sight whenever he could, lest he grow too morbid.

He rose and started once more toward the south, but the forest became more dense and tangled and the country rougher. In his weakened state he was not able to think with his usual clearness and precision, and he lost the sense of direction. He began to wander about aimlessly, and at last he stopped almost in despair.

He was in a desperate plight. He was unarmed, and a man alone and without weapons in the wilderness was usually as good as lost. He looked around, trying to study the points of the compass. The night was not dark. Trees and bushes stood up distinctly, and on a bough not far away, his eyes suddenly caught a flash of blue.

The flash was made by a small, glossy bird that wavered on a bough, and he was about to turn away, taking no further notice of it, when the bird flew slowly before him and in a direction which he now knew led straight toward the south. He remembered. Back to his mind rushed an earlier escape, and how he had followed the flight of a bird to safety. Had Tayoga's Manitou intervened again in his favour? Was it chance? Or did he in a dazed state imagine that he saw what he did not see?

The bird, an azure flash, flew on before him, and hope flowing in an invincible tide in his veins, he followed. He was in continual fear lest the blue flame fade away, but on he went, over hills and across valleys and brooks, and it was always just before him. He had been worn and weary before, but now he felt strong and active. Courage rose steadily in his veins, and he had no doubt that he would reach friends.

Near dawn the bird suddenly disappeared among the leaves. Robert stopped and heard a light foot-step in the bushes. Being apprehensive lest he be re-taken, he shrank away and then stopped. He listened a while, and the sound not being repeated, he hoped that he had been mistaken, but a voice called suddenly from a bush not ten feet away:

"Come, Dagaeoga! The Great Bear and I await you. Tododaho, watching on his star, has sent us into your path."

Robert, uttering a joyful cry, sprang forward, and the Onondaga and Willet, rising from the thicket, greeted him with the utmost warmth.

"I knew we'd find you again," said Willet "How did you manage to escape?"

"A way seemed to open for me," replied Robert. "The last man I saw in the French camp was St. Luc. After that I met no sentinel, although I passed where a sentinel would stand."

"Ah!" said Willet.

They gave him food, and after sunrise they started toward the south. Robert told how he had seen the great battle and the French victory.

"Tayoga, Black Rifle, Grosvenor and I were in the attack," said Willet, "but we went through it without a scratch. No troops ever fought more bravely than ours. The defeat was the fault of the commander, not theirs. But we'll put behind us the battle lost and think of the battle yet to be won."

"So we will," said Robert, as he looked around at the great curving forest, its deep green tinted with the light brown of summer. It was a friendly forest now. It no longer had the aspect of the night before, when the wolves, their jaws slavering in anticipation, howled in its thickets. Rabbits sprang up as they passed, but the little creatures of the wild did not seem to be afraid. They did not run away. Instead, they crouched under the bushes, and gazed with mild eyes at the human beings who made no threats. A deer, drinking at the edge of a brook, raised its head a little and then continued to drink. Birds sang in the dewy dawn with uncommon freshness and sweetness. The whole world was renewed.

Creature, as he was, of his moods, Robert's spirits soared again at his meeting with Tayoga and Willet, those staunch friends of his, bound to him by such strong ties and so many dangers shared. The past was the past, Ticonderoga was a defeat, a great defeat, when a victory had been expected, but it was not irreparable. Hope sang in his heart and his face flushed in the dawn. The Onondaga, looking at him, smiled.

"Dagaeoga already looks to the future," he said.

"So I do," replied Robert with enthusiasm. "Why shouldn't I? The night just passed has favoured me. I escaped. I met you and Dave, and it's a glorious morning."

The sun was rising in a splendid sea of colour, tinting the woods with red and gold. Never had the wilderness looked more beautiful to him. He turned his face in the direction of Ticonderoga.

"We'll come back," he said, his heart full of courage, "and we'll yet win the victory, even to the taking of Quebec."

"So we will," said the hunter.

"Aye, Stadacona itself will fall," said Tayoga.

Refreshed and strong, they plunged anew into the forest, travelling swiftly toward the south.

The Sun of Quebec

A Story of a Great Crisis

Foreword

The Sun of Quebec is the sixth and closing volume of the French and Indian War Series of which the predecessors have been *The Hunters of the Hills*, *The Shadow of the North*, *The Rulers of the Lakes*, *The Masters of the Peaks,* and *The Lords of the Wild.* The important characters in the earlier books reappear, and the mystery in the life of Robert Lennox, the central figure in all the romances, is solved.

Characters in the
French and Indian War Series

Robert Lennox	A lad of unknown origin
Tayoga	A young Onondaga warrior
David Willet	A hunter
Raymond Louis De St. Luc	A brilliant French officer
Aguste De Courcelles	A French officer
François De Jumonville	A French officer
Louis De Galisonnière	A young French officer
Jean De Mézy	A corrupt Frenchman
Armand Glandelet	A young Frenchman
Pierre Boucher	A bully and bravo
Philibert Drouillard	A French priest
The Marquis Duquesne	Governor-General of Canada
Marquis De Vaudreuil	Governor-General of Canada
François Bigot	Intendant of Canada
Marquis De Montcalm	French commander-in-chief
De Levis	A French general
Bourlamaque	A French general
Bougainville	A French general
Armand Dubois	A follower of St. Luc
M. De Chatillard	An old French Seigneur
Charles Langlade	A French partisan
The Dove	The Indian wife of Langlade
Tandakora	An Ojibway chief
Daganoweda	A young Mohawk chief

Hendrick	An old Mohawk chief
Braddock.	A British General
Abercrombie	A British general
Wolfe	A British general
Col. William Johnson	Anglo-American leader
Molly Brant	Col. Wm. Johnson's Indian wife
Joseph Brant	Young brother of Molly Brant; afterward the great Mohawk Chief Thayendanegea
Robert Dinwiddie	Lieutenant-Governor of Virginia
William Shirley	Governor of Massachusetts
Benjamin Franklin	Famous American patriot
James Colden	A young Philadelphia captain
William Wilton	A young Philadelphia lieutenant
Hugh Carson	A young Philadelphia lieutenant
Jacobus Huysman	An Albany burgher
Caterina	Jacobus Huysman's cook
Alexander Mclean	An Albany schoolmaster
Benjamin Hardy	A New York merchant
Johnathan Pillsbury	Clerk to Benjamin Hardy
Adrian Van Zoon	A New York merchant
The Slaver	A nameless rover
Achille Garay	A French spy
Alfred Grosvenor	A young English officer
James Cabell	A young Virginian
Walter Stuart	A young Virginian
Black Rifle	A famous "Indian fighter"
Elihu Strong	A Massachusetts colonel
Alan Hervey	A New York financier
Stuart Whyte	Captain of the British sloop Hawk
John Latham	Lieutenant of the British sloop Hawk
Edward Charteris	A young officer of the Royal Americans
Zebedee Crane	A young scout and forest runner
Robert Rogers	Famous Captain of American Rangers

CHAPTER 1

Old Friends

Mynheer Jacobus Huysman walked to the window and looked out at the neat red brick houses, the grass, now turning yellow, and the leaves, more brown than green. He was troubled, in truth his heart lay very heavy within him. He was thinking over the terrible news that had come so swiftly, as evil report has a way of doing. But he had cause for satisfaction, too, and recalling it, he turned to gaze once more upon the two lads who, escaping so many perils, had arrived at the shelter of his home.

Robert and Tayoga were thin and worn, their clothing was soiled and torn, but youth was youth and they were forgetting dangers past in a splendid dinner that the fat Caterina was serving for them while Mynheer Jacobus, her master, stood by and saw the good deed well done.

The dining room, large and furnished solidly, was wonderful in its neatness and comfort. The heavy mahogany of table, sideboard and chairs was polished and gleaming. No trace of dirt was allowed to linger anywhere. When the door to the adjoining kitchen opened, as Caterina passed through, pleasant odours floated in, inciting the two to fresh efforts at the trencher. It was all as it had been when they were young boys living there, attending the school of Alexander McLean and travelling by painful steps along the road to knowledge. In its snugness, its security and the luxury it offered it was a wonderful contrast to the dark forest, where death lurked in every bush. Robert drew a long sigh of content and poured himself another cup of coffee.

"And you escaped from the French after the great battle?" said Mynheer Jacobus, asking the same question over and over again.

"Yes, sir," replied Robert, "and it was not a difficult thing to do at all. The victory of the French was so remarkable, and I think so unexpected, that they were paying little attention to me. I just walked out of their camp, and the only man I met was the Chevalier de St. Luc, who did not seem at all interested in stopping me—a curious fact, but a fact all the same."

"A great leader and a fine man iss the Chevalier de St. Luc," said Mr. Huysman.

"He's both, as I've had many chances to learn, and I intend to know more about him some day."

"It may be that you will know even more than you think."

Robert looked sharply at the burgher, and he was about to ask questions, but he reflected that Mynheer Jacobus, if he were able to answer, would be evasive like all the others and so he checked the words at his lips.

"I suppose that time will disclose everything," he contented himself with saying. "Meanwhile, I want to tell you, sir, that Tayoga and I appreciate to the full your hospitality. It is noble, it always was noble, as we've had ample occasion to discover."

The full red face of Mynheer Jacobus bloomed into a smile. The corners of his mouth turned up, and his eyes twinkled.

"I must have had a premonition that you two were coming," he said, "and so I stocked the larder. I remembered of old your appetites, a hunger that could be satisfied only with great effort, and then could come back again an hour later, as fresh and keen as ever. You are strong and healthy boys, for which you should be grateful."

"We are," said Robert, with great emphasis.

"And you do not know whether Montcalm iss advancing with his army?"

"We don't, sir, but is Albany alarmed?"

"It iss! It iss alarmed very greatly. It wass not dreamed by any of us that our army could be defeated, that magnificent army which I saw go away to what I thought was certain victory. Ah, how could it have happened? How could it have happened, Robert?"

"We simply threw away our chances, sir. I saw it all. We underrated the French. If we had brought up our big guns it would have been easy. There was no lack of courage on the part of our men. I don't believe that people of British blood ever showed greater bravery, and that means bravery equal to anybody's."

Mynheer Jacobus Huysman sighed heavily.

"What a waste! What a waste!" he said. "Now the army hass retreated and the whole border iss uncovered. The tomahawk and scalping knife are at work. Tales of slaughter come in efery day, and it iss said that Montcalm iss advancing on Albany itself."

"I don't believe, sir, that he will come," said Robert. "The French numbers are much fewer than is generally supposed, and I can't think he will dare to attack Albany."

"It does not seem reasonable, but there iss great alarm. Many people are leaving on the packets for New York. Who would have thought it? Who could have thought it! But I mean to stay, and if Montcalm comes I will help fight in the defence."

"I knew you wouldn't leave, sir. But despite our defeat we've a powerful army yet, and England and the Colonies will not sit down and just weep."

"What you say iss so, Robert, my boy. I am not of English blood, but when things look worst iss the time when England shows best, and the people here are of the same breed. I do not despair. What did you say had become of Willet?"

"Shortly before we reached Albany he turned aside to see Sir William Johnson. We had, too, with us, a young Englishman named Grosvenor, a fine fellow, but he went at once to the English camp here to report for duty. He was in the battle at Ticonderoga and he also will testify that our army, although beaten, could have brought up its artillery and have fought again in a day or two. It would have gained the victory, too."

"I suppose so! I suppose so! But it did not fight again, and what might have been did not happen. It means a longer war in this country and a longer war all over the world. It spreads! It iss a great war, extending to most of the civilized lands, the greatest war of modern times and many think it will be the last war, but I know not. The character of mankind does not change. What do you two boys mean to do?"

"We have not decided yet," replied Robert, speaking for both. "We'll go back to the war, of course, which means that we'll travel once more toward the north, but we'll have to rest a few days."

"And this house iss for you to rest in—a few days or many days, as you please, though I hope it will be many. Caterina shall cook for you four, five meals a day, if you wish, and much at every meal. I do not forget how when you were little you raided the fruit trees, and the berry bushes and the vines. Well, the fruit will soon be ripe again und I will turn my back the other way. I will make that fat Caterina do the same, and you and Tayoga can imagine that you are little boys once more."

"I know you mean that, Mynheer Jacobus, and we thank you from the bottom of our hearts," said Robert, as the moisture came into his eyes.

"Here comes Master Alexander McLean," said Mr. Huysman, who

199

had turned back to the window. "He must have heard of your arrival and he wishes to see if your perils in the woods have made you forget your ancient history."

In a minute or two Master McLean, tall, thin, reddish of hair, and severe of gaze entered, his frosty blue eyes lighting up as he shook hands with the boys, though his manner remained austere.

"I heard that you had arrived after the great defeat at Ticonderoga," he said, "and you are fortunate to have escaped with your lives. I rejoice at it, but those who go into the woods in such times must expect great perils. It is of course well for all our young men to offer their lives now for their country, but I thought I saw in you at least, Robert Lennox, the germ of a great scholar, and it would be a pity for you to lose your life in some forest skirmish."

"I thank you for the compliment," said Robert, "but as I was telling Mynheer Jacobus I mean to go back into the woods."

"I doubt it not. The young of this generation are wise in their own conceit. It was hard enough to control Tayoga and you several years ago, and I cannot expect to do it now. Doubtless all the knowledge that I have been at such pains to instil into you will be lost in the excitement of trail and camp."

"I hope not, sir, though it's true that we've had some very stirring times. When one is in imminent danger of his life he cannot think much of his Latin, his Greek and his ancient history."

The severe features of Master Alexander McLean wrinkled into a frown.

"I do not know about that," he said. "Alexander the Great slept with his Homer under his pillow, and doubtless he also carried the book with him on his Asiatic campaigns, refreshing and strengthening his mind from time to time with dips into its inspiring pages. There is no crisis in which it is pardonable for you to forget your learning, though I fear me much that you have done so. What was the date, Robert, of the fall of Constantinople?"

"Mahomet the Second entered it, sir, in the year 1453 A. D."

"Very good. I begin to have more confidence in you. And why is Homer considered a much greater poet than Virgil?"

"More masculine, more powerful, sir, and far more original. In fact the Romans in their literature, as in nearly all other arts, were merely imitators of the Greeks."

The face of Master McLean relaxed into a smile.

"Excellent! Excellent!" he exclaimed. "You have done better than you claimed for yourself, but modesty is an attribute that becomes the young, and now I tell you again, Robert, that I am most glad you and Tayoga have come safely out of the forest. I wish to inform you also that Master Benjamin Hardy and his chief clerk, Jonathan Pillsbury, have arrived from New York on the fast packet, *River Queen*, and even now they are depositing their baggage at the George Inn, where they are expecting to stay."

Master Jacobus who had been silent while the schoolmaster talked, awoke suddenly to life.

"At the George Inn!" he exclaimed. "It iss a good inn, good enough for anybody, but when friends of mine come to Albany they stay with me or I take offense. Bide here, my friends, and I will go for them. Alexander, sit with the lads and partake of refreshment while I am gone."

He hastened from the room and Master McLean, upon being urged, joined Robert and Tayoga at the table, where he showed that he too was a good man at the board, thinness being no bar to appetite and capacity. As he ate he asked the boys many questions, and they, knowing well his kindly heart under his crusty manner, answered them all readily and freely. Elderly and bookish though he was, his heart throbbed at the tale of the great perils through which they had gone, and his face darkened when Robert told anew the story of Ticonderoga.

"It is our greatest defeat so far," he said, "and I hope our misfortunes came to a climax there. We must have repayment for it. We must aim at the heart of the French power, and that is Quebec. Instead of fighting on the defence, Britain and her colonies must strike down Canada."

"So it seems to me too, sir," said Robert. "We're permitting the Marquis de Montcalm to make the fighting, to choose the fields of battle, and as long as we do that we have to dance to his music. But, sir, that's only my opinion. I would not presume to give it in the presence of my superiors."

"You've had much experience despite your youth and you're entitled to your thoughts. But I hear heavy steps. 'Tis odds that it's Jacobus with his friends."

The door was opened and Mr. Huysman with many words of welcome ushered in his guests, who being simple and strong men brought their own baggage from the inn. Robert rose at once and faced Benjamin Hardy in whose eyes shone an undoubted gladness. The merchant did not look a day older than when Robert had last seen him in New York, and he was as robust and hearty as ever. Jonathan Pillsbury, tall, thin and dressed with meticulous care, also permitted himself a smile.

"Robert, my lad!" exclaimed Benjamin Hardy, dropping his baggage and holding out two sinewy hands. "'Tis a delight to find you and Tayoga here. I knew not what had become of you two, and I feared the worst, the times being so perilous. Upon my word, we've quite a reunion!"

Robert returned his powerful and friendly grasp. He was more than glad to see him for several reasons; for his own sake, because he liked him exceedingly, and because he was sure Master Benjamin held in his keeping those secrets of his own life which he was yet to learn.

"Sir," he said, "'tis not my house, though I've lived in it, and I know that Mr. Huysman has already given you a most thorough welcome, so I add that it's a delight to me to see you again. 'Twas a pleasant and most memorable visit that Tayoga and I had at your home in New York."

"And eventful enough, too. You came very near going to the Guineas on a slave trip. That was the kind of hospitality I offered you."

"No fault of yours, sir. I shall never forget the welcome you gave us in New York. It warms my heart now to think of it."

"I see you've not lost your gift of speech. Words continue to well from your lips, and they're good words, too. But I talk overmuch myself. Here is Jonathan waiting to speak to you. I told him I was coming to Albany. 'Upon what affair?' he asked. ''Tis secret,' I replied. 'Meaning you do not want to tell me of its nature,' he said. 'Yes,' I replied. Then he said, 'Whatever its gist, you'll need my presence and advice. I'm going with you.' And here he is. Doubtless he is right."

Jonathan Pillsbury clasped Robert's hand as warmly as he ever clasped anybody's and permitted himself a second smile, which was his limit, and only extraordinary occasions could elicit two.

"Our conversation has been repeated with accuracy," he said. "I do not yet know why I have come to Albany, but I feel sure it is well that I have come."

Mr. Huysman hustled about, his great red face glowing while fat Caterina brought in more to eat. He insisted that the new guests sit at the table and eat tremendously. It was a time when hospitality meant repeated offerings of food, which in America was the most abundant of all things, and Mr. Hardy and Mr. Pillsbury easily allowed themselves to be persuaded.

"And now, Robert, you must tell me something more about Dave," said the merchant as they rose from the table.

Young Lennox promptly narrated their adventures among the peaks and about the lakes while the older men listened with breathless attention. Nor did the story of the great hunter suffer in Robert's telling. He had an immense admiration for Willet and he spoke of his deeds with such vivid words and with so much imagery and embroidery that they seemed to be enacted again there in that quiet room before the men who listened.

"Ah, that is Dave! True as steel. As honest and brave as they ever make 'em," said Master Benjamin Hardy, when he had finished. "A man! a real man if ever one walked this earth!"

"And don't forget Tayoga here," said Robert. "The greatest trailer ever born. He saved us more than once by his ability to read the faintest sign the earth might yield."

"When Dagaeoga begins to talk he never knows how to stop," said Tayoga; "I but did the things all the warriors of my nation are taught to do. I would be unworthy to call myself a member of the clan of the Bear, of the nation Onondaga, of the great League of the Hodenosaunee, if I could not follow a trail. Peace, Dagaeoga!"

Robert joined in the laugh, and then the men began to talk about the prospects of an attack upon Albany by the French and Indians, though all of them inclined to Robert's view that Montcalm would not try it.

"As you were a prisoner among them you ought to know something about their force, Robert," said Mr. Hardy.

"I had opportunities to observe," replied the lad, "and from what I saw, and from what I have since heard concerning our numbers I judge that we were at least four to one, perhaps more. But we threw away all our advantage when we came with bare breasts against their wooden wall and sharpened boughs."

"It is a painful thing to talk about and to think about, but Britain never gives up. She marches over her mistakes and failures to triumph, and we are bone of her bone. And you saw St. Luc!"

"Often, sir. In the battle and in the preparations for it he was the right arm of the Marquis de Montcalm. He is a master of forest war."

"He is all that, Robert, my lad. A strange, a most brilliant man, he is one of our most formidable enemies."

"But a gallant one, sir. He did nothing to prevent my escape. I feel that at Ticonderoga as well as elsewhere I am greatly in his debt."

"Undoubtedly he favours you. It does not surprise me."

Intense curiosity leaped up in Robert's heart once more. What was he to St. Luc! What was St. Luc to him! All these elderly men seemed to hold a secret that was hidden from him, and yet it concerned him most. His lips twitched and he was about to ask a question, but he reflected that, as always before, it would not be answered, it would be evaded, and he restrained his eager spirit. He knew that all the men liked him, that they had his good at heart, and that when the time came to speak they would speak. The words that had risen to his lips were unspoken.

Robert felt that his elders wanted to talk, that something they would rather not tell to the lads was in their minds, and meanwhile the brilliant sunshine and free air outside were calling to him and the Onondaga.

"I think," he said, addressing them all collectively, "that Tayoga and I should go to see Lieutenant Grosvenor. He was our comrade in the forest, and he has been somewhat overcome by his great hardships."

"The idea would not be bad," said Master Benjamin Hardy. "Youth to youth, and, while you are gone, we old fellows will talk of days long ago as old fellows are wont to do."

And so they did want him and Tayoga to go! He had divined their wishes aright. He was quite sure, too, that when he and the Onondaga were away the past would be very little in their minds. These active men in the very prime of their powers were concerned most about the present and the future. Well, whatever it was he was sure they would discuss it with wisdom and foresight.

"Come, Tayoga," he said. "Outdoors is calling to us."

"And be sure that you return in time for supper," said Master Jacobus. "This house is to be your home as long as you are in Albany. I should be offended mortally if you went elsewhere."

"No danger of that," said Robert. "Tayoga and I know a good home when we find it. And we know friends, too, when we see them."

It was a bit of sentiment, but he felt it very deeply and he saw that all of the men looked pleased. As he and Tayoga went out he noticed that they drew their chairs about the dining-room table that Caterina had cleared, and before the door closed upon the two lads they were already talking in low and earnest tones.

"They have affairs of importance which are not for us," he said, when he and the Onondaga were outside.

"It is so," said Tayoga. "The white people have their chiefs and *sachems* like the nations of the Hodenosaunee, and their ranks are filled by age. The young warriors are for the trail, the hunt, and the war path, and not for the council. It is right that it should be thus. I do not wish to be a chief or a *sachem* before my time. I am glad, Dagaeoga, to enjoy youth, and let our elders do the hard thinking for us."

"So am I," said Robert joyfully as he filled his lungs with draught after draught of the fresh air. "No seat at the council for me! Not for twenty years yet! Give me freedom and action! Let others do the planning and take the responsibility!"

He felt a great elation. His sanguine temperament had made a complete rebound from the depression following Ticonderoga. Although he did not know it the result was partly physical—good food and abundant rest, but he did not seek to analyze the cause, the condition was sufficient. The colour in his cheeks deepened and his eyes glowed.

"Dagaeoga is feeling very, very good," said Tayoga.

"I am," replied Robert with emphasis. "I never felt better. I'm forgetting Ticonderoga; instead, I'm beholding our army at Quebec, and I'm seeing our flag wave over all Canada."

"Dagaeoga sees what he wants to see."

"It's not a bad plan. Then the lions die in your path."

"It is so. Dagaeoga speaks a great truth. We will now see how Red Coat feels."

A portion of the army that had retreated from Ticonderoga was camped on the flats near the town, and Robert and Tayoga walked swiftly toward the tents. It was a much more silent force, British and American, than that which had gone forth not so very long ago to what seemed certain victory. Officers and men were angry. They felt that they had been beaten when there was no reason why they should have been defeated. Obeying orders, they had retreated in sullen silence, when they had felt sure they could have gone on, fought a new battle, and have crushed Montcalm. Now they waited impatiently for another call to advance on Canada, and win back their lost laurels. Both lads felt the tension.

"They are like the wounded bear," said Tayoga. "They feel very sore, and they wish for revenge."

They learned that Grosvenor was in his tent and soon found him there lying upon his blankets. Some of the ruddy colour was gone from his cheeks, and he looked worn and thin. But he sat up, and welcomed Robert and Tayoga joyously.

"It's foolish of me to break down like this," he said, "but after we got back to civilization something seemed to cave in. I hope you chaps won't overlook the fact that I'm not as much used to the forest as you are, and bear in mind that I did my best."

"Red Coat's best was very good," said Tayoga in his grave, precise manner. "Few who have been in the forest as little as he could have done as much and have borne as much."

"Do you really think so, Tayoga? You're not merely flattering me?"

"Our wisest *sachem* would tell you so, Red Coat."

"Thanks, my friend. You make me feel better. I was lucky enough to go through the great battle with little hurt. It was a most ghastly slaughter, and I still dream of it. I stood up all right until we got back to Albany, and then I collapsed. But to-morrow I'll be on my feet again. Your friends, Colden, Wilton and Carson are all here. They showed great courage and they have some slight wounds, but not enough to trouble 'em."

Robert found the Philadelphians a little later, and they all went back to Grosvenor's tent, where they were joined in a half hour by the Virginians, Walter Stuart and James Cabell, who had been with them in Braddock's defeat and whom Robert had known at Williamsburg. It was a tight squeeze for them all in the tent, but there was another and joyous reunion. Youth responded to youth and hope was high.

"Stuart and I did not arrive in time for Ticonderoga," said Cabell, "but we mean to be in the next great battle."

"So we do!" exclaimed Cabell. "The Old Dominion had a taste of defeat at Fort Duquesne and you've had the like here. Now we'll all wait and see how victory agrees with us."

"Some of us have been in at both defeats," said Grosvenor rather sadly.

But the presence of so many friends and the cheerful talk made him feel so much better that he averred his ability to go anywhere and do anything at once.

"You've leave of absence if you wish it?" asked Cabell.

"For several days more," replied Grosvenor.

"Then let's all go into the town. I haven't had a good look at Albany yet. I want to see if it's as fine a place as Williamsburg."

"It's larger," said Robert.

"But size is not everything. That's where you northern people make your mistake."

"But you'll admit that Philadelphia's a fine city, won't you?" said Colden, "and you know it's the largest in the colonies."

"But it's comparatively near to Virginia," said Cabell briskly, "and our influence works wonders."

"We've our own conceit in Philadelphia," said Wilton, "but conceit and Virginia are just the same words, though they may have a different sound."

"Come on to the George Inn," said Grosvenor, "and you can argue it out there. Old England likes to see this healthy rivalry among her children. She doesn't mind your being bumptious."

"We're bumptious, because we're like our parent," said Cabell. "It's a matter of inheritance."

"Let the George Inn settle it. Come on, lads."

Grosvenor was feeling better and better. He was adaptable and this was a sprightly group, full of kindred spirits. The Virginians were as English as he was, and the others nearly as much so. He had acquitted himself well in the New World, in fields with which he was unfamiliar, and these lads were friends. Danger and hardships faded quite away into a forgotten past. He was strong and well once more.

"You shall all be my guests at the George Inn!" he exclaimed. "We shall have refreshment and talk, plenty of both."

"As we Virginians are the oldest people in the colonies, it's the right of Stuart and myself to be the hosts," said Cabell.

"Aye, so 'tis," said Stuart.

"As we're from Philadelphia, the greatest and finest city in the country, it's the right of Wilton, Carson and myself," said Colden.

But Grosvenor was firm. He had given the invitation first, he said, and nobody could take the privilege from him. So the others yielded gracefully, and in high good humour the eight, saying much and humming little songs, walked across the fields from the camp and into the town. Robert noticed the bustling life of Albany with approval. The forest made its appeal to him, and the city made another and different but quite as strong appeal. The old Fort Orange of the Dutch was crowded now, not only with troops but with all the forms of industry that follow in the train of an army. The thrifty Dutch, despite their apprehension over the coming of the French, were busy buying, selling, and between battles much money was made.

The George Inn, a low building but long and substantial was down by the river. The great doors stood wide open and much life flowed in and out, showing that it too profited by war. The eight found seats at a table on a sanded floor, and contented themselves with lemonade, which they drank slowly, while they talked and looked.

It was a motley and strange throng; American, English, Dutch, German, Indian, Swedish. A half dozen languages were heard in the great room, forerunner of the many elements that were to enter in the composition of the American nation. And the crowd was already cosmopolitan. Difference of race attracted no attention. Men took no notice of Tayoga because he was an Indian, unless to admire his tall, straight figure and proud carriage. Albany had known the Iroquois a century and a half.

Robert's spirits, like Grovenor's, mounted. Here he was with many friends of his own age and kindred mind. Everything took on the colour of rose. All of them were talking, but his own gift of speech was the finest. He clothed narrative with metaphor and illustration until it became so vivid that the others were glad to fall silent and listen to him, though Robert himself was unconscious of the fact. They made him relate once more his story of the battle as he saw it from inside the French lines at Ticonderoga, and, just as he came to the end of the tale, he caught a glimpse of a tall man entering the tavern.

"Tell us what you saw from the other side," he said to Grosvenor, and they compelled the reluctant Englishman to talk. Then Robert turned his eyes toward the tall man who was now sitting at a small table in the corner and drinking from a long glass. Something familiar in his walk had caught his attention as he came in, and, under cover of Grosvenor's talk, he wished to observe him again without being noticed even by his own comrades.

The stranger was sitting with the side of his face to Robert, and his features were not well disclosed. His dress was that of a seafaring man, rough but rather good in texture, and a belt held a long dirk in a scabbard which was usual at that time. The hand that raised the long glass to his lips was large, red and powerful. Robert felt that his first belief was correct. He had seen him before somewhere, though he could not yet recall where, but when he turned his head presently he knew. They had met under such circumstances that neither was ever likely to forget time or place.

He was amazed that the stranger had come so boldly into Albany, but second thought told him that there was no proof against him, it was merely Robert's word against his. Among people absorbed in a great war his own story would seem wildly improbable and the stranger's would have all the savour of truth. But he knew that he could not be mistaken. He saw now the spare face, clean shaven, and the hard eyes, set close together, that he remembered so well.

Robert did not know what to do. He listened for a little while to Grosvenor's narrative but his attention wandered back to the seafaring man. Then he decided.

"Will you fellows talk on and excuse me for a few minutes?" he said.

"What is it, Lennox?" asked Colden.

"I see an acquaintance on the other side of the room. I wish to speak to him."

"That being the case, we'll let you go, but we'll miss you. Hurry back."

"I'll stay only a few minutes. It's an old friend and I must have a little talk with him."

He walked with light steps across the room which was crowded, humming with many voices, the air heavy with smoke. The man was still at the small table, and, opposite him, was an empty chair in which Robert sat deliberately, putting his elbows on the table, and staring into the hard blue eyes.

"I'm Peter Smith," he said. "You remember me?"

There was a flicker of surprise in the Captain's face, but nothing more.

"Oh, yes, Peter," he said. "I know you, but I was not looking for you just at this moment."

"But I'm here."

"Perhaps you're coming back to your duty, is that it? Well, I'm glad. I've another ship now, and though you're a runaway seaman I can afford to let bygones be bygones."

"I hope your vessel has changed her trade. I don't think I'd care to sail again on a slaver."

"Always a particular sort of chap you were, Peter. It's asking a lot for me to change the business of my ship to suit you."

"But not too much."

The conversation was carried on in an ordinary tone. Neither raised his voice a particle. Nobody took any notice. His own comrades, engrossed in lively talk, seemed to have forgotten Robert for the moment, and he felt that he was master of the situation. Certainly the slaver would be more uncomfortable than he.

"I was wondering," he said, "how long you mean to stay in Albany."

"It's a pleasant town," said the man, "as I have cause to know since I've been here before. I may remain quite a while. Still, I shall decide wholly according to my taste."

"But there is a certain element of danger."

"Oh, the war! I don't think the French even if they come to Albany will have a chance to take me."

"I didn't have the war in mind. There are other risks of which I think that I, Peter Smith, who sailed with you once before ought to warn you."

"It's good of you, Peter, to think so much of my safety, but I don't believe I've any cause for fear. I've always been able to take care of myself."

The last words were said with a little snap, and Robert knew they were meant as a defiance, but he appeared not to notice.

"Ah, well you've shown that you know how to look out for number one," he said. "I'm only Peter Smith, a humble seaman, but I've the same faculty. I bid you good-day."

"Good-day, Peter. I hope there's no ill feeling between us, and that each will have whatever he deserves!"

Cool! wonderfully cool, Robert thought, but he replied merely: "I trust so, too, and in that case it is easy to surmise what one of us would get."

He sauntered back to his comrades, and, lest he attract their attention, he did not look toward the slaver again for a minute or two. When he glanced in that direction he saw the man walking toward the door, not in any hurried manner, but as if he had all the time in the world, and need fear nobody. Cool! wonderfully cool, Robert thought a second time.

The slaver went out, and Robert thought he caught a glimpse of a man meeting him, a second man in whose figure also there was something familiar. They were gone in an instant, and he was tempted to spring up and follow them, because the figure of which he had seen but a little at the door reminded him nevertheless of Achille Garay, the spy.

CHAPTER 2

The Chest of Drawers

It was but a fleeting glimpse that Robert had of the second man, but he believed that it was Garay. He not only looked like the spy, but he was convinced that it was really he. After the first moment or two he did not doubt his identity, and making an excuse that he wanted a little fresh air and would return in an instant he walked quickly to the door. He caught another and fugitive glimpse of two men, one tall and the other short, walking away together, and he could not doubt that they were the slaver and the spy.

Had he been alone Robert would have followed them, though he was quite certain that Garay must have had some place of sure refuge, else he would not have ventured into Albany. Even with that recourse his act was uncommonly bold. If the slaver was daring, the spy was yet more so. There was nothing against the slaver that they could prove, but the spy put his neck in the noose.

Robert whistled softly to himself, and he was very thoughtful. Willet, Tayoga and he had been so completely victorious over Garay in the forest that perhaps he had underrated him. Maybe he was a man to be feared. His daring appearance in Albany must be fortified by supreme cunning, and his alliance with the slaver implied a plan. Robert believed that the plan, or a part of it at least, was directed against himself. Well, what if it was? He could meet it, and he was not afraid. He had overcome other perils, and he had friends, as true and steadfast as were ever held to any man by hooks of steel. His heart beat high, he was in a glow, his whole soul leaped forward to meet prospective danger.

He went back into the inn and took his seat with the others. Now it was Stuart who was talking, telling them of life in the great Southern colony and of its delights, of the big houses, of the fields of tobacco, of the horse races, of the long visits to neighbours, and how all who were anybody were related, making Virginia one huge family.

"Now Cabell and I," he said, "belong to the same clan. My mother and his father are third cousins, which makes us fourth cousins, or fifth is it? But whether fourth or fifth, we're cousins just the same. All the people of our blood are supposed to stand together, and do stand together. Oh, it has its delights! It makes us sufficient unto ourselves! The old Dominion is a world in itself, complete in all its parts."

"But you have to come to Philadelphia to see a great city and get a taste of metropolitan life," said Colden.

Then a discussion, friendly but warm arose as to the respective merits of the Virginia and Pennsylvania provinces, and when it was at its height and the attention of all the others was absorbed in it, Tayoga leaned over and whispered to Robert:

"What did you see at the door, Dagaeoga?"

Robert was startled. So, the Onondago was watching, after all. He might have known that nothing would escape his attention.

"I saw Garay, the spy," he replied in the same tone.

"And the man at the little table was the captain of the slave ship on which you were taken?"

"The same."

"It bodes ill, Dagaeoga. You must watch."

"I will, Tayoga."

The crowd in the great room of the George Inn increased and the young group remained, eager to watch it. It was a reflex of the life in the colonies, at the seat of conflict, and throbbing with all the emotions of a great war that enveloped nearly the whole civilized world. A burly fellow, dressed as a teamster, finally made his voice heard above the others.

"I tell you men," he said, "that we must give up Albany! Our army has been cut to pieces! Montcalm is advancing with twenty thousand French regulars, and swarms of Indians! They control all of Lake George as well as Champlain! Hundreds of settlers have already fallen before the tomahawk, and houses are burning along the whole border! I have it from them that have seen the fires."

There was a sudden hush in the crowd, followed by an alarmed murmur. The man's emphasis and his startling statements made an impression.

"Go on, Dobbs! Tell us about it!" said one.

"What do you know?" asked another.

He stood up, a great tall man with a red face.

"My cousin has been in the north," he said, "and he's seen rangers, some that have just escaped from the Indians, barely saving their hair. He heard from them that the King of France has sent a big army to Canada, and that another just as big is on the way. It won't be a week before you see the French flag from the hills of Albany, and wise men are already packing ready to go to New York."

There was another alarmed hush.

"This fellow must be stopped," said Colden. "He'll start a panic."

"Dagaeoga has the gift of words," whispered a voice in Robert's ear, "and now is the time to use it."

Nothing more was needed. Robert was on fire in an instant, and, standing upon his chair, asked for attention.

"Your pardon a moment, Mr. Dobbs," he said, "if I interrupt you."

"Why it's only a boy!" a man exclaimed.

"A boy, it's true," said Robert, who now felt himself the centre of all eyes, and who, as usual, responded with all his faculties to such an opportunity, "but I was present at the Battle of Ticonderoga, and perhaps I've a chance to correct a few errors into which our friend, Mr. Dobbs, has fallen."

"What are those errors?" asked the man in a surly tone, not relishing his loss of the stage.

"I'll come to them promptly," said Robert in his mellowest tones. "They're just trifles, Mr. Dobbs, but still trifles should be corrected. I stood with the French army in the battle, and I know something about its numbers, which are about one-sixth of what Mr. Dobbs claims them to be."

"What were you doing with the French?"

"I happened to be a prisoner, Mr. Dobbs. I escaped a day or two later. But here are with me young officers of ours who were in the attack. Several of them felt the sting of French bullets on that day, so when they tell you what happened they know what they're talking about. Their reports don't come from their cousins, but are the product of their own eyes and ears. Peace, Mr. Dobbs! I've the floor, or rather the chair, and I must tell the facts. We were defeated at Ticonderoga, it's true, but we were not cut to pieces. Our generals failed to bring up our artillery. They underrated the French. They went with rifles, muskets and bayonets alone against breastworks, defended by a valiant foe, for the French are valiant, and they paid the price. But our army is in existence and it's as brave as ever. Albany is in no danger. Don't be alarmed."

"You're but a boy. You don't know," growled Dobbs.

"Peace, Mr. Dobbs! Give us peace. A boy who has seen may know better than a man who has not seen. I tell you once again, friends, that the Marquis de Montcalm will not appear before Albany. It's a long way from Ticonderoga to this city, too long a road for the French army to travel. Wise men are not packing for flight to New York. Wise men are staying right here."

"Hear! Hear!" exclaimed the Virginians and Philadelphians and Grosvenor, and "Hear! Hear!" was repeated from the crowd. Dobbs' red face grew redder, but now he was silent.

"My friends," continued Robert in his golden persuasive tones, "you're not afraid, you're all brave men, but you must guard against panic. Experience tells you that rumour is irresponsible, that, as it spreads, it grows. We're going to learn from our defeat. The French are as near to Albany as they'll ever come. The war is not going to move southward. Its progress instead will be toward Quebec. Remember that panic is always a bad counsellor; but that courage is ever a good one. Things are never as bad as they look."

"Hear! Hear!" exclaimed his young comrades again, and the echoes from the crowd were more numerous than before. The teamster began to draw back and presently slipped out of the door. Then Robert sat down amid great applause, blushing somewhat because he had been carried away by his feelings and apologizing to the others for making himself conspicuous.

"Nothing to apologize for," exclaimed Cabell. "'Twas well done, a good speech at the right time. You've the gift of oratory, Lennox. You should come to Virginia to live, after we've defeated the French. Our province is devoted to oratory. You've the gift of golden speech, and the people will follow you."

"I'm afraid I've made an enemy of that man, Dobbs," said Robert, "and I had enemies enough already."

His mind went back to the slaver and Garay, and he was troubled.

"We've had our little triumph here, thanks to Lennox," said Colden, "and it seems to me now that we've about exhausted the possibilities of the George. Besides, the air is getting thick. Let's go outside."

Grosvenor paid the score and they departed, a cheer following them. Here were young officers who had fought well, and the men in the George were willing to show respect.

"I think I'd better return to camp now," said Grosvenor.

"We'll go with you," said Colden, speaking for the Pennsylvanians.

"Stuart and I are detached for the present," said Cabell. "We secured a transfer from our command in Virginia, and we're hoping for commissions in the Royal Americans, and more active service, since the whole tide of war seems to have shifted to the north rather than the west."

"The Royal Americans are fine men," said Robert. "Though raised in the colonies, they rank with the British regulars. I had a good friend in one of the regiments, Edward Charteris, of New York, but he was taken at Ticonderoga. I saw the French bring him in a prisoner. I suppose they're holding him in Quebec now."

"Then we'll rescue him when we take Quebec," said Stuart valiantly.

The friends separated with promises to meet again soon and to see much of one another while they were in Albany, Grosvenor and the Pennsylvanians continuing to the camp, Cabell and Stuart turning back to the George for quarters, and Robert and Tayoga going toward the house of Mynheer Jacobus Huysman. But before they reached it young Lennox suggested that they turn toward the river.

"It is well to do so," said the Onondaga. "I think that Dagaeoga wishes to look there for a ship."

"That's in my mind, Tayoga, and yet I wouldn't know the vessel I'm looking for if I saw her."

"She will be commanded by the man whom we saw in the inn, the one with whom Dagaeoga talked."

"I've no doubt of it, Tayoga. Nothing escapes your notice."

"What are eyes for if not to see! And it is a time for all to watch; especially, it is a time for Dagaeoga to watch with his eyes, his ears and all his senses."

"I've that feeling myself."

"Something is plotting against you. The slaver did not meet the spy for nothing."

"Why should men bother about one as insignificant as I am, when the world is plunged into a great war?"

"It is because Dagaeoga is in the way of somebody. He is very much in the way or so much trouble and risk would not be taken to remove him."

"I wonder what it is Tayoga. I know that Mr. Hardy and Mr. Huysman and doubtless others hold the key to this lock, but I feel quite sure they are not going to put it in my hand just at present."

"No, they will not, but it must be for very good reasons. No one ever had better friends than Dagaeoga has in them. If they do not choose to tell him anything it will be wise for him not to ask questions."

"That's the way I feel about it, and so I'm going to ask no questions."

A hulking figure barred their way, a red face glowed at them, and a rough voice demanded satisfaction.

"You fellow with the slick tongue, you had 'em laughing at me in the tavern," said Dobbs, the teamster. "You just the same as told 'em I was a liar when I said the French were coming."

The man was full of unreasoning anger, and he handled the butt end of a heavy whip. Yet Robert felt quite cool. His pistol was in his belt, and Tayoga was at his elbow.

"You are mistaken, my good Mr. Dobbs," he said gaily. "I would never tell a man he was a liar, particularly one to whom I had not been introduced. I try to be choice in my language. I was trained to be so by Mr. Alexander McLean, a most competent schoolmaster of this city, and I merely tried to disseminate a thought in the minds of the numerous audience gathered in the George Inn. My thought was unlike your thought, and so I was compelled to use words that did not resemble the words used by you. I was not responsible for the results flowing from them."

"I don't know what you mean," growled Dobbs. "You string a lot of big words together, and I think you're laughing at me again."

"Impossible, Mr. Dobbs. I could not be so impolite. My risibilities may be agitated to a certain extent, but laugh in the face of a stranger, never! Now will you kindly let us pass? The street here is narrow and we do not wish to crowd."

Dobbs did not move and his manner became more threatening than ever, the loaded whip swaying in his hand. Robert's light and frolicsome humour did not depart. He felt himself wholly master of the situation.

"Now, good Mr. Dobbs, kind Mr. Dobbs, I ask you once more to move," he said in his most wheedling manner. "The day is too bright and pleasant to be disturbed by angry feelings. My own temper is always even. Nothing disturbs me. I was never known to give way to wrath, but my friend whom you see by my side is a great Onondaga chieftain. His disposition is haughty and fierce. He belongs to a race that can never bear the slightest suspicion of an insult. It is almost certain death to speak to him in an angry or threatening manner. Friends as we have been for years, I am always very careful how I address him."

The teamster's face fell and he stepped back. The heavy whip ceased to move in a menacing manner in his hand.

"Prudence is always a good thing," continued Robert. "When a great Indian chieftain is a friend to a man, any insult to that man is a double insult to the chieftain. It is usually avenged with the utmost promptitude, and place is no bar. An angry glance even may invite a fatal blow."

Dobbs stepped to one side, and Robert and Tayoga walked haughtily on. The Onondaga laughed low, but with intense amusement.

"Verily it is well to have the gift of words," he said, "when with their use one, leaving weapons undrawn, can turn an enemy aside."

"I could not enter into a street fight with such a man, Tayoga, and diplomacy was needed. You'll pardon my use of you as a menace?"

"I'm at Dagaeoga's service."

"That being the case we'll now continue the search for our slaver."

They hunted carefully along the shores of the Hudson. Albany was a busy river port at all times, but it was now busier than ever, the pressure of war driving new traffic upon it from every side. Many boats were bringing supplies from further south, and others were being loaded with the goods of timid people, ready to flee from Montcalm and the French. Albany caught new trade both coming and going. The thrifty burghers profited by it and rejoiced.

"We've nothing to go on," said Robert, "and perhaps we couldn't tell the slaver's ship if we were looking squarely at it. Still, it seems to me it ought to be a small craft, slim and low, built for speed and with a sneaky look."

"Then we will seek such a vessel," said Tayoga.

Nothing answered the description. The river people were quite willing to talk and, the two falling into conversation with them, as if by chance, were able to account for every craft of any size. There was no strange ship that could be on any mysterious errand.

"It is in my mind, Dagaeoga," said Tayoga, "that this lies deeper than we had thought. The slaver would not have shown himself and he would not have talked with you so freely if he had not known that he would leave a hidden trail."

"It looks that way to me, Tayoga," said Robert, "and I think Garay must be in some kind of disguise. He would not venture so boldly among us if he did not have a way of concealing himself."

"It is in my mind, too, that we have underestimated the spy. He has perhaps more courage and resolution than we thought, or these qualities may have come to him recently. The trade of a spy is very useful to Montcalm just now. After his victory at Ticonderoga he will be anxious to know what we are doing here at Albany, and it will be the duty of Garay to learn. Besides, we put a great humiliation upon him that time we took his letter from him in the forest, and he is burning for vengeance upon us. It is not in the nature of Dagaeoga to wish revenge, but he must not blind himself on that account to the fact that others cherish it."

"It was the fortune of war. We have our disasters and our enemies have theirs."

"Yet we must beware of Garay. I know it, Dagaeoga."

"At any rate we can't find out anything about him and the slaver along the river, and that being the case I suggest that we go on to the house of Mynheer Jacobus, where we're pretty sure of a welcome."

Their greetings at the burgher's home were as warm as anybody could wish. Master McLean had left, and the rest were talking casually in the large front room, but the keen eyes of the Onondaga read the signs infallibly. This was a trail that could not be hidden from him.

"Other men have been here," he said a little later to Robert, when they were alone in the room. "There has been a council."

"How do you know, Tayoga?"

"How do I know, Dagaeoga? Because I have eyes and I use them. It is printed all over the room in letters of the largest type and in words of one syllable. The floor is of polished wood, Dagaeoga, and there is a great table in the centre of the chamber. The chairs have been moved back, but eight men sat around it. I can count the faint traces made by the chairs in the polish of the floor. They were heavy men—most of the men of Albany are heavy, and now and then they moved restlessly, as they talked. That was why they ground the chair legs against the polish, leaving there little traces which will be gone in another hour, but which are enough while they last to tell their tale.

"They moved so, now and then because their talk was of great importance. They smoked also that they might think better over what they were saying. A child could tell that, because smoke yet lingers in the room, although Caterina has opened the windows to let it out. Some of it is left low down in the corners, and under the chairs now against the wall. A little of the ash from their pipes has fallen on the table, showing that although Caterina has opened the windows she has not yet had time to clean the room. You and I know, Dagaeoga, that she would never miss any ash on the table. Master McLean smoked much, perhaps more than any of the others. He uses the strongest Virginia tobacco that he can obtain, and I know its odour of old. I smell it everywhere in the room. I also know the odour of the tobacco that Mynheer Jacobus uses, and it is strongest here by the mantel, showing that in the course of the council he frequently got up and stood here. Ah, there is ash on the mantel itself! He tapped it now and then with his pipe to enforce what he was saying. Mynheer Jacobus was much stirred, or he would not have risen to his feet to make speeches to the others."

"Can you locate Master Hardy also?"

"I think I can, Dagaeoga."

He ran around the room like a hound on the scent, and, at last, he stopped before a large massive locked chest of drawers that stood in the corner, a heavy mahogany piece that looked as if it had been imported from France or Italy.

"Master Jacobus came here," said the Onondaga. "I smell his tobacco. Ah, and Master Hardy came, too! I now smell his tobacco also. I remember that when we were in New York he smoked a peculiar, bitter West India compound which doubtless is brought to him regularly in his ships—men nearly always have a favourite tobacco and will take every trouble to get it. I recognize the odour perfectly. There are traces of the ash of both tobaccos on the chest of drawers, and Master Huysman and Master Hardy came here, because there are papers in this piece of furniture which Master Huysman wished to show to Master Hardy. They are in the third drawer from the top, because there is a little dust on the others, but none on the third. It fell off when it was opened, and was then shut again strongly after they were through."

Robert gazed with intense curiosity at the third drawer. The papers in it might concern himself—he believed Tayoga implicitly—but it was not for him to pry into the affairs of two such good friends. If they wished to keep their secret a while longer, then they had good reasons for doing so.

"Did the others come to the chest of drawers also, and look at the papers?" he asked.

The Onondaga knelt down and examined the polished floor.

"I do not think so," he replied at length. "It is wholly likely that Master Jacobus and Master Hardy came to the chest of drawers after the others had gone, and that the papers had no bearing on the matters they talked over in the council. Yes, it is so! It is bound to be so! The odour of their two tobaccos is stronger than any of the other odours in the room, showing that they were in here much longer than the others. It may be that the papers in the third drawer relate to Dagaeoga."

"I had that thought myself, Tayoga."

"Does Dagaeoga wish me to go further with it?"

"No, Tayoga. What those men desire to hide from us must remain hidden."

"I am glad Dagaeoga has answered that way, because if he had not I should have refused to go on, and yet I knew that was the way in which he would answer."

They went to another room in which they found Mr. Huysman, Mr. Hardy and the clerk, and Robert told of his meeting with the slaver. The face of Benjamin Hardy darkened.

"Tayoga is right," he said. "That man's presence here bodes ill for you, Robert."

"I'm not afraid. Besides I've too many friends," said Robert quietly.

"Both your statements are true, but you must be careful just the same," interjected Master Jacobus. "Nevertheless, we'll not be apprehensive. Master McLean iss coming back for supper, and we're going to make it a great affair, a real reunion for all of us. Caterina, helped by two stout coloured women, has been cooking all the afternoon, and I hope that you two boys have had enough exercise and excitement to whet your appetites. How iss it?"

"We have, sir!" they replied together, and with emphasis.

"And now to your old room. You'll find there in a closet clothes for both of you, Tayoga's of his own kind, that Caterina has preserved carefully, and at six o'clock come in to supper, which to-day iss to be our chief meal. I would not have Benjamin Hardy to come all the way from New York and say that I failed to set for him as good a meal as he would set for me if I were his guest in his city. Not only my hospitality but the hospitality of Albany iss at stake."

"I know, sir, that your reputation will not suffer," said Robert with great confidence.

He and Tayoga in their room found their clothes preserved in camphor and quickly made the change. Then they stood by the window, looking out on the pleasant domain, in which they had spent so many happy hours. Both felt a glow.

"Master Jacobus Huysman is a good man," said Robert.

"A wise, fat chief," said the Onondaga. "A kind heart and a strong head. He is worthy to rule. If he belonged to the league of the Hodenosaunee we would put him in a high place."

"Though he holds no office, I think he sits in a high place here. It is likely that the men who were around the table to-day came to him for counsel."

"It seems a good guess to me, Dagaeoga. Perhaps they take measures to meet the threat of Montcalm."

"They're our elders, and we'll let them do the thinking on that point just now. Somehow, I feel light of heart, Tayoga, and I want to enjoy myself."

"Even though the slaver and the spy are here, and we all believe that they threaten you?"

"Even so. My heart is light, nevertheless. My mind tells me that I ought to be apprehensive and sad, but my heart has taken control and I am hopeful and gay?"

"It is the nature of Dagaeoga, and he should give thanks to Manitou that he has been made that way. It is worth much more to him than the white man's gold."

"I *am* thankful, Tayoga. I'm thankful for a lot of things. How does this coat look on me?"

"It is small. You have grown much in the last year or two. Your frame is filling out and you are bigger every way. Still, it is a fine coat, and the knee breeches, stockings and buckled shoes are very splendid. If Dagaeoga does not look like a chief it is only because he is not old enough, and he at least looks like the son of a chief."

Robert contemplated himself in a small mirror with much satisfaction. "I'm frightfully tanned," he said. "Perhaps they wouldn't take me for a model of fashion in Paris or London, but here nearly everybody else is tanned also, and, after all, it's healthy."

The Onondaga regarded him with an amused smile.

"If Dagaeoga had the time and money he would spend much of both on dress," he said. "He loves to make a fine appearance."

"You say nothing but the truth," said Robert frankly. "I hope some day to have the very best clothes that are made. A man who respects his clothes respects himself. I know no sin in trying to please the eyes of others and incidentally myself. I note, Tayoga, that on occasion you array yourself with great splendour, and that, at all times, you're very particular about your attire."

"It is so, Dagaeoga. I spoke in terms of approval, not of criticism. Are you satisfied with yourself?"

"As much as possible under the circumstances. If I could achieve the change merely by making a wish I'd have the coat and breeches of a somewhat richer hue, and the buckles on the shoes considerably larger, but they'll do. Shall we rest here until Caterina calls us for supper?"

"I think so, Dagaeoga."

But it was not long until the summons came, and they went into the great dining-room, where the elder company was already gathered. Besides Mr. Huysman, Benjamin Hardy, Jonathan Pillsbury, and Alexander McLean, there were Nicholas Ten Broeck and Oliver Suydam, two of Albany's most solid burghers, and Alan Hervey, another visitor from New York, a thin man of middle years and shrewd looks, whom Robert took to be a figure in finance and trade. All the elders seemed to know one another well, and to be on the best of terms.

Robert and Tayoga were presented duly, and made their modest acknowledgments, sitting together near the end of the table.

"These lads, young as they are," said Master Jacobus Huysman, "have had much experience of the present war. One of them was a prisoner of the French at Ticonderoga and saw the whole battle, while the other fought in it. Before that they were in innumerable encounters and other perils, usually with the great hunter, David Willet, of whom you all know, and who, I regret, is not here."

"It is no more than thousands of others have done," said Robert, blushing under his tan.

Hervey regarded him and Tayoga with interest. The Onondaga was in full Indian dress, but Albany was used to the Iroquois, and that fact was not at all exceptional.

"War is a terrible thing," he said, "and whether a nation is or is not to endure depends very much upon its youth."

"We always think that present youth is inferior to what our own youth was," said Mr. Hardy. "That, I believe, is a common human failing. But Master McLean ought to know. Forty years of youth, year after year have passed through his hands. What say you, Alexander?"

"Youth is youth," replied the schoolmaster, weighing his sentences, "and by those words I mean exactly what I say. I think it changes but little through all the ages, and it is probably the same to-day that it was in old Babylon. I find in my schoolroom that the youth of this year is just like the youth of ten years ago, just as the youth of ten years ago was exactly like the youth of twenty, thirty and forty years ago."

"And what are the cardinal points of this formative age, Alexander?" asked Master Jacobus.

"Speaking mildly, I would call it concentration upon self. The horizon of youth is bounded by its own eye. It looks no farther. As it sees and feels it, the world exists for youth. We elders, parents, uncles, guardians and such, live for its benefit. We are merely accessories to the great and main fact, which is youth."

"Do you believe that to be true, Robert?" asked Master Benjamin Hardy, a twinkle in his eye.

"I hope it's not, sir," replied Robert, reddening again under his tan.

"But it's true and it will remain true," continued the schoolmaster judicially. "It was equally true of all of us who passed our youth long ago. I do not quarrel with it. I merely state a fact of life. Perhaps if I could I would not strip youth of this unconscious absorption in self, because in doing so we might deprive it of the simplicity and directness, the artless beliefs that make youth so attractive."

"I hold," said Mr. Hervey, "that age is really a state of mind. We believe certain things at twenty, others at thirty, others at forty, and so on. The beliefs of twenty are true at twenty, we must not try them by the tests of thirty, nor must we try those of thirty by the tests of forty or fifty. So how are we to say which age is the wiser, when every age accepts as true what it believes, and, so makes it true? I agree, too, with Mr. McLean, that I would not change the character of youth if I could. Looking back upon my own youth I find much in it to laugh at, but I did not laugh at it at the time. It was very real to me then, and so must its feelings be to the youth of to-day."

"We wade into deep waters," said Mynheer Jacobus, "and we may go over our heads. Ah, here are the oysters! I hope that all of you will find them to your liking."

A dozen were served for every guest—it was the day of plenty, the fields and woods and waters of America furnishing more food than its people could consume—and they approached them with the keen appetites of strong and healthy men.

"Perhaps we do not have the sea food here that you have in New York, Alan," said Master Jacobus with mock humility, "but we give you of our best."

"We've the finest oysters in the world, unless those of Baltimore be excepted," said Hervey, "but yours are, in truth, most excellent. Perhaps you can't expect to equal us in a specialty of ours. You'll recall old Tom Cotton's inn, out by the East River, and how unapproachably he serves oyster, crab, lobster and every kind of fish."

"I recall it full well, Alan. I rode out the Bowery road when I was last in New York, but I did not get a chance to go to old Tom's. You and I and Benjamin have seen some lively times there, when we were a bit younger, eh, Alan?"

"Aye, Jacobus, you speak truly. We were just as much concentrated upon self as the youth of to-day. And in our elderly hearts we're proud of the little frivolities and dissipations that were committed then. Else we would never talk of 'em and chuckle over 'em to one another."

"And what is more, we're not too old yet for a little taste of pleasure, now and then, eh, Alexander?"

The schoolmaster, appealed to so directly, pursed his thin lips, lowered his lids to hide the faint twinkle in his eyes, and replied in measured tones:

"I cannot speak for you, Jacobus. I've known you a long time and your example is corrupting, but I trust that I shall prove firm against temptation."

The oysters were finished. No man left a single one untouched on his plate, and then a thick chicken soup was served by two very black women in gay cotton prints with red bandanna handkerchiefs tied like turbans around their heads. Robert could see no diminution in the appetite of the guests, nor did he feel any decrease in his own. Mr. Hervey turned to him.

"I hear you saw the Marquis de Montcalm himself," he said.

"Yes, sir," replied Robert. "I saw him several times, at Ticonderoga, and before that in the Oswego campaign. I've been twice a prisoner of the French."

"How does he look?"

"Of middle age, sir, short, dark and very polite in speech."

"And evidently a good soldier. He has proved that and to our misfortune. Yet, I cannot but think that we will produce his master. Now, I wonder who it is going to be. Under the English system the best general does not always come forward first, and perhaps we've not yet so much as heard the name of the man who is going to beat Montcalm. That he will be beaten I've no doubt. We'll conquer Canada and settle North American affairs for all time. Perhaps it will be the last great war."

Robert was listening with the closest attention, and it seemed to him that the New Yorker was right. With Canada conquered and the French power expelled it would be the last great war so far as North America was concerned? How fallible men are! How prone they are to think when they have settled things for themselves they have settled them also for all future generations!

"And then," continued Mr. Hervey, "New York will become a yet greater port than it now is. It may even hope to rival Philadelphia in size and wealth. It will be London's greatest feeder."

The soup, not neglected in the least, gave way to fish, and then to many kinds of meat, in which game, bear, deer and wild fowl were conspicuous. Robert took a little of everything, but he was absorbed in the talk. He felt that these men were in touch with great affairs, and, however much they diverged from such subjects they had them most at heart. It was a thrilling thought that the future of North America, in some degree at least, might be determined around that very table at which he was sitting as a guest. He had knowledge and imagination enough to understand that it was not the armies that determined the fate of nations, but the men directing them who stood behind them farther back, in the dark perhaps, obscure, maybe never to become fully known, but clairvoyant and powerful just the same. He was resolved not to lose a word. So he leaned forward just a little in his seat, and his blue eyes sparkled.

"Dagaeoga is glad to be here," said Tayoga in an undertone.

"So I am, Tayoga. They talk of things of which I wish to hear."

"As I told you, these be sachems with whom we sit. They be not chiefs who lead in battle, but, like the *sachems*, they plan, and, like the medicine men, they make charms and incantations that influence the souls of the warriors and also the souls of those who lead them to battle."

"The same thought was in my own mind."

Wine smuggled from France or Spain was served to the men, though young Lennox and the Onondaga touched none. In truth, it was not offered to them, Master Jacobus saying, with a glance at Robert:

"I have never allowed you and Tayoga to have anything stronger than coffee in my house, and although you are no longer under my charge I intend to keep to the rule."

"We wish nothing more, sir," said Robert.

"As for me," said the Onondaga, "I shall never touch any kind of liquor. I know that it goes ill with my race."

"Yours, I understand, is the Onondaga nation," said Mr. Hervey, looking at him attentively.

"The Onondaga, and I belong to the clan of the Bear," replied Tayoga proudly. "The Hodenosaunee have held the balance in this war."

"That I know full well. I gladly give the great League ample credit. It has been a wise policy of the English to deal honestly and fairly with your people. In general the French surpass us in winning and holding the affections of the native races, but some good angel has directed us in our dealings with the Six Nations. Without their Indians the French could have done little against us. I hear of one of their leaders who has endeared himself to them in the most remarkable manner. There has been much talk in New York of the Chevalier de St. Luc, and being nearer the seat of action you've perhaps heard some of it here in Albany, Jacobus!"

Robert leaned a little farther forward and concentrated every faculty on the talk, but he said nothing.

"Yes, we've heard much of him, Alan," replied Master Jacobus. "I think he's the most dangerous foe that we have among Montcalm's lieutenants. He passes like a flame along the border, and yet report speaks well of him, too. All our men who have come in contact with him say he is a gallant and chivalrous foe."

225

Robert glanced at Master Benjamin Hardy, but the great merchant's face was blank.

"Robert saw him, too, when he was a prisoner among the French," said Mr. Huysman.

Mr. Hervey looked at Robert, who said:

"I saw him several times at Ticonderoga, where he was the chief adviser of Montcalm during the battle, and I've seen him often elsewhere. All that they say about him is true. He's a master of forest warfare, and his following is devoted."

He glanced again at Benjamin Hardy, but the New Yorker was helping himself to an especially tender bit of venison and his face expressed nothing but appreciation of his food. Robert sighed under his breath. They would never do more than generalize about St. Luc. Tayoga and he asked presently to be excused. The men would sit much longer over their nuts and wine, and doubtless when the lads were gone they would enter more deeply into those plans and ventures that lay so near their hearts.

"I think I shall wander among the trees behind the house," said Tayoga, when they were out of the dining-room. "I want fresh air, and I wish to hear the wind blowing among the leaves. Then I can fancy that I am back in the great forest, and my soul will be in peace."

"And commune, perhaps, with Tododaho on his star," said Robert, not lightly but in all seriousness.

"Even so, Dagaeoga. He may have something to tell me, but if he does not it is well to be alone for a while."

"I won't let you be alone just yet, because I'm going out with you, but I don't mean to stay long, and then you can commune with your own soul."

It was a beautiful night, cooled by a breeze which came crisp and strong from the hills, rustling through the foliage, already beginning to take on the tints of early autumn. After the warm room and many courses of food it was very grateful to the two lads who stood under the trees listening to the pleasant song of the breeze. But in five minutes Robert said:

"I'm going back into the house now, Tayoga. I can see your star in the clear heavens, and perhaps Tododaho will speak to you."

"I shall see. Farewell for an hour, Dagaeoga."

Robert went in.

CHAPTER 3

The Pursuit of Garay

Robert paused a few moments in the hall. Sounds of voices came from the dining room, showing that the supper was still in progress. He thought of going back there to listen to the talk, but he reflected that the time for youth at the table had passed. They were in their secrets now, and he strolled toward the large room that contained the chest of drawers.

A dim light from an unshuttered window shone into the apartment and it was in his mind to wait there for Tayoga, but he stopped suddenly at the door and stared in astonishment. A shadow was moving in the room, thin, impalpable and noiseless, but it had all the seeming of a man. Moreover, it had a height and shape that were familiar, and it reminded him of the spy, Garay.

He was too much surprised to move, and so he merely stared. Garay knelt before the chest of drawers and began to work at it with a small sharp tool that he drew from his coat. Robert saw, too, that his attention was centred on the third drawer from the top. Then he came out of his catalepsy and started forward, but in doing so his foot made a slight noise on the floor.

Garay leaped to his feet, gave Robert one glance and then disappeared through the open window, with incredible dexterity and speed. Robert stared again. The man was there and then he was not. It could not be Garay, but his ghost, some illusion, a trick of the eye or mind. Then he knew it was no fancy. With extraordinary assurance the man had come there to rifle the drawer—for what purpose Robert knew not. He ran to the window, but saw nothing save the peaceful night, the waving trees and the quiet lawn lying beyond. Then he walked to the chest and examined the third drawer, noticing new scratches around the lock. There was not the slightest doubt that Garay had been trying to open it.

He went to the door, resolved to tell Mr. Huysman at once of the attempt upon the chest, but he stopped irresolute. The low sounds of talk still came from the dining-room. He was only a boy and his was a most improbable tale. They might think he had been dreaming, though he knew full well that he had seen straight and true. And then Garay was gone, leaving no trace. No, he would not interrupt Mr. Huysman now, but he would talk it over with Tayoga.

He found the Onondaga standing among the trees, gazing with rapt vision at his star.

"Did Tododaho speak to you?" asked Robert.

"He did," replied Tayoga earnestly.

"What did he say?"

"That the great war will go on, and that you and I and the Great Bear, who is away, will encounter many more perils. The rest is veiled."

"And while we take our ease, Tayoga, our enemies are at work."

"What does Dagaeoga mean?"

"I went into the room containing the chest of drawers, the story of which you read, and found there Garay, the spy, trying to open it."

"Dagaeoga does not dream?"

"Oh, I thought for a moment or two that I did, but it was reality. Garay escaped through the open window, and, on the lock of the third drawer, were scratches that he left where he had been working with a sharp tool. Come, Tayoga, and look at them."

The two went into the house. Robert lighted a lamp for better light, and Tayoga knelt before the drawer, giving it a long and close examination.

"Garay is a very clever man," he said at last, "much cleverer, perhaps, than we gave him the credit of being."

"I think so too," said Robert.

"As events show, he came into this house to obtain the papers in this drawer, and you and I feel quite certain that those papers concern you. And as you saw him and the slaver together, it indicates that they have some plot against you, what I know not. But the papers here have much to do with it."

"Do you think I should speak of it to Master Jacobus and Mr. Hardy now?"

"I think not, Dagaeoga. Whatever is the mystery about you it is evident that they do not wish to tell you of it yet. So, being what you are, you will not ask them, but wait until such time as they see fit. I think these scratches on the lock were made by the sharp point of a

228

hunting knife. Garay did not succeed in opening it, though it is likely that he would have done so if you had not interrupted him."

"When he saw me he was gone like a flash. I did not know a man could skip through a window with so much celerity."

"One has to be skilful at such things to carry on the trade of a spy. That is why he could have opened this lock, large and strong as it is, with the point of his hunting knife had he been allowed time, and that is why he flew through the window like a bird when you came upon him."

He examined the window, and then laughed a little.

"But he did not go without leaving further proof of himself," he said. "Here on the sill is the faintest trace of blood where he bruised his hand or wrist in his rapid flight."

"Suppose you try to trail him, Tayoga. I believe you could find out which way he went, even here in Albany. The men will talk in there a long time, and won't miss us. There's a fair moon."

"I will try," said Tayoga in his precise fashion. "First we will look at the ground under the window."

They went outside and the Onondaga examined the grass beneath it, the drop being five or six feet.

"As he had to come down hard, he ought to have left traces," said Robert.

"So he did, Dagaeoga. I find several imprints, and there also are two or three drops of blood, showing that he scratched his hand considerably when he went through the window. Here go the traces, leading north. Garay, of course, knows this immediate locality well, as he observed it closely when he made his attempt upon you before. It is lucky that it rained yesterday, leaving the ground soft. We may be able to follow him quite a distance."

"If anybody can follow him, you can."

"It is friendship that makes Dagaeoga speak so. The trail continues in its original course, though I think that sooner or later it will turn toward the river."

"Meaning that Garay will meet the slaver somewhere, and that the natural place of the latter is on the water."

"Dagaeoga reasons well. That, I think, is just what Garay will do. It is likely, too, that he will curve about the town. If he went upon a hard street we would lose him, since he would leave no trail there, but he will keep away because he does not wish to be seen. Ah, he now turns from the houses and into the fields! We shall be able to follow him. The moon is our friend. It is pouring down rays enough to disclose his trail, if trail he leaves."

They were soon beyond the houses and climbed three fences dividing the fields. At the third, Tayoga said:

"Garay paused here and rested. There is a drop of blood on the top rail. He probably sat there and looked back to see if he was followed. Ah, here is a splinter on a lower rail freshly broken!"

"What do you make of it, Tayoga?"

"The spy was angry, angry that his effort, made at such great risk, should have failed through the mere chance of your coming into the room at that particular time. He was angry, too, that he had bruised his hand so badly that it bled, and continued to bleed. So, his disappointment made him grind his heel against the rail and break the splinter."

"I'm glad he felt that way. A man in his trade ought to suffer many disappointments."

"When he had satisfied himself that no pursuit was in sight, he jumped to the ground. Here are deep imprints made by his descending weight, and now he becomes less careful. Albany is behind us, and he thinks all danger of pursuit has passed. I see a little brook ahead, and it is safe to say that he will kneel at it and drink."

"And also to bathe his wounded hand."

"Even so, Dagaeoga. Lo, it is as we said! Here are the imprints of his knees, showing that he refreshed himself with water after his hurried flight. The ground on the other side of the brook is soft and we shall be able to find his imprints there, even if it were pitch dark. Now I think they will turn very soon toward the river."

"Yes, they're curving. Here they go, Tayoga."

The trail led across a field, over a hill, and then through a little wood, where Tayoga was compelled to go slowly, hunting about like a hound, trying to trace a scent. But wherever he lost it he finally picked it up again, and, when they emerged from the trees, they saw the river not far ahead.

"Our trail will end at the stream," said Tayoga confidently.

As he had predicted, the imprints led directly to the river, and there ended their pursuit also. The Hudson flowed on in silence. There was nothing on its bosom.

"The slaver in a boat was waiting for him here," said Tayoga. "I think we can soon find proof of it."

A brief examination of the bank showed traces where the prow had rested.

"It was probably a boat with oars for two," he said. "The slaver sat in it most of the time, but he grew impatient at last and leaving the boat walked up the bank a little distance. Here go his steps, showing very plainly in the soft earth in the moonlight, and here come those of Garay to meet him. They stood at the top of the bank under this oak, and the spy told how he had failed. Doubtless, the slaver was much disappointed, but he did not venture to upbraid Garay, because the spy is as necessary to him as he is to the spy. After they talked it over they walked down the bank together—see their trails going side by side—entered the boat and rowed away. I wish the water would leave a trail, too, that we might follow them, but it does not."

"Do you think they'll dare go back to Albany?"

"The slaver will. What proof of any kind about anything have we? Down! Dagaeoga, down!"

Fitting the action to the word, the Onondaga seized Robert by the shoulders suddenly and dragged him to the earth, falling with him. As he did so a bullet whistled where Robert's head had been and a little puff of smoke rose from a clump of bushes on the opposite shore.

"They're there in their boat among the bushes that grow on the water's edge!" exclaimed Tayoga. "I ought to have thought of it, but I did see a movement among the bushes in time! I cannot see their faces or the boat, either, but I know it is Garay and the slaver."

"I have no weapon," said Robert. "It did not occur to me that I would need one."

"I have a pistol in my tunic. I always carry one when I am in the white man's country. It is wise."

"Under the circumstances, I think we'd better slip away and leave the spy and the slaver to enjoy the river as they please, for to-night at least."

He was about to rise, but Tayoga pulled him down a second time and a report heavier than the first came from the far shore. Another bullet passed over their heads and struck with a sough in the trunk of a big tree beyond them.

"That was from a rifle. The other was from a pistol," said Tayoga. "It is the slaver, of course, who has the rifle, and they mean to make it very warm for us. Perhaps an unexpected chance gives them hope to do here what they expected to achieve later on."

"Meaning a final disposition of me?"

"That was in my mind, Dagaeoga. I think it is you at whom they will shoot and you would better creep away. Lie almost flat and edge along until you come to the trees, which are about twenty yards behind us. There, you will be safe."

"And leave you alone, Tayoga! What have I ever done to make you think I'd do such a thing?"

"It is not Tayoga whom they want. It is Dagaeoga. I cannot go without taking a shot at them, else my pistol would burn me inside my tunic. Be wise as I am, Dagaeoga. Always carry a pistol when you are in the white man's towns. Life is reasonably safe only in the red man's forest."

"It looks as if you were right, Tayoga, but remember that I stay here with you as long as you stay."

"Then keep close to the earth. Roll back a bit and you will be sheltered better by that little rise."

Robert obeyed, and it was well that he did so, as the heavy rifle cracked a second time, and a ploughing bullet caused fine particles of earth to fly over him. Tayoga levelled his pistol at the flash and smoke, but did not pull the trigger.

"Why didn't you fire, Tayoga?" asked Robert.

"I could not see well enough. They and their boat are still hidden by the bushes in which they remain, because from there they can command the bank where we lie."

"Then it looks as if each side held the other. If they come out of the bushes you use your pistol on 'em, and if we retreat farther they use their rifle on us. You'll notice, Tayoga, that we're in a little dip, and if we go out of it on our far side in retreat we'll make a target of ourselves. If they leave the bushes on their far side to climb their own bank they come into view. It's checkmate for both."

"It is so, Dagaeoga. It is a difficult position for you, but not for me. We of the red races learn to have patience, because we are not in such a hurry to consume time as you white people are."

"That is true, but it is not a moment for a discussion of the relative merits of white and red."

"We are likely to have plenty of leisure for it, since I think we are doomed to a long wait."

"I think you're happy over it, Tayoga. Your voice has a pleased ring."

"I'm not unhappy. I see a chance to gratify a curiosity that I have long had. I wish to see whether the white race, even in great danger, where it is most needed, has as much patience as the red. Ah, Dagaeoga, you were incautious! Do not raise your head again. You, at least, do not have as much patience as the occasion requires."

The third bullet had passed so near Robert that cold shivers raced over his body and he resolved not to raise his head again a single inch, no matter what the temptation.

"Remember that it is you whom they want," said Tayoga in his precise, book English. "Having the rifle they can afford to try shots at longer range, but with the pistol I must wait until I can see them clearly. Well, Dagaeoga, it is a fine evening, not too cold, we need fresh air after a big supper, and perhaps one could not find a pleasanter place in which to pass the night."

"You mean that we may lie here until day?"

"Dagaeoga speaks as if that would be remarkable. My father waited once three days and three nights beside a run to obtain a deer. He neither ate nor drank during that time, but he went home with the deer. If he could wait so long for something to eat, cannot we wait as long when our lives are at stake?"

"According to the laws of proportion we should be willing to stay here a week, at least. Can you see anything moving in the bushes over there, Tayoga?"

"Not a thing. They too are patient men, the slaver and the spy, and having missed several times with the rifle they will bide a while, hoping that we will expose ourselves."

The Onondaga settled himself comfortably against the earth, his pistol lying on the little rise in front of him, over which his eyes watched the clump of bushes into which the boat had gone. If the slaver and the spy made any attempt to slip forth, whether on the water or up the bank, he would certainly see them, and he would not withhold the pressure of his finger on the trigger.

The full moon still shone down, clothing the world in a beautiful silver light. The stars in myriads danced in a sky of soft, velvety blue. The river flowed in an illuminated, molten mass. A light wind hummed a pleasant song among the brown leaves. Robert had a curious feeling of rest and safety. He was quite sure that neither the slaver nor the spy could hit him while he lay in the dip, and no movement of theirs would escape the observation of Tayoga, the incomparable sentinel. He relaxed, and, for a few moments, his faculties seemed to fall into a dreamy state.

"If I should go to sleep, Tayoga," he said, "wake me up when you need me."

"You will not go to sleep."

"How do you know? I feel a lot like it."

"It is because the worry you felt a little while ago has passed. You believe that in this duel of patience we shall conquer."

"I know that we'll conquer, Tayoga, because you are here."

"Dagaeoga's flattery is not subtle."

"It's not flattery. It's my real belief."

The night wore on. The breeze that rustled the leaves was warm and soothing, and Robert's sleepiness increased. But he fought against it. He used his will and brought his body roughly to task, shaking himself violently. He also told himself over and over again that they were in a position of great danger, that he must be on guard, that he must not leave the duty to the Onondaga alone. Such violent efforts gradually drove sleep away, and raising his head a few inches he looked over the rise.

The whole surface of the river still showed clearly in the moonlight, as it flowed slowly and peacefully on, silver in tint most of the time, but now and then disclosing shades of deep blue. Directly opposite was the clump of bushes in which the slaver and the spy had pushed their boat. An easy shot for a rifle, but a hard one for a pistol.

Robert studied the bushes very closely, trying to discern their enemies among them, but he saw nothing there save a slight movement of the leaves before the wind. It was possible that his foes had slipped away, going up the other bank in some manner unseen. Since he could discover no trace of them he began to believe that it was true, and he raised his head another inch for a better look.

Crack! went the rifle, and the bullet sang so close to his face that at first he thought he was hit. He stared for a moment at the puff of smoke rising from the bushes, his faculties in a daze. Then he came to himself all at once and dropped back abruptly, feeling his head gingerly to see that it was sound everywhere. But he was certain that the slaver and the spy were there.

"Dagaeoga was rash," said the Onondaga.

"I know now I was. Still, I feel much relief because I've settled a problem that was troubling me."

"What was it?"

"I wasn't sure that our enemies were still there. Now I am."

"If you feel like it yet, I think you may go to sleep. Nothing is likely to happen for a long time, and I can awaken you at any moment."

"Thank you, Tayoga, but I've banished the wish. I know I can't do anything without a weapon, but I can give you moral help. They're bound to try something sometime or other, because when the day comes other people may arrive—we're not so far from Albany—and they're guilty, we're not. We don't mind being seen."

"It is so, Dagaeoga. You talk almost like a man. At times you reason well. Finding that we are as patient as they are they will make a movement in an hour or two, though I think we are not likely to see it."

"An hour or two? Then I think I'd better make myself comfortable again."

He settled his body against the brown turf which was soft and soothing, and, in spite of himself, the wish for sleep returned. It was so quiet that one was really invited to go away to slumberland, and then he had eaten much at the big supper. After a long time, he was sinking into a doze when he was dragged back abruptly from it by a report almost at his ear that sounded like the roar of a cannon. He sat up convulsively, and saw Tayoga holding in his hand a smoking pistol.

"Did you hit anything?" he asked.

"I saw a stir in the bushes over there," replied the Onondaga, "and fired into them. I do not think my bullet found its target, but we will wait. I have ammunition in my pocket, and meanwhile I will reload."

He put in the powder and ball, still keeping an eye on the bushes. He waited a full half hour and then he handed the pistol to Robert.

"Watch, and use it if need be," he said, "while I swim over and get the boat."

"Get the boat! What are you talking about, Tayoga? Has the moon struck you with a madness?"

"Not at all, Dagaeoga. The slaver and the spy are gone, leaving behind them the boat which they could not take with them, and we might as well have it."

"Are you sure of what you are saying?"

"Quite sure, Dagaeoga. But for precaution's sake you can watch well with the pistol and cover my approach."

He thrust the weapon into Robert's hand, quickly threw off his clothing and sprang into the water, swimming with strong strokes toward the dense, high bushes that lined the opposite shore. Robert watched the lithe, brown figure cleave the water, disappear in the bushes and then reappear a moment or two later, rowing a boat. All had fallen out as the Onondaga had said, and he quickly came back to the western side.

"It is a good boat," he said, "a trophy of our victory, and we will use it. Take the oars, Dagaeoga, while I put on my clothes again. Our long wait is over."

Robert sprang into the boat, while Tayoga, standing upon the bank, shook himself, making the drops fly from him in a shower.

"Which way did they go?" asked Robert.

"They crept down the stream among the bushes between the water and the cliff. They could force their bodies that way but not the boat. I felt sure they had gone after my pistol shot, because I saw some of the bushes moving a little against the wind farther down the stream. It was proof. Besides, they had to go, knowing that day would soon be here."

235

He reclothed himself and stepped back into the boat, taking up the second pair of oars.

"Let us return to Albany in triumph by the river," he said.

"You think there is no danger of our being fired upon from ambush?"

"None at all. The slaver and spy will be anxious to get away and escape observation. They would be glad enough to shoot at us, but they would never dare to risk it."

"And so ours has been the triumph. Once more we've been victorious over our enemies, Tayoga."

"But they will strike again, and Dagaeoga must beware."

They rowed into the middle of the river and dropped slowly down the stream. Robert had so much confidence in the Onondaga that he felt quite safe for the present at least. It seemed to his sanguine temperament that as they had escaped every danger in the past so they would escape every one in the future. He was naturally a child of hope, in which he was fortunate.

The gray skies broke away in the east, and the dawn was unrolled, a blaze of rose and gold. The surface of the river glittered in the morning sun. The houses of Albany stood out sharp and clear in the first light of the morning.

"They'll be anxious about us at Mr. Huysman's," said Robert.

"So they will," said Tayoga. "As I have said to you before, Dagaeoga, it will be wise for us to return to the wilderness as soon as we can. The red man's forest still seems to be safer than the white man's town."

They reached Albany, tied up the boat, and walked in the early dawn to the house of Mynheer Jacobus Huysman, where Caterina met them at the door with a cry of joy. Master Jacobus appeared in a few moments, his face showing great relief.

"Where have you lads been?" he exclaimed.

"We have been in much danger," replied Robert soberly, "but we're out of it now, and here we are."

The others, all of whom had lain down fully dressed, came soon, and Robert told the story of the night, beginning with the spy's attempt upon the third drawer in the chest of drawers. Mr. Huysman and Mr. Hardy exchanged glances.

"That drawer does contain papers of value," said Mr. Huysman, "but I'll see that they're put today in a place into which no thief can break."

"And it would perhaps be well for young Mr. Lennox also to keep himself in a safe place," said Mr. Hervey, who had spent the night too in Mr. Huysman's house. "It seems that a most determined effort is being made against him."

"Thank you, sir, for your interest in me," said Robert, "and I'll do my best to be cautious."

He ate a hearty breakfast and then, on the insistence of Master Jacobus, lay down. Declaring that he would not sleep, he fell asleep nevertheless in ten minutes, and did not awake until the afternoon. He learned then that Albany was feeling better. Many of the rumours that Montcalm was advancing had been quieted. Scouts brought word that he was yet at Lake Champlain, and that he had not given any sign of marching upon Albany.

Robert learned also that the council in Mr. Huysman's house had been to take measures of offense as well as defence. Alan Hervey spoke for the leading men of New York and he was to tell Albany for them that they would make a mighty effort. A campaign had been lost, but another would be undertaken at once, and it would be won. They had no doubt that Boston, Baltimore and Charleston were doing the same. The strong men of the Colonies intended to assure England of their staunch support, and the English-speaking race not dreaming perhaps even then that it was to become such a mighty factor in the world, would fight to the bitter end for victory.

"I go back by sloop to New York tomorrow," said Mr. Hardy to him, "and of course Jonathan Pillsbury goes with me. There are important affairs of which I must speak to you some day, Robert, and believe me, my lad, I do not speak of them to you now because the reasons are excellent. I know you've borne yourself bravely in many dangers, and I know you will be as strong of heart in others to come. I'm sorry I have to go away without seeing Willet, but you could not be in safer hands than his."

"And I know, too," said Robert earnestly, "that I could have no better friend than you, Mr. Hardy, nor you, Mr. Pillsbury."

He spoke with the frank sincerity that always made such an appeal to everybody, and Mr. Hardy patted him approvingly on the shoulder.

"And don't forget me, Mr. Lennox," said Mr. Hervey. "I want you to be my guest in New York some day. We live in tremendous times, and so guard yourself well."

They left with a favouring breeze and the swift sloop that bore them was soon out of sight. Robert, Tayoga, Mr. Huysman and Master McLean, who had seen them off, walked slowly back up the hill to Mr. Huysman's house.

"I feel that they brought us new courage," said Master Jacobus.

"New York iss a great town, a full equal to Boston, though they are very unlike, and do not forget, Robert, that the merchants and financiers have much to say in a vast war like this which is vexing the world today."

"I do not forget it, sir," said Robert. "I have seen New York and its wealth and power. They say that it has nearly twenty thousand inhabitants—and some day I hope to see London too. Lieutenant Grosvenor is coming. Can we stop and speak to him?"

"Of course, my lad, but Master Alexander and I have pressing business and you will pardon us if we go on. If Lieutenant Grosvenor will come to my house as my guest bring him, and tell him to stay as long as he will."

"That I will, sir, and gladly," said Robert, as he and Tayoga turned aside to meet the young Englishman.

The meeting had all the warmth of youth and of real liking. Grosvenor was fully restored now and his intense interest in everything that was happening was undiminished. They strolled on together. Robert and Tayoga did not say anything for the present about their adventure of the preceding night with the slaver and the spy, but Robert delivered the invitation of Master Jacobus.

"If you can get leave come and stay a while with us in the house of Mr. Huysman," he said. "He bids me give you a most hospitable welcome, and when he says a thing he means not only what he says but a good deal more, too. You'll have a fine bed and you may have to eat more than you can well stand."

"It appeals to me," said Grosvenor, "and I'd come, but I'm leaving Albany in a day or two."

"Leaving Albany! I suppose I shouldn't ask where you're going."

"I'll tell you without the asking. I'm going with some other officers to Boston, where we're to await orders. Between you and me, Lennox, I think we shall take a sea voyage from Boston, maybe to Nova Scotia."

"And that, I think, indicates a new expedition from England and a new attack upon Canada and the French, but from another point. It's like the shadow of great events."

"It seems so to me, too. Come with us, Lennox. All your friends have got into the Royal Americans, and I think they too are going east. We could raise enough influence to secure you a lieutenant's commission."

Robert's heart swelled, but he shook his head.

"You tempt me, Grosvenor," he said. "I'd like to go. I think you and

238

the others will be in the thick of great events, but I could never desert Tayoga and Willet. I feel that my business, whatever it is, is here. But we may meet on the front again, though we'll come by different routes."

"If you can't you can't, and that's an end of it, but I'm glad, Lennox, that I've known you and Tayoga and Willet, and that we've shared perils. I'm to meet the Philadelphians and the Virginians at the George Inn again. Will you two come on?"

"Gladly," said Robert.

They found that the others had already arrived, and they were full of jubilation. Colden, Wilton and Carson were leaving their troop with regret, but the Royal Americans raised in the Colonies were a picked regiment ranking with the best of the British regulars. Stuart and Cabell, coming from the south, which was now more remote from the scene of war, were delighted at the thought that they would be in the heart of the conflict. They, too, were insistent that Robert come with them, but again he refused. When he and Tayoga left them and walked back to the house of Mr. Huysman the Onondaga said:

"Dagaeoga was right to stay. His world is centred here."

"That's so. I feel it in every bone of me. Besides, I'm thinking that we'll yet have to deal with Garay and that slaver. I'll be glad though when Willet comes. Then we can decide upon our next step."

Robert was too active to stay quietly at the house of Mr. Huysman. Only their host, Tayoga and he were present at their supper that evening, and, as the man was rather silent, the lads respected his preoccupation, believing that he was concerned with the great affairs in which he was having a part. After supper Tayoga left for the camp on the flats to see an Onondaga runner who had arrived that day, and Mr. Huysman, still immersed in his thoughts, withdrew into the room containing the great chest of drawers.

Robert spent a little while in the chamber that he and Tayoga had used, looking at the old, familiar things, and then he wandered restlessly outside, where he stood, glancing down at the lights of the town. He felt lonely for the moment. Everybody else was doing something, and he liked to be with people. Perhaps some of his friends had come to the George Inn. A light was burning there and he would go and see.

There was a numerous company at the inn, but it included nobody that Robert knew, and contenting himself with a look from the doorway, he turned back. Then the masts and spars in the river, standing up a black tracery against the clear, moonlit sky, interested him, and he walked casually to the bank. Some activity was still visible on the vessels, but tiring of them soon he turned away.

It was dark on the shore, but Robert started violently. If fancy were not playing tricks with him he saw the shadow of Garay once more. The figure had appeared about twenty yards ahead of him and then it was gone. Robert was filled with fierce anger that the man should show such brazen effrontery, and impulsively he pursued. Profiting by his experience with the spy, he now had a pistol in his pocket, and clutching the butt of it he hurried after the elusive shadow.

He caught a second glimpse. It was surely Garay, and he was running along the shore, up the stream.

Robert's anger rose by leaps. The spy's presumption was beyond all endurance, but he would make him pay for it this time. He drew his pistol that he might be ready should Garay turn and attack, though he did not believe that he would do so, and sped after him. But always the shadow flitted on before, and the distance between them did not seem to diminish.

They soon left all houses behind, although Robert, in his excitement, did not notice it, and then he saw that at last he was gaining.

"Stop, Garay! Stop, or I shoot!" he cried.

The spy halted, and Robert, covering him with his pistol, was about to approach when he heard a step behind him. He whirled, but it was too late. A stunning weight crashed down upon his head, and he fell into oblivion.

CHAPTER 4

Out to Sea

When Robert came back from the far country in which he had been dwelling, for a little space, he looked into a long face, with eyes set close and a curved nose. He was dimly conscious that it was a familiar countenance, but he could not yet remember where he had seen it before, because he could not concentrate his thoughts. His head was heavy and aching. He knew that he lived, but he did not know much more.

The staring face was distinctly unpleasant and menacing. He gazed into it, trying to recall the owner, but the effort was still too great. Then he became conscious that he was lying upon his back and that he was moving. Trees on his right and trees on his left, some distance away, were filing past. Two men on each side were pulling hard on oars, and then it slowly entered his mind that he was in a boat.

He made another and stronger effort to gather up his wandering faculties and then he realized with a jerk that the face looking into his was that of the slaver. Making a supreme effort he sat up. The slaver laughed.

"So, Peter Smith," he said, "you've decided to come back a second time. I knew that you couldn't stay away always from such a good, kind captain as I am. I saw the light of welcome in your eyes when we met so unexpectedly at the George Inn, and I decided that it was only a question of time until you came into my service again."

Robert stared at him. His mind, which would not work hitherto, recovered its power with great suddenness. All his faculties were keen and alert, and they coordinated smoothly and perfectly. He had been trapped. He had been struck from behind, while he pursued Garay with such eagerness. He had been careless, and once more he was in the power of the slaver. And there was the spy, too, in the prow of the boat, with his back to him, but that very back seemed to express insolent triumph. He felt a great sinking of the heart, but in a few moments recalled his courage. His was a spirit that could not be crushed. His head still ached and he was a prisoner, but his courage was invincible, and he put on a light manner.

"Yes, I've come back," he said. "You see, Captain, there are some things concerning you of which I'm not sure, and I couldn't part from you permanently until I learned them."

"I'm glad of it, Peter. You've an inquiring mind, I know, and you'll have plenty of opportunity to learn everything about me. We're likely to be together for quite a while."

Robert looked around. He was in a long boat, and there were four oarsmen, stout fellows, rough of looks and with hangers and pistols in their belts. Garay and the captain completed the party, and both the slaver and the spy were armed heavily. He saw that he had no earthly chance of escape at present, and he resigned himself for the moment. The slaver read his look.

"I'm glad, Peter," he said, "that you've given up the thought of leaving us that was flitting around in your head a minute or two ago. You're in a better state of mind now, and it was not possible anyway. Nor will there be any storm to send you away from me again. A chance like that wouldn't happen once in a hundred times. I suppose you understand where you are."

"I'm in a boat a few miles above Albany, and I think that before long you'll turn and go back down the stream."

"Why, Peter?"

"Because there's nothing for you to go to up the stream. If you kept on you'd arrive in the Indian country, and I doubt whether that's any part of your plan."

"Clever, Peter, clever! and well reasoned. I see that your intellect's as good as ever. You must rise above the place of a common seaman. When you're a little older there's a mate's berth for you."

Garay turned for the first time, and his malignant look of triumph was not veiled at all.

"You and Willet and the Indian thought you were very clever there in the forest when you compelled me to tell where the paper was hid," he said, "but you forgot that I might make repayment. We've taken you out of Albany from the very centre of your friends, and you'll never see them again."

"Theatricals! theatricals!" said Robert, preserving his gay manner, though his heart was low within him. "A cat has nine lives, but I have ten. I've been twice a prisoner of the French, and my presence here is proof that I escaped both times. When I tire of your society and that of the captain I'll leave you."

"No quarrelling! no quarrelling!" said the slaver. "I never allow it among my men. And now, Peter, I must insure your silence for a little while."

Two of the men who were rowing dropped their oars, seized him, bound and gagged him. He struggled at first against the indignity, but, soon realizing its futility, lay inert on the bottom of the boat.

"Good judgment, Peter," said the slaver, looking down at him. "It's never wise to struggle against a certainty. You've the makings of a fine officer in you."

The two resumed their oars, and the boat, turning abruptly, as Robert had surmised it would, went down the stream. The men ceased to talk and the lad on his back looked up at the sky in which but few stars twinkled. Heavy clouds floated past the moon, and the night was darkening rapidly. Once more his heart sank to the uttermost depths, and it had full cause to do so. For some reason he had been pursued with singular malice and cunning, and now it seemed that his enemies were triumphant. Tayoga could trail him anywhere on land, but water left no trail. He was sure that his captors would keep to the river.

The speed of the boat increased with the efforts of the rowers and the favour of the current. Soon it was opposite Albany and then the men rowed directly to a small schooner that lay at anchor, having come up the stream the day before. Robert was lifted on board and carried into the depths of the vessel, where they took out the gag and put him on the floor. The captain held a lantern over him and said:

"Garay is telling you good-bye, Peter. He's sorry he can't go with us, but he'll be having business on the Canadian frontier. He feels that the score is about even with you for that business of the letter in the forest, and that later on he'll attend also to the hunter and the Onondaga."

"And I wish you a pleasant life on the West Indian plantations," said Garay. "They still buy white labour there in both the French and British islands. It does not matter to me to which the captain sells you, for in either case it means a life of hard labour in the sugar cane. Few ever escape, and you never will."

Robert turned quite sick. So this was the plan. To sell him into slavery in the West Indies. Kidnapping was not at all uncommon then in both the Old World and the New, and they seemed to have laid their plans well. As the slaver had said, there was not one chance in a hundred of another storm. Again the captain read his mind.

"You don't like the prospect," he said, "and I'll admit myself that it's not a cheerful one. I've changed my opinion of you, Peter. I thought you'd make a fine sailor and that you might become a mate some day, but I've seen a light. You're not a good sailor at all. The stuff's not in you. But you're strong and hearty and you'll do well in the sugar cane. If the sun's too hot and your back bends too much just reflect that for a white man it's not a long life and your troubles will be over, some day."

Robert's old indomitable spirit flamed up.

"I never expect to see a West Indian plantation, not on this journey, at least," he said. "You and that miserable spy boast that you took me out of the very centre of my friends, and I tell you in reply that if I have enemies who follow me I also have friends who are truer in their friendship than you are in your hate, and they'll come for me."

"That's the spirit. I never heard another lad sling words in the noble fashion you do. You'll live a deal longer on the plantations than most of 'em. Now, Garay, I think you can go. It will be the last farewell for you two."

The exulting spy left the close little place, and Robert felt that a breath of hate went with him. His feet disappeared up a narrow little stair, and the slaver cut the cords that bound Robert.

"You'll be locked in here," he said, "and it's not worth while to damage good property by keeping it tied up too long."

"That's so," said Robert, trying to preserve a light manner. "You want to keep me strong and active for the work on the plantations. A white slave like a black one ought to be in good health."

The captain laughed. He was in high humour. Robert knew that he felt intense satisfaction because he was taking revenge for his mortification when he was defeated in the duel with swords before his own men by a mere boy. Evidently that would rankle long with one of the slaver's type.

"I'm glad to see you recognize facts so well, Peter," he said. "I see that you've an ambition to excel on the plantations, perhaps to be the best worker. Now, Garay, telling me of that little adventure of his in the forest with the hunter, the Indian and you, wanted me to be very careful about your rations, to put you on a sparing diet, so to speak. He thought it would be best not to let you have anything to eat for two or three days. His idea rather appealed to me, too, but, on the other hand, I couldn't impair your value, and so I decided against him."

"I'm not hungry," said Robert.

"No, but you will be. You're young and strong, and that wound on your head where I had to hit you with the butt of my pistol doesn't amount to much."

Robert put up his hands, felt of the back of his head, where the ache was, and found that the hair was matted together by congealed blood. But he could tell that the hurt was not deep.

"I'll leave you now," said the slaver in the same satisfied tone, "and I hope you'll enjoy the voyage down the river. There's a good wind blowing and we start in a half hour."

He went out, taking the lantern with him, and bolted the door heavily behind him. Then Robert felt despair for a while. It was much worse to be a prisoner on the ship than in the French camp or in the village of the partisan, Langlade. There he had been treated with consideration and the fresh winds of heaven blew about him, but here he was shut up in a close little hole, and his captors rejoiced in his misery.

It was quite dark in the tiny galley, and the only air that entered came from a small porthole high over a bunk. He stood upon the bank and brought his face level with the opening. It was not more than four inches across, but he was able to inhale a pure and invigorating breeze that blew from the north, and he felt better. The pain in his head was dying down also, and his courage, according to its habit, rose fast. In a character that nature had compounded of optimistic materials hope was always a predominant factor.

He could see nothing through the porthole save a dark blur, but he heard the creaking of cordage and the slatting of sails. He did not doubt that the slaver had told the truth when he said the schooner would soon start, and there was no possibility of escaping before then. Nevertheless, he tried the door, but could not shake it. Then he went back to the porthole for the sake of the air, and, because, if he could not have freedom for himself, he could at least see a little way into the open world.

The creaking of cordage and slatting of sails increased, he felt the schooner heave and roll beneath him, and then he knew that they were leaving Albany. It was the bitterest moment of his life. To be carried away in that ignominious manner, from the very centre of his friends, from a town in which he had lived, and that he knew so well was a terrible blow to his pride. For the moment apprehension about the future was drowned in mortification.

He heard heavy footsteps overhead, and the sound of commands, and the schooner began to move. He continued to stand on the bunk, with his eyes at the porthole. He was able to see a dark shore, moving past, slowly at first and then faster. The dim outlines of houses showed and he would have shouted for help, but he knew that it was impossible to make any one hear, and pride restrained.

The blurred outlines of the houses ceased and Albany was gone. Doubtless the schooner had appeared as an innocent trader with the proper licenses, and the slaver, having awaited its arrival, had come on ahead to the town. He was compelled to admit the thoroughness of the plan, and the skill with which it had been carried out, but he wondered anew why so much trouble had been taken in regard to him, a mere lad.

He stood at the porthole a long time, and the wind out of the north rose steadily. He heard its whistle and he also heard the singing of men above him. He knew that the schooner was making great speed down the stream and that Albany and his friends were now far behind. As the wise generally do, he resigned himself to inevitable fate, wasting no strength in impossible struggles, but waiting patiently for a better time. There was a single blanket on the hard bunk, and, lying down on it, he fell asleep.

When he awoke, day shining through the porthole threw a slender bar of light across the floor, which heaved and slanted, telling that the wind out of the north still blew strong and true. An hour later the door was opened and a sailor brought a rude breakfast on a tin plate. While he was eating it, and hunger made everything good, the slaver came in.

"You'll see, Peter, that I did not put you on the diet suggested by Garay," he said. "I'm at least a kind man and you ought to thank me for all I'm doing for you."

"For any kindness of yours to me I'm grateful," said Robert. "We're apt to do unto people as they do unto us."

"Quite a young philosopher, I see. You'll find such a spirit useful on the West India plantations. My heart really warms to you, Peter. I'd let you go on deck as we're running through good scenery now, but it's scarcely prudent. We'll have to wait for that until we pass New York and put out to sea. I hope you don't expect it of me, Peter?"

"No, I don't look for it. But if you don't mind I'd like to have a little more breakfast."

"A fine, healthy young animal, so you are! And you shall have it, too."

He called the sailor who brought a second helping and Robert fell to. He was really very hungry and he was resolved also to put the best possible face on the matter. He knew he would need every ounce of his strength, and he meant to nurse it sedulously.

"When do you expect to reach New York?" he asked.

"To-morrow some time, if the wind holds fair, but we won't stay there long. A few hours only to comply with the port regulations, and then ho! for the West Indies! It's a grand voyage down! And splendid islands! Green mountains that seem to rise straight up out of the sea! While you're working in the cane fields you can enjoy the beautiful scenery, Peter."

Robert was silent. The man's malice filled him with disgust. Undoubtedly the slaver had felt intense chagrin because of his former failure and his defeat in the duel of swords before his own men, but then one should not exult over a foe who was beaten for the time. He felt a bitter and intense hatred of the slaver, and, his breakfast finished, he leaned back, closing his eyes.

"So you do not wish to talk, but would meditate," said the man. "Perhaps you're right, but, at any rate, you'll have plenty of time for it."

When he went out Robert heard the heavy lock of the tiny room shove into place again, and he wasted no further effort in a new attempt upon it. Instead, he lay down on the bunk, closed his eyes and tried to reconcile himself, body and mind, to his present situation. He knew that it was best to keep quiet, to restrain any mental flutterings or physical quivers. Absolute calm, if he could command it, was good for the soul, placed as he was, and the mere act of lying still helped toward that. It was what Tayoga would do if he were in his place, and, spurred by a noble emulation, he resolved that he would not be inferior to the Onondaga.

An hour, two hours passed and he did not stir. His stillness made his hearing more acute. The trampling of feet over his head came to him with great distinctness. He heard the singing of wind at the porthole, and, now and then, the swish of waters as they swept past the schooner. He wondered what Tayoga was doing and what would Willet think when he came back to Albany and found him gone. It gave him a stab of agony. His pride was hurt, too, that he had been trapped so thoroughly. Then his resolution returned to his aid. Making a supreme effort of his will, he dismissed the thought, concentrating his mind on hope. Would Tayoga's Manitou help him? Would Tododaho on his remote star look down upon him with kindness? The Onondaga in his place would put his faith in them, and the Manitou of the Indian after all was but another name for his own Christian God. Resolving to hope he did hope. He refused to believe that the slaver could make him vanish from the face of the earth like a mist before the wind.

The air in the little cabin was dense and heavy already, but after a while he felt it grow thicker and warmer. He was conscious, too, of a certain sultriness in it. The tokens were for a storm. He thought with a leap of the heart of the earlier storm that had rescued him, but that was at sea; this, if it came, would be on a river, and so shrewd a captain as the slaver would not let himself be wrecked in the Hudson.

The heat and sultriness increased. Then he stood on the bunk and looked through the porthole. He caught glimpses of lofty shores, trees at the summit, and stretches of a dark and angry sky. Low thunder muttered, rolling up from the west. Then came flashes of lightning, and the thunder grew louder. By and by the wind blew heavily, making the schooner reel before it, and when it died somewhat rain fell in sheets.

Although he felt it rather than saw it, Robert really enjoyed the storm. It seemed a tonic to him, and the wilder it was the steadier grew his own spirit. The breath of the rain as it entered the porthole was refreshing, and the air in the cabin became clear and cool again. Then followed the dark, and his second night in the schooner.

A sailor brought him his supper, the slaver failing to reappear, and soon afterward he fell asleep. He made no surmise where they were the next morning, as he had no way of gauging their speed during the night, but he was allowed to go about under guard below decks for an hour or two. The slaver came down the ladder and gave him the greetings of the day.

"You will see, Peter," he said, "that I'm a much kinder man than Garay. He would restrict your food, but I not only give you plenty of it, I also allow you exercise, very necessary and refreshing to youth. I'm sorry I'll have to shut you up again soon, but in the afternoon we'll reach New York, and I must keep you away from the temptations of the great town."

Robert would have given much to be allowed upon the deck and to look at the high shores, but he could not sink his pride enough to ask for the privilege, and, when the time came for him to return to his cell of a cabin he made no protest.

He felt the schooner stop late in the afternoon and he was sure that they had reached New York. He heard the dropping of the anchor, and then the sounds became much dimmer. The light in the cabin was suddenly shut off, and he realized that the porthole had been closed from the outside. They were taking no chances of a call for help, and he tried to resign himself.

But will could not control feelings now. To know that he was in New York and yet was absolutely helpless was more than he could bear. He had never really believed that the schooner could pass the port and put out to sea with him a prisoner. It had seemed incredible, one of the things not to be contemplated, but here was the event coming to pass. Mind lost control of the body. He threw himself upon the door, pulled at it, and beat it. It did not move an inch. Then he shouted again and again for help. There was no response.

Gradually his panic passed, and ashamed of it he threw himself once more upon the bunk, where he tried to consider whatever facts were in his favour. It was certain they were not trying to take his life; had they wished they could have done that long ago, and while one lived one was never wholly lost. It was a fact that he would remember through everything and he would pin his faith to it.

He slept, after a while, and he always thought afterwards that the foul, dense air of the cabin added a kind of stupor to sleep. When he came out of it late the next day he was conscious of an immense heaviness in the head and of a dull, apathetic feeling. He sat up slowly and painfully as if he were an old man. Then he noticed that the porthole was open again, but, judging from the quality of the air in the cabin, it had not been open long.

So the slaver had been successful. He had stopped in the port of New York and had then put out to sea. Doubtless he had done so without any trouble. He was having his revenge in measure full and heaped over. Robert was bound to admit it, but he bore in mind that his own life was still in his body. He would never give up, he would never allow himself to be crushed.

He stood upon the bunk and put his eyes to the porthole, catching a view of blue water below and blue sky above, and the sea as it raced past showed that the vessel was moving swiftly. He heard, too, the hum of the strong wind in the rigging and the groaning timbers. It was enough to tell him that they were fast leaving New York behind, and that now the chances of his rescue upon a lone ocean were, in truth, very small. But once more he refused to despair.

He did not believe the slaver would keep him shut up in the cabin, since they were no longer where he could be seen by friends or those who might suspect, and his opinion was soon justified. In a half hour the door was opened by the man himself, who stood upon the threshold, jaunty, assured and triumphant.

"You can come on deck now, Peter," he said. "We've kept you below long enough, and, as I want to deliver you to the plantations strong and hearty, fresh air and exercise will do you good."

"I'll come willingly enough," said Robert, resolved to be jaunty too. "Lead the way."

The captain went up the ladder just outside the door and Robert followed him, standing at first in silence on the swaying deck and content to look at sky and ocean. How beautiful they were! How beautiful the world was to one who had been shut up for days in a close little room! How keen and sweet was the wind! And what a pleasant song the creaking of the ropes and the slatting of the sails made!

It was a brilliant day. The sun shone with dazzling clearness. The sea was the bluest of the blue. The wind blew steady and strong. Far behind them was a low line of land, showing but dimly on the horizon, and before them was the world of waters. Robert balanced himself on the swaying deck, and, for a minute or two, he enjoyed too much the sensation of at least qualified freedom to think of his own plight. While he stood there, breathing deeply, his lungs expanding and his heart leaping, the slaver who had gone away, reappeared, saluting him with much politeness.

"Look back, Peter," he said, "and you can get your last glimpse of your native soil. The black line that just shows under the sky is Sandy Hook. We won't see any more land for days, and you'll have a fine, uninterrupted voyage with me and my crew."

Robert in this desperate crisis of his life resolved at once upon a course of action. He would not show despair, he would not sulk, he would so bear himself and with such cheerfulness and easy good nature that the watch upon him might be relaxed somewhat, and the conditions of his captivity might become less hard. It was perhaps easier for him than for another, with his highly optimistic nature and his disposition to be friendly. He kissed his hand to the black line on the horizon and said:

"I'm going now, but I'll come back. I always come back."

"That's the right spirit, Peter," said the slaver. "Be pleasant. Always be pleasant, say I, and you'll get along much better in the world. Things will just melt away before you."

Robert looked over the schooner. He did not know much about ships, but she seemed to him a trim and strong craft, carrying, as he judged, about thirty men. A long eighteen-pound cannon was mounted in her stern, but that was to be expected in war, and was common in peace also when one sailed into that nest of pirates, the West Indies. The slaver carried pistol and dirk in his belt, and those of the crew whom he could see were sturdy, hardy men. The slaver read his eyes:

"Yes, she's a fine craft," he said. "Able to fight anything of her size we're likely to meet, and fast enough to run away from them that's too big for her. You can see as much of her as you want to. So long as we've no neighbour on the ocean you've the run of the craft. But if you should want to leave you needn't try to tempt any of my men to help you. They wouldn't dare do it, and they wouldn't want to anyhow. All their interests are with me. I'm something of a deity to them."

The slaver went away and Robert walked about the narrow deck, standing at last by the rail, where he remained a long time. No one seemed to pay any attention to him. He was free to come and go as he pleased within the narrow confines of the schooner. But he watched the black line of land behind them until it was gone, and then it seemed to him that he was cut off absolutely from all the life that he had lived. Tayoga, Willet, Master Jacobus, all the good friends of his youth had disappeared over the horizon with the lost land.

It had been so sudden, so complete that it seemed to him it must have been done with a purpose. To what end had he been wrenched away from the war and sent upon the unknown ocean? His wilderness had been that of the woods and not of the waters. He had imbibed much of Tayoga's philosophy and at times, at least, he believed that everything moved forward to an appointed end. What was it now?

He left the low rail at last, and finding a stool sat down upon the deck. The schooner was going almost due south, and she was making great speed. The slaver's boast that she could run away from anything too strong for her was probably true, and Robert judged also that she carried plenty of arms besides the eighteen-pounder. Most of the crew seemed to him to be foreigners, that is, they were chiefly of the races around the Mediterranean. Dark of complexion, short and broad, some of them wore earrings, and, without exception, they carried dirks and now and then both pistols and dirks in their belts. He sought among them for the face of one who might be a friend, but found none. They were all hardened and sinister, and he believed that at the best they were smugglers, at the worst pirates.

A heavy dark fellow whom Robert took to be a Spaniard was mate and directed the task of working the vessel, the captain himself taking no part in the commands, but casting an occasional keen glance at the sailors as he strolled about. Robert judged that he was an expert sailor and a leader of men. In truth, he had never doubted his ability from the first, only his scruples, or, rather, he felt sure that he had none at all.

The policy of ignoring the prisoner, evidently by order, was carried out by the men. For all save the captain he did not exist, apparently, and the slaver himself took no further notice of him for several hours. Then, continuing his old vein, he spoke to him lightly, as if he were a guest rather than a captive.

251

"I see that you're improving in both mind and body, Peter," he said. "You've a splendid colour in your cheeks and you look fine and hearty. The sea air is good for anybody and it's better for you to be here than in a town like Albany."

"Since I'm here," said Robert, "I'll enjoy myself as much as I can. I always try to make the best of everything."

"That's philosophical, and 'tis a surprisingly good policy for one so young."

Robert looked at him closely. His accent was that of an educated man, and he did not speak ungrammatically.

"I've never heard your name, captain," he said, "and as you know mine, I ought to know yours."

"We needn't mind about that now. Three-fourths of my men don't know my name, just calling me 'Captain.' And, at any rate, if I were to give it to you it wouldn't be the right one."

"I suspected as much. People who change their names usually do so for good reasons."

Colour came into the man's sun-browned cheeks.

"You're a bold lad, Peter," he said, "but I'll admit you're telling the truth. I rather fancy you in some ways. If I felt sure of you I might take you with me on a voyage that will not be without profit, instead of selling you to a plantation in the Indies. But to go with me I must have your absolute faith, and you must agree to share in all our perils and achievements."

His meaning was quite plain, and might have tempted many another, thinking, in any event, to use it as a plan for escape, but Robert never faltered for a moment. His own instincts were always for the right, and long comradeship with Willet and Tayoga made his will to obey those instincts all the stronger.

"Thank you, Captain," he replied, "but I judge that your cruises are all outside the law, and I cannot go with you on them, at least, not willingly."

The slaver shrugged his shoulder.

"'Tis just as well that you declined," he said. "'Twas but a passing whim of mine, and ten minutes later I'd have been sorry for it had you accepted."

He shrugged his shoulders again, took a turn about the deck and then went down to his cabin. Robert, notified by a sailor, the first man on the schooner outside of the slaver to speak to him, ate supper with him there. The food was good, but the captain was now silent, speaking only a few times, and mostly in monosyllables. Near the end he said:

"You're to sleep in the room you've been occupying. The door will not be bolted on you, but I don't think you'll leave the ship. The nearest land is sixty or seventy miles away, and that's a long swim."

"I won't chance it," said Robert. "Just now I prefer solid timber beneath my feet."

"A wise decision, Peter."

After supper the slaver went about his duties, whatever they were, and Robert, utterly free so far as the schooner was concerned, went on deck. It was quite dark and the wind was blowing strong, but the ship was steady, and her swift keel cut the waters. All around him curved the darkness, and the loneliness of the sea was immense at that moment. It was in very truth a long swim to the land, and just then the thought of escape was far from him. He shivered, and going down to the little cabin that had been a prison, he soon fell asleep.

CHAPTER 5

Music in the Moonlight

Several days passed and from the standpoint of the schooner the voyage was successful. The wind continued fresh and strong, and it came out of the right quarter. The days were clear, the sea was a dazzling colour, shifting as the sky over it shifted. The slaver was in high good humour. His crew seemed to be under perfect control and went about their work mostly in silence. They rarely sang, as sailors sing, but Robert, watching them on spar or mast, although he knew little about ships, knew that they were good sailors. He realized, too, that the crew was very large for a vessel of its size, and he believed that he understood the reason.

As for himself, he felt a vast loneliness. It was incredible, but he was there on the schooner far from all he had known. The forest, in which he had lived and the war that had concerned the whole world had sunk out of sight beyond the horizon. And on the schooner he had made no acquaintance save the slaver. He knew that the mate was called Carlos, but he had not yet spoken to him. He tried his best to be cheerful, but there were times when despair assailed him in spite of all his courage and natural buoyancy.

"Better reconsider," said the slaver one day, catching the look upon his face. "As I've told you, Peter, the life on the plantations is hard and they don't last long, no matter how strong they are. There's peril in the life I lead, I'll admit, but at least there's freedom also. Sport's to be found among the islands, and along the Spanish Main."

"I couldn't think of it," said Robert.

"Well, it's the second time I've made you the offer, and the last. I perceive you're bent on a life in the sugar cane, and you'll have your wish."

Robert, seeing no chance of escape from the ship now, began to hope for rescue from without. It was a time of war and all vessels were more than commonly wary, but one might come at last, and, in some way he would give a signal for help. How he did not know, but the character of the schooner was more than doubtful, and he might be able, in some way, yet unsuggested, to say so to any new ship that came.

But the surface of the sea, so far as their own particular circle of it was concerned, was untroubled by any keel save their own. It was as lone and desolate as if they were the first vessel to come there. They fell into a calm and the schooner rocked in low swells but made no progress. The sun shone down, brassy and hot, and Robert, standing upon the deck, looked at the sails flapping idly above. Although it carried him farther and farther away from all for which he cared, he wished that the wind would rise. Nothing was more tedious than to hang there upon the surface of the languid ocean. The slaver read his face.

"You want us to go on," he said, "and so do I. For once we are in agreement. I'd like to make a port that I know of much sooner than I shall. The war has brought privateersmen into these seas, and there are other craft that any ship can give a wide berth."

"If the privateer should be British, or out of one of our American ports why should you fear her?" asked Robert.

"I'm answering no such questions except to say that in some parts of the world you're safer alone, and this is one of the parts."

The dead calm lasted two days and two nights, and it was like forever to Robert. When the breeze came at last, and the sails began to fill, new life flowed into his own veins, and hope came back. Better any kind of action than none at all, and he drew long breaths of relief when the schooner once more left her trailing wake in the blue sea. The wind blew straight and strong for a day and night, then shifted and a long period of tacking followed. It was very wearisome, but Robert, clinging to his resolution, made the best of it. He even joined in some of the labour, helping to polish the metal work, especially the eighteen-pounder in the stern, a fine bronze gun. The men tolerated him, but when he tried to talk with them he found that most of them had little or no English, and he made scant progress with them in that particular. The big first mate, Carlos, rebuffed him repeatedly, but he persisted, and in time the rebuffs became less brusque. He also noticed a certain softening of the sailors toward him. His own charm of manner was so great that it was hard to resist it when it was continuously exerted, and sailors, like other men, appreciate help when it is given to them continuously. The number of frowns for him decreased visibly.

He still ate at the captain's table, why he knew not, but the man seemed to fancy his company; perhaps there was no other on the schooner who was on a similar intellectual level, and he made the most of the opportunity to talk.

"Peter," he said, "you seem to have ingratiated yourself to a certain extent with my crew. I'm bound to admit that you're a personable young rascal, with the best manners I've met in a long time, but I warn you that you can't go far. You'll never win 'em over to your side, and be able to lead a mutiny which will dethrone me, and put you in command."

"I've no such plan in my mind," said Robert laughing. "I don't know enough about sailing to take command of the ship, and I'd have to leave everything to Carlos, whom I'd trust, on the whole, less than I do you."

"You're justified in that. Carlos is a Spaniard out of Malaga, where he was too handy with the knife, just as he has been elsewhere. Whatever I am, you're safer with me than you would be with Carlos, although he's a fine sailor and loyal to me."

"How long will it be before we make any of the islands?"

"It's all with the wind, but in any event it will be quite a while yet. It's a long run from New York down to the West Indies. Moreover, we may be blown out of our course at any time."

"Are we in the stormy latitudes?"

"We are. Hurricanes appear here with great suddenness. You noticed how hot it was to-day. We're to have another calm, and the still, intense heat is a great breeder of storms. I think one will come soon, but don't put any faith in its helping you, Peter. To be saved that way once is all the luck you can expect. If we were wrecked here you'd surely go down; it's too far from land."

"I'm not expecting another wreck, nor am I hoping for it," said Robert. "I'm thinking the land will be better for me. I'll make good my escape there. I've been uncommonly favoured in that way. Once I escaped from you and twice from the French and Indians, so I think my future will hold good."

"Maybe it will, Peter. As resolute an optimist as you ought to succeed. If you escape after I deliver you to the plantation 'twill be no concern to me at all. On the whole I'm inclined to hope you will, for I'm rather beginning to like you, spite of all the trouble you've caused me and that time you beat me with the swords before my own men."

Robert's heart leaped up. Could the man be induced to relent in his plan, whatever it was? But his hope fell the next moment, when the slaver said:

"Though I tell you, Peter, I'm going to stick to my task. You'll be handed over to the plantation, whatever comes. After that, it's for others to watch you, and I rather hope you'll get the better of 'em."

The storm predicted by the slaver arrived within six hours, and it was a fearful thing. It came roaring down upon them, and the wind blew with such frightful violence that Robert did not see how they could live through it, but live they did. Both the captain and mate revealed great seamanship, and the schooner was handled so well and behaved so handsomely that she drove through it without losing a stick.

When the hurricane passed on the sea resumed its usual blue colour, and, the dead, heavy heat gone, the air was keen and fresh. Robert, although he did not suffer from seasickness, had been made dizzy by the storm, and he felt intense relief when it was over.

"You'll observe, Peter," said the slaver, "that we're coming into regions of violence both on land and sea. You've heard many a tale of the West Indies. Well, they're all true, whatever they are, earthquakes, hurricanes, smugglers, pirates, wild Englishmen, Frenchmen, Americans, Spaniards, Portuguese, deeds by night that the day won't own, and the prize for the strongest. It's a great life, Peter, for those that can live it."

The close-set eyes flashed, and the nostrils dilated. Despite the apparent liking that the slaver had shown for him, Robert never doubted his character. Here was a man to whom the violent contrasts and violent life of the West Indian seas appealed. He wondered what was the present mission of the schooner, and he thought of the bronze eighteen-pounder, and of the dirks and pistols in the belts of the crew.

"I prefer the north," he said. "It's cooler there and people are more nearly even, in temper and life."

"Your life there has been in peril many times from the Indians."

"That's true, but I understand the Indians. Those who are my friends are my friends, and those who are my enemies are my enemies. I take it that in the West Indies you never know what change is coming."

"Correct, Peter, but it's all a matter of temperament. You like what you like, because you're made that way, and you can't alter it, but the West Indies have seen rare deeds. Did you ever hear of Morgan, the great buccaneer?"

"Who hasn't?"

"There was a man for you! No law but his own! Willing to sack the biggest and strongest cities on the Spanish Main and did it, too! Ah, Peter, 'twould have been a fine thing to have lived in his day and to have done what he did."

"I shouldn't care to be a pirate, no matter how powerful, and no matter how great the reward."

"Again it's just a matter of temperament. I'm not trying to change you, and you couldn't change me."

Came another calm, longer than the first. They hung about for days and nights on a hot sea, and captain and crew alike showed anxiety and impatience. The captain was continually watching the horizon with his glasses, and he talked to Robert less than usual. It was obvious that he felt anxiety.

The calm was broken just before nightfall. Dark had come with the suddenness of the tropic seas. There was a puff of wind, followed by a steady breeze, and the schooner once more sped southward. Robert, anxious to breathe the invigorating air, came upon deck, and standing near the mainmast watched the sea rushing by. The captain paused near him and said to Robert in a satisfied tone:

"It won't be long now, Peter, until we're among the islands, and it may be, too, that we'll see another ship before long. We've been on a lone sea all the way down, but you'll find craft among the islands."

"It might be a hostile vessel, a privateer," said Robert.

"It's not privateers of which I'm thinking."

The light was dim, but Robert plainly saw the questing look in his eyes, the look of a hunter, and he drew back a pace. This man was no mere smuggler. He would not content himself with such a trade. But he said in his best manner:

"I should think, captain, it was a time to avoid company, and that you would be better pleased with a lone sea."

"One never knows what is coming in these waters," said the slaver. "It may be that we shall have to run away, and I must not be caught off my guard."

But the look in the man's eyes did not seem to Robert to be that of one who wished to run away. It was far more the look of the hunter, and when the hulking mate, Carlos, passed near him his face bore a kindred expression. The sailors, too, were eager, attentive, watching the horizon, as if they expected something to appear there.

No attention was paid to Robert, and he remained on the deck, feeling a strong premonition that they were at the edge of a striking event, one that had a great bearing upon his own fate, no matter what its character might be.

The wind rose again, but it did not become a gale. It was merely what a swift vessel would wish, to show her utmost grace and best speed. The moon came out and made a silver sea. The long white wake showed clearly across the waters. The captain never left the deck, but continued to examine the horizon with his powerful glasses.

Robert, quick to deduce, believed that they were in some part of the sea frequented by ships in ordinary times and that the captain must be reckoning on the probability of seeing a vessel in the course of the night. His whole manner showed it, and the lad's own interest became so great that he lost all thought of going down to his cabin. Unless force intervened he would stay there and see what was going to happen, because he felt in every fibre that something would surely occur.

An hour, two hours passed. The schooner went swiftly on toward the south, the wind singing merrily through the ropes and among the sails. The captain walked back and forth in a narrow space, circling the entire horizon with his glasses at intervals seldom more than five minutes apart. It was about ten o'clock at night when he made a sharp, decisive movement, and a look of satisfaction came over his face. He had been gazing into the west and the lad felt sure that he had seen there that for which he was seeking, but his own eyes, without artificial help, were not yet able to tell him what it was.

The captain called the mate, speaking to him briefly and rapidly, and the sullen face of the Spaniard became alive. An order to the steersman and the course of the schooner was shifted more toward the west. It was evident to Robert that they were not running away from whatever it was out there. The slaver for the first time in a long while took notice of Robert.

"There's another craft in the west, Peter," he said, "and we must have a look at her. Curiosity is a good thing at sea, whatever it may be on shore. When you know what is near you you may be able to protect yourself from danger."

His cynical, indifferent air had disappeared. He was gay, anticipatory, as if he were going to something that he liked very much. The close-set eyes were full of light, and the thin lips curved into a smile.

"You don't seem to expect danger," said Robert. "It appears to me that you're thinking of just the opposite."

"It's because I've so much confidence in the schooner. If it's a wicked ship over there we'll just show her the fastest pair of heels in the West Indies."

He did not speak again for a full quarter of an hour, but he used the glasses often, always looking at the same spot on the western horizon. Robert was at last able to see a black dot there with his unassisted eyes, and he knew that it must be a ship.

"She's going almost due south," said the captain, "and in two hours we should overhaul her."

"Why do you wish to overhaul her?" asked Robert.

"She may be a privateer, a Frenchman, even a pirate, and if so we must give the alarm to other peaceful craft like ourselves in these waters."

He raised the glasses again and did not take them down for a full five minutes. Meantime the strange ship came nearer. It was evident to Robert that the two vessels were going down the sides of a triangle, and if each continued on its course they would meet at the point.

The night was steadily growing brighter. The moon was at its fullest, and troops of new stars were coming out. Robert saw almost as well as by day. He was soon able to distinguish the masts and sails of the stranger, and to turn what had been a black blur into the shape and parts of a ship. He was able, too, to tell that the stranger was keeping steadily on her course, but the schooner, obeying her tiller, was drawing toward her more and more.

"They don't appear to be interested in us," he said to the captain.

"No," replied the man, "but they should be. They show a lack of that curiosity which I told you is necessary at sea, and it is my duty to overtake them and tell them so. We must not have any incautious ships sailing in these strange waters."

Ten minutes later he called the mate and gave a command. Cutlasses and muskets with powder and ball were put at convenient points. Every man carried at least one pistol and a dirk in his belt. The captain himself took two pistols and a cutlass.

"Merely a wise precaution, Peter," he said, "in case our peaceful neighbour, to whom we wish to give a useful warning, should turn out to be a pirate."

Robert in the moonlight saw his eyes gleam and his lips curve once more into a smile. He had seen enough of men in crucial moments to know that the slaver was happy, that he was rejoicing in some great triumph that he expected to achieve. In spite of himself he shivered and looked at the stranger. The tracery of masts and spars was growing clearer and the dim figures of men were visible on her decks.

"Oh, we'll meet later," said the captain exultantly. "Don't deceive yourself about that. There is a swift wind behind us and the speed of both ships is increasing."

Robert looked over the side. The sea was running in white caps and above his head the wind was whistling. The schooner rolled and his footing grew unsteady, but it was only a fine breeze to the sailors, just what they loved. Suddenly the captain burst into a great laugh.

"The fools! the fools!" he exclaimed. "As I live, they're pleasuring here in the most dangerous seas in the world! Music in the moonlight!"

"What do you mean?" asked Robert, astonished.

"Just what I say! A madness hath o'ercome 'em! Take a look through the glasses, Peter, and see a noble sight, but a strange one at such a time."

He clapped the glasses to Robert's eyes. The other ship, suddenly came near to them, and grew fourfold in size. Every detail of her stood out sharp and vivid in the moonlight, a stout craft with all sails set to catch the good wind, a fine merchantman by every token, nearing the end of a profitable voyage. Discipline was not to say somewhat relaxed, but at least kindly, the visible evidence of it an old sailor sitting with his back against the mast playing vigorously upon a violin, while a dozen other men stood around listening.

"Look at 'em, Peter. Look at 'em," laughed the captain. "It's a most noble sight! Watch the old fellow playing the fiddle, and I'll lay my eyes that in a half minute or so you'll have some of the sailormen dancing."

Robert shuddered again. The glee in the slaver's voice was wicked. The cynical jesting tone was gone and in its place was only unholy malice. But Robert was held by the scene upon the deck of the stranger.

"Yes, two of the sailors have begun to dance," he said. "They're young men and clasping each other about the shoulders, they're doing a hornpipe. I can see the others clapping their hands and the old fellow plays harder than ever."

"Ah, idyllic! Most idyllic, I vow!" exclaimed the captain. "Who would have thought, Peter, to have beheld such a sight in these seas! 'Tis a childhood dream come back again! 'Tis like the lads and maids sporting on the village green! Ah, the lambs! the innocents! There is no war for them. It does my soul good, Peter, to behold once more such innocent trust in human nature."

The shudder, more violent than ever, swept over Robert again. He felt that he was in the presence of something unclean, something that exhaled the foul odour of the pit. The man had become wholly evil, and he shrank away.

"Steady, Peter," said the slaver. "Why shouldn't you rejoice with the happy lads on yon ship? Think of your pleasant fortune to witness such a play in the West Indian seas, the merry sailormen dancing to the music in the moonlight, the ship sailing on without care, and we in our schooner bearing down on 'em to secure our rightful share in the festival. Ah, Peter, we must go on board, you and I and Carlos and more stout fellows and sing and dance with 'em!"

Robert drew back again. It may have been partly the effect of the moonlight, and partly the mirror of his own mind through which he looked, but the captain's face had become wholly that of a demon. The close-set eyes seemed to draw closer together than ever, and they were flashing. His hand, sinewy and strong, settled upon the butt of a pistol in his belt, but, in a moment, he raised it again and took the glasses from Robert. After a long look he exclaimed:

"They dream on! They fiddle and dance with their whole souls, Peter, my lad, and such trusting natures shall be rewarded!"

Robert could see very well now without the aid of the glasses. The sailor who sat on a coil of rope with his back against a mast, playing the violin, was an old man, his head bare, his long white hair flying. It was yet too far away for his face to be disclosed, but Robert knew that his expression must be rapt, because his attitude showed that his soul was in his music. The two young sailors, with their arms about the shoulders of each other, were still dancing, and two more had joined them.

The crowd of spectators had thickened. Evidently it was a ship with a numerous crew, perhaps a rich merchantman out of Bristol or Boston. No flag was flying over her. That, however, was not unusual in those seas, and in times of war when a man waited to see the colours of his neighbour before showing his own. But Robert was surprised at the laxity of discipline on the stranger. They should be up and watching, inquiring into the nature of the schooner that was drawing so near.

"And now, Peter," said the captain, more exultant than ever, "you shall see an unveiling! It is not often given to a lad like you, a landsman, to behold such a dramatic act at sea, a scene so powerful and complete that it might have been devised by one of the great Elizabethans! Ho, Carlos, make ready!"

He gave swift commands and the mate repeated them as swiftly to the men. The two ships were rapidly drawing nearer, but to Robert's amazement the festival upon the deck of the stranger did not cease. Above the creaking of the spars the wailing strains of the violin came to him across the waters. If they were conscious there of the presence of the schooner they cared little about it. For the moment it occurred to Robert that it must be the *Flying Dutchman*, or some other old phantom ship out of the dim and legendary past.

"And now, Carlos!" exclaimed the captain in a full, triumphant voice, "we'll wake 'em up! Break out the flag and show 'em what we are!"

A coiled piece of cloth, dark and menacing, ran up the mainmast of the schooner, reached the top, and then burst out, streaming at full length in the strong wind, dark as death and heavy with threat. Rob-

262

ert looked up and shuddered violently. Over the schooner floated the black flag, exultant and merciless.

The tarpaulin was lifted and the long bronze gun in the stern was uncovered. Beside her stood the gunners, ready for action. The boatswain's whistle blew and the dark crew stood forth, armed to the teeth, eager for action, and spoil. Carlos, a heavy cutlass in hand, awaited his master's orders. The captain laughed aloud.

"So you see, Peter, what we are!" he exclaimed. "And it's not too late for you to seize a cutlass and have your share. Now, my lads, we'll board her and take her in the good old way."

The mate shouted to the steersman, and the schooner yawed. Robert, filled with horror, scarcely knew what he was doing; in truth, he had no conscious will to do anything, and so he ended by doing nothing. But he heard the fierce low words of the pirates, and he saw them leaning forward, as if making ready to leap on the deck of the stranger and cut down every one of her crew.

Then he looked at the other ship. The old man who had been playing the violin suddenly dropped it and snatched up a musket from behind the coil of rope on which he had been sitting. The dancers ceased to dance, sprang away, and returned in an instant with muskets also. Heavy pistols leaped from the shirts and blouses of the spectators, and up from the inside of the ship poured a swarm of men armed to the teeth. A piece of cloth swiftly climbed the mainmast of the stranger also, reached the top, broke out there triumphantly, and the flag of England, over against the black flag, blew out steady and true in the strong breeze.

"God! A sloop of war!" exclaimed the captain. "About, Carlos! Put her about!"

But the sloop yawed quickly, her portholes opened, bronze muzzles appeared, tampions fell away, and a tremendous voice shouted: "Fire!"

Robert saw a sheet of flame spring from the side of the sloop, there was a terrific crash, a dizzying column of smoke and the schooner seemed fairly to leap from the water, as the broadside swept her decks and tore her timbers. The surly mate was cut squarely in two by a round shot, men screaming in rage and pain went down and the captain staggered, but recovered himself. Then he shouted to the steersman to put the schooner about and rushing among the sailors he ordered them to another task than that of boarding.

"It was a trick, and it trapped us most damnably!" he cried. "A fool I was! Fools we must all have been to have been caught by it! They lured us on! But now, you rascals, to your work, and it's for your lives! We escape together or we hang together!"

263

The night had darkened much, clouds trailing before the moon and stars, but Robert clearly saw the slaver's face. It was transformed by chagrin and wrath, though it expressed fierce energy, too. Blood was running from his shoulder down his left arm, but drawing his sword he fairly herded the men to the sails; that is, to those that were left. The helmsman put the shattered schooner about and she drove rapidly on a new course. But the sloop of war, tacking, let go her other broadside.

Robert anticipated the second discharge, and by impulse rather than reason threw himself flat upon the deck, where he heard the heavy shot whistling over his head and the cries of those who were struck down. Spars and rigging, too, came clattering to the deck, but the masts stood and the schooner, though hit hard, still made way.

"Steady! Keep her steady, my boys!" shouted the captain. "We've still a clean pair of heels, and with a little luck we'll lose the sloop in the darkness!"

He was a superb seaman and the rising wind helped him. The wounded schooner had gained so much that the third broadside did but little damage and killed only one man. Robert stood up again and looked back at the pursuing vessel, her decks covered with men in uniform, the gunners loading rapidly while over the sloop the flag of England that was then the flag of his own country too, streamed straight out in the wind, proud and defiant.

He felt a throb of intense, overwhelming pride. The black flag had been overmatched by the good flag. In the last resort, those who lived right had proved themselves more than equal to those who lived wrong. Law and order were superior to piracy and chaos. Forgetful of his own safety, he hoped that the sloop would overtake the schooner, and obeying his impulse he uttered a shout of triumph. The captain turned upon him fiercely.

"You cheer the wrong ship," he said. "If they overtake us, you being with us, I'll swear that you were one of the hardiest men in my crew!"

Robert laughed, he could not help it, though the act was more or less hysterical, and replied:

"I'll chance it! But, Captain, didn't you have the surprise of your whole life, and you so cunning, too!"

The man raised his cutlass, but dropped it quickly.

"Don't try me that way again," he said. "It was my impulse to cut you down, and the next time I'd do it. But you're right. It was a surprise, though we'll escape 'em yet, and we'll let 'em know we're not just a hunted rabbit, either!"

The Long Tom in the stern of the schooner opened fire. The first shot splashed to the right of the sloop, and the second to the left, but the third struck on board, and two men were seen to go down. The captain laughed.

"That's a taste of their own medicine," he said.

A big gun on the sloop thundered, and a round shot cut away one of the schooner's spars. Another flashed and a load of grape hissed over the decks. Two men were killed and three more wounded. The captain shouted in anger and made the others crack on all the sail they could. She was a staunch schooner, and though hurt grievously she still made speed. Swifter than the sloop, despite her injuries, she gradually widened the gap between them, while the wind rose fast, and the trailing blackness spread over the sea.

Although still close at hand, the outline of the pursuing sloop became dim. Robert was no longer able to trace the human figures on her deck, but the banner of law and right flying from her topmast yet showed in the dusk. Forgetful as before of his own danger, he began to have a fear that the pirate would escape. Under his breath he entreated the avenging sloop to come on, to sail faster and faster, he begged her gunners to aim aright despite the darkness, to rake the decks of the schooner with grape and to send the heavy round shot into her vitals.

The sloop kept up a continuous fire with her bow guns. The heavy reports crashed through the darkness, the sounds rolling sullenly away, and not every shot went wild. There was a tearing of sails, a splintering of spars, a shattering of wood, and now and then the fall of a man. Under the insistent and continuous urging of the captain the men on the schooner replied with the Long Tom in her stern, and, when one of the shots swept the deck of the sloop, the fierce, dark sailors shouted in joy. Robert saw with a sinking of the heart that the gap between the two vessels was still widening, while almost the last star was gone from the heavens, and it was now so dark that everything was hidden a few hundred yards away.

"We'll lose her! We'll lose her yet!" cried the captain. "Winds and the night fight for us. See you, Peter, we must be the chosen children of fortune, for this can hardly be chance!"

Robert said nothing, because it seemed for the time at least that the captain's words were true. A sudden and tremendous gust of wind caught the schooner and drove her on, ragged and smashed though she was, at increased speed, while the same narrow belt of wind seemed to miss the sloop. The result was apparent at once. The gap between them became a gulf. The flag flying so proudly on the topmast of the sloop was gone in the dusk. Her spars and sails faded away, she showed only a dim, low hulk on the water from which her guns flashed.

The schooner tacked again. A new bank of blackness poured down over the sea, and the sloop was gone.

"It was a trap and we sailed straight into it," exclaimed the captain, "but it couldn't hold us. We've escaped!"

He spoke the truth. They drove steadily on a long time, and saw no more of the sloop of war.

CHAPTER 6

The Island

Robert came out of his benumbed state. It had all seemed a fantastic dream, but he had only to look around him to know that it was reality. Three or four battle lanterns were shining and they threw a ghostly light over the deck of the schooner, which was littered with spars and sails, and the bodies of men who had fallen before the fire of the sloop. Streams of blood flowed everywhere. He sickened and shuddered again and again.

The captain, a savage figure, stained with blood, showed ruthless energy. Driving the men who remained unwounded, he compelled them to cut away the wreckage and to throw the dead overboard. Garrulous, possessed by some demon, he boasted to them of many prizes they would yet take, and he pointed to the black flag which still floated overhead, unharmed through all the battle. He boasted of it as a good omen and succeeded in infusing into them some of his own spirit.

Robert was still unnoticed and at first he wandered about his strait territory. Then he lent a helping hand with the wreckage. His own life was at stake as well as theirs, and whether they wished it or not he could not continue to stand by an idler. Circumstance and the sea forced him into comradeship with men of evil, and as long as it lasted he must make the best of it. So he fell to with such a will that it drew the attention of the captain.

"Good boy, Peter!" he cried. "You'll be one of us yet in spite of yourself! Our good fortune is yours, too! You as well as we have escaped a merry hanging! I'll warrant you that the feel of the rope around the neck is not pleasant, and it's well to keep one's head out of the noose, eh, Peter?"

Robert did not answer, but tugged at a rope that two other men were trying to reeve. He knew now that while they had escaped the sloop of war their danger was yet great and imminent. The wind was still rising, and now it was a howling gale. The schooner had been raked heavily. Most of her rigging was gone, huge holes had been smashed in her hull, half of her crew had been killed and half of the rest were wounded, there were not enough men to work her even were she whole and the weather the best. As the crest of every wave passed she wallowed in the trough of the sea, and shipped water steadily. The exultant look passed from the captain's eyes.

"I'm afraid you're a lad of ill omen, Peter," he said to Robert. "I had you on board another ship once and she went to pieces. It looks now as if my good schooner were headed the same way."

A dark sailor standing near heard him, and nodded in approval, but Robert said:

"Blame the sloop of war, not me. You would lay her aboard, and see what has happened!"

The captain frowned and turned away. For a long time he paid no further attention to Robert, all his skill and energy concentrated upon the effort to save his ship. But it became evident even to Robert's inexperienced eye that the schooner was stricken mortally. The guns of the sloop had not raked and slashed her in vain. A pirate she had been, but a pirate she would be no more. She rolled more heavily all the time, and Robert noticed that she was deeper in the water. Beyond a doubt she was leaking fast.

The captain conferred with the second mate, a tall, thin man whom he called Stubbs. Then the two, standing together near the mast, watched the ship for a while and Robert, a little distance away, watched them. He was now keenly alive to his own fate. Young and vital, he did not want to die. He had never known a time when he was more anxious to live. He was not going to be sold into slavery on a West India plantation. Fortune had saved him from that fate, and it might save him from new perils. In a storm on a sinking vessel he was nevertheless instinct with hope. Somewhere beyond the clouds Tayoga's Tododaho on his great star was watching him. The captain spoke to him presently.

"Peter," he said, "I think it will be necessary for us to leave the ship soon. That cursed sloop has done for the staunchest schooner that ever sailed these seas. I left you on board a sinking vessel the other time, but as it seemed to bring you good luck then, I won't do it now. Besides, I'm tempted to keep you with me. You bore yourself bravely during the battle. I will say that for you."

"Thanks for taking me, and for the compliment, too," said Robert. "I've no mind to be left here alone in the middle of the ocean on a sinking ship."

"'Tis no pleasant prospect, nor have we an easy path before us in the boats, either. On the whole, the chances are against us. There's land not far away to starboard, but whether we'll make it in so rough a sea is another matter. Are you handy with an oar?"

"Fairly so. I've had experience on lakes and rivers, but none on the sea."

"'Twill serve. We'll launch three boats. Hooker, the boatswain, takes one, Stubbs has the other, and I command the last. You go with me."

"It would have been my choice."

"I'm flattered, Peter. I may get a chance yet to sell you to one of the plantations."

"I think not, Captain. The stars in their courses have said 'no.'"

"Come! Come! Don't be Biblical here."

"The truth is the truth anywhere. But I'm glad enough to go with you."

One of the boats was launched with great difficulty, and the boatswain, Hooker, and six men, two of whom were wounded, were lowered into it. It capsized almost immediately, and all on board were lost. Those destined for the other two boats hung back a while, but it became increasingly necessary for them to make the trial, no matter what the risk. The schooner rolled and pitched terribly, and a sailor, sent to see, reported that the water was rising in her steadily.

The captain showed himself a true seaman and leader. He had been wounded in the shoulder, but hurt had been bound up hastily and he saw to everything. Each of the boats contained kegs of water, arms, ammunition and food. A second was launched and Stubbs and his crew were lowered into it. A great wave caught it and carried it upon its crest, and Robert, watching, expected to see it turn over like the first, but the mate and the crew managed to restore the balance, and they disappeared in the darkness, still afloat.

"There, lads," exclaimed the captain, "you see it can be done. Now we'll go too, and the day will soon come when we'll have a new ship, and then, ho! once more for the rover's free and gorgeous life!"

The unwounded men raised a faint cheer. The long boat was launched with infinite care, and Robert lent a hand. The pressure of circumstances made his feeling of comradeship with these men return. For the time at least his life was bound up with theirs. Two wounded sailors were lowered first into the boat.

"Now, Peter, you go," said the captain. "As I told you, I may have a chance yet to sell you to a plantation, and I must preserve my property."

Robert slid down the rope. The captain and the others followed, and they cast loose. They were eight in the boat, three of whom were wounded, though not badly. The lad looked back at the schooner. He saw a dim hulk, with the black flag still floating over it, and then she passed from sight in the darkness and driving storm.

He took up an oar, resolved to do his best in the common struggle for life, and with the others fought the sea for a long time. The captain set their course south by west, apparently for some island of which he knew, and meanwhile the men strove not so much to make distance as to keep the boat right side up. Often Robert thought they were gone. They rode dizzily upon high waves, and they sloped at appalling angles, but always they righted and kept afloat. The water sprayed them continuously and the wind made it sting like small shot, but that was a trifle to men in their situation who were straining merely to keep the breath in their bodies.

After a while—Robert had no idea how long the time had been—the violence of the wind seemed to abate somewhat, and their immense peril of sinking decreased. Robert sought an easier position at the oar, and tried to see something reassuring, but it was still almost as dark as pitch, and there was only the black and terrible sea around them. But the captain seemed cheerful.

"We'll make it, lads, before morning," he said. "The storm is sinking, as you can see, and the island is there waiting for us."

In another hour the sea became so much calmer that there was no longer any danger of the boat overturning. Half of the men who had been rowing rested an hour, and then the other half took their turn. Robert was in the second relay, and when he put down his oar he realized for the first time that his hands were sore and his bones aching.

"You've done well, Peter," said the captain. "You've become one of us, whether or no, and we'll make you an honoured inhabitant of our island when we come to it."

Robert said nothing, but lay back, drawing long breaths of relief. The danger of death by drowning had passed for the moment and he had a sense of triumph over nature. Despite his weariness and soreness, he was as anxious as ever to live, and he began to wonder about this island of which the captain spoke. It must be tropical, and hence in his imagination beautiful, but by whom was it peopled? He did not doubt that they would reach it, and that he, as usual, would escape all perils.

Always invincible, his greatest characteristic was flaming up within him. He seemed to have won, in a way, the regard of the captain, and he did not fear the men. They would be castaways together, and on the land opportunities to escape would come. On the whole he preferred the hazards of the land to those of the sea. He knew better how to deal with them. He was more at home in the wilderness than on salt water. Yet a brave heart was alike in either place.

"We'd better take it very easy, lads," said the captain. "Not much rowing now, and save our strength for the later hours of the night."

"Why?" asked Robert.

"Because the storm, although it has gone, is still hanging about in the south and may conclude to come back, assailing us again. A shift in the wind is going on now, and if it hit us before we reached the island, finding us worn out, we might go down before it."

It was a good enough reason and bye and bye only two men kept at the oars, the rest lying on the bottom of the boat or falling asleep in their seats. The captain kept a sharp watch for the other boat, which had gone away in the dark, but beheld no sign of it, although the moon and stars were now out, and they could see a long distance.

"Stubbs knows where the island is," said the captain, "and if they've lived they'll make for it. We can't turn aside to search all over the sea for 'em."

Robert after a while fell asleep also in his seat, and despite his extraordinary situation slept soundly, though it was rather an unconsciousness that came from extreme exhaustion, both bodily and mental. He awoke some time later to find that the darkness had come back and that the wind was rising again.

"You can take a hand at the oar once more, Peter," said the captain. "I let you sleep because I knew that it would refresh you and we need the strength of everybody. The storm, as I predicted, is returning, not as strong as it was at first, perhaps, but strong enough."

He wakened the other men who were sleeping, and all took to the oars. The waves were running high, and the boat began to ship water. Several of the men, under instructions from the captain, dropped their oars and bailed it out with their caps or one or two small tin vessels that they had stored aboard.

"Luckily the wind is blowing in the right direction," said the captain. "It comes out of the northeast, and that carries us toward the island. Now, lads, all we have to do is to keep the boat steady, and not let it ship too much water. The wind itself will carry us on our way."

But the wind rose yet more, and it required intense labour and vigilance to fight the waves that threatened every moment to sink their craft. Robert pulled on the oar until his arms ached. Everybody toiled except the captain, who directed, and Robert saw that he had all the qualities to make him a leader of slavers or pirates. In extreme danger he was the boldest and most confident of them all, and he stood by his men. They could see that he would not desert them, that their fortune was his fortune. He was wounded, Robert did not yet know how badly, but he never yielded to his hurt. He was a figure of strength in the boat, and the men drew courage from him to struggle for life against the overmastering sea. Somehow, for the time at least, Robert looked upon him as his own leader, obeying his commands, willingly and without question.

He was drenched anew with the salt water, but as they were in warm seas he never thought of it. Now and then he rested from his oar and helped bail the water from the boat.

A pale dawn showed at last through the driving clouds, but it was not encouraging. The sea was running higher than ever, and there was no sign of land. One of the men, much worse wounded than they had thought, lay down in the bottom of the boat and died. They tossed his body unceremoniously overboard. Robert knew that it was necessary, but it horrified him just the same. Another man, made light of head by dangers and excessive hardships, insisted that there was no island, that either they would be drowned or would drift on in the boat until they died of thirst and starvation. The captain drew a pistol and looking him straight in the eye said:

"Another word of that kind from you, Waters, and you'll eat lead. You know me well enough to know that I keep my word."

The man cowered away and Robert saw that it was no vain threat. Waters devoted his whole attention to an oar, and did not speak again.

"We'll strike the island in two or three hours," the captain said with great confidence.

The dawn continued to struggle with the stormy sky, but its progress was not promising. It was only a sullen gray dome over a gray and ghastly sea, depressing to the last degree to men worn as they were. But in about two hours the captain, using glasses that he had taken from his coat, raised the cry:

"Land ho!"

He kept the glasses to his eyes a full two minutes, and when he took them down he repeated with certainty:

"Land ho! I can see it distinctly there under the horizon in the west, and it's the island we've been making for. Now, lads, keep her steady and we'll be there in an hour."

All the men were vitalized into new life, but the storm rose at the same time, and spray and foam dashed over them. All but two or three were compelled to work hard, keeping the water out of the boat, while the others steadied her with the oars. Robert saw the captain's face grow anxious, and he began to wonder if they would reach the island in time. He wondered also how they would land in case they reached it, as he knew from his reading and travellers' tales that most of the little islands in these warm seas were surrounded by reefs.

The wind drove them on and the island rose out of the ocean, a dark, low line, just a blur, but surely land, and the drooping men plucked up their spirits.

"We'll make it, lads! Don't be down-hearted!" cried the captain. "Keep the boat above water a half hour longer, and we'll tread the soil of mother earth again! Well done, Peter! You handle a good oar! You're the youngest in the boat, but you've set an example for the others! There's good stuff in you, Peter."

Robert, to his own surprise, found his spirit responding to this man's praise, slaver and pirate though he was, and he threw more strength into his swing. Soon they drew near to the island, and he heard such a roaring of the surf that he shuddered. He saw an unbroken line of white and he knew that behind it lay the cruel teeth of the rocks, ready to crunch any boat that came. Every one looked anxiously at the captain.

"There's a rift in the rocks to the right," he said, "and when we pass through it we'll find calm water inside. Now, lads, all of you to the oars and take heed that you do as I say on the instant or we'll be on the reef!"

They swung to the right, and so powerful were wind and wave that it seemed to Robert they fairly flew toward the island. The roaring of the surf grew and the long white line rose before them like a wall. He saw no opening, but the captain showed no signs of fear and gave quick, sharp commands. The boat drove with increased speed toward the island, rising on the crests of great waves, then sinking with sickening speed into the trough of the sea, to rise dizzily on another wave. Robert saw the rocks, black, sharp and cruel, reaching out their long, savage teeth, and the roar of wind and surf together was now so loud that he could no longer hear the captain's commands. He was conscious that the boat was nearly full of water, and when he was not blinded by the flying surf he saw looks of despair on the faces of the men.

An opening in the line of reefs disclosed itself, and the boat shot toward it. He heard the captain shout, but did not understand what he said, then they were wrenched violently to the left by a powerful current. He saw the black rocks frowning directly over him, and felt the boat scrape against them. The whole side of it was cut away, and they were all hurled into the sea.

Robert was not conscious of what he did. He acted wholly from impulse and the instinctive love of life that is in every one. He felt the water pour over him, and fill eye, ear and nostril, but he was not hurled against rock. He struck out violently, but was borne swiftly away, not knowing in which direction he was taken.

He became conscious presently that the force driving him on was not so great and he cleared the water from his eyes enough to see that he had been carried through the opening and toward a sandy beach. His mind became active and strong in an instant. Chance had brought him life, if he only had the presence of mind to take it. He struck out for the land with all his vigour, hoping to reach it before he could be carried back by a returning wave.

The wave caught him, but it was not as powerful as he had feared, and, when he had yielded a little, he was able to go forward again. Then he saw a head bobbing upon the crest of the next retreating wave and being carried out to sea. It was the captain, and reaching out a strong arm Robert seized him. The shock caused him to thrust down his feet, and to his surprise he touched bottom. Grasping the captain with both hands he dragged him with all his might and ran inland.

It was partly an instinctive impulse to save and partly genuine feeling that caused him to seize the slaver when he was being swept helpless out to sea. The man, even though in a malicious, jeering way, had done him some kindnesses on the schooner and in the boat, and he could not see him drown before his eyes. So he settled his grasp upon his collar, held his head above the water and strove with all his might to get beyond the reach of the cruel sea. Had he been alone he could have reached the land with ease, but the slaver pulled upon him almost a dead weight.

Another returning wave caught him and made him stagger, but he settled his feet firmly in the sand, held on to the unconscious man, and when it had passed made a great effort to get beyond the reach of any other. He was forced half to lift, half to drag the slaver's body, but he caught the crest of the next incoming wave, one of unusual height and strength, and the two were carried far up the beach. When it died in foam and spray he lifted the man wholly and ran until he fell exhausted on the sand. When another wave roared inland it did not reach him, and no others came near. As if knowing they were baffled, they gave up a useless pursuit.

Robert lay a full half hour, supine, completely relaxed, only half conscious. Yet he was devoutly thankful. The precious gift of life had been saved, the life that was so young, so strong and so buoyant in him. The sea, immense, immeasurable and savage might leap for him, but it could no longer reach him. He was aware of that emotion, and he was thankful too that an Infinite Hand had been stretched out to save him in his moment of direst peril.

He came out of his cataleptic state, which was both a mental and physical effect, and stood up. The air was still dim with heavy clouds and the wind continuously whistled its anger. He noticed for the first time that it was raining, but it was a trifle to him, as he had already been thoroughly soaked by the sea.

The sea itself was as wild as ever. Wave after wave roared upon the land to break there, and then rush back in masses of foam. As far as Robert could see the surface of the water, lashed by the storm, was wild and desolate to the last degree. It was almost as if he had been cast away on another planet. A feeling of irrepressible, awful loneliness overpowered him.

"Well, Peter, we're here."

It was a feeble voice, but it was a human one, the voice of one of his own kind, and, in that dreary wilderness of the ocean, it gave welcome relief as it struck upon his ear. He looked down. The slaver, returned to consciousness, had drawn himself into a sitting position and was looking out at the gray waters.

"I've a notion, Peter," he said, "that you've saved my life. The last I remember was being engulfed in a very large and very angry ocean. It was kind of you, Peter, after I kidnapped you away from your friends, meaning to sell you into slavery on a West India plantation."

"I couldn't let you drown before my eyes."

"Most men in your place would have let me go, and even would have helped me along."

"Perhaps I felt the need of company. 'Twould have been terrible to be alone here."

"There may be something in that. But at any rate, you saved me. I'm thinking that you and I are all that's left. I was a fool, Peter, ever to have mixed in your business. I can see it now. When I carried you away from New York I lost my ship. I kidnap you away again from Albany, and I lose my ship and all my crew. I would have lost my own life, too, if it had not been for you. It was never intended by the fates that I should have been successful in my attempts on you. The first time should have been enough. That was a warning. Well, I've paid the price of my folly. All fools do."

He tried to stand up, but fresh blood came from his shoulder and he quickly sat down again. It was obvious that he was very weak.

"I'll do the best I can for us both," said Robert, "but I don't know the nature of this land upon which we're cast. I suppose it's an island, of course. I can see trees inland, but that's all I can discover at present."

"I know a deal more," said the slaver. "That's why I had the boat steered for this point, hoping to make the little bay into which the opening through the reefs leads. It's an island, as you say, seven or eight miles long, half as broad and covered thickly with trees and brush. There's a hut about half a mile inland, and if you help me there we'll both find shelter. I'll show the way. As trying too steadily to do you evil brought me bad luck I'll now try to do you good. You can put it down to logic, and not to any sudden piety in me."

Yet Robert in his heart did not ascribe it wholly to logic. He was willing to believe in a kindly impulse or two in everybody, there was a little good hidden somewhere deep down even in Tandakora, though it might have to struggle uncommonly hard for expression. He promptly put his arm under the man's and helped him to his feet.

"Give me the direction," he said, "and I'll see that we reach the hut."

"Bear toward the high hill ahead and to the right. And between you and me, Peter, I'm glad it's inland. I've had enough of the sea for a while and I don't want to look at it. How is it behaving now?"

Robert, looking back, saw a great wave rushing upon the beach as if it thought it could overtake them, and it gave him an actual thrill of delight to know the effort would be in vain.

"It's as wild, as desolate and as angry as ever," he said, "and we're well away from it for the present."

"Then go on. I fear I shall have to lean upon you rather hard. A bit of grape shot from that cursed sloop has bitten pretty deep into my shoulder. I've been doubly a fool, Peter, in kidnapping you a second time after the first warning, and in allowing myself to be tolled up under the broadside of that sloop. It's the last that hurts me most. I behaved like any youngster on his first cruise."

Robert said nothing, but did his best to support the wounded man, who was now bearing upon him very heavily. His own strength was largely factitious, coming from the hope that they would soon find shelter and a real place in which to rest, but such as it was it was sufficient for the time being.

He did not look back again. Like the slaver, he wanted to shut out the sea for the present. It was a raging, cruel element, and he felt better with it unseen. But he became conscious, instead, of the rain which was driving hard. He suddenly realized that he was cold, and he shivered so violently that the slaver noticed it.

"Never mind, Peter," he said. "We're going to a palace, or at least 'twill seem a palace by power of contrast. There you'll be snug and warm."

"And you can bind up your wound again and get back your strength."

"Aye, we can bind it up again, but it's not so sure about my getting back my strength. I tell you again, lad, that the grape bit deep. It hurts me all the time to think I was lured under those guns by a silly old fiddler and a couple of silly sailors dancing to his silly tune. You're a good lad, Peter, I give you credit for it, and since, beside myself, only one on board the schooner was saved, I'm glad it was you and not a member of the crew."

"We don't know that others were not saved. We haven't had time yet to see."

"I know they weren't. It's only a miracle that we two came through the reefs. Miracles may happen, Peter, but they don't happen often. Nobody else will appear on the island. Keep steering for the hill. I'll be glad when we get there, because, between you and me, Peter, it will be just about as far as I can go and I'll need a long, long rest."

He bore so heavily upon Robert now that their progress was very slow, and the lad himself began to grow weak. It was impossible for any one, no matter how hardy of body and soul, to endure long, after going through what he had suffered. He too staggered.

"I'm leaning hard on you, Peter," said the slaver. "I know it, but I can't help it. What a difference a whiff of grapeshot makes!"

Robert steadied himself, made a mighty effort, and they went on. The wind shifted now and the rain drove directly in his face. It was cold to him, but it seemed to whip a little increase of vigour and strength into his blood, and he was able to go somewhat faster. As he pulled along with his burden he looked curiously at the region through which he was travelling. The ground was rough, often with layers of coral, and he saw on all sides of him dense groves of bushes, among which he recognized the banana by the fruit. It gave him a thrill of relief. At all events here was food of a kind, and they would not starve to death. It was the first time he had thought of food. Hitherto he had been occupied wholly with the struggle for immediate life.

A belt of tall trees shut out the hill toward which he had been steering, and he was uncertain. But the man gave him guidance.

"More to the right, Peter," he said. "I won't let you go astray, and it's full lucky for us both that I know this island."

A half hour of painful struggle and Robert saw the dark shape of a small house in the lee of a hill.

"It's the hut, Peter," said the slaver, "and you've done well to bring us here. You're not only a good lad, but you're strong and brave, too. You needn't knock at the door. No one will answer. Push it open and enter. It really belongs to me."

Robert obeyed while the man steadied himself sufficiently to stand alone. He thrust his hand against the door, which swung inward, revealing a dark interior. A musty odour entered his nostrils, but the hut, whatever its character, was dry. That was evident, and so it was welcome. He went in, helping the wounded man along with him, and standing there a moment or two everything became clear.

It was more than a hut. He was in a room of some size, containing articles of furniture, obviously brought across the sea, and clothing hanging from the wall on hooks. A couch was beside one wall, and two doors seemed to lead to larger chambers or to small closets. The captain staggered across the room and lay down on the couch.

"Well, how do you like it, Peter?" he asked. "'Twill serve in a storm, will it not?"

"It will serve grandly," replied Robert. "How does it come to be here?"

"I had it built. The islands all the way from the Bahamas to South America and the waters around them are the great hunting ground for people in my trade, and naturally we need places of refuge, secluded little harbours, so to speak, where we can commune with ourselves and refresh our minds and bodies. Even rovers must have periods of relaxation, and you'll find a lot of such places scattered about the islands, or, rather, you won't find 'em because they're too well hidden. I had this built myself, but I never dreamed that I should come back to it in the way I have."

"It's a palace just now," said Robert, "yes, it's more than a palace, it's a home. I see clothing here on the wall, and, by your leave, I'll change you and then myself into some of those dry garments."

"You're lord of the manor, Peter, by right of strength. I'm in no condition to resist you, even had I the wish, which I haven't."

Assisted by the man himself, he removed the captain's garments and put him in dry clothing, first looking at the wound in his shoulder, which his experience told him was very serious. The piece of grapeshot had gone entirely through, but the loss of blood had been large, and there was inflammation.

"I must bathe that with fresh water a little later and devise some kind of dressing," said Robert. "I've had much experience in the wilderness with wounds."

"You're a good lad, Peter," said the slaver. "I've told you that before, but I repeat it now."

Robert then arrayed himself in dry garments. He was strangely and wonderfully attired in a shirt of fine linen with lace ruffles, a short, embroidered jacket of purple velvet, purple velvet knee-breeches, silk stockings and pumps, or low shoes, with large silver buckles. It was very gorgeous, and, just then, very comfortable.

"You look the dandy to the full, Peter," said the slaver. "The clothes have hung here more than a year. They came from a young Spaniard who had the misfortune to resist too much when we took the ship that carried him. They've come to a good use again."

Robert shuddered, but in a moment or two he forgot the origin of his new raiment. He had become too much inured to deadly peril to be excessively fastidious. Besides, he was feeling far better. Warmth returned to his body and the beat of the rain outside the house increased the comfort within.

"I think, Peter," said the slaver, "that you'd better go to sleep. You've been through a lot, and you don't realize how near exhaustion you are."

Without giving a thought to the question of food, which must present itself before long, Robert lay down on the floor and fell almost at once into a sound slumber.

CHAPTER 7

The Pirate's Warning

When the lad awoke it was quite dark in the house, but there was no sound of rain. He went to the door and looked out upon a fairly clear night. The storm was gone and he heard only a light wind rustling through palms. There was no thunder of beating surf in the distance. It was a quiet sky and a quiet island.

He went back and looked at the slaver. The man was asleep on his couch, but he was stirring a little, and he was hot with fever. Robert felt pity for him, cruel and blood-stained though he knew him to be. Besides, he was the only human companion he had, and he did not wish to be left alone there. But he did not know what to do just then, and, lying down on the floor, he went to sleep again.

When he awoke the second time day had come, and the slaver too was awake, though looking very weak.

"I've been watching you quite a while, Peter," he said. "You must have slept fifteen or sixteen hours. Youth has a wonderful capacity for slumber and restoration. I dare say you're now as good as ever, and wondering where you'll find your breakfast. Well, when I built this house I didn't neglect the plenishings of it. Open the door next to you and you'll find *boucan* inside. '*Boucan*,' as you doubtless know, is dried beef, and from it we got our name the buccaneers, because in the beginning we lived so much upon dried beef. Enough is in that closet to last us a month, and there are herds of wild cattle on the island, an inexhaustible larder."

"But we can't catch wild cattle with our hands," said Robert.

The slaver laughed. "You don't think, Peter," he said, "that when I built a house here and furnished it I neglected some of the most necessary articles. In the other closet you'll find weapons and ammunition. But deal first with the *boucan*."

Robert opened the closet and found the *boucan* packed away in sheets or layers on shelves, and at once he became ravenously hungry.

"On a lower shelf," said the slaver, "you'll find flint and steel, and with them it shouldn't be hard for a wilderness lad like you to start a fire. There are also kettles, skillets and pans, and I think you know how to do the rest."

Robert went to work on a fire. The wood, which was abundant outside, was still damp, but he had a strong clasp knife and he whittled a pile of dry shavings which he succeeded in igniting with the flint and steel, though it was no light task, requiring both patience and skill. But the fire was burning at last and he managed to make in one of the kettles some soup of the dried beef, which he gave to the captain. The man had no appetite, but he ate a little and declared that he felt stronger. Then Robert broiled many strips for himself over the coals and ate ravenously. He would have preferred a greater variety of food, but it was better than a castaway had a right to expect.

His breakfast finished, he continued his examination of the house, which was furnished with many things, evidently captured from ships. He found in one of the closets a fine fowling piece, a hunting rifle, two excellent muskets, several pistols, ammunition for all the fire-arms and a number of edged weapons.

"You see, Peter, you're fitted for quite an active defence should enemies come," said the slaver. "You'll admit, I think, that I've been a good housekeeper."

"Good enough," said Peter. "Are there any medicines?"

"You'll find some salves and ointments on the top shelf in the second closet, and you can make a poultice for this hurt of mine. Between you and me, Peter, I've less pain, but much more weakness, which is a bad sign."

"Oh, you'll be well in a few days," said Robert cheerfully. "One wound won't carry off a man as strong as you are."

"One wound always suffices, provided it goes in deep enough, but I thank you for your rosy predictions, Peter. I think your good wishes are genuinely sincere."

Robert realized that they were so, in truth. In addition to the call of humanity, he had an intense horror of being left alone on the island, and he would fight hard to save the slaver's life. He compounded the poultice with no mean skill, and, after bathing the wound carefully with fresh water from a little spring behind the hut, he applied it.

"It's cooling, Peter, and I know it's healing, too," said the man, "but I think I'll try to go to sleep again. As long as I'm fastened to a couch that's about the only way I can pass the time. Little did I think when I built this house that I'd come here without a ship and without a crew to pass some helpless days."

He shut his eyes. After a while, Robert, not knowing whether he was asleep or not, took down the rifle, loaded it, and went out feeling that it was high time he should explore his new domain.

In the sunlight the island did not look forbidding. On the contrary, it was beautiful. From the crest of the hill near the house he saw a considerable expanse, but the western half of the island was cut off from view by a higher range of hills. It was all in dark green foliage, although he caught the sheen of a little lake about two miles away. As far as he could see a line of reefs stretched around the coast, and the white surf was breaking on them freely.

From the hill he went back to the point at which he and the captain had been swept ashore, and, as he searched along the beach he found the bodies of all those who had been in the boat with them. He had been quite sure that none of them could possibly have escaped, but it gave him a shock nevertheless to secure the absolute proof that they were dead. He resolved if he could find a way to bury them in the sand beyond the reach of the waves, but, for the present, he could do nothing, and he continued along the shore several miles, finding its character everywhere the same, a gentle slope, a stretch of water, and beyond that the line of reefs on which the white surf was continually breaking, reefs with terrible teeth as he well knew.

But it was all very peaceful now. The sea stretched away into infinity the bluest of the blue, and a breeze both warm and stimulating came out of the west. Robert, however, looked mostly toward the north. Albany and his friends now seemed a world away. He had been wrenched out of his old life by a sudden and unimaginable catastrophe. What were Tayoga and Willet doing now? How was the war going? For him so far as real life was concerned the war simply did not exist. He was on a lost island with only a wounded man for company and the struggle to survive and escape would consume all his energies.

Presently he came to what was left of their boat. It was smashed badly and half buried in the sand. At first he thought he might be able to use it again, but a critical examination showed that it was damaged beyond any power of his to repair it, and with a sigh he abandoned the thought of escape that way.

He continued his explorations toward the south, and saw groves of wild banana, the bushes or shrubs fifteen or twenty feet high, some of them with ripe fruit hanging from them. He ate one and found it good, though he was glad to know that he would not have to depend upon bananas wholly for food.

A mile to the south and he turned inland, crossing a range of low hills, covered with dense vegetation. As he passed among the bushes he kept his rifle ready, not knowing whether or not dangerous wild animals were to be found there. He had an idea they were lacking in both the Bahamas and the West Indies, but not being sure, he meant to be on his guard.

Before he reached the bottom of the slope he heard a puff, and then the sound of heavy feet. All his wilderness caution was alive in a moment, and, drawing back, he cocked the rifle. Then he crept forward, conscious that some large wild beast was near. A few steps more and he realized that there were more than one. He heard several puffs and the heavy feet seemed to be moving about in an aimless fashion.

He came to the edge of the bushes, and, parting them, he looked cautiously from their cover. Then his apprehensions disappeared. Before him stretched a wide, grassy savannah and upon it was grazing a herd of wild cattle, at least fifty in number, stocky beasts with long horns. Robert looked at them with satisfaction. Here was enough food on the hoof to last him for years. They might be tough, but he had experience enough to make them tender when it came to fire and the spit.

"Graze on in peace until I need you," he said, and crossing the savannah he found beyond, hidden at first from view by a fringe of forest, the lake that he had seen from the crest of the hill beside the house. It covered about half a square mile and was blue and deep. He surmised that it contained fish good to eat, but, for the present he was content to let them remain in the water. They, like the wild cattle, could wait.

Feeling that he had been gone long enough, he went back to the house and found the slaver asleep or in a stupor, and, when he looked at him closely, he was convinced that it was more stupor than sleep. He was very pale and much wasted. It occurred suddenly to Robert that the man would die and the thought gave him a great shock. Then, in very truth, he would be alone. He sat by him and watched anxiously, but the slaver did not come back to the world for a full two hours.

"Aye, Peter, you're there," he said. "As I've told you several times, you're a good lad."

"Can I make you some more of the beef broth?" asked Robert.

"I can take a little I think, though I've no appetite at all."

"And I'd like to dress your wound again."

"If it's any relief to you, Peter, to do so, go ahead, though I think 'tis of little use."

"It will help a great deal. You'll be well again in a week or two. It isn't so bad here. With a good house and food it's just the place for a wounded man."

"Plenty of quiet, eh Peter? No people to disturb me in my period of convalescence."

"Well, that's a help."

Robert dressed the wound afresh, but he noticed during his ministrations that the slaver's weakness had increased, and his heart sank. It was a singular fact, but he began to feel a sort of attachment for the man who had done him so much ill. They had been comrades in a great hazard, and were yet. Moreover, the fear of being left alone in a tremendous solitude was recurrent and keen. These motives and that of humanity made him do his best.

"I thank you, Peter," said the wounded man. "You're standing by me in noble fashion. On the whole, I'm lucky in being cast away with you instead of one of my own men. But it hurts me more than my wound does to think that I should have been tricked, that a man of experience such as I am should have been lured under the broadside of the sloop of war by an old fellow playing a fiddle and a couple of sailors dancing. My mind keeps coming back to it. My brain must have gone soft for the time being, and so I've paid the price."

Robert said nothing, but finished his surgeon's task. Then he made a further examination of the house, finding more *boucan* stored in a small, low attic, also clothing, both outer and inner garments, nautical instruments, including a compass, a pair of glasses of power, and bottles of medicine, the use of some of which he knew.

Then he loaded the fowling piece and went back toward the lake, hoping he might find ducks there. Beef, whether smoked or fresh, as an exclusive diet, would become tiresome, and since they might be in for a long stay on the island he meant to fill their larder as best he could. On his way he kept a sharp watch for game, but saw only a small coney, a sort of rabbit, which he left in peace. He found at a marshy edge of the lake a number of ducks, three of which he shot, and which he dressed and cooked later on, finding them to be excellent.

Robert made himself a comfortable bed on the floor with blankets from one of the closets and slept soundly through the next night. The following morning he found the slaver weaker than ever and out of his head at times. He made beef broth for him once more, but the man was able to take but little.

"'Tis no use, Peter," he said in a lucid interval. "I'm sped. I think there's no doubt of it. When that sloop of war lured us under her guns she finished her task; she did not leave a single thing undone. My schooner is gone, my crew is gone, and now I'm going."

"Oh, no," said Robert. "You'll be better to-morrow."

The man said nothing, but seemed to sink back into a lethargic state. Robert tried his pulse, but could hardly feel its beat. In a half hour he roused himself a little.

"Peter," he said. "You're a good lad. I tell you so once more. You saved me from the sea, and you're standing by me now. I owe you for it, and I might tell you something, now that my time's at hand. It's really come true that when I built this house I was building the place in which I am to die, though I didn't dream of it then."

Robert was silent, waiting to hear what he would tell him. But he closed his eyes and did not speak for five minutes more. The lad tried his pulse a second time. It was barely discernible. The man at length opened his eyes and said:

"Peter, if you go back to the province of New York beware of Adrian Van Zoon."

"Beware of Van Zoon! Why?"

"He wants to get rid of you. I was to put you out of the way for him, at a price, and a great price, too. But it was not intended, so it seems, that I should do so."

"Why does Adrian Van Zoon want me put out of the way?"

"That I don't know, Peter, but when you escape from the island you must find out."

His eyelids drooped and closed once more, and when Robert felt for his pulse a third time there was none. The slaver and pirate was gone, and the lad was alone.

Robert felt an immense desolation. Whatever the man was he had striven to keep him alive, and at the last the captain had shown desire to undo some of the evil that he had done to him. And so it was Adrian Van Zoon who wished to put him out of the way. He had suspected that before, in fact he had been convinced of it, and now the truth of it had been told to him by another. But, why? The mystery was as deep as ever.

Robert had buried the bodies of the sailors in the sand in graves dug with an old bayonet that he had found in the house, and he interred the captain in the same manner, only much deeper. Then he went back to the house and rested a long time. The awful loneliness that he had feared came upon him, and he wrestled with it for hours.

That night it became worse than ever, but it was so acute that it exhausted itself, and the next morning he felt better.

Resolved not to mope, he took down the rifle, put some of the smoked beef in his pocket, and started on a long exploration, meaning to cross the high hills that ran down the centre of the island, and see what the other half was like.

In the brilliant sunshine his spirits took another rise. After all, he could be much worse off. He had a good house, arms and food, and in time a ship would come. A ship must come, and, with his usual optimism, he was sure that it would come soon.

He passed by the lakes and noted the marshy spot where he had shot the ducks. Others had come back and were feeding there now on the water grasses. Doubtless they had never seen man before and did not know his full destructiveness, but Robert resolved to have duck for his table whenever he wanted it.

A mile or two farther and he saw another but much smaller lake, around the edge of which duck also were feeding, showing him that the supply was practically unlimited. Just beyond the second lake lay the range of hills that constituted the backbone of the island, and although the sun was hot he climbed them, their height being about a thousand feet. From the crest he had a view of the entire island, finding the new half much like the old, low, hilly, covered with forest, and surrounded with a line of reefs on which the surf was breaking.

His eyes followed the long curve of the reefs, and then stopped at a dark spot that broke their white continuity. His blood leaped and instantly he put to his eyes the strong glasses that he had found in the house and that fortunately he had brought with him. Here he found his first impression to be correct. The dark spot was a ship!

But it was no longer a ship that sailed the seas. Instead it was a wrecked and shattered ship, with her bow driven into the sand, and her stern impaled on the sharp teeth of the breakers. Then his heart leaped again. A second long look through the glasses told him that the lines of the ship, bruised and battered though she was, were familiar.

It was the schooner. The storm had brought her to the island also, though to the opposite shore, and there she lay a wreck held by the sand and rocks. He descended the hills, and, after a long walk, reached the beach. The schooner was not broken up as much as he had thought, and as she could be reached easily he decided to board her.

The vessel was tipped partly over on her side, and all her spars and sails were gone. She swayed a little with the swell, but she was held fast by sand and rocks. Robert, laying his clothes and rifle on the beach, waded out to her, and, without much difficulty, climbed aboard, where he made his way cautiously over the slanting and slippery deck.

His first motive in boarding the wreck was curiosity, but it now occurred to him that there was much treasure to be had, treasure of the kind that was most precious to a castaway. A long stay on the island had not entered into his calculations hitherto, but he knew now that he might have to reckon on it, and it was well to be prepared for any event.

He searched first the cabins of the captain and mates, taking from them what he thought might be of use, and heaping the store upon the beach. He soon had there a pair of fine double-barrelled pistols with plenty of ammunition to fit, another rifle, one that had been the captain's own, with supplies of powder and ball, a half dozen blankets, a medicine chest, well supplied, and a cutlass, which he took without any particular thought of use.

Then he invaded the carpenter's domain, and there he helped himself very freely, taking out two axes, two hatchets, two saws, a hammer, two chisels, several augers, and many other tools, all of which he heaped with great labour upon the beach.

Then he explored the cook's galley, gleaning three large bags of flour, supplies of salt and pepper, five cured hams, four big cheeses, several bottles of cordial and other supplies such as were carried on any well-found ship. It required great skill and caution to get all his treasures safely ashore, but his enthusiasm rose as he worked, and he toiled at his task until midnight. Then he slept beside the precious heap until the next day.

He lighted a fire with his flint and steel, which he made a point to carry with him always, and cooked a breakfast of slices from one of the hams. Then he planned a further attack upon the schooner, which had not altered her position in the night.

Robert now felt like a miser who never hoards enough. Moreover, his source of supply once gone, it was not likely that he would find another, and there was the ship. The sea was in almost a dead calm, and it was easier than ever to approach her. So he decided to board again and take off more treasure.

He added to the heap upon the beach another rifle, two muskets, several pistols, a small sword and a second cutlass, clothing, a considerable supply of provisions and a large tarpaulin which he meant to spread over his supplies while they lay on the sand. Then he launched a dinghy which he found upon the ship with the oars inside.

The dinghy gave him great pleasure. He knew that it would be an arduous task to carry all his supplies on his back across the island to the house, and it would lighten the labour greatly to make trips around in the boat. So he loaded into the dinghy as much of the most precious of his belongings as he thought it would hold, and began the journey by water that very day, leaving the rest of the goods covered with the tarpaulin in the event of rain.

It was a long journey, and he had to be careful about the breakers, but fortunately the sea remained calm. He was caught in currents several times, but he came at last to the opening in the rocks through which he and the captain had entered and he rowed in joyfully. He slept that night in the house and started back in the morning for another load. One trip a day in the dinghy he found to be all that he could manage, but he stuck to his work until his precious store was brought from the beach to the house.

He could not make up his mind even then to abandon the schooner entirely. There might never be another magazine of supply, and he ransacked her thoroughly, taking off more tools, weapons, clothing and ammunition. Even then he left on board much that might be useful in case of emergency, such as cordage, sails, and clothing that had belonged to the sailors. There was also a large quantity of ammunition for the Long Tom which he did not disturb. The gun itself was still on board the ship, dismounted and wedged into the woodwork, but practically as good as ever. Robert, with an eye for the picturesque, thought it would have been fine to have taken it ashore and to have mounted it before the house, but that, of course, was impossible. He must leave it to find its grave in the ocean, and that, perhaps, was the best end to a gun used as the Long Tom had been.

Part of his new treasures he took across the island on his back, and part he carried around it in the boat, which he found to be invaluable, and of which he took the utmost care, drawing it upon the beach at night, beyond the reach of tide or storm.

More than two weeks passed in these labours, and he was so busy, mind and body, that he was seldom lonely except at night. Then the feeling was almost overpowering, but whenever he was assailed by it he would resolutely tell himself that he might be in far worse case. He had shelter, food and arms in plenty, and it would not be long before he was taken off the island. Exerting his will so strongly, the periods of depression became fewer and shorter.

But the silence and the utter absence of his own kind produced a marked effect upon his character. He became graver, he thought more deeply upon serious things than his years warranted. The problem of his own identity was often before him. Who was he? He was sure that Benjamin Hardy knew. Jacobus Huysman must know, too, and beyond a doubt Adrian Van Zoon did, else he would not try so hard to put him out of the way. And St. Luc must have something to do with this coil. Why had the Frenchman really pointed out to him the way of escape when he was a prisoner at Ticonderoga? He turned these questions over and over and over in his mind, though always the answer evaded him. But he resolved to solve the problem when he got back to the colonies and as soon as the great war was over. It was perhaps typical of him that he should want his own personal fortunes to wait upon the issue of the mighty struggle in which he was so deeply absorbed.

Then his thoughts turned with renewed concentration to the war. Standing far off in both mind and body, he was able to contemplate it as a whole and also to see it in all its parts. And the more he looked at it the surer he was that England and her colonies would succeed. Distance and perspective gave him confidence. The French generals and French soldiers had done wonders, nobody could be braver or more skilful than they, but they could not prevail always against superior might and invincible tenacity.

Sitting on the ground and looking at the white surf breaking on the rocks, he ended the war in the way he wished. The French and Canada were conquered completely and his own flag was victorious everywhere. Braddock's defeat and Ticonderoga were but incidents which could delay but which could not prevent.

But he did not spend too much time in reflection. He was too young for that, and his years in the wilderness helped him to bear the burden of being alone. Rifle on shoulder, he explored every part of the island, finding that his domain presented no great variety. There was much forest, and several kinds of tropical fruits were for his taking, but quadruped life was limited, nothing larger than small rodents. Well-armed as he was, he would have preferred plenty of big game. It would have added spice to his life, much of which had been spent in hunting with Willet and Tayoga. Excitement might have been found in following bear or deer, but he knew too well ever to have expected them on an island in summer seas.

There was some sport in fishing. Plenty of tackle had been found among the ship's stores, and he caught good fish in the larger lake. He also tried deep sea fishing from the dinghy, but the big fellows bit so fast that it soon ceased to be of interest. The fish, though, added freshness and variety to his larder, and he also found shellfish, good and wholesome when eaten in small quantities, along the shore.

He went often to the highest hill in the centre of the island, where he would spend long periods, examining the sea from horizon to horizon with his strong glasses, searching vainly for a sail. He thought once of keeping a mighty bonfire burning every night, but he reconsidered it when he reflected on the character of the ship that it might draw.

Both the Bahamas and the West Indies—he did not know in which group he was—swarmed then with lawless craft. For nearly two hundred years piracy had been common, and in a time of war especially the chances were against a ship being a friend. He decided that on the whole he would prefer a look at the rescuer before permitting himself to be rescued.

The weather remained beautiful. He had been a month on the island, and the sea had not been vexed by another storm since his arrival. The schooner was still wedged in the sand and on the rocks, and he made several more trips to her, taking off many more articles, which, however, he left in a heap well back of the beach covered with a tarpaulin and the remains of sails. He felt that they could lie there awaiting his need. Perhaps he would never need them at all.

His later visits to the schooner were more from curiosity than from any other motive. He had a strong desire to learn more about the captain and his ship. There was no name anywhere upon the vessel, nor could he find any ship's log or manifest or any kind of writing to indicate it. Neither was the name of the slaver known to him, nor was there any letter nor any kind of paper to disclose it. It was likely that it would always remain hidden from him unless some day he should wrench it from Adrian Van Zoon.

Robert went into the sea nearly every morning. As he was a powerful swimmer and the weather remained calm, he was in the habit of going out beyond the reefs, but one day he noticed a fin cutting the water and coming toward him. Instantly he swam with all his might toward the reefs, shivering as he went. When he drew himself up on the slippery rocks he did not see the formidable fin. He was quite willing to utter devout thanks aloud. It might not have been a shark, but it made him remember they were to be expected in those waters. After that he took no chances, bathing inside the reefs and going outside in the dinghy only.

A few days later he was upon his highest hill watching the horizon when he saw a dark spot appear in the southwest. At first he was hopeful that it was a sail, but as he saw it grow he knew it to be a cloud. Then he hurried toward the house, quite sure a storm was coming.

Knowing how the southern seas were swept by hurricanes, it was surprising that none had come sooner, and he ran as fast as he could for the shelter of the house.

Robert made the door just in time. Then the day had turned almost as dark as night and, with a rush and a roar, wind and rain were upon him. Evidently the slaver had known those regions, and so he had built a house of great strength, which, though it quivered and rattled under the sweep of the hurricane, nevertheless stood up against it.

The building had several small windows, closed with strong shutters, but as wind and rain were driving from the west he was able to open one on the eastern side and watch the storm. It was just such a hurricane as that which had wrecked the shattered schooner. It became very dark, there were tremendous displays of thunder and lightning, which ceased, after a while, as the wind grew stronger, and then through the dark he saw trees and bushes go down. Fragments struck against the house, but the stout walls held.

The wind kept up a continuous screaming, as full of menace as the crash of a battle. Part of the time it swept straight ahead, cutting wide swathes, and then, turning into balls of compressed air, it whirled with frightful velocity, smashing everything level with the ground as if it had been cut down by a giant sword.

Robert had seen more than one hurricane in the great northern woods and he watched it without alarm. Although the house continued to rattle and shake, and now and then a bough, wrenched from its trunk, struck it a heavy blow, he knew that it would hold. There was a certain comfort in sitting there, dry and secure, while the storm raged without in all its violence. There was pleasure too in the knowledge that he was on the land and not the sea. He remembered the frightful passage that he and the slaver had made through the breakers, and he knew that his escape then had depended upon the slimmest of chances. He shuddered as he recalled the rocks thrusting out their savage teeth.

The storm, after a while, sank into a steady rain, and the wind blew but little. The air was now quite cold for that region, and Robert, lying down on the couch, covered himself with a blanket. He soon fell asleep and slept so long, lulled by the beat of the rain, that he did not awaken until the next day.

Then he took the dinghy and rowed around to the other side of the island. As he had expected, the schooner was gone. The storm had broken her up, and he found many of her timbers scattered along the beach, where they had been brought in by the waves. He felt genuine sadness at the ship's destruction and disappearance. It was like losing a living friend.

Fortunately, the tarpaulin and heavy sails with which he had covered his heap of stores high up the beach, weighting them down afterward with huge stones, had held. Some water had entered at the edges, but, as the goods were of a kind that could not be damaged much, little harm was done. Again he resolved to preserve all that he had accumulated there, although he did not know that he would have any need of them.

When he rowed back in the dinghy he saw a formidable fin cutting the water again, and, laying down the oars, he took up the rifle which he always carried with him. He watched until the shark was almost on the surface of the water, and then he sent a bullet into it. There was a great splashing, followed by a disappearance, and he did not know just then the effect of his shot, but a little later, when the huge body of the slain fish floated to the surface he felt intense satisfaction, as he believed that it would have been a man-eater had it the chance.

CHAPTER 8

Making the Best of It

After his return in the dinghy Robert decided that he would have some fresh beef and also a little sport. Although the island contained no indigenous wild animals of any size, there were the wild cattle, and he had seen they were both long of horn and fierce. If he courted peril he might find it in hunting them, and in truth he rather wanted a little risk. There was such an absence of variety in his life, owing to the lack of human companionship, that an attack by a maddened bull, for instance, would add spice to it. The rifle would protect him from any extreme danger.

He knew he was likely to find cattle near the larger lake, and, as he had expected, he saw a herd of almost fifty grazing there on a flat at the eastern edge. Two fierce old bulls with very long, sharp horns were on the outskirts, as if they were mounting guard, while the cows and calves were on the inside near the lake.

Robert felt sure that the animals, although unharried by man, would prove wary. For the sake of sport he hoped that it would be so, and, using all the skill that he had learned in his long association with Willet and Tayoga, he crept down through the woods. The bulls would be too tough, and as he wanted a fat young cow it would be necessary for him to go to the very edge of the thickets that hemmed in the little savannah on which they were grazing.

The wind was blowing from him toward the herd and the bulls very soon took alarm, holding up their heads, sniffing and occasionally shaking their formidable horns. Robert picked a fat young cow in the grass almost at the water's edge as his target, but stopped a little while in order to disarm the suspicion of the wary old guards. When the two went back to their pleasant task of grazing he resumed his cautious advance, keeping the fat young cow always in view.

Now that he had decided to secure fresh beef, he wanted it very badly, and it seemed to him that the cow would fulfil all his wants. A long experience in the wilderness would show him how to prepare juicy and tender steaks. Eager to replenish his larder in so welcome a way, he rose and crept forward once more in the thicket.

The two bulls became suspicious again, the one on the right, which was the larger, refusing to have his apprehension quieted, and advancing part of the way toward the bushes, where he stood, thrusting forward angry horns. His attitude served as a warning for the whole herd, which, becoming alarmed, began to move.

Robert was in fear lest they rush away in a panic, and so he took a long shot at the cow, bringing her down, but failing to kill her, as she rose after falling and began to make off. Eager now to secure his game he drew the heavy pistol that he carried at his belt, and, dropping his rifle, rushed forward from the thicket for a second shot.

The cow was not running fast. Evidently the wound was serious, but Robert had no mind for her to escape him in the thickets, and he pursued her until he could secure good aim with the pistol. Then he fired and had the satisfaction of seeing the cow fall again, apparently to stay down this time.

But his satisfaction was short. He heard a heavy tread and an angry snort beside him. He caught the gleam of a long horn, and as he whirled the big bull was upon him. He leaped aside instinctively and escaped the thrust of the horn, but the bull whirled also, and the animal's heavy shoulder struck him with such force that he was knocked senseless.

When Robert came to himself he was conscious of an aching body and an aching head, but he recalled little else at first. Then he remembered the fierce thrusts of the angry old bull, and he was glad that he was alive. He felt of himself to see if one of those sharp horns had entered him anywhere, and he was intensely relieved to find that he had suffered no wound. Evidently it had been a collision in which he had been the sufferer, and that he had fallen flat had been a lucky thing for him, as the fierce bull had charged past him and had then gone on.

Robert was compelled to smile sourly at himself. He had wanted the element of danger as a spice for his hunting, and he had most certainly found it. He had been near death often, but never nearer than when the old bull plunged against him. He rose slowly and painfully, shook himself several times to throw off as well as he could the effect of his heavy jolt, then picked up his rifle at one point and his pistol at another.

The herd was gone, but the cow that he had chosen lay dead, and, as her condition showed him that he had been unconscious not more than five minutes, there was his fresh beef after all. As his strength was fast returning, he cut up and dressed the cow, an achievement in which a long experience in hunting had made him an expert. He hung the quarters in a dense thicket of tall bushes where vultures or buzzards could not get at them, and took some of the tenderest steaks home with him.

He broiled the steaks over a fine bed of coals in front of the house and ate them with bread that he baked himself from the ship's flour. He enjoyed his dinner and he was devoutly grateful for his escape. But how much pleasanter it would have been if Willet and Tayoga, those faithful comrades of many perils, were there with him to share it! He wondered what they were doing. Doubtless they had hunted for him long, and they had suspected and sought to trace Garay, but the cunning spy doubtless had fled from Albany immediately after his capture. Willet and Tayoga, failing to find him, would join in the great campaign which the British and Americans would certainly organize anew against Canada.

It was this thought of the campaign that was most bitter to Robert. He was heart and soul in the war, in which he believed mighty issues to be involved, and he had seen so much of it already that he wanted to be in it to the finish. When these feelings were strong upon him it was almost intolerable to be there upon the island, alone and helpless. All the world's great events were passing him by as if he did not exist. But the periods of gloom would not last long. Despite his new gravity, his cheerful, optimistic spirit remained, and it always pulled him away from the edge of despair.

Although he had an abundance of fresh meat, he went on a second hunt of the wild cattle in order to keep mind and body occupied. He wanted particularly to find the big bull that had knocked him down, and he knew that he would recognize him when he found him. He saw a herd grazing on the same little savannah by the lake, but when he had stalked it with great care he found that it was not the one he wanted.

A search deeper into the hills revealed another herd, but still the wrong one. A second day's search disclosed the right group grazing in a snug little valley, and there was the big bull who had hurt so sorely his body and his pride. A half hour of creeping in the marsh grass and thickets and he was within easy range. Then he carefully picked out that spot on the bull's body beneath which his heart lay, cocked his rifle, took sure aim, and put his finger to the trigger.

But Robert did not pull that trigger. He merely wished to show to himself and to any invisible powers that might be looking on that he could lay the bull in the dust if he wished. If he wanted revenge for grievous personal injury it was his for the taking. But he did not want it. The bull was not to blame. He had merely been defending his own from a dangerous intruder and so was wholly within his rights.

"Now that I've held you under my muzzle you're safe from me, old fellow," were Robert's unspoken words.

He felt that his dignity was restored and that, at the same time, his sense of right had been maintained. Elated, he went back to the house and busied himself, arranging his possessions. They were so numerous that he was rather crowded, but he was not willing to give up anything. One becomes very jealous over his treasures when he knows the source of supplies may have been cut off forever. So he rearranged them, trying to secure for himself better method and more room, and he also gave them a more minute examination.

In a small chest which he had not opened before he found, to his great delight, a number of books, all the plays of Shakespeare, several by Beaumont and Fletcher, others by Congreve and Marlowe, Monsieur Rollin's Ancient History, a copy of Telemachus, translations of the Iliad and Odyssey, Ovid, Horace, Virgil and other classics. Most of the books looked as if they had been read and he thought they might have belonged to the captain, but there was no inscription in any of them, and, on the other hand, they might have been taken from a captured ship.

With plenty of leisure and a mind driven in upon itself, Robert now read a great deal, and, as little choice was left to him, he read books that he might have ignored otherwise. Moreover, he thought well upon what he read. It seemed to him as he went over his Homer again and again that the gods were cruel. Men were made weak and fallible, and then they were punished because they failed or erred. The gods themselves were not at all exempt from the sins, or, rather, mistakes for which they punished men. He felt this with a special force when he read his Ovid. He thought, looking at it in a direct and straight manner, that Niobe had a right to be proud of her children, and for Apollo to slay them because of that pride was monstrous.

His mind also rebelled at his Virgil. He did not care much for the elderly lover, Aeneas, who fled from Carthage and Dido, and when Aeneas and his band came to Italy his sympathies were largely with Turnus, who tried to keep his country and the girl that really belonged to him. He was quite sure that something had been wrong in the mind of Virgil and that he ought to have chosen another kind of hero.

Shakespeare, whom he had been compelled to read at school, he now read of his own accord, and he felt his romance and poetry. But he lingered longer over the somewhat prosy ancient history of Monsieur Rollin. His imaginative mind did not need much of a hint to attempt the reconstruction of old empires. But he felt that always in them too much depended upon one man. When an emperor fell an empire fell, when a king was killed a kingdom went down.

He applied many of the lessons from those old, old wars to the great war that was now raging, and he was confirmed in his belief that England and her colonies would surely triumph. The French monarchy, to judge from all that he had heard, was now in the state of one of those old oriental monarchies, decayed and rotten, spreading corruption from a poisoned centre to all parts of the body. However brave and tenacious the French people might be, and he knew that none were more so, he was sure they could not prevail over the strength of free peoples like those who fought under the British flag, free to grow, whatever their faults might be. So, old Monsieur Rollin, who had brought tedium to many, brought refreshment and courage to Robert.

But he did not bury himself in books. He had been a creature of action too long for that. He hunted the wild cattle over the hills, and, now and then, taking the dinghy he hunted the sharks also. Whenever he found one he did not spare the bullets. His finger did not stop at the trigger, but pulled hard, and he rarely missed.

But in spite of reading and action, time dragged heavily. The old loneliness and desolation would return and they were hard to dispel. He could not keep from crying aloud at the cruelty of fate. He was young, so vital, so intensely alive, so anxious to be in the middle of things, that it was torture to be held there. Yet he was absolutely helpless. It would be folly to attempt escape in the little dinghy, and he must wait until a ship came. He would spend hours every day on the highest hill, watching the horizon through his glasses for a ship, and then, bitter with disappointment, he would refuse to look again for a long time.

Whether his mind was up or down its essential healthiness and sanity held true. He always came back to the normal. Had he sought purposely to divest himself of hope he could not have done it. The ship was coming. Its coming was as certain as the rolling in of the tide, only one had to wait longer for it.

Yet time passed, and there was no sign of a sail on the horizon. His island was as lonely as if it were in the South Seas instead of the Atlantic. He began to suspect that it was not really a member of any group, but was a far flung outpost visited but rarely. Perhaps the war and its doubling the usual dangers of the sea would keep a ship of any kind whatever from visiting it. He refused to let the thought remain with him, suppressing it resolutely, and insisting to himself that such a pleasant little island was bound to have callers some time or other, some day.

But the weeks dragged by, and he was absolutely alone in his world. He had acquired so many stores from the schooner that life was comfortable. It even had a touch of luxury, and the struggle for existence was far from consuming all his hours. He found himself as time went on driven more and more upon his books, and he read them, as few have ever read anything, trying to penetrate everything and to draw from them the best lessons. As a student, in a very real sense of the term, Robert became more reconciled to his isolation. His mind was broadening and deepening, and he felt that it was so. Many things that had before seemed a puzzle to him now became plain. He was compelled, despite his youth, to meditate upon life, and he resolved that when he took up its thread again among his kind he would put his new knowledge to the best of uses.

He noted a growth of the body as well as of the mind. An abundant and varied diet and plenty of rest gave him a great physical stimulus. It seemed to him that he was taller, and he was certainly heavier. Wishing to profit to the utmost, and, having a natural neatness, he looked after himself with great care, bathing inside the reefs once every day, and, whether there was work to be done or not, taking plenty of exercise.

He lost count of the days, but he knew that he was far into the autumn, that in truth winter must have come in his own and distant north. That thought at times was almost maddening. Doubtless the snow was already falling on the peaks that had seen so many gallant exploits by his comrades and himself, and on George and Champlain, the lakes so beautiful and majestic under any aspect. Those were the regions he loved. When would he see them again? But such thoughts, too, he crushed and saw only the ship that was to take him back to his own.

Some change in the weather came, and he was aware that the winter of the south was at hand. Yet it was not cold. There was merely a fresh sparkle in the air, a new touch of crispness. Low, gray skies were a relief, after so much blazing sunshine, and the cool winds whipped his blood to new life. The house had a fireplace and chimney and often he built a low fire, not so much for the sake of warmth as for the cheer that the sparkling blaze gave. Then he could imagine that he was back in his beloved province of New York. Now the snow was certainly pouring down there. The lofty peaks were hidden in clouds of white, and the ice was forming around the edges of Andiatarocte and Oneadatote. Perhaps Willet and Tayoga were scouting in the snowy forests, but they must often hang over the blazing fires, too.

The coldness without, the blaze on the hearth, and the warmth within increased his taste for reading and his comprehension seemed to grow also. He found new meanings in the classics and he became saturated also with style. His were the gifts of an orator, and it was often said in after years, when he became truly great, that his speech, in words, in metaphor and in illustration followed, or at least were influenced, by the best models. Some people found in him traces of Shakespeare, the lofty imagery and poetry and the deep and wide knowledge of human emotions, of life itself. Others detected the mighty surge of Homer, or the flow of Virgil, and a few discerning minds found the wit shown in the comedies of the Restoration, from which he had unconsciously plucked the good, leaving the bad.

It is but a truth to say that every day he lived in these days he lived a week or maybe a month. The stillness, the utter absence of his kind, drove his mind inward with extraordinary force. He gained a breadth of vision and a power of penetration of which he had not dreamed. He acquired toleration, too. Looking over the recent events in his perilous life, he failed to find hate for anybody. Perhaps untoward events had turned the slaver into his evil career, and at the last he had shown some good. The French were surely fighting for what they thought was their own, and they struck in order that they might not be struck. Tandakora himself was the creature of his circumstances. He hated the people of the English colonies, because they were spreading over the land and driving away the game. He was cruel because it was the Ojibway nature to be cruel. He would have to fight Tandakora, but it was because conditions had made it necessary.

His absorption as a student now made him forget often that he was alone, and there were long periods when he was not unhappy, especially when he was trying to solve some abstruse mental problem. He regretted sometimes that he did not have any book on mathematics, but perhaps it was as well for him that he did not. His mind turned more to the other side of life, to style, to poetry, to the imagination, and, now, as he was moving along the line of least resistance, under singularly favourable circumstances, he made extraordinary progress.

Heavy winds came and Robert liked them. He had plenty of warm clothing and it pleased him to walk on the beach, his face whipped by the gale, and to watch the great waves come in. It made him stronger to fight the storm. The response to its challenge rose in his blood. It was curious, but at such times his hope was highest. He stood up, defying the lash of wind and rain, and felt his courage rise with the contest. Often, he ran up and down the beach until he was soaked through, letting the fierce waves sweep almost to his feet, then he would go back to the house, change to dry clothing, and sleep without dreams.

There was no snow, although he longed for it, as do those who are born in northern regions. Once, when he stood on the crest of the tallest hill on the island, he thought he saw a few tiny flakes floating in the air over his head, but they were swept away by the wind, as if they were down, and he never knew whether it was an illusion or reality. But he was glad that it had happened. It gave him a fleeting touch of home, and he could imagine once more, and, for a few seconds, that he was not alone on the island, but back in his province of New York, with his friends not far away.

Then came several days of fierce and continuous cold rain, but he put on an oilskin coat that he found among the stores and spent much of the time out of doors, hunting ducks along the edges of the larger lake, walking now and then for the sake of walking, and, on rare occasions, seeking the wild cattle for fresh meat. The herds were in the timber most of the time for shelter, but he was invariably able to secure a tender cow or a yearling for his larder. He saw the big bull often, and, although he was charged by him once again, he refused to pull trigger on the old fellow. He preferred to look upon him as a friend whom he had met once in worthy combat, but with whom he was now at peace. When the bull charged him he dodged him easily among the bushes and called out whimsically:

"Let it be the last time! I don't mean you any harm!"

The fierce leader went peacefully back to his grazing, and it seemed to Robert that he had been taken at his word. The old bull apparently realized at last that he was in no danger from the human being who came to look at him at times, and he also was willing to call a truce. Robert saw him often after that, and invariably hailed him with words of friendship, though at a respectful distance. The old fellow would look up, shake his big head once or twice in a manner not at all hostile, and then go on peacefully with his grazing. It pleased Robert to think that in the absence of his own kind he had a friend here, and—still at a respectful distance—he confided to him some of his opinions upon matters of importance. He laughed at himself for doing so, but he was aware that he found in it a certain relief, and he continued the practice.

The dinghy became one of his most precious possessions. A little farther to the north he had found a creek that flowed down from the centre of the island, rising among the hills. It was narrow and shallow, except near the mouth, but there it had sufficient depth for the boat, and he made of it a safe anchorage and port during the winter storms. He slept more easily now, as he knew that however hard the wind might blow there was no danger of its being carried out to sea. He thought several times of rigging a mast and sails for it and trying to make some other island, but he gave up the idea, owing to the smallness of the boat, and his own inexperience as a sailor. He was at least safe and comfortable where he was, and a voyage of discovery or escape meant almost certain death.

But he used the dinghy in calm weather for bringing back some of the stores that he had left on the other side of the island. The lighter articles he brought by land. There was not room for all of them in the house, but he built a shed under which he placed those not of a per-ishable nature, and covered them over with the tarpaulin and sails. He still had the feeling that he must not lose or waste anything, because he knew that in the back of his head lay an apprehension lest his time on the island should be long, very long.

He kept in iron health. His life in the wilderness had taught him how to take care of himself, and, with an abundant and varied diet and plenty of exercise, he never knew a touch of illness. He did not forget to be grateful for it. A long association with Tayoga had taught him to remember these things. It might be true that he was being guarded by good spirits. The white man's religion and the red man's differed only in name. His God and Tayoga's Manitou were the same, and the spirits of the Onondaga were the same as his angels of divine power and mercy.

Often in the moonlight he looked up at the great star upon which Tayoga said that Tododaho dwelled, that wise Onondaga chieftain who had gone away to the skies four hundred years before. Once or twice he thought he could see the face of Tododaho with the wise snakes, coil on coil in his hair, but, without his full faith, it was not given to him to have the full vision of Tayoga. He found comfort, however, in the effort. It gave new strength to the spirit, and, situated as he was, it was his soul, not his body, that needed fortifying.

He decided that Christmas was near at hand, and he decided to celebrate it. With the count of time lost it was impossible for him to know the exact day, but he fixed upon one in his mind, and re-solved to use it whether right or wrong in date. The mere fact that he celebrated it would make it right in spirit. It might be the 20th or the 30th of December, but if he chose to call it the 25th, the 25th it would be. Endowed so liberally with fancy and with such a power of projecting the mind, it was easy for him to make believe, to turn imagination into reality. And this power was heightened by his loneliness and isolation, and by the turning in of his mind so tremendously upon itself.

After the thought of a Christmas dinner was struck out by his fancy it grew fast, and he made elaborate preparations. Ducks were shot, a yearling from the wild cattle was killed, the stores from the ship were drawn upon liberally, and he even found among them a pudding which could yet be made savoury. Long experience had made him an excellent cook and he attended to every detail in the most thorough manner.

The dinner set, he arrayed himself in the finest clothes to be found in his stock, and then, when all was ready, he sat down to his improvised board. But there was not one plate alone, there were four, one for Willet opposite him, one for Tayoga at his right hand and one for Grosvenor at his left. And for every thing he ate he placed at least a small portion on every plate, while with unspoken words he talked with these three friends of his.

It was a dark day, very cold and raw for the island, and while there was no Christmas snow there was a cold rain lashing the windows that could very well take its place. A larger fire than usual, crackling and cheerful, was blazing on the hearth, throwing the red light of its flames over the table, and the three places where his invisible friends sat.

His power of evocation was so vivid and intense that he could very well say that he saw his comrades around the table. There was Willet big, grave and wise, but with the lurking humour in the corner of his eye, there was Tayoga, lean, calm, inscrutable, the young philosopher of the woods and the greatest trailer in the world, and there was Grosvenor, ruddy, frank, tenacious, eager to learn all the lore of the woods. Yes, he could see them and he was glad that he was serving Christmas food to them as well as to himself. Willet loved wild duck and so he gave him an extra portion. Tayoga was very partial to cakes of flour and so he gave him a double number, and Grosvenor, being an Englishman, must love beef, so he helped him often to steak.

It was fancy, but fancy breeds other and stronger fancies, and the feeling that it was all reality grew upon him. Dreams are of thin and fragile texture, but they are very vivid while they last. Of course Willet, Tayoga and Grosvenor were there, and when the food was all served, course by course, he filled four glasses, one at each plate, from a bottle of the old cordial that he had saved from the ship, lifted his own to his lips, tasted it and said aloud:

"To the victory of our cause under the walls of Quebec!"

Then he shut his eyes and when he shut them he saw the three tasting their own glasses, and he heard them say with him:

"To the victory of our cause under the walls of Quebec!"

CHAPTER 9

The Voice in the Air

Robert slept long and peacefully the night after his Christmas dinner, and, when he rose the next morning, he felt more buoyant and hopeful than for days past. The celebration had been a sort of anchor to his spirit, keeping him firm against any tide of depression that in his situation might well have swept him toward despair. As he recalled it the day after, Tayoga, Willet and Grosvenor were very vivid figures at his table, sitting opposite him, and to right and left. They had responded to his toast, he had seen the flash in their eyes, and their tones were resonant with hope and confidence. It was clear they had meant to tell him that rescue was coming.

He accepted these voices out of the distance as definite and real. It could not be long until he saw the hunter, the Onondaga and the young Englishman once more. His lonely life caused him, despite himself, to lend a greater belief to signs and omens. Tayoga was right when he peopled the air with spirits, and most of the spirits on that island must be good spirits, since all things, except escape, had been made easy for him, house, clothes, food and safety.

The day itself was singularly crisp and bright, inciting to further cheerfulness. It was also the coldest he had yet felt on the island, having a northern tang that stirred his blood. He could shut his eyes and see the great forests, not in winter, but as they were in autumn, glowing in many colours, and with an air that was the very breath of life. The sea also sang a pleasant song as it rolled in and broke on the rocks, and Robert, looking around at his island, felt that he could have fared far worse.

Rifle on shoulder he went off for a long and brisk walk, and his steps unconsciously took him, as they often did, toward the high hill in the centre of the island, a crest that he used as a lookout. On his way he passed his friend, the old bull, grazing in a meadow, and, watching his herd, like the faithful guardian he was. Robert called to him cheerfully. The big fellow looked up, shook his horns, not in hostile fashion but in the manner of comrade saluting comrade, and then went back, with a whole and confident heart, to his task of nipping the grass. Robert was pleased. It was certain that the bull no longer regarded him with either fear or apprehension, and he wanted to be liked.

It was nearly noon when he reached his summit, and as he was warm from exercise he sat down on a rock, staying there a long time and scouring the horizon now and then through the glasses. The sea was a circle of blazing blue, and the light wind sang from the southwest.

He had brought food with him and in the middle of the day he ate it. With nothing in particular to do he thought he would spend the afternoon there, and, making himself comfortable, he waited, still taking occasional glances through the glasses. While he sat, idling more than anything else, his mind became occupied with Tayoga's theory of spirits in the air—less a theory however than the religious belief of the Indians.

He wanted to believe that Tayoga was right, and his imagination was so vivid and intense that what he wished to believe he usually ended by believing. He shut his eyes and tested his power of evocation. He knew that he could create feeling in any part of his body merely by concentrating his mind upon that particular part of it and by continuing to think of it. Physical sensation even came from will. So he would imagine that he heard spirits in the air all about him, not anything weird or hostile, but just kindly people of the clouds and winds, such as those created by the old Greeks.

Fancying that he heard whispers about him and resolved to hear them, he heard them. If a powerful imagination wanted to create whispers it could create them. The spirits of the air, Tayoga's spirits, the spirits of old Hellas, were singing in either ear, and the song, like that of the sea, like the flavour breathed out by his Christmas celebration, was full of courage, alive with hope.

He had kept his eyes closed a full half hour, because, with sight shut off, the other senses became much more acute for the time. The power that had been in the eyes was poured into their allies. Imagination, in particular, leaped into a sudden luxuriant growth. It was true, of course it was quite true, that those friendly spirits of the air were singing all about him. They were singing in unison a gay and brilliant song, very pleasant to hear, until he was startled by a new note that came into it, a note not in harmony with the others, the voice of Cassandra herself. He listened and he was sure. Beyond a doubt it was a note of warning.

Robert opened his eyes and everything went away. There was the pleasant, green island, and there was the deep blue sea all about it. He laughed to himself. He was letting imagination go too far. One could make believe too much. He sat idly a few minutes and then, putting the glasses to his eyes, took another survey of the far horizon where blue sky and blue water met. He moved the focus slowly around the circle, and when he came to a point in the east he started violently, then sprang to his feet, every pulse leaping.

He had seen a tiny black dot upon the water, one that broke the continuity of the horizon line, and, for a little while, he was too excited to look again. He stood, the glasses in his trembling fingers and stared with naked eyes that he knew could not see. After a while he put the glasses back and then followed the horizon. He was afraid that it was an illusion, that his imagination had become too vivid, creating for him the thing that was not, and now that he was a little calmer he meant to put it to the proof.

He moved the glasses slowly from north to east, following the line where sky and water met, and then the hands that held them trembled again. There was the black spot, a trifle larger now, and, forcing his nerves to be calm, he stared at it a long time, how long he never knew, but long enough for him to see it grow and take form and shape, for the infinitesimal but definite outline of mast, sails and hull to emerge, and then for a complete ship to be disclosed.

The ship was coming toward the island. The increase in size told him that. It was no will-o'-the-wisp on the water, appearing a moment, then gone, foully cheating his hopes. If she kept her course, and there was no reason why she should not, she would make the island. He had no doubt from the first that a landing there was its definite purpose, most likely for water.

When he took the glasses from his eyes the second time he gave way to joy. Rescue was at hand. The ship, wherever she went, would take him to some place where human beings lived, and he could go thence to his own country. He would yet be in time to take part in the great campaign against Quebec, sharing the dangers and glory with Willet, Tayoga, Grosvenor and the others. The spirits in the air had sung to him a true song, when his eyes were shut, and, in his leaping exultation, he forgot the warning note that had appeared in their song, faint, almost buried, but nevertheless there.

He put the glasses to his eyes a third time. The ship was tacking, but that was necessary, and it was just as certain as ever that her destination was the island. Owing to the shifts and flaws in the wind it would be night before she arrived, but that did not matter to him. Having waited months he could wait a few hours longer. Likely as not she was an English ship out of the Barbadoes, bound for the Carolinas. He must be somewhere near just such a course. Or, maybe she was a colonial schooner, one of those bold craft from Boston. There was a certain luxury in speculating on it, and in prolonging a doubt which would certainly be solved by midnight, and to his satisfaction. It was not often that in real life one looked at a play bound to develop within a given time to a dramatic and satisfying finish.

He remained on the crest until late in the afternoon, watching the ship as she tacked with the varying winds, but, in the end, always bearing toward the island. He was quite sure now that her arrival would be after dark. She would come through the opening in the reefs that he and the slaver had made so hardly in the storm, but on the night bound to follow such a day it would be as easy as entering a drawing room, with the doors held open, and the guest made welcome. He would be there to give the welcome.

He was able to see more of the ship now. As he had surmised, she was a schooner, apparently very trim and handled well. Doubtless she was fast. The faster the better, because he was eager to get back to the province of New York.

Late in the afternoon, he left the hill and went swiftly back to his house, where he ate an early supper in order that he might be on the beach to give welcome to the guest, and perhaps lend some helpful advice about making port. There was none better fitted than he. He was the oldest resident of the island. Nobody could be jealous of his position as adviser to the arriving vessel.

This was to be a great event in his life, and it must be carried out in the proper manner with every attention to detail. He put on the uniform of an English naval officer that he had found on the ship, and then rifle on shoulder and small sword in belt went through the forest toward the inlet.

The night was bright and beautiful, just fitted for a rescue, and an escape from an island. All the stars had come out to see it, and, with his head very high, he trod lightly as he passed among the trees, approaching the quiet beach. Before he left the wood he saw the top of the schooner's mast showing over a fringe of bushes. Evidently she had anchored outside the reefs and was sending in a boat to look further. Well, that was fit and proper, and his advice and assistance would be most timely.

The wind rose a little and it sang a lilting melody among the leaves. His imagination, alive and leaping, turned it into the song of a troubadour, gay and welcoming. Tayoga's spirits were abroad again, filling the air in the dusk, their favourite time, and he rejoiced, until he suddenly heard once more that faint note of warning, buried under the volume of the other, but nevertheless there.

Alone, driven in upon himself for so many months, he was a creature of mysticism that night. What he imagined he believed, and, obedient to the warning, he drew back. All the caution of the northern wilderness returned suddenly to him. He was no longer rushing forward to make a welcome for guests awaited eagerly. He would see what manner of people came before he opened the door. Putting the rifle in the hollow of his arm he crept forward through the bushes.

A large boat was coming in from the schooner, and the bright moonlight enabled him to see at first glance that the six men who sat in it were not men of Boston. Nor were they men of England. They were too dark, and three of them had rings in their ears.

Perhaps the schooner was a French privateer, wishing to make a secret landing, and, if so, he had done well to hold back. He had no mind to be taken a prisoner to France. The French were brave, and he would not be ill-treated, but he had other things to do. He withdrew a little farther into the undergrowth. The door of welcome was open now only a few inches, and he was peering out at the crack, every faculty alive and ready to take the alarm.

The boat drew closer, grounded on the beach, and the men, leaping out, dragged it beyond the reach of the low waves that were coming in. Then, in a close group, they walked toward the forest, looking about curiously. They were armed heavily, and every one of them had a drawn weapon in his hand, sword or pistol. Their actions seemed to Robert those of men who expected a stranger, as a matter of course, to be an enemy. Hence, they were men whose hands were against other men, and so also against young Robert Lennox, who had been alone so long, and who craved so much the companionship of his kind.

He drew yet deeper into the undergrowth and taking the rifle out of the hollow of his arm held it in both hands, ready for instant use. The men came nearer, looking along the edge of the forest, perhaps for water, and, as he saw them better, he liked them less. The apparent leader was a short, broad fellow of middle years, and sinister face, with huge gold rings in his ears. All of them were seamed and scarred and to Robert their looks were distinctly evil.

The door of welcome suddenly shut with a snap, and he meant to bar it on the inside if he could. His instinct gave him an insistent warning. These men must not penetrate the forest. They must not find his house and treasures. Fortunately the dinghy was up the creek, hidden under overhanging boughs. But the event depended upon chance. If they found quickly the water for which they must be looking, they might take it and leave with the schooner before morning. He devoutly hoped that it would be so. The lad who had been so lonely and desolate an hour or two before, longing for the arrival of human beings, was equally eager, now that they had come, that they should go away.

The men began to talk in some foreign tongue, Spanish or Portuguese or a Levantine jargon, perhaps, and searched assiduously along the edges of the forest. Robert, lurking in the undergrowth, caught the word *aqua* or *agua*, which he knew meant water, and so he was right in his surmise about their errand. There was a fine spring about two hundred yards farther on, and he hoped they would soon stumble upon it.

All his skill as a trailer, though disused now for many months, came back to him. He was able to steal through the grass and bushes without making any noise and to creep near enough to hear the words they said. They went half way to the spring, then stopped and began to talk. Robert was in fear lest they turn back, and a wider search elsewhere would surely take them to his house. But the men were now using English.

"There should be water ahead," said the swart leader. "We're going down into a dip, and that's just the place where springs are found."

Another man, also short and dark, urged that they turn back, but the leader prevailed.

"There must be water farther on," he said. "I was never on this island before, neither were you, José, but it's not likely the trees and bushes would grow so thick down there if plenty of water didn't soak their roots."

He had his way and they went on, with Robert stalking them on a parallel line in the undergrowth, and now he knew they would find the water. The spirit of the island was watching over its own, and, by giving them what they wanted at once, would send these evil characters away. The leader uttered a shout of triumph when he saw the water gleaming through the trees.

"I told you it was here, didn't I, José?" he said. "Trust me, a sailor though I am, to read the lay of the land."

The spring as it ran from under a rock formed a little pool, and all of the men knelt down, drinking with noise and gurglings. Then the leader walked back toward the beach, and fired both shots from a double-barrelled pistol into the air. Robert judged that it was a signal, probably to indicate that they had found water. Presently a second and larger boat, containing at least a dozen men, put out from the schooner. A third soon followed and both brought casks which were filled at the spring and which they carried back to the ship.

Robert, still and well hidden, watched everything, and he was glad that he had obeyed his instinct not to trust them. He had never seen a crew more sinister in looks, not even on the slaver, and they were probably pirates. They were a jumble of all nations, and that increased his suspicion. So mixed a company, in a time of war, could be brought together only for evil purposes.

It was hard for him to tell who was the captain, but the leader who had first come ashore seemed to have the most authority, although nearly all did about as they pleased to the accompaniment of much talk and many oaths. Still they worked well at filling the water casks, and Robert hoped they would soon be gone. Near midnight, however, one of the boats came back, loaded with food, and kegs and bottles of spirits. His heart sank. They were going to have a feast or an orgy on the beach and the day would be sure to find them there. Then they might conclude to explore the island, or at least far enough to find his house.

They dragged up wood, lighted a fire, warmed their food and ate and drank, talking much, and now and then singing wild songs. Robert knew with absolute certainty that this was another pirate ship, a rover of the Gulf or the Caribbean, hiding among the islands and preying upon anything not strong enough to resist her.

The men filled him with horror and loathing. The light of the flames fell on their faces and heightened the evil in them, if that were possible. Several of them, drinking heavily of the spirits, were already in a bestial state, and were quarrelling with one another. The others paid no attention to them. There was no discipline.

Apparently they were going to make a night of it, and Robert watched, fascinated by the first sight of his own kind in many months, but repelled by their savagery when they had come. Some of the men fell down before the fires and went to sleep. The others did not awaken them, which he took to be clear proof that they would remain until the next day.

A drop of water fell on his face and he looked up. He had been there so long, and he was so much absorbed in what was passing before his eyes that he had not noted the great change in the nature of the night. Moon and stars were gone. Heavy clouds were sailing low. Thunder muttered on the western horizon, and there were flashes of distant lightning.

Hope sprang up in Robert's heart. Perhaps the fear of a storm would drive them to the shelter of the ship, but they did not stir. Either they did not dread rain, or they were more weather-wise than he. The orgy deepened. Two of the men who were quarrelling drew pistols, but the swart leader struck them aside, and spoke to them so fiercely that they put back their weapons, and, a minute later, Robert saw them drinking together in friendship.

The storm did not break. The wind blew, and, now and then, drops of rain fell, but it did not seem able to get beyond the stage of thunder and lightning. Yet it tried hard, and it became, even to Robert, used to the vagaries of nature, a grim and sinister night. The thunder, in its steady growling, was full of menace, and the lightning, reddish in colour, smelled of sulphur. It pleased Robert to think that the island was resenting the evil presence of the men from the schooner.

The ruffians, however, seemed to take no notice of the change. It was likely that they had not been ashore for a long time before, and they were making the most of it. They continued to eat and the bottles of spirits were passed continuously from one to another. Robert had heard many a dark tale of piracy on the Spanish Main and among the islands, but he had never dreamed he would come into such close contact with it as he was now doing for the second time.

He knew it was lucky for the men that the storm did not break. The schooner in her position would be almost sure to drag her anchor and then would drive on the rocks, but they seemed to have no apprehensions, and, it was quite evident now, that they were not going back to the vessel until the next day. The ghastly quality of the night increased, however. The lightning flared so much and it was so red that it was uncanny, it even had a supernatural tinge, and the sullen rumbling of the distant thunder added to it.

The effect upon Robert, situated as he was and alone for many months, was very great. Something weird, something wild and in touch with the storm that threatened but did not break, crept into his own blood. He was filled with hatred and contempt of the men who caroused there. He wondered what crimes they had committed on those seas, and he had not the least doubt that the list was long and terrible. He ought to be an avenging spirit. He wished intensely that Tayoga was with him in the bush. The Onondaga would be sure to devise some plan to punish them or to fill them with fear. He felt at that moment as if he belonged to a superior race or order, and would like to stretch forth his hand and strike down those who disgraced their kind.

The swart leader at last took note of the skies and their sinister aspect. Robert saw him walking back and forth and looking up. More than half of his men were stretched full length, either asleep or in a stupor, but some of the others stood, and glanced at the skies. Robert thought he saw apprehension in their eyes, or at least his imagination put it there.

A wild and fantastic impulse seized him. These men were children of the sea, superstitious, firm believers in omens, and witchcraft, ready to see the ghosts of the slain, all the more so because they were stained with every crime, then committed so freely under the black flag. He had many advantages, too. He was a master of woodcraft, only their wilderness was that of the waters.

He gave forth the long, melancholy hoot of the owl, and he did it so well that he was surprised at his own skill. The note, full of desolation and menace, seemed to come back in many echoes. He saw the swart leader and the men with him start and look fearfully toward the forest that curved so near. Then he saw them talking together and gazing at the point from which the sound had come. Perhaps they were trying to persuade themselves the note was only fancy.

Robert laughed softly to himself. He was pleased, immensely pleased with his experiment. His fantastic mood grew. He was a spirit of the woods himself; one of those old fauns of the Greeks, and he was really there to punish the evil invaders of his island. His body seemed to grow light with his spirit and he slid away among the trees with astonishing ease, as sure of foot and as noiseless as Tayoga himself. Then the owl gave forth his long, lonely cry with increased volume and fervour. It was a note filled with complaint and mourning, and it told of the desolation that overspread a desolate world.

Robert knew now that the leader and his men were disturbed. He could tell it by the anxious way in which they watched the woods, and, gliding farther around the circle, he sent forth the cry a third time. He was quite sure that he had made a further increase in its desolation and menace, and he saw the swart leader and his men draw together as if they were afraid.

The owl was not the only trick in Robert's trade. His ambition took a wide sweep and fancy was fertile. He had aroused in these men the fear of the supernatural, a dread that the ghosts of those whom they had murdered had come back to haunt or punish them. He had been an apt pupil of Tayoga before the slaver came to Albany, and now he meant to show the ruffians that the owl was not the only spirit of fate hovering over them.

The deep growl of a bear came from the thicket, not the growl of an ordinary black bear, comedian of the forest, but the angry rumble of some great ursine beast of which the black bear was only a dwarf cousin. Then he moved swiftly to another point and repeated it.

He heard the leader cursing and trying to calm the fears of the men while it was evident that his own too were aroused. The fellow suddenly drew a pistol and fired a bullet into the forest. Robert heard it cutting the leaves near him. But he merely lay down and laughed. His fantastic impulse was succeeding in more brilliant fashion than he had hoped.

Imitating their leader, six or eight of the men snatched out pistols and fired at random into the woods. The cry of a panther, drawn out, long, full of ferocity and woe, plaintive on its last note, like the haunting lament of a woman, was their answer. He heard a gasp of fear from the men, but the leader, of stauncher stuff, cowed them with his curses.

Robert moved back on his course, and then gave forth the shrill, fierce yelp of the hungry wolf, dying into an angry snarl. It was, perhaps, a more menacing note than that of the larger animals, and he plainly saw the ruffians shiver. He was creating in them the state of mind that he wanted, and his spirits flamed yet higher. All things seemed possible to him in his present mood.

He moved once more and then lay flat in the dense bushes. He fancied that the pirates would presently fire another volley into the shadows, and, in a moment of desperate courage, might even come into the forest. His first thought was correct, as the leader told off the steadier men, and, walking up and down in front of the forest, they raked it for a considerable distance with pistol shots. All of them, of course, passed well over Robert's head, and as soon as they finished he went back to his beginnings, giving forth the owl's lament.

He heard the leader curse more fiercely than ever before, and he saw several of the men who had been pulling trigger retreat to the fire. It was evident to him that the terror of the thing was entering their souls. The night itself, as if admiring his plan, was lending him the greatest possible aid. The crimson lightning never ceased to quiver and the sullen rumble of the distant thunder was increasing. It was easy enough for men, a natural prey to superstition, and, with the memories of many crimes, to believe that the island was haunted, that the ghosts of those they had slain were riding the lightning, and that demons, taking the forms of animals, were waiting for them in the bushes.

But the swart leader was a man of courage and he still held his ruffians together. He cursed them fiercely, told them to stand firm, to reload their pistols and to be ready for any danger. Those who still slumbered by the fire were kicked until they awoke, and, with something of a commander's skill, the man drew up his besotted band against the mystic dangers that threatened so closely.

But Robert produced a new menace. He was like one inspired that night. The dramatic always appealed to him and his success stimulated him to new histrionic efforts. He had planted in their minds the terror of animals, now he would sow the yet greater terror of human beings, knowing well that man's worst and most dreaded enemy was man.

He uttered a deep groan, a penetrating, terrible groan, the wail of a soul condemned to wander between the here and the hereafter, a cry from one who had been murdered, a cry that would doubtless appeal to every one of the ruffians as the cry of his own particular victim. The effect was startling. The men uttered a yell of fright, and started in a panic run for the boats, but the leader threatened them with his levelled pistol and stopped them, although the frightful groan came a second time.

"There's nothing in the bush!" Robert heard him say. "There can't be! The place has no people and we know there are no big wild animals on the islands in these seas! It's some freak of the wind playing tricks with us!"

He held his men, though they were still frightened, and to encourage them and to prove that no enemy, natural or supernatural, was near, he plunged suddenly into the bushes to see the origin of the terrifying sounds. His action was wholly unexpected, and chance brought him to the very point where Robert was. The lad leaped to his feet and the pirate sprang back aghast, thinking perhaps that he had come face to face with a ghost. Then with a snarl of malignant anger he levelled the pistol that he held in his hand. But Robert struck instantly with his clubbed rifle, and his instinctive impulse was so great that he smote with tremendous force. The man was caught full and fair on the head, and, reeling back from the edge of the bushes in which they stood, fell dead in the open, where all his men could see.

It was enough. The demons, the ghosts that haunted them for their crimes, were not very vocal, but they struck with fearful power. They had smitten down the man who tried to keep them on their island, and they were not going to stay one second longer. There was a combined yell of horror, the rush of frightened feet, and, reaching their boats, they rowed with all speed for the schooner, leaving behind them the body of their dead comrade.

Robert, awed a little by his own success in demonology, watched until they climbed on board the ship, drawing the boats after them. Then they hoisted the anchor, made sail, and presently he saw the schooner tacking in the wind, obviously intending to leave in all haste that terrible place.

She became a ghost ship, a companion to the *Flying Dutchman*, outlined in red by the crimson lightning that still played at swift intervals. Now she turned to the colour of blood, and the sea on which she swam was a sea of blood. Robert watched her until at last, a dim, red haze, she passed out of sight. Then he turned and looked at the body of the man whom he had slain.

He shuddered. He had never intended to take the leader's life. Five minutes before it occurred he would have said such a thing was impossible. It was merely the powerful impulse of self-protection that had caused him to strike with such deadly effect, and he was sorry. The man, beyond all doubt, was a robber and murderer who had forfeited his life a dozen times, and still he was sorry. It was a tragedy to him to take the life of any one, no matter how evil the fallen might be.

He went back to the house, brought a shovel, one of the numerous ship's stores, and buried the body at once high up the beach where the greatest waves could not reach it and wash it away. He did his task to the rumble of thunder and the flash of lightning, but, when he finished it, dawn came and then the storm that had threatened but that had never burst passed away. He felt, though, that it had not menaced him. To him it was a good storm, kindly and protecting, and giving sufficient help in his purpose that had succeeded so well.

It was a beautiful day, the air crisp with as much winter as the island ever knew, and shot with the beams from a brilliant sun, but Robert was exhausted. He had passed through a night of intense emotions, various, every one of them poignant, and he had made physical and mental efforts of his own that fairly consumed the nerves. He felt as if he could lie down and sleep for a year, that it would take at least that long to build up his body and mind as they were yesterday.

He dragged himself through the woods, forced his unwilling muscles to cook a breakfast which he ate. Then he laid himself down on his bed, his nerves now quiet, and fell asleep at once. When he awoke it was night and he lay giving thanks for his great escape until he slept again. When he awoke a second time day had returned, and, rising, he went about his usual tasks with a light heart.

CHAPTER 10

The Sloop of War

Robert ate a light breakfast and went out to look at his domain, now unsullied. What a fine, trim, clean island it was! And how desirable to be alone on it, when the Gulf and the Caribbean produced only such visitors as those who had come two nights before! He looked toward the little bay, fearing to see the topmast of the schooner showing its tip over the trees, but the sky there, an unbroken blue, was fouled by no such presence. He was rid of the pirates—and forever he hoped.

It seemed to him that he had passed through an epic time, one of the great periods of his life. He wondered now how he had been able to carry out such a plan, how he had managed to summon up courage and resources enough, and he felt that the good spirits of earth and air and water must have been on his side. They had fought for him and they had won for him the victory.

He shouldered his rifle and strolled through the woods toward the beach. He had never noticed before what a fine forest it was. The trees were not as magnificent as those of the northern wilderness, but they had a beauty very peculiarly their own, and they were his. There was not a single other claimant to them anywhere in the world.

It was a noble beach too, smooth, sloping, piled with white sand, gleaming now in the sun, and the little frothy waves that ran up it and lapped at his feet, like puppies nibbling, were just the friendliest frothy little waves in the world. But there were the remains of the fire left by the ruffians to defile it, and broken bottles and broken food were scattered about. The litter hurt his eyes so much that he gathered up every fragment, one by one, and threw them into the sea. When the last vestige of the foul invasion was cleared away he felt that he had his lonely, clean island back again, and he was happy.

He strolled up and down the glistening beach, feeling a great content. After a while, he threw off his clothes and swam in the invigorating sea, keeping well inside the white line of the breakers, in those waters into which the sharks did not come. When he had sunned himself again on the sand he went to the creek, took his dinghy from the bushes, where it had been so well hidden, and rowed out to sea, partly to feel the spring of the muscles in his arms, and partly to sit off at a distance and look at his island. Surely if one had to be cast away that was the very island on which he would choose to be cast! Not too big! Not too hot! And not too cold! Without savage man or savage beasts, but with plenty of wild cattle for the taking, and good fish in the lakes, and in the seas about it. Plenty of stores of all kinds from the slaver's schooner, even books to read. So far from being unfortunate he was one of the lucky. A period of retirement from the companionship of his own kind might be trying on the spirit, but it also meant meditation and mental growth.

His joy over the departure of the pirates was so great and his temperament was such that he felt a mighty revulsion of the spirits. He had a period of extravagant elation. He took off his cap and saluted his island. He made little speeches of glowing compliment to it, he called it the pearl of its kind, the choicest gem of the Gulf or the Caribbean, and, if pirates came again while he was there, he would drive them away once more with the aid of the good spirits.

He rowed back, hid his boat in the old covert among the bushes at the edge of the creek, and, rifle on shoulder, started through the forest toward his peak of observation. On the way, he passed the lake and saw the herd of wild cattle grazing there, the old bull at its head. The big fellow, assured now by use and long immunity, cocked his head on one side and regarded him with a friendly eye. But the bull had a terrible surprise. He heard the sharp ping of a rifle and a fearful yell. Then he saw a figure capering in wild gyrations, and thinking that this human being whom he had learned to trust must have gone mad, he forgot to be angry, but was very much frightened. Enemies he could fight, but mad creatures he dreaded, and, bellowing hoarsely to his convoy, as a signal, he took flight, all of them following him, their tails streaming straight out behind them, so fast they ran.

Robert leaped and danced as long as one of them was in sight. When the last streaming tail had disappeared in the bushes he sobered down. He realized that he had given his friend, the bull, a great shock. In a way, he had been guilty of a breach of faith, and he resolved to apologize to him in some fashion the next time they met. Yet he had been so exultant that it was impossible not to show it, and he was only a lad in years.

When he reached the crest of his peak he scanned the sea on all sides. Eagerly as he had looked before for a sail he now looked to see that there was none. Around and around the circle of the horizon his eyes travelled, and when he assured himself that no blur broke the bright line of sea and sky his heart swelled with relief.

In a day or so, his mind became calm and his thoughts grew sober. Then he settled down to his studies. The battle of life occupied only a small portion of his time, and he resolved to put the hours to the best use. He pored much over Shakespeare, the other Elizabethans and the King James Bible, a copy of which was among the books. It was his intention to become a lawyer, an orator, and if possible a statesman. He knew that he had the gift of speech. His mind was full of thoughts and words always crowded to his lips. It was easy enough for him to speak, but he must speak right. The thoughts he wished to utter must be clothed in the right kind of words arranged in the right way, and he resolved that it should be so.

The way in which men thought and the way in which their thoughts were put in the Bible and the great Elizabethans fascinated him. That was the way in which he would try to think, and the way in which he would try to put his thoughts. So he recited the noble passages over and over again, he memorized many of them, and he listened carefully to himself as he spoke them, alike for the sense and the music and power of the words.

It was then perhaps that he formed the great style for which he was so famous in after years. His vocabulary became remarkable for its range, flexibility and power, and he developed the art of selection. His rivals even were used to say of him that he always chose the best word. He learned there on the island that language was not given to man merely that he might make a noise, but that he might use it as a great marksman uses a rifle.

Work and study together filled his days. They kept far from him also any feeling of despair. He had an abiding faith that a ship of the right kind would come in time and take him away. He must not worry about it. It was his task now to fit himself for the return, to prove to his friends when he saw them once more that all the splendid opportunities offered to him on the island had not been wasted.

Almost unconsciously, he began to reason more deeply, to look further into the causes of things, and his mind turned particularly to the present war. The more he thought about it the greater became his conviction that England and the colonies were bound to win. Courage and numbers, resources and tenacity must prevail even over great

317

initial mistakes. Duquesne and Ticonderoga would be brushed away as mere events that had no control over destiny.

He remembered Bigot's ball in Quebec that Willet and Tayoga and he had attended. It came before him again almost as vivid as reality. He realized now in the light of greater age and experience how it typified decadence. A power that was rotten at the top, where the brain should be, could never defeat one that was full of youthful ardour and strength, sound through and through, awkward and ill directed though that strength might be. The young French leaders and their soldiers were valiant, skilful and enduring—they had proved it again and again on sanguinary fields—but they could not prevail when they had to receive orders from a corrupt and reckless court at Versailles, and, above all when they had to look to that court for help that never came.

His reading of the books in the slaver's chest told him that folly and crime invariably paid the penalty, if not in one way then in another, and he remembered too some of the ancient Greek plays, over which he had toiled under the stern guidance of Master Alexander McLean. Their burden was the certainty of fate. You could never escape, no matter how you writhed, from what you did, and those old writers must have told the truth, else men would not be reading and studying them two thousand years after they were dead. Only truth could last twenty centuries. Bigot, Cadet, Péan, and the others, stealing from France and Canada and spending the money in debauchery, could not be victorious, despite all the valour of Montcalm and St. Luc and De Levis and their comrades.

He remembered, too, the great contrast between Quebec and New York that had struck him when he arrived at the port at the mouth of the Hudson with the hunter and the Onondaga. The French capital in Canada was all of the state; it was its creature. If the state declined, it declined, there was little strength at the roots, little that sprang from the soil, but in New York, which men already forecast as the metropolis of the New World, there was strength everywhere. It might be a sprawling town. There might be no courtliness to equal the courtliness at the heart of Quebec, but there was vigour, vigour everywhere. The people were eager, restless, curious, always they worked and looked ahead.

He saw all these things very clearly. Silence, loneliness and distance gave a magnificent perspective. Facts that were obscured when he was near at hand, now stood out sharp and true. His thoughts in this period were often those of a man double his age. His iron health too remained. His was most emphatically the sound mind in the sound body, each helping the other, each stimulating the other to greater growth.

It was a fact, however, that the Onondaga belief, peopling the air and all sorts of inanimate objects with spirits, grew upon him; perhaps it is better to say that it was a feeling rather than a belief. According to Tayoga the good spirits fought with the bad, and on his island the good had prevailed. They had told him that a ship was coming, and then they had warned him that it would be a ship of pirates. They had shown him how to drive away the ruffians. His inspiration had not been his own, it had come from them and he thankfully acknowledged it.

He told himself now as he went about his island that he heard the good spirits singing among the leaves and he told it to himself so often that he ended by believing it. It was such a pleasant and consoling belief too. He listened to hear them say that he would leave the island when the time was ripe and his imagination was now so extraordinarily vivid that what he expected to hear he heard. The spirits assured him that when the time came to go he would go. They did not tell him exactly when he would go, but that could not be asked. No one must anticipate a complete unveiling of the future. It was sufficient that intimations came out of it now and then.

It was this feeling, amounting to a conviction, that bore him up on a shield of steel. It soothed the natural impatience of his youth and temperament. Why grieve over not going when he knew that he would go? Yet, a long time passed and there was no sail upon the sea, though the fact failed to shake his faith. Often he climbed his peak of observation and studied the circling horizon through the glasses, only to find nothing, but he was never discouraged. There was never any fall of the spirits. No ship showed, but the ship that was coming might even then be on the way. She had left some port, probably one in England, not dreaming that it was a most important destiny and duty of hers to pick up a lone lad cast away on an island in the Gulf or the Caribbean—at least it was most important to him.

Now came a time of storms that seemed to him to portend a change in the seasons. The island was swept by wind and rain, but he liked to be lashed by both. He even went out in the dinghy in storms, though he kept inside the reefs, and fought with wave and undertow and swell, until, pleasantly exhausted, he retreated to the beach, drawing his little boat after him, where he watched the sea, vainly struggling to reach the one who had defied it. It was after such contests that he felt strongest of the spirit, ready to challenge anything.

He plunged deeper and deeper into his studies, striving to understand everything. The intensity of his application was possible only because he was alone. Forced to probe, to examine and to ponder, his mind acquired new strength. Many things which otherwise would have been obscure to him became plain. Looking back upon his own eventful life since that meeting with St. Luc and Tandakora in the forest, he was better able to read motives and to understand men. The reason why Adrian Van Zoon wished him to vanish must be money, because only money could be powerful enough to make such a man risk a terrible crime. Well, he would have a great score to settle with Van Zoon. He did not yet know just how he would settle it, but he did not doubt that the day of reckoning would come.

A cask of oil and several lanterns were among his treasures from the ship, and, making use of them, he frequently read late at night, often with the rain beating hard on walls and roof. Then it seemed to him that his mind was clearest, and he resolved again and again that when he returned to his own he would make full use of what he learned on the island. It seemed to him sometimes that his being cast away was a piece of luck and not a misfortune.

A clear day came, and, taking his rifle, he strolled toward his peak of observation, passing on the way the herd of wild cattle with the old bull at its head. The big fellow looked at him suspiciously, as if fearing that his friend might be suffering from one of his mad spells again. But Robert's conduct was quite correct. He walked by in a quiet and dignified manner, and, reassured, the bull went back to his task of reducing the visible grass supply.

He saw nothing from the peak except the green island and the blue sea all about it, but there was a singing wind among the leaves and it was easy for him to sit down on a rock and fall into a dreaming state. The good spirits were abroad, and it was their voices that he heard among the leaves. Their chant too was full of courage, hope and promise, and his spirits lifted as he listened. They were watching over him, guarding him from evil, and he felt, at last, that they were telling him something.

It is not always easy to know the exact burden of a song, even if it is uplifting, and Robert listened a long time, trying to decipher exactly what the good spirits were saying to him. It was just such a song as they sang to him before the pirate ship came, saving one strain and that was most important. There was no underlying note of warning. Hunt for it as he would, with his fullest power of hearing, he could detect no trace of it. Then he became convinced. Another ship was coming, and this time it was no pirate craft.

He roused himself from his dreaming state and shook his head, but the vision did not depart. The ship was coming and it was for him to receive it. The news of it had been written too deeply upon the sensitive plate of his brain to be effaced, and, as he walked back toward the house, it seemed to grow more vivid. He was too much excited to study that day, and he spent the time building a great heap of wood upon the beach. Even if one were helped by good spirits he must do his own part. They might bring the ship to the horizon's rim, but it was for him to summon it from there, and he would have a great bonfire ready.

The brilliance of the day departed in the afternoon, and it became apparent that the season of rain and storm was not yet over. Clouds marched up in grim battalions from the south and west, rain came in swift puffs and then in long, heavy showers, the sea heaved, breaking into great waves and the surf dashed fiercely on the sharp teeth of the rocks.

Robert's spirits fell. This was not the way in which a rescuing ship should come, under a sombre sky and before driving winds. Perhaps he had read the voices of the spirits wrong, or at least the ship, instead of coming now, was coming at some later time, a month or two months away maybe. He watched through the rest of the afternoon, hoping that the clouds would leave, but they only thickened, and, long before the time of sunset, it was almost as dark as night. He was compelled to remain in the shelter of the house, and, in a state of deep depression, he ate his supper without appetite.

The storm was one of the fiercest he had seen while on the island. The rain drove in sheets, beating upon the walls and roof of the house like hail, and the wind kept up a continuous whistling and screaming. All the while the house trembled over him. Nor was there any human voice in the wind. The good spirits, if such existed, would not dare the storm, but had retreated to cover. All the illusion was gone, he was just a lonely boy on a lonely island, listening to the wrath of a hurricane, a ship might or might not come, most probably never, or if it did it would be another pirate.

The storm did not seem to abate as the evening went on, perhaps it was the climax of the season. Tired of hearing its noise he lay down on his couch and at last fell asleep. He was awakened from slumber by an impact upon the drum of his ear like a light blow, but, sitting up, he realized that it was a sound. The storm had not abated. He heard the beat of wind and rain as before, but he knew it was something else that had aroused him. The noise of the storm was regular, it was going on when he fell asleep, and it had never ceased while he slept. This was something irregular, something out of tune with it, and rising above it. He listened intently, every nerve and pulse alive, body and mind at the high pitch of excitement, and then the sound came again, low but distinct, and rising above the steady crash of the storm.

He knew the note. He had heard it often, too often on that terrible day at Ticonderoga. It could be but one thing. It was the boom of a cannon, and it could come only from a ship, a ship in danger, a ship driven by the storm, knowing nothing of either sea or island, sending forth her signal of distress which was also a cry for help.

It was his ship! The ship of rescue! But he must first rescue *it*! Now he heard the voices of the good spirits, the voices that had been silent all through the afternoon and evening, singing through the storm, calling to him, summoning him to action. He had not taken off his clothes and he leaped from the couch, snatched up a lighted lantern, stuffed flint and steel in his pocket, and ran out into the wind and rain, of which he was now scarcely conscious.

The boom came to his ears a second time, off to the east, and now distinctly the report of a cannon. He waited a little, watching, and, when the report came a third time, he saw dimly the flash of the gun, but it was too dark for him to see anything of the ship. She was outside the reefs, how far he could not tell, but he knew by the difference in the three reports that she was driving toward the island.

It was for him to save the unknown vessel that was to save him, and in the darkness and storm he felt equal to the task. His soul leaped within him. His whole body seemed to expand. He knew what to do, and, quick as lightning, he did it. He ran at full speed through the woods, his lighted lantern swinging on his arm, and twice on the way he heard the boom of the cannon, each time a little nearer. The reports merely made him run faster. Time was precious, and in the moment of utmost need he was not willing to lose a second.

He reached the great heap of wood that he had built up on the beach, worked frantically with flint and steel, shielding the shavings at the bottom with his body, and quickly set fire to them. The blaze crackled, leaped and grew. He had built his pyramid so well, and he had selected such inflammable material, that he knew, if the flames once took hold, the wind would fan them so fiercely the rain could not put them out.

Higher sprang the blaze, running to the crest of the pyramid, roaring in the wind and then sending out defiant hissing tongues at the rain. The boom of the cannon came once more, and, then by the light of his splendid bonfire, he looked. There was the ship outside the reefs which his great pyramid of flame now enabled her to see.

He shouted in his joy, and threw on more wood. If he could only build that pyramid high enough they would see the opening too and make for it.

He worked frantically, throwing on driftwood, the accumulation of many years, and the flames biting into every fresh log, roared and leaped higher. The ship ceased to fire her signal guns, and now he saw, with a great surge of joy, that she was beating up in the storm and trying for the opening in the reef, her only chance, the chance that he had given her. He had done his part and he could do no more but feed the fire.

As he threw on wood he watched. His pyramid of flame roared and threw out sparks in myriads. The ship, a sloop, was having a desperate struggle with wind and wave, but his beacon was always there, showing her the way, and he never doubted for a moment that she would make the haven. He was sure of it. It was a terrible storm, and there was a fierce sea beating on the reefs, but a master mind was on the sloop, the mind of a great sailor, and that mind, responding to his signal of the fire, the only one that could have been made, was steering the ship straight for the opening in the reef.

His glasses were always in his pocket, and, remembering them now for the first time, he clapped them to his eyes. The sloop and her tracery of mast and spars became distinct. He saw guns on the deck and men, men in uniform, and he could see well enough, a moment or two later, to tell that they wore the uniform of Britain. His heart gave a wild throb. The spirits in the air were good spirits, and the storm had never been able to drive them away. They had been calling to him when he thought they were silent, only he had not been able to hear them.

He gave a wild shout of joy that could be heard above the crash of the storm. Triumph was assured. He was rescuing, and he would be rescued. He did not realize until that instant how eager he was to be taken from the island, how he longed, with all his soul, to rejoin his own kind, to see his friends again and to take a part in the great events that were shaking the world. He uttered his wild shout over and over, and, in between, he laughed, laughed with a joy that he could not control.

The sloop entered the opening. It seemed to him that the rocks, those fearful sharks' teeth, almost grazed her on either side, and his heart stood still, but she went safely past them, drew into the little harbour where she was safe from the wildest storm that ever blew, dropped anchor, and was at rest.

Robert in his exultation had never permitted his fire to die down an inch. Rather he had made it grow higher and higher until it was a vast core of light, throwing a red glare over the beach and the adjacent waves, and sending off vast showers of sparks. But when the ship cast anchor in her port he stood still before it, a dark figure, a perfect silhouette outlined against a blazing background, and watched, while a boat was launched from the sloop.

He saw five figures descend into the boat. Four were sailors and one an officer in uniform, and he knew well that they were coming to see him, the human being by the fire who had saved them. Pride was mingled with his joy. If he had not been there the sloop and probably all on board of her would have perished. It was touch and go, only a brief opportunity to save had been allowed him, but he had used it. So he raised himself to his full height, straightened his clothes, for which he always had respect despite the storm, and waited on. He had a full sense of drama, and he felt that this was one of the most dramatic moments of his life.

The boat came up the beach on a wave, the men sprang out, held it as the wave retreated, and then dragged it after them until it was beyond the reach of invading water. Robert meanwhile never stirred, and the great fire behind him enlarged his figure to heroic proportions.

The officer, young, handsome, in the British naval uniform, walked forward, with the four sailors following in a close group behind, but he stopped again, and looked at the strange figure before him. Evidently something in its pose, in its whole appearance, in truth, made an extraordinary impression upon him. He passed his hands before his eyes as if to make sure that it was no blur of the vision, and then he went forward again, the sailors keeping close behind, as if they were in fear lest the figure prove to be supernatural.

"Who are you?" called the young officer.

"Robert Lennox, of Albany, the Province of New York, and the wilderness," replied Robert. "Welcome to my island."

His sense of drama was still strong upon him, and he replied in his fullest and clearest voice. The officer stared, and then said:

"You've saved the ship and all our lives."

"I think that's what I was here for, though it's likely that you've saved me, too. What ship it that?"

"His Majesty's sloop of war, *Hawk*, Captain Stuart Whyte, from Bridgetown in the Barbadoes, for Boston."

Robert thrilled when he heard the word "Boston." It was not New York, but it was a port for home, nevertheless.

"Who are you?" continued the officer, on fire with curiosity. "You've told me your name, but what are you? and where are the other people of the island?"

"There are no other people. It's my island. I'm sole lord of the isle, and you're most welcome."

"You heard our signal guns?"

"Aye, I heard 'em, but I knew before you fired a shot that you were coming."

"'Tis impossible!"

"It's not! I knew it, though I can't explain how to you. Behold my bonfire! Do you think I could have built such a pyramid of wood between the firing of your first shot and your coming into my harbour? No, I was ready and waiting for you."

"That's convincing."

"I repeat that I welcome you to Lennox Island. My house is but a short distance inland in a beautiful forest. I should like to receive Captain Whyte there as an honoured guest, and you, too."

"Your house?"

"Aye, my house. And it's well built and well furnished. You'd be surprised to know how much comfort it can offer."

The officer—a lieutenant—and the men, coming closer, inspected Robert with the most minute curiosity. Lone men on desert islands were likely to go insane, and it was a momentary thought of the officer that he was dealing with some such unhappy creature, but Robert's sentences were too crisp, and his figure too erect and trim for the thought to endure more than a few seconds.

"It's raining heavily," he said, "and Captain Whyte will be glad to be a guest at your home later. I'll admit that for a moment I doubted the existence of your house, but I don't now. Are you willing to go on board the *Hawk* with us and meet Captain Whyte?"

"Gladly," replied Robert, who felt that his dramatic moment was being prolonged. "The storm is dying now. Having done its worst against you, and, having failed, it seems willing to pass away."

"But we don't forget that you saved us," said the officer. "My name is Lanham, John Lanham, and I'm a lieutenant on the *Hawk*."

The storm was, in truth, whistling away to the westward and its rage, so far as Robert's island was concerned, was fully spent. The waves were sinking and the night was lightening fast. The sloop of war, heaving at her anchorage, stood up sharp and clear, and it seemed to Robert that there was something familiar in her lines. As he looked he was sure. Coincidence now and then stretches forth her long arm, and she had stretched it now.

The sailors, when the sea died yet more, relaunched the boat. Lanham and Robert sprang in, and the men bent to the oars.

325

CHAPTER 11

Back to the World

Captain Stuart Whyte of His Majesty's gallant sloop of war, the *Hawk*, was standing on his own quarterdeck, looking curiously at the scene about him, and, taking it in, as well as he could, by the light of a great bonfire blazing on the beach some distance away. He was a young officer and his immense relief predominated over his curiosity. The *Hawk* was a fine sloop, and he loved her, but there had been a terrible time that night when he thought she was lost and her crew and himself with her.

He had seen more than one storm in these sudden seas, but this was perhaps the worst. All bearings were gone, and then the signs showed breakers. He was a brave man and he had brave officers, but every one of them had despaired, until suddenly a light, a pillar of fire, rose in the darkness and the storm, almost from the heart of the ocean, as if it had been evoked by his own signal guns. Then, by this marvellous beacon, they had scraped between the rocks and into safety. Clearly it was a miracle, and young Captain Whyte felt a deep and devout gratitude. He had then sent one of his best officers ashore to see the man who had saved them, and, meanwhile, he had stood by, watching through his glasses.

He saw the man of the island get into the boat with Lanham and approach the sloop. The storm had now sunk much, and it was not difficult to come aboard, but Captain Whyte, still intensely curious, but with a proper sense of his own dignity, withdrew to his cabin where he might receive the lord of the isle in state.

He rose politely, and then stared at the tall youth who came in with Lieutenant Lanham, the water running from his clothes. Yet the stranger had a dignity fully equal to his own, and there was also something very uncommon about him, a look of strength and confidence extraordinary in one so young.

"Won't you sit down?" said Captain Whyte.

Robert glanced at his clothes.

"I bring the storm with me," he said—he often spoke in the language that he had unconsciously imbibed in much reading of the Elizabethans.

"Never mind that. Water won't hurt my cabin, and if it did you're welcome just the same. I suppose you represent the people of the island, to whom my crew and I owe so much."

"I am the people of the island."

"You mean that you're here alone?"

"Exactly that. But tell me, before we go any further, Captain, what month this is."

"May."

"And the year?"

"1759."

"I wanted to be sure. I see that I've been on the island eight or nine months, but I lost all count of time, and, now and then it seemed like eight or nine years. As I've already told Lieutenant Lanham, I'm Robert Lennox, of Albany, the Province of New York, and the wilderness. I was kidnapped at Albany and carried down the Hudson and out to sea by a slaver and pirate."

"'Tis an extraordinary tale, Mr. Lennox."

"But a true one, Captain Whyte."

"I meant no insinuation that it wasn't. Extraordinary things happen in the world, and have been happening in these seas, ever since Columbus first came into them."

"Still mine is such an unusual story that it needs proof, and I give it. Did you not last autumn pretend that yours was a merchant ship, have a sailor play the violin on deck while others danced about, and lure under your guns a pirate with the black flag at her masthead?"

Captain Whyte stared in astonishment.

"How do you know that?" he exclaimed.

"Did you not shatter the pirate ship with your broadsides but lose her afterwards in a great storm that came up suddenly?"

"Aye, so I did, and I've been looking for her many a time since then."

"You'll never find her, Captain. Your guns were aimed well enough, and they took the life out of her. She couldn't weather the storm. Of all the people who were aboard her then I'm the only survivor. Her captain escaped with me to this island, but he died of wounds and I buried him. I can show you his grave."

"How do I know that you, too, are not one of the pirates?"

"By taking me back on your ship to the colonies, and proving my tale. If you don't find that every word I tell you is true you can hang me to your own yardarm."

Captain Whyte laughed. It was a fair and frank offer, but he was a reader of men, and he felt quite sure that the strange youth was telling the absolute truth.

"He's given me, sir, quite correct accounts of events that happened in the colonies last year," said Lanham. "He was at Ticonderoga and his narrative of the battle agrees fully with the accounts that we received."

And just at that moment coincidence stretched out her long arm again, as she does so often.

"I had a cousin at Ticonderoga," said Captain Whyte. "A splendid young fellow, name of Grosvenor. I've seen a letter from him in which he says 'twas a terrible fight, but that we threw away our chances before we went upon the field."

"Grosvenor! Grosvenor!" exclaimed Robert eagerly. "Why, I knew him! He was a friend of mine! We were in the forest together, in combat and escape. His first name was Alfred. Did he say nothing in his letter of Robert Lennox?"

"Of course he did! I was so much interested in you that I paid little attention to your name, and it glided past me as if I'd not heard it. He told of a friend of his, name of yours, who had been lost, murdered they all believed by some spy."

"And did he say nothing also of Tayoga, a wonderful Onondaga Indian, and of David Willet, a great hunter?"

"Aye, so he did. I recall those names too. Said the Indian was the most marvellous trailer the world had ever known, could trace the flight of a bird through the air, and a lot more that must have been pure romance."

"It's all true! every word of it. I'll see that you meet Tayoga, and then you'll believe, and you must know Willet, too, one of the grandest men that ever lived, soul of honour, true as steel, all those things."

"I believe you! Every word you say! But I can't keep you talking here with the water dripping from you. We really couldn't question your truth, either, after you'd saved our ship and all our lives. I see you have a naval uniform of ours. Well, we'll give you a dry one in its place. See that the best the *Hawk* has is his, Lanham."

Robert was taken to a small cabin that was vacant and he exchanged into dry clothing. He went back a little later to the captain's room with Lanham, where they insisted upon his taking refreshment, and then Captain Whyte sent him to bed.

"I've a million questions to ask you, Mr. Lennox," he said, "but I won't ask 'em until to-morrow. You must sleep."

Robert's manner had been calm, but he found when he lay down that he was surcharged with excitement. It was inside him and wanted to get it out, but he kept it bottled up, and after an hour spent in quieting his nerves he fell asleep. When he awoke, dressed and went on deck, all trace of the storm had gone. The *Hawk* swung quietly at anchor and to him she seemed the very finest ship that had ever sailed on any sea from the day of the galley to the day of the three-decker. He noticed with pleasure how trim everything was, how clean was the wood, how polished the brass, and how the flag of Britain snapped in the breeze overhead. He noticed too the eighteen pounders and he knew these were what had done the business for the slaver and pirate. Lanham gave him a hearty welcome.

"It's half way to noon," he said, "and you slept long and well, as you had a right to do, after saving His Majesty's twenty-two gun sloop, *Hawk*, from the rocks. We had a boat's crew ashore this morning, not because we doubted your word, but to see that everything was trim and snug on your island, and they found your house. On my word, quite a little castle, and well furnished. We didn't disturb a thing. It's yours, you know."

"I merely inherited it," said Robert. "The slaver and pirate who kidnapped me built it as a place for a refuge or a holiday, and he came back here to die. He furnished it partly, and the rest came from his wrecked ship."

After breakfast Robert went ashore also with the captain and Lanham, and he showed them about the island. They even saw the old bull at the head of his herd, and Robert waved him a friendly farewell. The house and its contents they decided to leave exactly as they were.

"They may shelter some other castaway," said Robert.

"We'll even leave the guns and ammunition," said Captain Whyte. "We don't need 'em. You rescued 'em from the ship and they belong to you. The *Hawk* has no claim on 'em."

"I'd like for 'em to stay here," said Robert. "Nobody may ever be cast away on this island again, and on the other hand it might happen next week. You can't tell. But it's been a good island to me, and, though I say farewell, I won't forget it."

"You take the right view of it," said Captain Whyte, "and even if I didn't feel your way about it, although I do, I'd be bound to give you your wish since you saved us. You've also taken quite a burden off my mind. It's always been a source of grief to me that the pirate eluded us in the storm, but since you've shown me that we were really responsible for her sinking I feel a lot better about it."

On the *Hawk* Lanham told him what had been passing in the world.

"There's a great expedition out from England under that young general, Wolfe, who distinguished himself at Louisbourg," he said. "It aims at the taking of Quebec, and we're very hopeful. The rendezvous is Louisbourg, on Cape Breton Island and army and navy, I suppose, are already there. Your own Royal Americans will be in it, and what we lost at Ticonderoga we propose to regain—and more—before Quebec. The *Hawk* is bound for Louisbourg to join the fleet, but she puts in at Boston first. If you choose to go on to Louisbourg with us you won't fare ill, because the captain has taken a great fancy for you."

"I thank you much," said Robert, gratefully. "I'm almost tempted to join the great expedition from Louisbourg into the St. Lawrence, but I feel that I must leave the ship at Boston. I'm bound to hunt up Willet and Tayoga, and we'll come by land. We'll meet you before the heights of Quebec."

Everything seemed to favour the northward voyage of the *Hawk*. Good winds drove her on, and Robert's heart leaped within him at the thought that he would soon be back in his own country. Yet he made little outward show of it. The gravity of mind and manner that he had acquired on the island remained with him. Habits that he had formed there were still very powerful. It was difficult for him to grow used to the presence of other people, and at times he longed to go out on his peak of observation, where he might sit alone for hours, with only the rustling of the wind among the leaves in his ears. The sound of the human voice was often strange and harsh, and now and then only his will kept him from starting when he heard it, as one jumps at the snarl of a wild animal in the bush.

But the friendship between him, Captain Whyte, Lieutenant Lanham and the other young officers grew. People instinctively liked Robert Lennox. Whether in his gay mood or his grave he had a charm of manner that few could resist, and his story was so strange, so picturesque that it invested him with compelling romance. He told all about his kidnapping and his life upon the island, but he said nothing of Adrian Van Zoon. He let it be thought that the motive of the slaver in seizing him was merely to get a likely lad for sale on a West India plantation. But his anger against Van Zoon grew. He was not one to cherish wrath, but on this point it was concentrated, and he intended to have a settlement. It was not meant that he should be lost, it was not meant that Adrian Van Zoon should triumph. He had been seized and carried away twice, and each time, when escape seemed impossible, a hand mightier than that of man had intervened in his favour.

He spoke a little of his thought once or twice when he stood on the deck of the *Hawk* on moonlight nights with Captain Whyte and Lieutenant Lanham.

"You can't live with the Indians as much as I have," he said, "especially with such a high type of Indian as the Iroquois, without acquiring some of their beliefs which, after all, are about the same as our own Christian religion. The difference is only in name. They fill the air with spirits, good and evil, and have 'em contending for the mastery. Now, I felt when I was on the island and even before that I was protected by the good spirits of the Iroquois, and that they were always fighting for me with the bad."

"I take it," said Captain Whyte, "that the Indian beliefs, as you tell them, are more like the mythology of the old Greeks and Romans. I'm a little rusty on my classics, but they had spirits around everywhere, good and bad, always struggling with one another, and their gods themselves were mixtures of good and evil, just like human beings. But I'm not prepared to say, Mr. Lennox, that you weren't watched over. It seems strange that of all the human beings on the slaver you should have been the only one saved and you the only one not stained with crime. It's a fact I don't undertake to account for. And you never found out the name of the pirate captain?"

"Neither his nor that of his ship. It had been effaced carefully from the schooner and all her boats."

"I suppose it will remain one of the mysteries of the sea. But tell me more about my cousin, Grosvenor. He was really becoming a trailer, a forest runner?"

"He was making wonderful progress. I never saw anybody more keen or eager."

"A fine lad, one of our best. I'm glad that you two met. I'd like to meet too that Frenchman, St. Luc, of whom you've spoken so often. We Englishmen and Frenchmen have been fighting one another for a thousand years, and it seems odd, doesn't it, Mr. Lennox, that it should be so? Why, the two countries can see each other across the Channel on clear days, and neighbours ought to be the best of friends, instead of the most deadly enemies. It seems that the farther a nation is from another the better they get along together. What is there in propinquity, Mr. Lennox, to cause hostility?"

"I don't know, but I suppose it's rivalry, the idea that if your neighbour grows he grows at your expense. Your hostility carries over to us in America also. We're your children and we imitate our parents. The French in Canada hate the English in the Provinces and the English in the Provinces hate the French in Canada, when there's so much of the country of each that they're lost in it."

"It's a queer world, Mr. Lennox. In spite of what you say and which I endorse, I'm going with an eager heart in the great expedition against Quebec, and so will you. I'll be filled with joy if it succeeds and so will you."

Robert admitted the fact.

"And I'd be delighted if we could meet a French sloop of about our own size and armament," continued the captain. "Every man on board the *Hawk* would go into battle with her eagerly, and yet I don't hate the French individually. They're a brave and gallant nation, and this St. Luc, of whom you speak, seems to be the very flower of chivalry."

The captain's wish to meet a French sloop of war of his own size was not granted. He had high hopes the fourth day when they saw a sail, but it proved to be a schooner out of Newport returning from Jamaica with a cargo of sugar and molasses. The *Hawk* showed her heels in disgust, and pursued her way northward.

As the time to reach Boston drew near, Robert's heart filled again. He would be back in his own land, and his world would be before him once more. He had already decided that he would go at once to Albany and there pick up the thread of his old life. He was consumed, too, by curiosity. What had happened since he was gone? His feeling that he had been in the island eight or nine years instead of eight or nine months remained. While it was his own world to which he was returning, it was also a new world.

Came the day when the harbour lights of the port of Boston showed through a haze and Robert, standing on the deck of the *Hawk*, watched the city rise out of the sea. He was dressed in a good suit of civilian clothing that he had found on the island, and he had some money that had never been taken from him when he was kidnapped, enough to pay his way from Boston to Albany. His kindly English friends wanted to lend him more, but he declined it.

"You can pay us back in Quebec," said White.

"I don't need it," replied Robert, "but I'll keep the rendezvous there with you both."

As the *Hawk* was to stay two or three days in port in order to take on supplies, they went ashore together, and the three were full of curiosity when they entered, for the first time, the town of which they had heard so much. Boston had already made such impress upon the imagination that all the English colonists were generally known to the French in Canada as Bostonnais. In England it had a great name, and there were often apprehensions about it. It was the heart and soul of the expedition when the New Englanders surprised the world by taking the great French fortress of Louisbourg, and it had an individuality and a personality which it has never lost.

"I don't know how I'm going to like it," said Captain Whyte, as they left the sloop. "I hear that they're very superior here, and consider us English a rather backward lot. Don't you think you'd better reconsider, Lennox, and go on with us to Louisbourg?"

Robert laughed. "I'm not afraid of the Bostonians," he said. "I met some very competent ones on the shores of Lake George. There was one Elihu Strong, a colonel of Massachusetts infantry, whom I like to remember. In truth, Captain, what I see here arouses my admiration. You noticed the amount of shipping in the port. The Bostonians are very keen traders, and they say there are sharp differences in character between them and the people of our southern provinces, but as I come from a middle province, New York, I am, in a sense, neutral. The New Englanders have a great stake in the present war. Their country has been ravaged for more than a century by French and Indians from Canada, and this province of Massachusetts is sending to it nearly every man, and nearly every dollar it has."

"We know of their valour and tenacity in England," said Captain Whyte, "but we know also that they're men of their own minds."

"Why shouldn't they be? That's why they're English."

"Since you put it that way, you're right. But here we are."

The town, about the size of New York, looked like a great city to Robert. He had come from a land that contained only one inhabitant, himself, and it was hard for him now to realize there were so many people in the world. The contrast put crowds everywhere, and, at times, it was very confusing, though it was always interesting. The men were mostly tall, thin, and with keen but composed eyes. They were of purer British blood than those in New York, but it seemed to Robert that they had departed something from type. They were more strenuous than the English of Old England, and the New Yorkers, in character if not in blood and appearance, were more nearly English than the Bostonians. He also thought, and he was not judging now so much from a glimpse of Boston as from the New England men whom he had met, that they were critical both of themselves and others, and that they were a people who meant to have their way at any cost.

333

But his attempts to estimate character and type were soon lost in his huge delight at being back in his own country. Robert's mind was a mirror. It always reflected his surroundings. Quickly adaptable, he usually perceived the best of everything, and now busy and prosperous Boston in its thin, crisp air, delighted him immeasurably. His feelings were much as they had been when he visited New York. Here was a great city, that is, great for his country and time, and it was destined to be much greater.

As usual with sailors Captain Whyte and Lieutenant Lanham wished to go to a coffee house, and Robert, nothing loath, accompanied them to one of good quality to which they were directed near the water front. Here they found numerous guests in the great common room and much talk going forward, mostly talk of the war, as was natural. There was much criticism of the British Government, not restrained at all, rather increased, by the uniforms of the two naval officers.

"'Tis reported that the new expedition gathered at Louisbourg will go the way of the one that was repulsed at Ticonderoga," said a thin, elderly man. "I hear 'tis commanded by young Wolfe, who is sickly and much given to complaint. Abercrombie, who led us at Ticonderoga, was fat, old and slothful, and now Wolfe, who leads the new force is young, sickly and fretful. It seems that England can't choose a middle course. Why doesn't she send us a man?"

"That I can't tell you, Master Carver," said the man whom he was addressing, "but I do know that if England would consult Massachusetts more we'd fare better in this war. We should have marched over the French army at Ticonderoga. I can't understand to this day how we lost that battle."

"It seems that in very truth we lacked something there."

Robert was sitting not ten feet from them and their tone being so very critical, he could not restrain a word or two.

"Your pardon, if I interrupt," he said, "but hearing you speak in a somewhat slighting manner of Ticonderoga I'm bound to advise you that you're wrong, since I was there. The English and Scotch troops, with our own Americans, showed the very greatest valour on that sad occasion. 'Twas no fault of theirs. Our defeat was due to the lack of artillery, the very skilful arrangements of the French commander, the Marquis de Montcalm, and the extreme courage of the French army."

The two, who seemed to be merchants or shipping men, regarded him with interest but with no appearance of resentment because of his interference in their conversation. Apparently the criticism that they permitted so freely to themselves they were willing also to allow to others.

"But you are English," said the first who had spoken, "and 'tis most natural for you to defend the generals who are sent out from the home country."

"I am not English. I am a native of the Province of New York, and being a colonial like yourselves, I think we allow too little credit to the old country in the war. I speak as one who through the force of circumstances has been an eye witness to many of the facts. My name is Robert Lennox, sir, and my companions are Captain Stuart Whyte and Lieutenant John Lanham of His Majesty's twenty-two gun sloop of war *Hawk*, now in Boston harbour."

"And I, sir," responded the thin man with much courtesy, "am Samuel Carver, wholesale dealer in cloth and leather, and my friend is Lemuel Mason, owner of shipping plying principally to the West Indies. We're pleased to meet His Majesty's officers and also you, Mr. Lennox, who we can see is very young to have had so much experience in the wars. We trust that all of you will pardon our freedom of criticism, but we're at the heart of affairs here, and we see very clearly. It's not a freedom that we'll give up."

Captain Whyte laughed easily.

"If what we hear in England of Boston is true," he said, "'tis a privilege that nothing can make you give up. Perhaps 'tis as well. I'm all for free speech myself. Through it affairs are well threshed out. But I assure you you're wrong about General Wolfe. 'Tis true that he's young and that he's sickly, but he's been chosen by Mr. Pitt for most solid reasons. He has a great gift for arms. I've been fortunate enough to meet him once or twice, and I can assure you that he makes a most favourable impression. Moreover, the fact that he's been chosen by Mr. Pitt is proof of his worth. Mr. Pitt is a very great man and he has that highest of all talents, the ability to know other men and to direct them."

Captain Whyte spoke with much warmth and his words carried conviction.

"I can well believe you, sir, when you speak so highly of Mr. Pitt," said Mr. Carver. "'Tis evident that he has the honour and glory of England at heart and 'tis evident, too, that he does not mean to neglect the interests of the colonies, a matter of the utmost importance. 'Tis only Mr. Pitt among the home statesmen who have recognized our greatness on this side of the ocean."

"Believe me, sir, I'm not blind to the growth and prosperity of the colonies," said Captain Whyte. "I've seen your cities and I know how much the Americans have done in the present war."

"Then 'tis a pity that England also doesn't know it," said Mr. Mason somewhat sharply.

But Captain Whyte refused to be either angry or disconcerted.

"The width of our ocean always promotes ignorance, and misunderstandings," he said. "And 'tis true too that the closest of kin will quarrel, but families usually unite against an alien foe."

"'Tis so," admitted Mr. Mason, "and 'tis the business of statesmanship to smooth down the quarrels that arise between the different parts of a great kingdom. I trust that ours will always be equal to the task."

"Do you know a merchant of this city, Elihu Strong, who is also a colonel of the Massachusetts infantry?" asked Robert. "I met him in a strenuous business before Ticonderoga, where he also had a gallant part."

"We could scarce be Bostonians and not know Elihu Strong," said Mr. Carver. "One of the most active of our merchants, he has ships of his own that ply between here and England, and he has also taken a very zealous part in the war. The regiment that he commanded was equipped partly at his expense."

"Commanded?" exclaimed Robert.

"I used the past tense, not because he has fallen, my young friend, but Elihu was unfortunate enough to receive a severe wound in the leg some months after Ticonderoga, and he is now recuperating at his own home here near the Common. 'Tis not dangerous. He will not lose the leg, but he will not be able to walk on it for some months yet. A great pity, say I, that Elihu Strong is out of active service for a while, as His Majesty's government might profit greatly by his advice and leadership in the field."

"I've no doubt of it," said Captain Whyte with the greatest sincerity. "I'm all for cooperation with the experienced men of the colonies, and so is a far greater than I, the illustrious Mr. Pitt. They're on the ground, they've lived their lives here and they ought to know."

"Our hope is in Mr. Pitt," said Mr. Carver. "You speak well of him, Captain Whyte, and 'tis pleasing to our ears to hear you, because you cannot know how his name inspires confidence in the colonies. Why, sir, we look upon him as almost the half of England!"

It was so. And it was destined to remain so. Whatever happened between England and America, the name of the elder Pitt, the great Englishman, kept and keeps its place in the hearts of Americans, who in some respects are the most sentimental and idealistic of all peoples.

Robert saw that the two young English officers and the two middle aged Boston merchants were arriving at an understanding, that good relations were established already, and he thought it wise to leave them.

"I think," he said, "that I will visit Colonel Strong at his house, and as my time in Boston must be short 'twill be best for me to go now."

Both Mr. Carver and Mr. Mason urged him to spend the night at their houses, and Captain Whyte and Lieutenant Lanham were zealous for his return with them to the *Hawk*, but he declined the offer, though saying he would certainly visit the sloop before he left Boston. He judged that it would be wise to leave the four together, in the coffee-house, and, after receiving careful instructions how to reach the mansion of that most respectable and worthy Bostonian, Colonel Elihu Strong, he went into the street.

He found the Strong home to be a goodly house, one of the best in the city, partly of brick and partly of wood, with columns in front, all very spacious and pleasing. He knocked with a heavy brass knocker and a trim coloured maid responded.

"Is Colonel Strong at home?" he asked.

"He is, sir," she responded in English as good as his own, "though confined to his chair with a wound in the leg which makes his temper a trifle short at times."

"Naturally. So would mine be if I couldn't walk. I wish to see him."

"What name, sir, shall I say?"

"Tell him 'tis one who served with him in wilderness fighting, on the eve of Ticonderoga."

She looked at him doubtfully, but her face cleared in a moment. Robert's frank, open gaze invited everybody's confidence.

"Come into the hall, sir," she said, and then led the way from the hall into a large room opening upon a lawn, well-shaded by many fine, large trees. Elihu Strong sat in a chair before one of the windows, and his wounded leg, swathed heavily, reposed in another chair.

Robert paused, and his heart beat rather hard. This was the first friend of his old life that he had seen. Now, he was coming in reality back to his world. He stood a few moments, irresolute, and then advancing lightly he said:

"Good morning, Colonel Strong!"

The wounded man wheeled in his chair and looked at him, inquiry in his face. Robert did not know what changes his life on the island had made in his appearance, his expression rather, but he saw that Colonel Strong did not know him, and it pleased him to play for a minute or so with the fact.

"You did not receive this bullet, sir, when you saved us from St. Luc," he said. "It must have been much later, but I know it was a bad moment for the Province of Massachusetts when the hostile lead struck you."

Colonel Strong stared.

"Who are you?" he exclaimed.

"There was a battle on the shores of Lake George, at a point where our men had been building boats. They were besieged by a mixed force of French and Indians, commanded by the great French partisan leader, St. Luc. They beat off the attacks, but they would have been overcome in time, if you had not hurried to their relief, with a strong force and two brass cannon."

"That is true and if the Governor and Legislature of Massachusetts had done their full duty we'd have had twice as many men and four, six, or even eight cannon in place of two. But what do you know about those things?"

"There were two boys, one Indian and one white, who came on the lake, telling you of the plight of the boat builders. The Indian was Tayoga of the Clan of the Bear, of the Nation Onondaga, of the Great League of the Hodenosaunee, the finest trailer in the world. The white boy was Robert Lennox, of the Province of New York."

"Aye, you speak truly. Full well do I remember them. How could I forget them? Tayoga is back there now with the hunter Willet, doing some great service in the war, what I know not, but it is something surely great. The white boy, Robert Lennox, is dead. A great loss, too! A fine and gallant lad."

"How do you know he is dead?"

"I had it in a letter from Master Benjamin Hardy of New York, with whom I often transact affairs of business, and he, in turn, had it from one Jacobus Huysman, a burgher of Albany in most excellent standing. Parts of the matter are obscure, but the result is certain. It seems that the lad was stalked by a spy, one Garay, and was murdered by him. His body, they think, was thrown into the Hudson and was carried away. At least it was never found. A most tragic business. I could have loved that lad as if he had been my own son. It caused great grief to both Hardy and Huysman,—and to me, too."

A lump came into Robert's throat. He did have friends, many and powerful, and they mourned him. He seemed to have the faculty of inspiring liking wherever he went. He had been standing in the shadow, while the wounded man sat where the sunlight from the windows poured upon him. He moved a little nearer where he could be more clearly seen, and said: "But what if I tell you that Robert Lennox is not dead, that he survived a most nefarious plot against him, that he was, in truth, kidnapped and carried far away to sea, but was rescued in a most remarkable manner and has come back to his own land."

"'Tis impossible! 'Tis a wild tale, though God knows I wish it were true, because he was a fine and gallant lad."

"'Tis a wild tale, sir, that I confess, but 'tis not impossible, for it has happened. I am that Robert Lennox who came with Tayoga, the Onondaga, in the canoe, through the fog on Lake George, to you, asking that you hurry to the relief of the boat builders! You will remember, sir, the fight at the ford, when they sought to ambush us, and how we routed them with the cannon. You'll recall how St. Luc drew off when we reached the boat builders. I've been away a long time, where every month counted as a year, and perhaps I've changed greatly, but I'm that same Robert Lennox to whom you said more than once that if the Governor and Legislature of the Province of Massachusetts had done their full duty your force would have been three or four times as strong."

"What? What? No stranger could know as much as you know! Come farther into the light, boy! The voice is nearly the same as I remember it, but the face has changed. You're older, graver, and there's a new look! But the eyes are like his! On my soul I believe it's Robert Lennox! Aye, I know 'tis Robert! Come, lad, and shake hands with me! I would go to you but this wretched wound holds me in my chair! Aye, boy, yours is the grasp of a strong and honest hand, and when I look into your eyes I know 'tis you, Robert, your very self. Sit you down and tell me how you have risen from the grave, and why you've come to comfort an old man with this most sudden and welcome news!"

The moisture rose in Robert's eyes. Truly he had friends, and not least among them was this thin, shrewd Bostonian. He drew a chair close to the colonel and spun the wonderful tale of his kidnapping, the sea fight, the wreck, the island and his rescue by the *Hawk*. Colonel Strong listened intently and seldom interrupted, but when Robert had finished he said:

"'Tis clear, lad, that your belief in the good spirits was well placed. We lose nothing by borrowing a little from the Iroquois beliefs. Their good spirits are our angels. 'Tis all the same in the essence, only the names are different. 'Tis clear, too, that they were watching over you. And now this house is your home so long as you stay in Boston. We're full of the great war, as you'll soon learn. Mr. Pitt has sent over a new commander and a mighty attempt will be made on Quebec, though if the King and Parliament of Britain did their full duty, the expedition would be three times as large, and, if the Legislature and Governor of Massachusetts also did their full duty, they would give three times as much help."

"I'll stay gladly with you to-night, sir, but I must go in the morning. I wish to reach Albany as soon as possible and show that I'm not dead. You're the first, sir, of all my friends, to learn it. I must tell my comrades of the *Hawk* good-bye too. They've been very good to me, and their ship is in your harbour."

"But you spend the night here. That's promised, and I can give you news of some of your friends, those gallant lads who were with us in the great adventure by the lake. The young Englishman, Grosvenor, the Philadelphians, Colden, Wilton and Carson, and the Virginians, Stuart and Cabell, have all been to see me. Grosvenor joins a regiment with Wolfe, the Grenadiers, I think, and the Philadelphians and Virginians are transferred to the Royal Americans, for the term of the war, at least."

"I hope to see them all, sir, under the walls of Quebec. Captain Whyte of the *Hawk* offered to take me in his ship to the rendezvous at Louisbourg, but I felt that I must go first to Albany and then join Willet and Tayoga. We'll go by land and meet the army and fleet coming down the St. Lawrence."

"A proper plan, and a proper ambition, my lad. I would that I could be with you, but this wound may hold me here. As for going to Albany, I may assist you in that matter. A company of Boston merchants are sending a despatch, that is, a stage, to Albany to-morrow. I am one of that company and I can provide a place for you."

"My very great thanks are yours, sir."

"Say no more about it. 'Tis just what I ought to do. 'Tis a long journey, but 'tis a fine time of the year, and you'll have a pleasant trip. Would that I had your youth and your unwounded leg and I'd be with you under the walls of Quebec, whether we take the city or not."

His eyes sparkled and his thin cheeks flushed with his intense fire. Robert knew that there was no more valiant soldier than the shrewd Boston merchant, and he appreciated his intense earnestness.

"Perhaps, sir," he said, "your recovery will be in full time for the campaign."

"I fear not, I'm sure not, Mr. Lennox, and yet I wish with all my soul to be there. I foresee victory, because I think victory is due. 'Tis not in nature for the French in Canada, who are few and who receive but little help from their own country, to hold back forever the whole might of Britain and her colonies. They have achieved the impossible already in stemming the flood so long, and because it's about time for the weight, in spite of everything, to break over the dam, I think that victory is at hand. And then, Britain will be supreme on the North American continent from the Spanish domains northward to the Pole."

"And that means a tremendous future, sir, for England and her colonies!"

The face of Elihu Strong clouded.

"I do not know," he cried. "I hope so, and yet, at times, I fear not. You think only of united hearts in England and America and a long future under one flag. I repeat that I wish it could be so and yet the old always regard the new with patronage, and the new always look upon the old with resentment. There are already differences between the English and Americans, questions of army rank, disputes about credit in the field, different points of view, created by the width of an ocean."

"But if we are victorious and overrun Canada, they will be settled."

"There lies the greatest danger, my lad. 'Tis the common peril that holds us together for the time. When this shadow in the north which has overhung us so long, is removed, the differences will grow the greater, and each side will assert itself. 'Tis in our common blood. The English are a free people and freedom brings diversities, differing opinions and a strenuous expression of them. I see already great issues between the colonies and the mother country, and I pray that temperate men may have the handling of them. The wrong will not be all on one side, nor the right either. But enough of an old man's forebodings! Why should I poison your happy return from an adventure, in which your chance of escape was not one in ten?"

Robert talked with him a while longer, and then he suggested that he go to the *Hawk* and tell his friends there good-bye, as they had probably returned to the ship by this time.

"But be sure you're back here by nightfall," said Colonel Strong. "You favour me, lad, by coming. It refreshes me to see you and to talk with one who had a share with me in an eventful campaign. And have you money enough for this trip to Albany? I take it that you were not accumulating much treasure while you were on the island, and a loan may be timely."

Robert thanked him, but said he had enough for his needs. He promised also to be back by nightfall, and, having said farewell to the officers of the sloop, he returned to Colonel Strong's mansion at the appointed time.

CHAPTER 12

The Wilderness Again

The full hospitality of Colonel Strong's house was for Robert, and he sat late that night, listening to the talk of his host, merchant and warrior, and politician too. There were many like him in the colonies, keen men who had a vision for world affairs and who looked far into the future. He was so engrossed in these matters that he did not notice that he was doing nearly all the talking, but Robert was content to listen.

As Robert sat with Colonel Strong he felt to the full the reality of his own world to which he had returned, and his long life on the island became for the time a dream, something detached, that might have happened on another planet. Yet its effects remained. His manner was grave, and his thoughts were those of one much beyond his years. But mingled with his gravity were an elation and a sanguine belief in his future. He had survived so much that coming dangers could not daunt him.

The special coach departed the next morning and Robert sat upon the seat with the driver. All things were auspicious. The company in the coach was good, the driver was genial and the weather fine. It was a long trip and they slept several nights in inns by the way, but Robert always had pleasant memories of that journey. He was seeing his country under the most favourable conditions, well cultivated, trim and in the full freshness of spring.

They reached Albany and his heart beat hard once more. He realized now that he was one risen from the dead. His reception by Colonel Strong had shown him that, but he believed the joy of his friends would be great when they saw him. The coach drew up at the George Inn, and, leaving it there, he started through the streets, taking no baggage.

It was the same busy little city with its thrifty Dutch burghers. The tide of war had brought added prosperity to Albany, and he saw about him all the old signs of military preparations. It was yet a base for the great campaigns to the northward. Evidently the fear of an attack by Montcalm had passed, as he did not see apprehension or depression in the faces of the people.

He went directly to the house of Master Jacobus Huysman, that staunch friend of his and Tayoga's, and the solid red brick building with its trim lawns and gardens looked as neat and comfortable as ever. It was hard to believe that he had gone away, that he had been so long on an island. Nothing had been changed except himself and he felt different, much older.

He lifted the heavy brass knocker, and struck thrice. The sound of footsteps came from within, and he knew at once that they were Caterina's. Middle-aged, phlegmatic and solid she had loved both him and Tayoga, despite tricks and teasing, but he knew her very phlegm would keep her from being startled too much. Only an earthquake could shake the poise of Caterina.

The door swung slowly open. The nature of Caterina was cautious and she never opened a door quickly.

"Good-morning, Caterina," said Robert. "Is Master Jacobus in? I stayed away a bit longer than I intended, and I wish to make my apologies to him, if I've caused him any inconvenience."

The mouth of Caterina, a wide cleft, opened full as slowly as the door and full as steadily, and her eyes seemed to swell at the same time. But she did not utter a word. Words might be forming in her throat, though they were not able to pass her lips. But Robert saw amazement and joy in her eyes. She knew him. That was evident. It was equally evident that she had been struck dumb, so he grasped her large and muscular hand and said:

"I've come back, Caterina, a trifle late 'tis true, but as you see I'm here. It's not my fault that I've been delayed a little. I hope that Master Jacobus is well. I know he's in his study as the odour of his pipe comes floating to me, a pleasant odour too, Caterina; I've missed it."

"Aye! Aye!" said Caterina. It was all she could manage to say, but suddenly she seized his hand, and fell to kissing it.

"Don't do that, Caterina!" exclaimed Robert, pulling his hand away. "You're glad to see me and I'm glad to see you. I'm no ghost. I'm solid and substantial, at least ten pounds heavier than I was when I went away suddenly at the invitation of others. And now, Caterina, since you've lost your voice I'll go in and have a talk with Master Jacobus."

Caterina's mouth and eyes were still opening wider and wider, but as Robert gave her an affectionate pat on the shoulder she managed to gasp:

"You haf come back! you wass dead, but you wouldn't stay dead."

"Yes, that's it, Caterina, I wouldn't stay dead, or rather I was lost, but I wouldn't stay lost. I'll go in now and see Master Jacobus."

He walked past her toward the odour of the pipe that came from the study and library of Mr. Huysman, and Caterina stood by the door, still staring at him, her mouth opening wider and wider. No such extraordinary thing had ever happened before in the life of Caterina, and yet it was a happy marvel, one that filled her with gratitude.

The door of Mr. Huysman's room was open and Robert saw him very clearly before he entered, seated in a great chair of mahogany and hair cloth, smoking his long hooked pipe and looking thoughtfully now and then at some closely written sheets of foolscap that he held in his hand. He was a solid man of the most solid Dutch ancestry, solid physically and mentally, and he looked it. Nothing could shake his calm soul, and it was a waste of time to try to break anything to him gently. Good news or bad news, it was well to be out with it, and Robert knew it. So he stepped into the room, sat down in a chair near that of Mr. Huysman and said:

"I hope, sir, that I've not caused you any inconvenience. I didn't mean to keep you waiting so long."

Master Jacobus turned and regarded him thoughtfully. Then he took one long puff at his pipe, removed it from his mouth, and blew the smoke in spirals towards the ceiling.

"Robert," he said, after an inspection of a full minute, "why were you in such a hurry about coming back? Are you sure you did everything you should before you came? You wass sometimes a hasty lad."

"I can't recall, sir, anything that I've neglected. Also, I wiped my shoes on the porch and I shut the door when I came in, as Caterina used to bid me do."

"It iss well. It shows that you are learning at last. Caterina and I haf had much trouble teaching manners to you and that young Onondaga scamp, Tayoga."

"As we grow older, sir, we have more desire to learn. We're better able to perceive the value of good advice."

Master Jacobus Huysman put the stem of his long pipe back in his mouth, took the very longest draught upon it that he had ever drawn, removed it again, sent the smoke rushing in another beautiful spear of spirals toward the ceiling, and, then, for the first and last time in his life, he lost all control over himself. Springing to his feet he seized Robert by both hands and nearly wrung them off.

"Robert, my lost lad!" he exclaimed. "It iss you! it iss really you! I knew that you wass dead, and, yet when you walked into the room, I knew that it wass you alive! Your face iss changed! your look iss changed! your manner iss changed! you are older, but I would have known you anywhere and at the first glance! You do not understand how much you took out of my life when you went, and you do not know how much you have brought back when you come again! I do not ask why you left or where you have been, you can tell it all when you are ready! It iss enough that you are here!"

Tears rose in Robert's eyes and he was not ashamed of them. He knew that his welcome would be warm, but it had been even warmer than he had expected.

"I did not go away of my own accord, sir," he said. "I could not have been so heartless as that. I've a wonderful tale to tell, and, as soon as you give me all the news about my friends, I'll tell it."

"Take your time, Robert, take your time. Maybe you are hungry. The kitchen iss full of good things. Let me call Caterina, and she will bring you food."

The invitation of the good Mynheer Jacobus, a very natural thought with him, eased the tension. Robert laughed.

"I thank you, sir," he said, "but I cannot eat now. Later I'll show you that I haven't lost my ability at the trencher, but I'd like to hear now about Tayoga and Dave."

"They're gone into the northern forests to take part in the great expedition that's now arranging against Quebec. We hunted long, but we could discover no trace of you, not a sign, and then there was no conclusion left but the river. You had been murdered and thrown into the Hudson. Your body could not disappear in any other way, and we wass sure it must have been the spy Garay who did the foul deed. Only Tayoga kept any hope. He said that you wass watched over by Manitou and by his own patron saint, Tododaho, and though you might be gone long, Manitou and Tododaho would bring you back again. But we thought it wass only a way he had of trying to console himself for the loss of his friend. Willet had no hope. I wass sorry, sorry in my soul for David. He loved you as a son, Robert, and the blow wass one from which he could never have recovered. When all hope wass gone he and Tayoga plunged into the forest, partly I think to forget, and I suppose they have been risking the hair on their heads every day in battle with the French and Indians."

"It is certain that they won't shirk any combat," said Robert. "Valiant and true! No one was ever more valiant and true than they are!"

"It iss so, and there wass another who took it hard, very hard. I speak of Benjamin Hardy of New York. I wrote him the letter telling him all that we knew, and I had a reply full of grief. He took it as hard as Willet."

"It was almost worth it to be lost a while to discover what good and powerful friends I have."

"You have them! You have them! And now I think, Robert, that the time draws nigh for you to know who you are. No, not now! You must wait yet a little longer. Believe me, Robert, it iss for good reasons."

"I know it, Mr. Huysman! I know it must be so! But I know also there is one who will not rejoice because I've come back! I mean Adrian Van Zoon!"

"Why, Robert, what do you know of Adrian Van Zoon?"

"I was told by a dying man to beware of him, and I've always heard that dying men speak the truth. And this was a dying man who was in a position to know. I'm sure his advice was meant well and was based on knowledge. I think, Mr. Huysman, that I shall have a large score to settle with Adrian Van Zoon."

"Well, maybe you have. But tell me, lad, how you were lost and how you came back."

So, Robert told the long story again, as he had told it to Elihu Strong, though he knew that he was telling it now to one who took a deeper and more personal interest in him than Colonel Strong, good friend though the latter was. Jacobus Huysman had settled back into his usual calm, smoking his long pipe, and interrupting at rare intervals with a short question or two.

"It iss a wonderful story," he said, when Robert finished, "and I can see that your time on the island wass not wholly lost. You gained something there, Robert, my lad. I cannot tell just what it iss, but I can see it in you."

"I feel that way myself, sir."

"No time iss ever lost by the right kind of a man. We can put every hour to some profit, even if it iss not the kind of profit we first intended. But I will not preach to one who hass just risen from the dead. Are you sure, Robert, you will not have a dinner now? We have some splendid fish and venison and sausage and beef! Just a plate of each! It will do you good!"

Robert declined again, but his heart was very full. He knew that Master Jacobus felt deep emotion, despite his calmness of manner, and this was a way he had of giving welcome. To offer food and to offer it often was one of the highest tributes he could pay.

"I could wish," he said, "that you would go to New York and stay with Benjamin Hardy, but as you will not do it, I will not ask it. I know that nothing on earth can keep you from going into the woods and joining Willet and Tayoga, and so I will help you to find them. Robert Rogers, the ranger leader, will be here to-morrow, and he starts the next day into the north with a force of his. He can find Willet and Tayoga, and you can go with him."

"Nothing could be better, sir. I know him well. We've fought side by side in the forest. Is he going to lead his rangers against Quebec?"

"I do not know. Maybe so, and maybe he will have some other duty, but in any event he goes up by the lakes, and you're pretty sure to find Tayoga and Willet in that direction. I know that you will go, Robert, but I wish you would stay."

"I must go, and if you'll pardon me for saying it, sir, you won't wish in your heart that I would stay. You'd be ashamed of me, if I were to do so."

Mr. Huysman made no answer, but puffed a little harder on his pipe. Very soon he sent for Master Alexander McLean, and that thin dry man, coming at once, shook hands with Robert, released his hand, seized and shook it a second and a third time with more energy than ever. Mr. McLean, an undemonstrative man, had never been known to do such a thing before, and he was never known to do it again. Master Jacobus regarded him with staring eyes.

"Alexander iss stirred! He iss stirred mightily to make such a display of emotion," he said under his breath.

"Robert hass been away on an island all by himself, eight or nine months or more," he added, aloud.

"And of course," said Master McLean, who had recovered his usual calm, "he forgot all his classical learning while he was there. I do not know where his island is, but desert islands are not conducive to a noble education."

"On the contrary, sir," said Robert, "I learned more about good literature when I was there than I ever did anywhere else, save when I sat under you."

"'Tis clearly impossible. In such a place you could make no advancement in learning save by communing with yourself."

"Nevertheless, sir, happy chance gave me a supply of splendid books. I had Shakespeare, Marlowe, Beaumont and Fletcher, translations of Homer and of other great Greeks and Latins."

Mr. McLean's frosty eyes beamed.

"What a wonderful opportunity!" he said. "Eight or nine months on a desert island with the best of the classics, and nobody to disturb you! No such chance will ever come to me, I fear. Which book of the Iliad is the finest, Robert?"

"The first, I think. 'Tis the noble opening, the solemn note of tragedy that enchains the attention of us all."

"Well answered. But I wish to make a confession to you and Jacobus, one that would shock nearly all scholars, yet I think that I must speak it out, to you two at least, before I die. There are times when my heart warms to the Odyssey more than it does to the Iliad. The personal appeal is stronger in the Odyssey. There is more romance, more charm. The interest is concentrated in Ulysses and does not scatter as it does in the Iliad, where Hector is undoubtedly the most sympathetic figure. And the coming home of Ulysses arouses emotion more than anything in the Iliad. Now, I have made my confession—I suppose there is something in the life of every man that he ought to hide—but be the consequences what they may I am glad I have made it."

Mr. McLean rose from his chair and then sat down again. Twice that day he had been shaken by emotion as never before, once by the return of the lad whom he loved, risen from the dead, and once by the confession of a terrible secret that had haunted him for years.

"When I was on the island I reread both books in excellent translations," said Robert, the utmost sympathy showing in his voice, "and I confess, sir, though my opinion is a poor one, that it agrees with yours. Moreover, sir, you have said it ahead of me. I shall maintain it, whenever and wherever it is challenged."

Mr. McLean's frosty blue eyes gleamed again, and his sharp strong chin set itself at a firm defiant angle. It was clear that he was relieved greatly.

"Have a pipe, Alexander," said Master Jacobus. "A good pipe is a splendid fortifier of both body and soul, after a great crisis."

Mr. McLean accepted a pipe and smoked it with methodical calm. Robert saw that a great content was settling upon both him and Mr. Huysman, and, presently, the burgher began to tell him news of vital importance, news that they had not known even in Boston when he left. It seemed that the Albany men had channels through Canada itself, by which they learned quickly of great events in the enemy's camp.

"Wolfe with his fleet and army will be in the Gulf of St. Lawrence very soon," said Master Jacobus, "and by autumn they will certainly appear before Quebec. Whatever happens there it will not be another Duquesne, nor yet a Ticonderoga. You must know, Robert, that the great merchants of the great ports get the best of information from

England and from France too, because it is to their interest to do so. Mr. Pitt iss a great minister, the greatest that England hass had in centuries, a very great man."

"Colonel Strong said the same, sir."

"Colonel Strong hass the same information that we have. He iss one of our group. And the new general, Wolfe, iss a great man too. Young and sickly though he may be, he hass the fire, the genius, the will to conquer, to overcome everything that a successful general must have. I feel sure that he will be more than a match for Montcalm, and so does Alexander. As you know, Robert, Wolfe iss not untried. He was the soul of the Louisbourg attack last year. People said the taking of the place was due mostly to him, and they've called him the 'Hero of Louisbourg.'"

"You almost make me wish, sir, that I had accepted the offer of Captain Whyte and had gone on to Louisbourg."

"Do not worry yourself. If you find Willet and Tayoga, as you will, you can reach Quebec long before Wolfe can achieve much. He hass yet to gather his forces and go up the St. Lawrence. Armies and fleets are not moved in a day."

"Do you know what Rogers' immediate duties are?"

"I do not, but I think he iss to help the movement that General Amherst is going to conduct with a strong force against Ticonderoga and Crown Point. Oh, Mr. Pitt hass a great plan as becomes a great man, and Canada will be assailed on all sides. I hear talk too that Rogers will also be sent to punish the St. Francis Indians who have ravaged the border."

They talked a while longer, and Robert listened, intent, eager. The burgher and the schoolmaster had the vision of statesmen. They were confident that England and the colonies would achieve complete success, that all defeats and humiliations would be wiped away by an overwhelming triumph. Their confidence in Pitt was wonderful. That sanguine and mighty mind had sent waves of energy and enthusiasm to the farthest limits of the British body politic, whether on one side of the Atlantic or the other, and it was a singular, but true, fact, that the wisest were those who believed in him most.

Mr. McLean went away, after a while, and Robert took a walk in the town, renewing old acquaintances and showing to them how one could really rise from the dead, a very pleasant task. Yet he longed with all his soul for the forest, and his comrades of the trail. His condition of life on the island had been mostly mental. It had been easy there to subsist. His physical activities had not been great, save when he chose to make them so, and now he swung to the other extreme. He wished to think less and to act more, and he shared with Mr. Huysman and Mr. McLean the belief that the coming campaign would win for England and her colonies a complete triumph.

He too thrilled at the name of Pitt. The very sound of the four letters seemed to carry magic everywhere, with the young English officers on the ship, in Boston, in Albany, and he had noticed too that it inspired the same confidence at the little towns at which they stopped on their way across Massachusetts. Like a blast on the horn of the mighty Roland, the call of Pitt was summoning the English-speaking world to arms. Robert little dreamed then, despite the words of Colonel Strong, that the great cleavage would come, and that the call would not be repeated until more than a century and a half had passed, though then it would sound around the world summoning new English-speaking nations not then born.

Rogers, the famous ranger, upon whom Tayoga had bestowed the name Mountain Wolf, arrived the next day, bringing with him fifty men whom he supplied with ammunition for one of his great raids. The rest of his band was waiting for him near the southern end of Lake George, and he could stay only a few hours in Albany. He gave Robert a warm welcome.

"I remember you well, Mr. Lennox," he said. "We've had some hard fighting together around Lake George against St. Luc, Tandakora and the others, but I think the battle line will shift far northward now. Amherst is going to swoop down on Ticonderoga and Crown Point, and Sir William Johnson, well of his wound, is to march against Niagara. I'll punish the St. Regis Indians for all their barbarities. Oh, it's to be a great campaign, and I'll tell you a secret too."

"What is it?" asked Robert.

"We're to have St. Luc against us near the lakes once more. Could you ask for a better antagonist?"

Robert smiled at the man's eagerness, but his heart throbbed, as always, at the mention of the great French chevalier's name.

"He'll give us all we can do," he said.

"That's why I want to meet him," said Rogers. "The whole northern frontier is going to be ablaze."

Robert left that very day with Rogers and his men. Mr. Huysman purchased for him a splendid equipment which he forced him to accept, and he and Mr. McLean bade him good-by, while Caterina wept in her apron.

"Don't fear for me," said Robert, who was much moved. "Mr. Pitt will bring us all victory. His first efforts failed at Ticonderoga, as we know, but now he has all his forces moving on all fronts, and he's bound to succeed. You've said that yourselves."

"So we have, Robert," said Mr. Huysman, "and we shall watch for your return, confident that you'll come."

The next day the rangers, Robert with them, were far to the north of Albany, and then they plunged into the deep woods. Robert rejoiced at the breath of the forest now in its freshest green, not yet faded by summer heats. He had grown to love his island, but it was not like the mighty wilderness of North America, in which he had spent so much of his life. He kept at the head of the column, side by side with the Mountain Wolf, and his step was so strong and elastic that Rogers took approving notice.

"You like the woods, Robert," he said. "Well, so do I. It's the only place where a man can live a free life."

"I like the woods and the towns too," said Robert. "Each in its place. Where do we camp to-night?"

"By a little lake, a few miles farther on, and as we're not yet in the Indian country we'll make it a fire camp."

The lake covered only two or three acres, but it was set in high hills, and it was as clear as crystal. A great fire was built near the shore, two or three of the rangers caught plenty of fish for all, and they were broiled over the coals. Game had become so plentiful, owing to the ravages of the war, that a fat deer was shot near the water, and, when they added coffee and *samp* from their own stores, they had a feast.

Robert ate with a tremendous appetite, and then, wrapping himself in his blanket, lay down under a tree. But he did not go to sleep for a long time. He was full of excitement. All the omens and signs told him that he was coming into the thick of events once more, and he felt also that he would soon see Willet and Tayoga again. He would encounter many perils, but for the present at least he did not fear them. Much of his vivid youth was returning to him.

He saw the surface of the lake from where he lay, a beautiful silver in the clear moonlight, and he could even perceive wild fowl swimming at the far edge, unfrightened by the presence of man, or by the fires that he built. The skies were a great silver curve, in which floated a magnificent moon and noble stars in myriads. There was the one on which Tayoga's Tododaho lived, and so powerful was Robert's fancy that he believed he could see the great Onondaga sage with the wise snakes in his hair. And there too was the star upon which Hayowentha lived and the Onondaga and the Mohawk undoubtedly talked across space as they looked down on their people.

Out of the forest came the calls of night birds, and Robert saw one shoot down upon the lake and then rise with a fish in its talons. He almost expected to see the dusky figure of Tandakora creep from the bush, and he knew at least that the Ojibway chief would be somewhere near the lakes. Beyond a doubt they would encounter him and his warriors as they pressed into the north. Rogers, noticing that he was not asleep, sat down beside him and said:

"I suppose, Mr. Lennox, when you find Tayoga and Willet that you'll go with Amherst's army against Ticonderoga and Crown Point. A great force has gathered to take those places."

"I'm not sure," said Robert, "I think it depends largely upon what Tayoga and Dave have planned, but I want to go against Quebec, and I think they will too. Still, I'd like to see our defeat at Ticonderoga atoned for. It's a place that we ought to have, and Crown Point too."

"A scout that I sent out has come in," said Rogers, "and he says he's seen an Indian trail, not big enough to be of any danger to us, but it shows we'll have 'em to deal with before long, though this is south of their usual range. I hear an owl hooting now, and if I didn't know it was a real owl I could think it was Tandakora himself."

"I hear it too," said Robert, "and I'm not so sure that it's a real owl. Do you think that any band will try to cut us off before we reach Amherst and the lake?"

"I can't say, but my faith in the owl, Robert, is beginning to shake too. It may be an Indian belonging to the band that the scout told about, but I still don't think we're in any danger of attack. We're in too small force to try it down here, but they might cut off a straggler."

"I'd like to help keep the watch."

"We won't need you to-night, but I may call on you to-morrow night, so it's my advice to you to sleep now."

The Mountain Wolf walked away to look at his outposts—he was not one ever to neglect any precaution—and Robert, knowing that his advice was good, closed his eyes, trying to sleep. But his hearing then became more acute, and the long, lonesome note of the owl came with startling dreams. Its cry was in the west, and after a while another owl in the north answered it. Robert wished that Tayoga was with him. He would know, but as for himself he could not tell whether or no the owls were real. They might be Indians, and if so they would probably, when they gathered sufficient force, throw themselves across the path of the rangers and offer battle. This presence too indicated that Tayoga and Willet might be near, because it was against just such bands that they guarded, and once more his heart beat fast.

He opened his eyes to find that the beauty of the night had deepened, if that were possible. The little lake was molten silver, and the forest seemed silver too under silver skies. The moon, large and benignant, smiled down on the earth, not meant, so Robert thought, for battle. But the two owls were still calling to each other, and now he was convinced that they were Indians and not owls. He was really back in the wilderness, where there was no such thing as peace, the wilderness that had seldom ever known peace. But believing with Rogers that the force was too strong to be attacked he fell asleep, at last, and awoke to another bright summer day.

They resumed the advance with great caution. Rogers did not go directly toward the force of Amherst, but bore more toward the west, thinking it likely that he would have to meet the force of Sir William Johnson who was to cooperate with Prideaux in the attack on Niagara.

"Sir William has entirely recovered from the wound he received at the Battle of Lake George," Rogers said to Robert, "and he's again taking a big part in the war. We have Louisbourg and Duquesne, and now, if we take Niagara and Ticonderoga and Crown Point, we can advance in great force on Quebec and Montreal."

"So we can," said Robert, "but there are those owls again, hooting in the daytime, and I'm quite sure now they're Indians."

"I think so too, and it begins to look as if they meant an attack. Every mile here brings us rapidly nearer to dangerous country. I'll send out two more scouts."

Two of his best men were dispatched, one on either flank, but both came in very soon with reports of imminent danger. Trails were seen, and they had grown in size. One found the trace of a gigantic moccasin, and it was believed to be that of Tandakora. Many scouts knew his footstep. There was no other so large in the north. Rogers' face was grave.

"I think they're going to try to cut us off before we reach the bigger part of my force," he said. "If so, we'll give 'em a fight. You'll be in the thick of it much earlier than you expected, Robert."

Robert also was inclined to that opinion, but he was still confident they could not be menaced by any very large party, and he remained in that belief the next night, when they made their camp on a little hill, covered with bushes, but with open country on every side, an excellent site for defence. They ate another plentiful supper, then put out their fire, posted sentinels and waited.

Robert was among the sentinels, and Rogers, who had made

him second in command until he was reunited with his main force, stood by him in the first hour while they waited. There was again a splendid moon and plenty of fine stars, shedding a brilliant glow over the forest, and they believed they could see any enemy who tried to approach, especially as the hill was surrounded on all sides by a stretch of open.

"It's a good place for a camp," said the Mountain Wolf, looking around with approval. "I believe they'll scarce venture to attack us here."

"But there are the owls," said Robert. "They're at least thinking about it."

The long mournful cry came from the depths of the forest, and then it was repeated a second and a third time at other points.

"The owls that send forth those calls," said Robert, "don't sit on the boughs of trees."

"No," said Rogers; "it's the warriors, not a doubt of it, and they'll be stealing in on us before long."

But several hours passed before there was any stir in the forest beyond the open. Then a rifle cracked there, but no one heard the impact of the bullet. Rogers laughed scornfully.

"Their lead fell short," he said. "How could they expect to hit any of us at such a range, and they not the best of marksmen even in the daylight. They can't hope to do any more than to keep us awake."

The rangers made no reply to the shot, they would not deign it with such notice, but the guard was doubled, while the others remained in their blankets. A half hour more passed, and a second shot came, but from a point much nearer.

"They're trying to steal forward through the grass that grows tall down there," said Rogers. "They're more bent on battle than I thought they'd be. It seems that they mean to stalk us, so we'll just stalk 'em back."

Four of the rangers, fine sharpshooters, edged their way along the slope, and, when the warriors among the trees fired, pulled trigger by the flash of their rifles. It was difficult to hit any one in such a manner, and more than twenty shots were fired by the two sides, before a death shout was uttered. Then it came from the forest, and Robert knew that one warrior was gone. He was taking no present part in the battle himself, held like the bulk of the force in reserve, but he was an intent observer. Rogers, the daring leader of the rangers, still standing by his side, took it all as a part of his daily work, which in truth it was.

"I think it was Thayer who brought down that warrior," he said. "Thayer is one of the bravest men I ever saw, and a great scout and trailer. He'd be worthy to go with Willet and Tayoga and you. Ah, there goes a second death shout! Any one who seeks a brush with these boys of mine does it at his own risk."

He spoke proudly, but one of his own men came creeping back presently with a wound in his shoulder. Rogers himself bound it up and the man lay down in his blanket, confident that in a week he could resume his place in the campaign. Those who lived the life he did had, of necessity, bodies as hard as iron.

The deadly skirmishing died down repeatedly, but, after a little while, it was always renewed. Though the warriors were getting the worst of it, they persisted in the attack, and Robert knew they must have some motive, not yet evident.

"Either they hope to frighten us back, or they mean to hold us until a much bigger force comes up," he said.

"One or the other," said Rogers, "but I don't believe any big band would venture down here. The hope to frighten us seems the more likely."

The combat, drawn out long and with so little result, annoyed Robert intensely. As he saw it, it could have no decisive effect upon anything and was more than futile, it was insensate folly. The original time set for his watch was over long since and he wanted to roll himself in his blanket and find slumber, but those ferocious warriors would not let him. Despite their losses, they still hung around the hill, and, giving up the attempt to stalk the defenders through the grass, fired long shots from the cover of the forest. Another ranger was wounded by a chance bullet, but Rogers, skilful and cautious, refused to be drawn from the shelter of the bushes on the hill.

Thus the fitful and distant combat was waged until dawn. But with the rise of a brilliant sun, throwing a clear light over the whole wilderness, the warriors drew off and the rangers resumed their march.

CHAPTER 13

The Reunion

Willet, the hunter, and Tayoga, the great young Onondaga trailer, were walking through the northern woods, examining forest and bush very cautiously as they advanced, knowing that the danger from ambushed warriors was always present. Willet was sadder and sterner than of old, while the countenance of the Onondaga was as grave and inscrutable as ever, though he looked older, more mature, more the mighty forest runner.

"Think you, Tayoga," said the hunter, "that Tandakora and his men have dared to come into this region again?"

"Tandakora will dare much," replied the Onondaga. "Though he is full of evil, we know that well. The French still hold Ticonderoga, and he can use it as a base for bands much farther south."

"True, but I don't think they'll have Ticonderoga, or Crown Point, either, long. Amherst is gathering too big an army and there is no Montcalm to defend them. The Marquis will have his hands full and overflowing, defending Quebec against Wolfe. We've held both Duquesne and Louisbourg a long while now. We've smashed the French line at both ends, and Mr. Pitt is going to see that it's cut in the centre too. How I wish that Robert were alive to see the taking of Ticonderoga! He saw all the great defeat there and he was entitled to this recompense."

He sighed deeply.

"It may be, Great Bear," said Tayoga, "that Dagaeoga will see the taking of Ticonderoga. No one has ever looked upon his dead body. How then do we know that he is dead?"

Willet shook his head.

"'Tis no use, Tayoga," he said. "The lad was murdered by Garay and the river took his body away. Why, it will be a year this coming au-

356

tumn since he disappeared, and think you if he were alive he couldn't have come back in that time! 'Tis the part of youth to hope, and it does you credit, but the matter is past hope now. We've all given up except you."

"When only one hopes, Great Bear, though all others have failed, there is still hope left. Last night I saw Tododaho on his star very clearly. He looked down at me, smiled and seemed to speak. I could not hear his words, but at the time I was thinking of Dagaeoga. Since Tododaho sits with the great gods, and is one of them, he knew my thoughts, and, if he smiled when I was thinking of Dagaeoga, he meant to give me hope."

The hunter again shook his head sadly.

"You thought you saw it, because you wished it so much," he said, "or maybe the promise of Tododaho was for the future, the hereafter."

"For the hereafter we need no special promise, Great Bear. That has always been made to all of us by Manitou himself, but I was thinking of Dagaeoga alive, present with us in this life, when Tododaho smiled down on me. I hold it in my heart, Great Bear, as a sign, a promise."

Willet shook his head for the third time, and with increasing sadness, but said nothing more. If Tayoga cherished such a hope it was a consolation, a beautiful thing, and he was not one to destroy anybody's faith.

"Do you know this region?" he asked.

"I was through here once with the Mohawk chief, Daganoweda," replied Tayoga. "It is mostly in heavy forest, and, since the war has gone on so long and the settlers have gone away, there has been a great increase in the game."

"Aye, I know there'll be no trouble on that point. If our own supplies give out it won't take long to find a deer or a bear. It's a grand country in here, Tayoga, and sometimes it seems a pity to one that it should ever be settled by white people, or, for that matter, by red either. Let it remain a wilderness, and let men come in, just a little while every year, to hunt."

"Great Bear talks wisdom, but it will not be done his way. Men have been coming here a long time now to fight and not to hunt. See, Great Bear, here is a footprint now to show that some one has passed!"

"'Twas made by the moccasin of a warrior. A chance hunter."

"Suppose we follow it, Great Bear. It is our business to keep guard and carry word to Amherst."

"Good enough. Lead and I'll follow."

"It is not the step of a warrior hunting," said Tayoga, as they pursued the traces. "The paces are even, regular and long. He goes swiftly, not looking for anything as he goes, but because he wishes to reach a destination as soon as possible. Ah, now he stopped and he leaned against this bush, two of the stems of which are broken! I do not know what he stopped for, Great Bear, but it may have been to give a signal, though that is but a surmise. Now he goes on, again walking straight and swift. Ah, another trail coming from the west joining his and the two warriors walk together!"

The two followed the double trail a mile or more in silence, and then it was joined by the traces of three more warriors. The five evidently had stood there, talking a little while, after which they had scattered.

"Now, what does that mean?" exclaimed the hunter.

"I think if we follow every one of the five trails," said Tayoga, "we will find that the men lay down in the bush. It is certain in my mind, Great Bear, that they were preparing for a battle, and they were but a part of a much larger force hidden in these thickets."

"Now, that's interesting, Tayoga. Let's look around and see if we can find where more of the warriors lay."

They circled to the right, and presently they came upon traces where three men had knelt behind bushes. The imprints of both knees and toes were plain.

"They were here a long time," said Tayoga, "because they have moved about much within a little space. In places the ground is kneaded by their knees. And lo! Great Bear, here on the bush several of the young leaves are burned. Now, you and I know well what alone would do that at such a time."

"It was done by the flash from a big musket, such a musket as those French Indians carry."

"It could have been nothing else. I think if we go still farther around the curve we will find other bushes behind which other warriors kneeled and fired, and maybe other leaves scorched by the flash of big muskets."

A hundred yards more and they saw that for which they looked. The signs were just the same as at the other places.

"Now, it is quite clear to you and me, Great Bear," said the Onondaga, "that these men, posted along a curving line, were firing at something. They were here a long time, as the numerous and crowded footprints at every place show. They could not have been firing at game, because there were too many of them, and the game would not have stayed to be fired at so long. Therefore, Great Bear, and you know it as well as I, they must have been in battle. All the points of ambush to which we have come are at an almost equal distance from some other point."

"Which, Tayoga, is that hill yonder, crowned with bushes, but with bare slopes, a good place for a defence, and just about a long rifle or musket shot from the forest here."

"So it is, Great Bear. It could be nothing else. The defenders lay among the bushes on top of the hill, and the battle was fought in the night, because those who attacked were not numerous enough to push a combat in the day. The defenders must have been white men, as we know from the footprints here that the assailants were warriors. Ah, here are other traces, Great Bear, and here are more, all trodden about in the same manner, indicating a long stay, and all at about an equal distance from the hill! I think the warriors lay in the forest all night firing upon the hill, and probably doing little damage. But they suffered more hurt themselves. See, here are faint traces of blood, yet staining the grass, and here is a trail leading out of the bushes and into the grass that lines the slopes of the hill. The trail goes forward, and then it comes back. It is quite clear to both of us, Dagaeoga, that a warrior, creeping through the long grass, tried to stalk the hill, but met a bullet instead. Those who lay upon the hill and defended themselves were not asleep. They could detect warriors who tried to steal forward and secure good shots at them. And they could fire at long range and hit their targets. Now, soldiers know too little of the forest to do that, and so it must have been scouts or rangers."

"Perhaps some of the rangers belonging to Rogers. We know that he's operating in this region."

"It was in my thought too, Great Bear, that the rangers of the Mountain Wolf lay on the hill. See, here is a second trace of blood, and it also came from a warrior who tried to stalk the hill, but who had to come back again after he had been kissed by a bullet. The men up there among the bushes never slept, and they allowed no one of their enemies to come near enough for a good shot with a musket. The chances are ninety-nine out of a hundred that they were rangers, Great Bear, and we may speak of them as rangers. Now, we come to a spot where at least a dozen warriors lay, and, since their largest force was here, it is probable that their chief stayed at this spot. See, the small bones of the deer picked clean are lying among the bushes. I draw from it the opinion, and so do you, Great Bear, that the warriors kept up the siege of the hill until dawn, because at dawn they would be most likely to eat their breakfast, and these little bones of the deer prove that they did eat this breakfast here. Now, it is very probable that they went away, since they could win nothing from the defenders of the hill."

"Here's their broad trail leading directly from the hill."

They followed the trail a little distance, finding those of other warriors joining, until the total was about forty. Willet laughed with quiet satisfaction.

"They had all they wanted of the hill," he said, "and they're off swiftly to see if they can't find easier prey elsewhere."

"And you and I, Great Bear, will go back and see what happened on the hill, besides discovering somewhat more about the identity of the defenders."

"Long words, Tayoga, but good ones upon which we can act. I'm anxious about the top of that hill myself."

They went back and walked slowly up the hill. They knew quite well that nobody was there now. The entire forest scene had vanished, so far as the actors were concerned, but few things disappear completely. The actors could go, but they could not do so without leaving traces which the two great scouts were able to read.

"How long ago do you think all this happened, Tayoga?" asked Willet.

"Not many hours since," replied the Onondaga. "It is mid-morning now, and we know that the warriors departed at dawn. The people on the hill would stay but a little while after their enemies had gone, and since they were rangers they would not long remain blind to the fact that they had gone."

They pushed into the bushes, and were soon among the traces left by the defenders.

"Here is where the guard knelt," said Tayoga, as they walked around the circle of the bushes, "and behind them is where the men slept in their blankets. That is farther proof that they were rangers. They had so much experience, and they felt so little alarm that most of them slept placidly, although they knew warriors were watching below seeking to shoot them down. The character of the footprints indicates that all of the defenders were white men. Here is a trail that I have seen many times before, so many times that I would know it anywhere. It is that of the Mountain Wolf. He probably had a small part of his rangers here and was on his way to join his main force, to act either with Amherst or Waraiyageh (Sir William Johnson). Of course he would depart with speed as soon as his enemy was beaten off."

"Altogether reasonable, Tayoga, and I'm glad Rogers is in these parts again with his rangers. Our generals will need him."

"The Mountain Wolf stood here a long time," said Tayoga. "He walked now and then to the right, and also to the left, but he always came back to this place. He stood here, because it is a little knoll, and from it he could see better than from anywhere else into the forest that hid the enemy below. The Mountain Wolf is a wise man, a great forest fighter, and a great trailer, but he was not alone when he stood here."

"I suppose he had a lieutenant of course, a good man whom he could trust. Every leader has such a helper."

The Onondaga knelt and examined the traces minutely. When he rose his eyes were blazing.

"He did have a good helper, an able assistant, O Great Bear!" he said. "He had one whom he trusted, one whom I could trust, one whom you could trust. The Mountain Wolf stood by this bush and talked often with one whom we shall be very glad to see, O Great Bear, one whom the Mountain Wolf himself was both surprised and glad to see."

"Your meaning is beyond me, Tayoga."

"It will not be beyond you very long, O Great Bear! When Tododaho, reading my thoughts, looked down on me last night from the great star on which he has lived four hundred years, and smiled upon me, his smile meant what it said. The Hodenosaunee are the children of Todohado and Hayowentha, and they never make sport of them, nor of any one of them."

"I'm still in the dark of the matter, Tayoga!"

"Does not Great Bear remember what I was thinking about when Todohado smiled? What I said and always believed is true, O Great Bear! I believed it against all the world and I was right. Look at the traces beside those of the Mountain Wolf! They are light and faint, but look well at them, O Great Bear! I would know them anywhere! I have seen them thousands of times, and so has the Great Bear! Dagaeoga has come back! He stood here beside the Mountain Wolf! He was on this hill among the bushes all through the night, while the rangers fought the warriors among the trees below! He and the Mountain Wolf talked together and consulted while they looked at the forest! Lo! my brother Dagaeoga has come back out of the mists and vapours into which he went nearly a year ago, for he is my brother, though my skin is red and his is white, and he has been my brother ever since we were little children together! Lo! Great Bear, Dagaeoga has come back as I told you, as I alone told you he would, and my heart sings a song of joy within me, because I have loved my brother! Look! look, Great Bear, and see where the living Dagaeoga has walked, not six hours since!"

Willet knelt and examined the traces. He too was a great trailer, but he did not possess the superhuman instinct that had come down through the generations to the Onondaga. He merely saw traces, lighter than those made by Rogers. But if his eyes could not, his mind did tell him that Tayoga was right. The ring of conviction was so strong in the voice of the Onondaga that Willet's faith was carried with it.

"It must be as you tell me, Tayoga," he said. "I do not doubt it. Robert has been here with Rogers. He has come back out of the mists and vapours that you tell about, and he walked this hill in the living flesh only a few hours ago. Where could he have been? How has it happened?"

"That does not concern us just now, Great Bear. It is enough to know that he is alive, and we rejoice in it. Before many hours we shall speak with him, and then he can tell his tale. I know it will be a strange and wonderful one, and unless Degaeoga has lost his gift of words, which I think impossible, it will lose no colour in the telling."

"Let him spin what yarn he pleases, I care not. All I ask is to put eyes on the lad again. It seems, when I think of it in cold blood, that it can scarce be true, Tayoga. You're sure you made no mistake about the footsteps?"

"None, Great Bear. It is impossible. I know as truly that the living Dagaeoga stood on this hill six hours ago as I know that you stand before me now."

"Then lead on, Tayoga, and we'll follow the trail of the rangers. We ought to overtake 'em by noon or soon after."

The broad path, left by the rangers, was like the trail of an army to Tayoga, and they followed it at great speed, keeping a wary eye for a possible ambush on either side. The traces grew fresher and fresher, and Tayoga read them with an eager eye.

"The Mountain Wolf, Dagaeoga and the rangers are walking rapidly," he said. "I think it likely that they are going to join Amherst in his advance on Ticonderoga or Crown Point, or maybe they will turn west and help Waraiyageh, but, in either case, they do not feel any alarm about the warriors with whom they fought last night. Now and then the trail of a scout branches off from their main trail, but it soon comes back again. They feel quite sure that the warriors were only a roving band, and will not attack them again. The Mountain Wolf and Dagaeoga walk side by side, and we can surmise, Great Bear, that they talk much together. Perhaps Dagaeoga was telling the Mountain Wolf where he has been these many months, why he went away, and why he chose to come back when he did out of the mists and vapours. Dagaeoga is strong and well. Look how his footprints show the length of his stride and how steady and even it is! He walks stride for stride with the Mountain Wolf, who as we know is six feet tall. Dagaeoga has grown since he went away. He was strong before he left, but he is stronger now. I think we shall find, Great Bear, that while Dagaeoga was absent his time was not lost. It may be that he gained by it."

"I'm not thinking whether he has or not, Tayoga. I'm glad enough to get the lad back on any terms. We're making great speed now, and I think we ought to overtake 'em before long. The trail appears to grow a lot fresher."

"In an hour, Great Bear, we can signal to them. It will be best to send forth a call, since one does not approach in the forest, in war, without sending word ahead that he is a friend, else he may be met by a bullet."

"That's good and solid truth, Tayoga. We couldn't have our meeting with Robert spoiled at the last moment by a shot. But it's much too early yet to send out a call."

"So it is, Great Bear. I think, too, the rangers have increased their speed. Their stride has lengthened, but, as before, the Mountain Wolf and Dagaeoga keep together. They are great friends. You will recall that they fought side by side on the shores of Andiatarocte."

"I remember it well enough, Tayoga. Nobody could keep from liking Robert. 'Tis a gallant spirit he has."

"It is so, Great Bear. He carries light wherever he goes. Such as he are needed among us. Because of that I never believed that Manitou had yet taken him to himself. The rangers stopped here, sat on these fallen logs, and ate food at noonday. There are little bones that they threw away, and the birds, seeking shreds of food, are still hopping about."

"That's clear, Tayoga, and since they would probably stay about fifteen minutes we ought to come within earshot of them in another half hour."

They pressed on at speed, and, within the appointed time, they sank down in a dense clump of bushes, where Tayoga sent forth the mellow, beautiful song of a bird, a note that penetrated a remarkable distance in the still day.

"It is a call that Dagaeoga knows," he said. "We have used it often in the forest."

In a few minutes the reply, exactly the same, faint but clear, came back from the north. When the sound died away, Tayoga imitated the bird again, and the second reply came as before.

"Now we will go forward and shake the hand of Dagaeoga," said the Onondaga.

Rising from the bush, the two walked boldly in the direction whence the reply had come, and they found a tall, straight young figure advancing to meet them.

"Robert, my lad!" exclaimed Willet.

"Dagaeoga!" said the Onondaga.

Each seized a hand of Robert and shook it. Their meeting was not especially demonstrative, but their emotions were very deep. They were bound together by no common ties.

"You've changed, Robert," said Willet, merely as a sort of relief to his feelings.

"And you haven't, Dave," said Robert, with the same purpose in view. "And you, Tayoga, you're the great Onondaga chief you always were."

"I hope to be a chief some day," said Tayoga simply, "and then, when I am old enough, to be a sachem too, but that rests with Tododaho and Manitou. Dagaeoga has been away a long time, and we do not know where he went, but since he has come back out of the mists and vapours, it is well."

"I understood your call at once," said Robert, "and as you know I gave the reply. I came from Albany with Rogers to find you, and I found you quicker than I had hoped. We had a meeting with hostile warriors last night, but we beat 'em off, and we've been pushing on since then."

"Your encounter last night was what enabled us to find you so quickly," said Willet. "Tayoga read on the ground the whole story of the combat. He understood every trace. He recognized the footprints of Rogers and then your own. He always believed that you'd come back, but nobody else did. He was right, and everybody else was wrong. You're bigger, Robert, and you're graver than you were when you went away."

"I've been where I had a chance to become both, Dave. I'll tell you all about it later, for here's Rogers now, waiting to shake hands with you too."

"Welcome, old friend," said Rogers, grasping the hunter's powerful hand in his own, almost as powerful, "and you too Tayoga. If there's a finer lad in the wilderness anywhere, I don't know it."

They said little more at present, joining the group of rangers and going on steadily until nightfall. On the way Robert gave Willet and Tayoga an outline of what had happened to him, not neglecting the dying words of the slaver.

"It was the hand of Van Zoon," he said.

"Aye, it was Van Zoon," said the hunter. "It was his hand too that was raised against you that time in New York. I've feared him on your account, Robert. It's one reason why we've been so much in the forest. You wonder why Huysman or Hardy or I don't tell you about him, but all in good time. If we don't tell you now it's for powerful reasons."

"The others have told me so too," said Robert, "and I'm not asking to know anything I oughtn't to know now. If you put off such knowledge, Dave, I'm sure it ought to be put off."

They overtook the main body of the rangers that night, and Rogers now had a force of more than two hundred men, but information from his second in command decided him to join in the great movement of Sir William Johnson and Prideaux against Niagara. The duties of Willet and Tayoga called them to Amherst, and of course Robert went with them. So the next morning they parted from Rogers.

"I think there'll be big things to tell the next time we meet," said Willet to Rogers. "Mr. Pitt doesn't make his plans for nothing. He not only makes big plans, but he prepares big armies and fleets to carry 'em out."

"We have faith in him everywhere here," said Rogers, "and I hear they've the same faith in him on the other side of the Atlantic. The failure before Ticonderoga didn't seem to weaken it a particle. Take care of yourselves, my friends."

It was a sincere farewell on both sides, but quickly over, and the three pressed on to Amherst's camp, in the valley near the head of Lake George, that had already seen so many warlike gatherings. Here a numerous and powerful army, bent upon taking Ticonderoga and Crown Point, was being trained already, and Robert, after visiting it, looked once more and with emotion upon the shores of Andiatarocte.

Fate was continually calling him back to this lake and Champlain, around which so much of American story is wrapped. The mighty drama known as the Seven Years' War, that involved nearly all the civilized world, found many of its springs and also much of its culmination here. The efforts made by the young British colonies, and by the mother country, England, were colossal, and the battles were great for the time. To the colonies, and to those in Canada as well, the campaigns were a matter of life or death. For the English colonies the war, despite valour and heroic endurance, had been going badly in the main, but now almost all felt that a change was coming, and it seemed to be due chiefly to one man, Pitt. It was Napoleon who said later that "Men are nothing, a man is everything," but America, as well as England, knew that in the Seven Years' War Pitt, in himself, was more than an army—he was a host. And America as well as England has known ever since that there was never a greater Englishman, and that he was an architect who built mightily for both.

The future was not wholly veiled to Robert as he looked down anew upon the glittering waters of Andiatarocte. He had come in contact with the great forces that were at work, he had vision anew and greater vision, and he knew the gigantic character of the stakes for which men played. If the French triumphed here in America, then the old Bourbon monarchy, which Willet told him was so diseased and corrupt, would appear triumphant to all the world. It would invent new tyrannies, the cause of liberty and growth would be set back generations, and nobody would be trodden under the heel more than the French people themselves. Robert liked the French, and sometimes the thought occurred to him that the English and Americans were fighting not only their own battle but that of the French as well.

He knew as he stood with Willet and Tayoga looking at Lake George that the great crisis of the war was at hand. All that had gone before was mere preparation. He had felt the difference at once when he came back from his island. The old indecision, doubt and despondency were gone; now there was a mighty upward surge. Everybody was full of hope, and the evidence of one's own eyes showed that the Anglo-American line was moving forward at all points. A great army would soon be converging on Ticonderoga, where a great army had been defeated the year before, but now there would be no Montcalm to meet. He must be in Quebec to defend the very citadel and heart of New France against the army and fleet of Wolfe. The French in Canada were being assailed on all sides, and the decaying Bourbon monarchy could or would send no help. Robert's occasional thought, that the English and Americans might be fighting for the French as well as themselves, did not project itself far enough to foresee that out of the ashes left by the fall of Canada might spring another and far stronger France.

"I'm glad I'm back here to join in the new advance on Ticonderoga," said Robert. "As I was with Montcalm and saw our army defeated when it ought not to have been, I think it only a just decree of fate that I should be here when it wins."

"We'll take Ticonderoga this time, Robert. Never fear," said Willet. "We'll advance with our artillery, and the French have no force there that can stop us. Amherst is building a fort that he calls Edward, but we'll never need it. He's very cautious, but it's as well, our curse in this war has been the lack of caution, lack of caution by both English and Americans. Still, that over-confidence has a certain strength in it. You've noticed how we endure disaster. We've had heavy defeats, but we rise after every fall, and go into the combat once more, stronger than we went before."

The three spent some time with Amherst, and saw his great force continue its preparation and drilling, until at last the general thought they were fit to cope with anything that lay before them. Then, a year lacking but a few days after Abercrombie embarked with his great army for the conquest of Ticonderoga, Amherst with another army, mostly Americans, embarked upon the same waters, and upon the same errand.

Robert, Tayoga and Willet were in a canoe in the van of the fleet. They were roving scouts, held by the orders of nobody, and they could do as they pleased, but for the present they pleased to go forward with the army. Robert and Tayoga were paddling with powerful strokes, while Willet watched the shores, the lake and the long procession. The sun was brilliant, but there was a strong wind off the mountains and the boats rocked heavily in the waves. Nevertheless, the fleet, carrying its artillery with it, bore steadily on.

"The French have as big a force at Ticonderoga as they had when Montcalm defeated Abercrombie," said the hunter, "and it's commanded by Bourlamaque."

"A brave and skilful man," said Robert. "I saw him when I was a prisoner of the French."

"But he knows Amherst will not make the mistake Abercrombie did," said Willet. "Our big guns will talk for us, and they'll say things that wooden walls can't listen to long. I'm thinking that Bourlamaque won't stand. I've heard that he'll retreat to the outlet of Lake Champlain and make a last desperate defence at Isle-aux-Noix. If he's wise, and I think he is, he'll do it."

"Do you know whether St. Luc is with him or if he has gone to Quebec with Montcalm?" asked Robert.

"I haven't heard, but I think it's likely that he's here, because he has so much influence with the Indians, who are far more useful in the woods than in a fortress like Quebec. It's probable that we'll hear from him in the morning when we try a landing."

"You mean we'll spend the night on the lake?"

"Aye, lad. It's blowing harder, and we've a rough sea here, though 'tis a mountain lake. We make way but slowly, and we must be full of caution, or risk a shipwreck, with land in sight on both sides of us."

Night drew on, dark and blowy, with the army still on the water, as Willet had predicted, and much of it seasick. The lofty shores, green by day, were clothed in mists and vapour, and the three saw no trace of the French or the Indians, but they were quite sure they were watching from the high forests. Robert believed now that St. Luc was there, and that once again they would come into conflict.

"Do you think we'd better try the shore to-night?" he asked.

Willet shook his head.

"'Twould be too risky," he replied, "and, even if we succeeded, 'twould do no good. We'll find out in the morning all we want to know."

They tied their canoe to one of the long boats, and, going on board the latter, slept a little. But slumber could not claim Robert long. All about, it was a battle-ground to him, whether land or water. Armies had been passing and repassing, and fighting here from the beginning. It was the centre of the world to him, and in the morning they would be in battle again. If St. Luc held the shore they would not land unscorched. He tried to see signals on the mountain, but the French did not have to talk to one another. They and their red allies lay silent and unseen in the dark woods and waited.

Dawn came, and the three were back in their canoe. The wind had died, and the fleet, bearing the army, moved forward to the landing. Officers searched the woods with their strongest glasses, while the scouts in their canoes, daring every peril, shot forward and leaped upon the shore. Then a sheet of musketry and rifle fire burst from the woods. Men fell from the boats into the water, but others held on to the land that they had gained.

Robert, Tayoga and Willet among the first fired at dusky figures in the woods, and once or twice they caught the gleam of French uniforms.

"It is surely St. Luc," said Robert, when he heard the notes of a silver whistle, "but he can't keep us from landing."

"Aye, it's he," said Willet, "and he's making a game fight of it against overwhelming forces."

Cannon from the boats also swept the forest with grape and round shot, and the troops began to debark. It was evident that the French and Indians were not in sufficient numbers to hold them back. Not all the skill of St. Luc could avail. The three soon had evidence that the formidable Ojibway chief was there also. Tayoga saw a huge trace in the earth, and called the attention of Willet and Robert to it.

"Tandakora is in the bush," he said. "Sharp Sword does not like him, but Manitou has willed that they must often be allies. Now the battle thickens, but the end is sure."

The shores of Lake George, so often the scene of fierce strife, blazed with the fury of the combat. The mountains gave back the thunder of guns on the big boats, and muskets and rifles crackled in the forest. Now and then the shouts of the French and the Indian yell rose, but the triumphant American cheer always replied. The troops poured ashore and the odds against St. Luc rose steadily.

"The Chevalier can't hold us back many minutes longer," said Willet. "If he doesn't give ground, he'll be destroyed."

A few minutes more of resolute fighting and they heard the long, clear call of the silver whistle. Then the forces in front of them vanished suddenly, and not a rifle replied to their fire. French, Canadians and Indians were gone, as completely as if they had never been, but, when the Americans advanced a little farther, they saw the dead, whom St. Luc had not found time to take away. Although the combat had been short, it had been resolute and fierce, and it left its proofs behind.

"Here went Tandakora," said Tayoga. "His great footsteps are far apart, which shows that he was running. Perhaps he hopes to lay an ambush later on. The heart of the Ojibway was full of rage because he could not withstand us."

"And I imagine that the heart of the Chevalier de St. Luc is also heavy," said Robert. "He knows that General Amherst is bringing his artillery with him. When I was at Ticonderoga last year and General Abercrombie advanced, the French, considering the smallness of their forces, were in doubt a long time about standing, and I know from what I heard that they finally decided to defend the place because we did not bring up our guns. We're making no such mistake now; we're not underrating the enemy in that way. It's glorious, Dave, to come back over the ground where you were beaten and retrieve your errors."

"So it is, Robert. We'll soon see this famous Ticonderoga again."

Robert's heart beat hard once more. All the country about him was familiar. So much had been concentrated here, and now it seemed to him that the climax was approaching. Many of the actors in last year's great drama were now on another stage, but Bourlamaque and St. Luc were at hand, and Tandakora had come too with his savages. He looked around it the splendid landscape of lake and mountain and green forest, and the pulses in his temples throbbed fast.

"Aye, Dagaeoga," said Tayoga, who was looking at him, "it is a great day that has come."

"I think so," said Robert, "and what pleases me most is the sight of the big guns. Look how they come off the boats! They'll smash down that wooden wall against which so many good men hurled themselves to death last year. We've got a general who may not be the greatest genius in the world, but he'll have neither a Braddock's defeat nor a Ticonderoga disaster."

Caution, supreme caution, was evident to them all as they moved slowly forward, with the bristling guns at the front. Robert's faith in the cannon was supreme. He looked upon them as their protectors. They were to be the match for Ticonderoga.

On they went, winding through the forest and valleys, but they met nothing. The green woods were silent and deserted, though much was there for Tayoga to read.

"Here still goes Tandakora," he said, "and his heart is as angry as ever. He is bitter against the French, too, because he fears now that he has taken the wrong side. He sees the power of his enemies growing and growing, and Montcalm is not here to lead the French. I do not think Tandakora will go into the fort with St. Luc and Bourlamaque. His place is not inside the walls. He wants the great forest to roam in."

"In that Tandakora is right," said Willet; "he acts according to his lights. A fortress is no place for an Indian."

"Tandakora is now going more slowly," resumed the Onondaga. "His paces shorten. It may be that he will stop to talk with some one. Ah! he does, and it is no less a man than Sharp Sword himself. I have looked upon Sharp Sword's footprints so often that I know them at a glance. He and Tandakora stood here, facing each other, and talked. Neither moved from his tracks while he spoke, and so I think it was not a friendly conference. It is likely that the Ojibway spoke of the defeat of the French, and Sharp Sword replied that in defeat as well as victory true allies stand together. Moreover, he said that defeat might be followed by victory and one must always hope. But Tandakora was not convinced. It is the custom of the Indian to run away when he knows that his enemy is too strong for him, and it may be wise. Now Tandakora turns from the course and goes toward the west. And, lo! his warriors all fall in behind him! Here is their great trail. Sharp Sword heads in another direction. He is going with the French and Canadians to the fortress."

The army, under the shadow of its great guns, moved slowly on, and presently they came upon the terrible field of the year before. Before them lay the wall, stronger than ever with earth and logs, but not a man held it. The French and Canadians were in the fortress, and the Americans and English were free to use the entrenchments as a shelter for themselves if they chose.

"It's going to be a siege," said Willet.

The cannon of Ticonderoga soon opened, and Amherst's guns replied, the cautious general moving his great force forward in a manner that betokened a sure triumph, though it might be slow. But on the following night the whole French army, save a few hundred men under Hebecourt, left to make a last desperate stand, stole away and made for Isle-aux-Noix. Hebecourt replied to Amherst's artillery with the numerous guns of the fort for three days. Amherst still would not allow his army to move forward for the assault, having in mind the terrible losses of last year and knowing that he was bound to win.

The brave Hebecourt and his soldiers also left the fort at last, escaping in boats, and leaving a match burning in the magazine. One of the bastions of Ticonderoga blew up with a tremendous explosion, and then the victorious army marched in. Ticonderoga, such a looming and tremendous name in America, a fortress for which so much blood had been shed, had fallen at last. Robert did not dream that in another war, less than twenty years away, it would change hands three times.

They found, a little later, that Crown Point, the great fortress upon which the French king had spent untold millions, had been abandoned also and was there for the Anglo-American army to take whenever it chose. Then Amherst talked of going on into Canada and cooperating with Wolfe, but, true to his cautious soul, he began to build forts and arrange for the mastery of Lake Champlain.

Robert, Tayoga and Willet grew impatient as the days passed. The news came that Prideaux had been killed before Niagara, but Sir William Johnson, the Waraiyageh of the Mohawks, assuming command in his stead, had taken the place, winning a great victory. After the long night the dawn had come. Everything seemed to favour the English and Americans, and now the eyes of the three turned upon Quebec. It was evident that the war would be won or lost there, and they could bear the delays no longer. Saying farewell to their comrades of Amherst's army, they plunged into the northern wilderness, taking an almost direct course for Quebec.

They were entering a region haunted by warriors, and still ranged by daring French partisans, but they had no fear. Robert believed that the surpassing woodcraft of the hunter and the Onondaga would carry them safely through, and he longed for Quebec, upon which the eyes of both the New World and the Old now turned. They had heard that Wolfe had suffered a defeat at the Montmorency River, due largely to the impetuosity of his men, but that he was hanging on and controlled most of the country about Quebec. But Montcalm on the great rock was as defiant as ever, and it seemed impossible to get at him.

"We'll be there in ample time to see the result, whatever it is," said Willet.

"And we may find the trail of Sharp Sword and Tandakora who go ahead of us," said Tayoga.

"But the Ojibway turned away at Ticonderoga," said Robert. "Why do you think he'll go to Quebec?"

"Because he thinks he will get profit out of it, whatever the event. If our army is defeated, he may have a great scalping, such as there was at Fort William Henry; if the French are beaten, it will be easy enough for him to get away in time. But as long as the issue hangs in the balance, Tandakora means to be present."

"Sound reasoning," said the hunter, "and we'll watch for the trail of both St. Luc and the Ojibway. And now, lads, with eyes and ears open, we'll make speed."

And northward they went at a great rate, watching on all sides for the perils that were never absent from the woods and peaks.

Chapter 14

Before Quebec

True to the predictions of Tayoga, they struck the trail of St. Luc and Tandakora far up in the province of New York and west of Lake Champlain. Ever since the white man came, hostile forces had been going north or south along well-defined passes in these regions, and, doubtless, bands of Indians had been travelling the same course from time immemorial; so it was not hard for them to come upon the traces of French and Indians going to Quebec to make the great stand against Wolfe and his fleet.

"It is a broad trail because many Frenchmen and Indians make it," said the Onondaga. "As I have said, Sharp Sword and Tandakora do not like each other, but circumstances make them allies. They have rejoined and they go together to Quebec. Here is the trail of at least three hundred men, perhaps two hundred Frenchmen and a hundred warriors. The footsteps of Sharp Sword are unmistakable, and so are those of Tandakora. Behold their great size, Dagaeoga; and here are the prints of boots which belong to De Courcelles and Jumonville. I have seen them often before, Dagaeoga. How could you believe they might have been left by somebody else?"

"I see nothing but some faint traces in the earth," said Robert. "If you didn't tell me, I wouldn't be even sure that they were made by a man."

"But they are plain to us who were born in the woods, and whose ancestors have lived in the woods since the beginning of the world. It is where we are superior to the white man, much as the white man thinks of his wisdom, though there be those, like the Great Bear, the Mountain Wolf and Black Rifle, who know much. But the feet of the two Frenchmen who love not Dagaeoga have passed here."

"It is true they do not love me, Tayoga. I wounded one of them last year, shortly before Ticonderoga, as you know, and I fancy that I'd receive short shrift from either if I fell into his hands."

"That is so. But Dagaeoga will not let himself be captured again. He has been captured often enough now."

"I don't seem to be any the worse for it," said Robert, laughing. "You're right, though, Tayoga. For me to be captured once more would be once too much. As St. Luc doesn't like Tandakora, I imagine you don't see him walking with them."

"I do not, Dagaeoga. Sharp Sword keeps by himself, and now De Courcelles and Jumonville walk with the Ojibway chief. Here are their three trails, that of Tandakora between the other two. Doubtless the two Frenchmen are trying to make him their friend, and it is equally sure that they speak ill to him of St. Luc. But Sharp Sword does not care. He expects little from Tandakora and his warriors. He is thinking of Quebec and the great fight that Montcalm must make there against Wolfe. He is eager to arrive at Stadacona, which you call Quebec, and help Montcalm. He knows that it is all over here on Andiatarocte and Oneadatote, that Ticonderoga is lost forever, that Crown Point is lost forever, and that Isle-aux-Noix must go in time, but he hopes for Stadacona. Yet Sharp Sword is depressed. He does not walk with his usual spring and courage. His paces are shorter, and they are shorter because his footsteps drag. Truly, it was a dagger in the heart of Sharp Sword to give up Ticonderoga and Crown Point."

"I can believe you, Tayoga," said Willet. "It's bitter to lose such lakes and such a land, and the French have fought well for them. Do you think there's any danger of our running into an ambush? It would be like Tandakora to lie in wait for pursuers."

"I am not sure, Great Bear. He, like the Frenchman, is in a great hurry to reach Stadacona."

An hour or two later they came to a dead campfire of St. Luc's force, and, a little farther on, a new trail, coming from the west, joined the Chevalier's. They surmised that it had been made by a band from Niagara or some other fallen French fort in that direction, and that everywhere along the border Montcalm was drawing in his lines that he might concentrate his full strength at Quebec to meet the daring challenge of Wolfe.

"But I take it that the drawing in of the French won't keep down scalping parties of the warriors," said Willet. "If they can find anything on the border to raid, they'll raid it."

"It is so," said Tayoga. "It may be that Tandakora and his warriors will turn aside soon to see if they cannot ambush somebody."

"In that case it will be wise for us to watch out for ourselves. You think Tandakora may leave St. Luc and lie in wait, perhaps, for us?"

"For any one who may come. He does not yet know that it is the Great Bear, Dagaeoga and I who follow. Suppose we go on a while longer and see if he leaves the main trail. Is it the wish of Great Bear and Dagaeoga?"

"It is," they replied together.

They advanced several hours, and then the great trail split, or rather it threw off a stem that curved to the west.

"It is made by about twenty warriors," said Tayoga, "and here are the huge footsteps of Tandakora in the very centre of it. I think they will go northwest a while, and then come back toward the main trail, hoping to trap any one who may be rash enough to follow Sharp Sword. But, if the Great Bear and Dagaeoga wish it, we will pursue Tandakora himself and ambush him when he is expecting to ambush others."

The dark eyes of the Onondaga gleamed.

"I can see, Tayoga, that you're hoping for a chance to settle that score between you and the Ojibway," said the hunter. "Maybe you'll get it this time, and maybe you won't, but I'm willing to take the trail after him, and so is Robert here. We may stop a lot of mischief."

It was then about two o'clock in the afternoon, and, as Tayoga said that Tandakora's trail was not more than a few hours old, they pushed on rapidly, hoping to stalk his camp that very night. The traces soon curved back toward St. Luc's and they knew they were right in their surmise that an ambush was being laid by the Ojibway. He and his warriors would halt in the dense bush beside the great trail and shoot down any who followed.

"We'll shatter his innocent little plan," said Willet, his spirits mounting at the prospect.

"Tandakora will not build a fire to-night," said Tayoga. "He will wait in the darkness beside Sharp Sword's path, hoping that some one will come. He will lie in the forest like a panther waiting to spring on its prey."

"And we'll just disturb that panther a little," said Robert, appreciating the merit of their enterprise, which now seemed to all three a kind of great game.

"Aye, we'll make Tandakora think all the spirits of earth and air are after him," said Willet.

They now moved with great caution as the trail was growing quite fresh.

"We will soon be back to Sharp Sword's line of march," said Tayoga, "and I think we will find Tandakora and his warriors lying in the bushes not more than a mile ahead."

They redoubled their caution, and, when they approached a dense thicket, Robert and Willet lay down and Tayoga went on, creeping on hands and knees. In a half hour he came back and said that Tandakora and his band were in the thicket watching the great trail left by St. Luc.

"The Ojibway does not dream that he himself is being watched," said the Onondaga, "and now I think we would better eat a little food from our knapsacks and wait until the dark night that is promised has fully come."

Tayoga's report was wholly true. Tandakora and twenty fierce warriors lay in the thicket, waiting to fall upon those who might follow the trail of St. Luc. He had no doubt that a force of some kind would come. The Bostonnais and the English always followed a retreating enemy, and experience never kept them from walking into an ambush. Tandakora was already counting the scalps he would take, and his savage heart was filled with delight. He had been aghast when Bourlamaque abandoned Ticonderoga and Crown Point. Throughout the region over which he had been roaming for three or four years the Bostonnais would be triumphant. Andiatarocte and Oneadatote would pass into their possession forever. The Ojibway chief belonged far to the westward, to the west of the Great Lakes, but the great war had called him, like so many others of the savage tribes, into the east, and he had been there so long that he had grown to look upon the country as his own, or at least held by him and his like in partnership with the French, a belief confirmed by the great victories at Duquesne and Oswego, William Henry and Ticonderoga.

Now Tandakora's whole world was overthrown. The French were withdrawing into Canada. St. Luc, whom he did not like, but whom he knew to be a great warrior, was retreating in haste, and the invincible Montcalm was beleaguered in Quebec. He would have to go too, but he meant to take scalps with him. Bostonnais were sure to appear on the trail, and they would come in the night, pursuing St. Luc. It was a good night for such work as his, heavy with clouds and very dark. He would creep close and strike before his presence was even suspected.

Tandakora lay quiet with his warriors, while night came and its darkness grew, and he listened for the sound of men on the trail. Instead he heard the weird, desolate cry of an owl to his left, and then the equally lone and desolate cry of another to his right. But the warriors still lay quiet. They had heard owls often and were not afraid of them. Then the cry came from the north, and now it was repeated from the south. There was a surfeit of owls, very much too many of them, and they called to one another too much. Tandakora did not like it. It was almost like a visitation of evil spirits. Those weird, long-drawn cries, singularly piercing on a still night, were bad omens. Some of his warriors stirred and became uneasy, but Tandakora quieted them sternly and promised that the Bostonnais would soon be along. Hope aroused again, the men plucked up courage and resumed their patient waiting.

Then the cry of the panther, long drawn, wailing like the shriek of a woman, came from the east and the west, and presently from the north and the south also, followed soon by the dreadful hooting of the owls, and then by the fierce growls of the bear. Tandakora, in spite of himself, in spite of his undoubted courage, in spite of his vast experience in the forest, shuddered. The darkness was certainly full of wicked spirits, and they were seeking prey. So many owls and bears and panthers could not be abroad at once in a circle about him. But Tandakora shook himself and resolved to stand fast. He encouraged his warriors, who were already showing signs of fright, and refused to let any one go.

But the forest chorus grew. Tandakora heard the gobble of the wild turkey as he used to hear it in his native west, only he was sure that the gobble now was made by a spirit and not by a real turkey. Then the owl hooted, the panther shrieked and the bear growled. The cry of a moose, not any moose at all, as Tandakora well knew, but the foul emanation of a wicked spirit, came, merely to be succeeded by the weird cries of night birds which the Ojibway chief had never seen, and of which he had never dreamed. He knew, though, that they must be hideous, misshapen creatures. But he still stood fast, although all of his warriors were eager to go, and the demon chorus came nearer and nearer, multiplying its cries, and adding to the strange notes of birds the equally strange notes of animals, worse even than the growl of bear or shriek of panther.

Tandakora knew now that the wicked spirits of earth and air were abroad in greater numbers than he had ever known before. They fairly swarmed all about him and his warriors, continually coming closer and closer and making dire threats. The night was particularly suited to them. The heavy black clouds floating before the moon and stars were met by thick mists and vapours that fairly oozed out of the damp earth. It was an evil night, full of spells and magic, and the moment came when the chief wished he was in his own hunting grounds far to the west by the greatest of the Great Lakes.

The darkness was not too great for him to see several of his warriors trembling and he rebuked them fiercely, though his own nerves, tough as they were, were becoming frayed and uneasy. He forgot to watch the trail and listen for the sound of footsteps. All his attention was centred upon that horrible and circling chorus of sound. The Bostonnais might come and pass and he would not see them. He went into the forest a little way, trying to persuade himself that they were really persecuted by animals. He would find one of these annoying panthers or bears and shoot it, or he would not even hesitate to send a bullet through an owl on a bough, but he saw nothing, and, as he went back to his warriors, a hideous snapping and barking of wolves followed him.

The note of the wolf had not been present hitherto in the demon chorus, but now it predominated. What it lacked in the earliness of coming it made up in the vigour of arrival. It had in it all the human qualities, that is, the wicked or menacing ones—hunger, derision, revenge, desire for blood and threat of death. Tandakora, veteran of a hundred battles, one of the fiercest warriors that ever ranged the woods, shook. His blood turned to water, ice water at that, and the bones of his gigantic frame seemed to crumble. He knew, as all the Indians knew, that the souls of dead warriors, usually those who had been wicked in life, dwelled for a while in the bodies of animals, preferably those of wolves, and the wolves about him were certainly inhabited by the worst warriors that had ever lived. In every growl and snap and bark there was a threat. He could hear it, and he knew it was meant for him. But what he feared most of all was the deadly whine with which growl, snap and bark alike ended. Perspiration stood out on his face, but he could not afford to show fear to his men, and, retreating slowly, he rejoined them. He would make no more explorations in the haunted wood that lay all about them.

As the chief went back to his men the snarling and snapping of the demon wolves distinctly expressed laughter, derision of the most sinister kind. They were not only threatening him, they were laughing at him, and his bones continued to crumble through sheer weakness and fear. It was not worth while for him to fire at any of the sounds. The bullet might go through a wolf, but it would not hurt him, it would merely increase his ferocity and make him all the more hungry for the blood of Tandakora.

The band pressed close together as the wolves growled and snapped all about them, but the warriors still saw nothing. How could they see anything when such wolves had the power of making themselves invisible? But their claws would tear and their teeth would rend just the same when they sprang upon their victims, and now they were coming so close that they might make a spring, the prodigious kind of spring that a demon wolf could make.

It was more than Tandakora and his warriors could stand. Human beings, white or red, they would fight, but not the wicked and powerful spirits of earth and air which were now closing down upon them. The chief could resist no longer. He uttered a great howl of fear, which was taken up and repeated in a huge chorus by his warriors. Then, and by the same impulse, they burst from the thicket, rushed into St. Luc's trail and sped northward at an amazing pace.

Tayoga, Willet and Robert emerged from the woods, lay down in the trail and panted for breath.

"Well, that's the easiest victory we ever gained," said Robert. "Even easier than one somewhat like it that I won on the island."

"I don't know about that," gasped Willet. "It's hard work being an owl and a bear and a panther and a wolf and trying, too, to be in three or four places at the same time. I worked hardest as a wolf toward the last; every muscle in me is tired, and I think my throat is the most tired of all. I must lie by for a day."

"Great Bear is a splendid animal," said Tayoga in his precise, book English, "nor is he wanting as a bird, either. I think he turned himself into birds that were never seen in this world, and they were very dreadful birds, too. But he excelled most as a wolf. His growling and snapping and whining were better than that of ninety-nine out of a hundred wolves, only a master wolf could have equalled it, and when I stood beside him I was often in fear lest he turn and tear me to pieces with tooth and claw."

"Tandakora was in mortal terror," said Robert, who was not as tired as the others, who had done most of the work in the demon chorus. "I caught a glimpse of his big back, and I don't think I ever saw anybody run faster. He'll not stop this side of the St. Lawrence, and you'll have to postpone your vengeance a while, Tayoga."

"I could have shot him down as he stood in the woods, shaking with fear," said the Onondaga, "but that never would have done. That would have spoiled our plan, and I must wait, as you say, Dagaeoga, to settle the score with the Ojibway."

"I think we'd better go into the bushes and sleep," said the hunter. "Being a demon is hard work, and there is no further danger from the warriors."

But Robert, who was comparatively fresh, insisted on keeping the watch, and the other two, lying down on their blankets, were soon in deep slumber. The next day they shot a young bear, and had a feast in the woods, a reward to which they thought themselves entitled after the great and inspired effort they had made the night before. As they sat around their cooking fire, eating the juicy steaks, they planned how they should enter Canada and join Wolfe, still keeping their independence as scouts and skirmishers.

"Most of the country around the city is held by the English, or at least they overrun it from time to time," said Willet, "and we ought to get past the French villages in a single night. Then we can join whatever part of the force we wish. I think it likely that we can be of most use with the New England rangers, who are doing a lot of the scouting and skirmishing for Wolfe."

"But I want to see the Royal Americans first," said Robert. "I heard in Boston that Colden, Wilton, Carson, Stuart and Cabell had gone on with them, and I know that Grosvenor is there with his regiment. I should like to see them all again."

"And so would I," said the hunter. "A lot of fine lads. I hope that all of them will come through the campaign alive."

They travelled the whole of the following night and remained in the forest through the day, and following this plan they arrived before Quebec without adventure, finding the army of Wolfe posted along the St. Lawrence, his fleet commanding the river, but the army of Montcalm holding Quebec and all the French elated over the victory of the Montmorency River. Robert went at once to the camp of the Royal Americans, where Colden was the first of his friends whom he saw. The Philadelphian, like all the others, was astounded and delighted.

"Lennox!" he exclaimed, grasping his hand. "I heard that you were dead, killed by a spy named Garay, and your body thrown into the Hudson, where it was lost! Now, I know that reports are generally lies! And you're no ghost. 'Tis a solid hand that I hold in mine!"

"I'm no ghost, though I did vanish from the world for a while," said Robert. "But, as you see, I've come back and I mean to have a part in the taking of Quebec."

Wilton and Carson, Stuart and Cabell soon came, and then Grosvenor, and every one in his turn welcomed Robert back from the dead, after which he gave to them collectively a rapid outline of his story.

"'Tis a strange tale, a romance," said Grosvenor. "It's evident that it's not intended you shall lose your life in this war, Lennox. What has become of that wonderful Onondaga Indian, Tayoga, and the great hunter, Willet?"

"They're both here. You shall see them before the day is over. But what is the feeling in the army?"

"We're depressed and the French are elated. It's because we lost the Montmorency battle. The Royal Americans and the Grenadiers were too impulsive. We tried to rush slopes damp and slippery from rain, and we were cut up. I received a wound there, and so did Wilton, but neither amounts to anything, and I want to tell you, Lennox, that, although we're depressed, we're not withdrawing. Our general is sick a good deal, but the sicker he grows the braver he grows. We hang on. The French say we can continue hanging on, and then the winter will drive us away. You know what the Quebec winter is. But we'll see. Maybe something will happen before winter comes."

As Robert turned away from the little group he came face to face with a tall young officer dressed with scrupulousness and very careful of his dignity.

"Charteris!" he exclaimed.

"Lennox!"

They shook hands with the greatest surprise and pleasure.

"When I last saw you at Ticonderoga you were a prisoner of the French," said Robert.

"And so were you."

"But I escaped in a day or two."

"I escaped also, though not in a day or two. I was held a prisoner in Quebec all through the winter and spring and much befell me, but at last I escaped to General Wolfe and rejoined my old command, the Royal Americans."

"And he took part in the battle of Montmorency, a brave part too," said Colden.

"No braver than the others. No more than you yourself, Colden," protested Charteris.

"And 'tis said that, though he left Quebec in the night, he left his heart there in the possession of a very lovely lady who speaks French better than she speaks English," said Colden.

"'Tis not a subject of which you have definite information," rejoined Charteris, flushing very red and then laughing.

But Colden, suspecting that his jest was truth rather, had too much delicacy to pursue the subject. Later in the day Robert returned with Willet and Tayoga and they had a reunion.

"When we take Quebec," said Tayoga to Grosvenor, "Red Coat must go back with us into the wilderness and learn to become a great warrior. We can go beyond the Great Lakes and stay two or three years."

"I wish I could," laughed Grosvenor, "but that is one of the things I must deny myself. If the war should be finished, I shall have to return to England."

"St. Luc is in Quebec," said Willet. "We followed his trail a long distance."

"Which means that our task here will be the harder," said Colden.

Robert went with Willet, Charteris and Tayoga the next day to Monckton's camp at Point Levis, whence the English batteries had poured destruction upon the lower town of Quebec, firing across the St. Lawrence, that most magnificent of all rivers, where its channel was narrow. He could see the houses lying in ashes or ruins, but above them the French flag floated defiantly over the upper city.

"Montcalm and his lieutenants made great preparations to receive General Wolfe," said Charteris. "As I was in Quebec then, I know something about them, and I've learned more since I escaped. They threw up earthworks, bastions and redoubts almost all the way from Quebec to Montcalm's camp at Beauport. Over there at Beauport the Marquis' first headquarters were located in a big stone house. Across the mouth of the St. Charles they put a great boom of logs, fastened together by chains, and strengthened further by two cut-down ships on which they mounted batteries. Forces passing between the city and the Beauport camp crossed the St. Charles on a bridge of boats, and each entrance of the bridge was guarded by earthworks. In the city they closed and fortified every gate, except the Palace Gate, through which they passed to the bridge or from it. They had more than a hundred cannon on the walls, a floating battery carried twelve more guns, and big ones too, and they had a lot of gun-boats and fire ships and fire rafts. They gathered about fifteen thousand men in the Beauport camp, besides Indians, with the regulars in the centre, and the militia on the flank. In addition to these there were a couple of thousand in the city itself under De Ramesay, and I think Montcalm had, all told, near to twenty thousand men, about double our force, though 'tis true many of theirs are militia and we have a powerful fleet. I suppose their numbers have not decreased, and it's a great task we've undertaken, though I think we'll achieve it."

Robert looked again and with great emotion upon Quebec, that heart and soul of the French power in North America. Truly much water had flowed down the St. Lawrence since he was there before. He could not forget the thrill with which he had first approached it, nor could he forget those gallant young Frenchmen who had given him a welcome, although he was already, in effect, an official enemy. And then, too, he had seen Bigot, Péan, Cadet and their corrupt group who were doing so much to wreck the fortunes of New France. Not all the valour of Montcalm, De Levis, Bourlamaque, St. Luc and the others could stay the work of their destructive hands.

The mills of God grind slowly, but they grind exceeding small. It was true! The years had passed. The French victories in North America had been numerous. Again and again they had hurled back the English and Americans, and year after year they had dammed the flood. They had struck terrible blows at Duquesne and Oswego, at William Henry and at Ticonderoga. But the mills of God ground on, and here at last was the might of Britain before Quebec, and Robert's heart, loyal as he was to the mother country, always throbbed with pride when he recalled that his own Americans were there too, the New England rangers and the staunch regiment of Royal Americans, the bravest of the brave, who had already given so much of their blood at Montmorency. In these world-shaking events the Americans played their splendid part beside their English kin, as they were destined to do one hundred and fifty-nine years later upon the soil of Europe itself, closing up forever, as most of us hope, the cleavage between nations of the same language and same ideals.

Robert looked long at Quebec on its heights, gleaming now in the sun which turned it into a magic city, increasing its size, heightening the splendour of the buildings and heightening, too, the formidable obstacles over which Wolfe must prevail. Nature here had done wonders for the defence. With its mighty river and mighty cliffs it seemed that a capable general and a capable army could hold the city forever.

"Aye, it's strong, Lennox," said Charteris, who read his thoughts. "General Wolfe, as I know, has written back to England that it's the strongest place in the world, and he may be right, but we've had some successes here, mingled with some failures. Aside from the Battle of Montmorency most of the land fighting has been in our favour, and our command of the river through our fleet is a powerful factor in our favour. Yet, the short Quebec summer draws to a close, and if we take the city we must take it soon. General Wolfe is lying ill again in a farm house, but his spirit is not quenched and all our operations are directed from his sick bed."

As Charteris spoke, the batteries on the Heights of Levis opened again, pouring round shot, grape and canister upon the Lower Town. Fragments of buildings crashed to the earth, and other fragments burst into flames. Cannon on the frigates in the river also fired upon the devoted city and from the great rock cannon replied. Coils of smoke arose, and, uniting into a huge cloud, floated westward on the wind. It was a great spectacle and Robert's heart throbbed. But he was sad too. He had much pity for the people of Quebec, exposed to that terrible siege and the rain of death.

"We've ravaged a good deal of the country around Quebec," continued Charteris. "It's hard, but we're trying to cut off the subsistence of the French army, and, on the other hand, bands of their Indian allies raid our outposts and take scalps. It's the New England rangers mostly that deal with these war parties, in which the French and Canadians themselves take a part."

"Then Tandakora will find plenty of employment here," said Willet. "Nothing will give him more joy than to steal upon a sentinel in the dark and cut him down."

"And while Tandakora hunts our people," said Tayoga, "we will hunt him. What better work can we do, Great Bear, than to meet these raiding parties?"

"That's our task, Tayoga," replied the hunter.

As they turned away from the Heights of Levis the batteries were still thundering, pouring their terrible flood of destruction upon the Lower Town, and far up on the cliffs cannon were firing at the ships in the river. Robert looked back and his heart leaped as before. The eyes of the world he knew were on Quebec, and well it deserved the gaze of the nations. It was fitting that the mighty drama should be played out there, on that incomparable stage, where earth rose up to make a fitting channel for its most magnificent river.

"It's all that you think it is," said Charteris, again reading his thoughts; "a prize worth the efforts of the most warlike nations."

"The Quebec of the English and French," said Tayoga, "but the lost Stadacona of the Mohawks, lost to them forever. Whatever the issue of the war the Mohawks will not regain their own."

The others were silent, not knowing what to say. A little later a tall, lank youth to whom Charteris gave a warm welcome met them.

"Been taking a look at the town, Leftenant?" he said.

"Aye, Zeb," replied Charteris. "I've been showing it to some friends of mine who, however, have seen it before, though not under the same conditions. These gentlemen are David Willet, Robert Lennox and Tayoga, the Onondaga, and this is Zebedee Crane, a wonderful scout to whom I owe my escape from Quebec."

Willet seized the lank lad's hand and gave it a warm grasp.

"I've heard of you, Zeb Crane," he said. "You're from the Mohawk Valley and you're one of the best scouts and trailers in the whole Province of New York, or anywhere, for that matter."

"And I've heard uv all three uv you," said the boy, looking at them appreciatively. "I wuz at Ticonderogy, an' two uv you at least wuz thar. I didn't git to see you, but I heard uv you. You're a great hunter, Mr.

Willet, whom the Iroquois call the Great Bear, an' ez fur Tayoga I know that he belongs to the Clan of the Bear uv the nation Onondaga, an' that he's the grandest trailer the world hez ever seed."

Tayoga actually blushed under his bronze.

"The flattery of my friends should be received at a heavy discount," he said in his prim, precise English.

"It ain't no flattery," said Zebedee. "It's the squar' an' solid truth. I've heard tales uv you that are plum' impossible, but I know that they hev happened all the same. Ef they wuz to tell me that you had tracked the wild goose through the air or the leapin' salmon through the water I'd believe 'em."

"It would be very little exaggeration," said Robert, earnestly. "Be quiet, Tayoga! If we want to sing your praises we'll sing 'em and you can't help it."

The five recrossed the river together, and went to Wolfe's camp below the town facing the Montmorency, Charteris going back into camp with the Royal Americans to whom he belonged, and the others going as free lances with the New England rangers. Robert also resumed his acquaintance with Captain Whyte and Lieutenant Lanhan of the *Hawk*, who were delighted to meet him again.

Soon they found that there was much for them to do. Robert's heart bled at the sight of the devastated country. Houses and farms were in ruins and their people fled. Everywhere war had blazed a red path. Nor was it safe for the rangers unless they were in strong parties. Ferocious Indians roamed about and cut off all stragglers, sometimes those of their own French or Canadian allies. Once they came upon the trail of Tandakora. They found the dead bodies of four English soldiers lying beside an abandoned farm house, and Tayoga, looking at the traces in the earth, told the tale as truly as if he had been there.

"Tandakora and his warriors stood behind these vines," he said, going to a little arbour. "See their traces and in the centre of them the prints left by the gigantic footsteps of the Ojibway chief. The house had been plundered by some one, maybe by the warriors themselves, before the soldiers came. Then the Ojibway and his band hid here and waited. It was easy for them. The soldiers knew nothing of wilderness war, and they came up to the house, unsuspecting. They were at the front door, when Tandakora and his men fired. Three of them fell dead where they lie. The fourth was wounded and tried to escape. Tandakora ran from behind the vines. Here goes his trail and here he stopped, balanced himself and threw his tomahawk."

"And it clove the wounded soldier's head," said Robert. "Here he lies, telling the rest of the tale."

They buried the four, but they found new tragedies. Thus the month of August with its successes and failures, its attacks and counter-attacks dragged on, as the great siege of Quebec waged by Phipps and the New Englanders nearly three-quarters of a century before had dragged.

CHAPTER 15

The Lone Château

Despite his courage and the new resolution that he had acquired during his long months on the island, Robert's heart often sank. They seemed to make no progress with the siege of Quebec. Just so far had they gone and they could go no farther. The fortress of France in the New World appeared impregnable. There it was, cut clear against the sky, the light shining on its stone buildings, proud and defiant, saying with every new day to those who attacked it that it could not be taken, while Montcalm, De Levis, Bougainville, St. Luc and the others showed all their old skill in defence. They heard too that Bourlamaque after his retreat from Ticonderoga and Crown Point was sitting securely within his lines and entrenchments at Isle-aux-Noix and that the cautious Amherst would delay longer and yet longer.

It was now certain that no help could be expected from Amherst and his strong army that year. The most that he would do would be to keep Bourlamaque and his men from coming to the relief of Quebec. So far as the capital of New France was concerned the issue must be fought out by the forces now gathered there for the defence and the offense, the French and the Indians against the English and the Americans.

Robert realized more keenly every day that the time was short and becoming shorter. Hot summer days were passing, nights came on crisp and cool, the foliage along the king of rivers and its tributaries began to glow with the intense colours of decay, there was more than a touch of autumn in the air. They must be up and doing before the fierce winter came down on Quebec. Military operations would be impossible then.

In this depressing time Robert drew much courage from Charteris, who had been a prisoner a long time in Quebec, and who understood even more thoroughly than young Lennox the hollowness of the French power in North America.

"It is upheld by a few brave and skilful men and a small but heroic army," he said. "In effect, New France has been deserted by the Bourbon monarchy. If it were not for the extraordinary situation of Quebec, adapted so splendidly to purposes of defence, we could crush the Marquis de Montcalm in a short time. The French regulars are as good as any troops in the world and they will fight to the last, but the Canadian militia is not disciplined well, and is likely to break under a fierce attack. You know, Lennox, what militiamen always are, no matter to what nation they belong. They may fight and die like heroes at one time, and, at another time, they may run away at the first fire, struck with panic. What we want is a fair chance at the French army in the open. General Wolfe himself, though cursed by much illness, never loses hope. I've had occasion to talk with him more than once owing to my knowledge of Quebec and the surrounding country, and there's a spirit for you, Lennox. It's in an ugly body but no man was ever animated by a finer temper and courage."

Robert and Charteris formed a great friendship, a true friendship that lasted all their long lives. But then Robert had a singular faculty for making friends. Charteris interested him vastly. He had a proud, reserved and somewhat haughty nature. Many people thought him exclusive, but Robert soon learned that his fastidiousness was due to a certain shy quality, and a natural taste for the best in everything. Under his apparent coldness lay a brave and staunch nature and an absolute integrity.

Robert's interest in Charteris was heightened by the delicate cloud of romance that floated about him, a cloud that rose from the hints thrown forth now and then by Zebedee Crane. The young French lady in Quebec who loved him was as beautiful as the dawn and she had the spirit of a queen. Charteris lived in the hope that they might take Quebec and her with it. But Robert was far too fine of feeling ever to allude to such an affair of the heart to Charteris, or in truth to any one else.

It was a period of waiting and yet it was a period of activity. The partisans were incessant in their ways. Robert heard that his old friend, Langlade, was leading a numerous band against the English, and the evidences of Tandakora's murderous ferocity multiplied. Nor were the outlying French themselves safe from him. News arrived that he intended an attack upon a château called Chatillard farther up the river but within the English lines. A band of the New England rangers, led by Willet, was sent to drive him off, and to destroy the Ojibway pest, if possible. Robert, Tayoga and Zeb Crane went with him.

They arrived at the château just before twilight. It was a solid stone building overlooking the St. Lawrence, and the lands about it had a narrow frontage on the river, but it ran back miles after the old French custom in making such grants, in order that every estate might have a river landing. Willet's troops numbered about forty men, and, respecting the aged M. de Chatillard, who was quite ill and in bed, they did not for the present go into the house, eating their own supper on the long, narrow lawn, which was thick with dwarfed and clipped pines and other shrubbery.

But they lighted no fires, and they kept very quiet, since they wished for Tandakora to walk into an ambush. The information, most of which had been obtained by Zeb Crane, was to the effect that Tandakora believed a guard of English soldiers was in the house. After his custom he would swoop down upon them, slaughter them, and then be up and away. It was a trick in which the savage heart of the Ojibway delighted, and he had achieved it more than once.

The August night came down thick and dark. A few lights shone in the Château de Chatillard, but Willet and his rangers stood in black gloom. Almost at their feet the great St. Lawrence flowed in its mighty channel, a dim blue under the dusky sky. Nothing was visible there save the slow stream, majestic, an incalculable weight of water. Nothing appeared upon its surface, and the far shore was lost in the night. It seemed to Robert, despite the stone walls of the château by their side, that they were back in the wilderness. It was a northern wilderness too. The light wind off the river made him shiver.

The front door of the house opened and a figure outlined against the light appeared. It was an old man in a black robe, tall, thin and ascetic, and Robert seeing him so clearly in the light of a lamp that he held in his hand recognized him at once. It was Father Philibert Drouillard, the same whom he had defeated in the test of oratory in the vale of Onondaga before the wise sachems, when so much depended on victory.

"Father Drouillard!" he exclaimed impulsively, stepping forward out of the shadows.

"Who is it who speaks?" asked the priest, holding the lamp a little higher.

"Father Drouillard, don't you know me?" exclaimed Robert, advancing within the circle of light.

"Ah, it is young Lennox!" said the priest. "What a meeting! And under what circumstances!"

"And there are others here whom you know," said Robert. "Look, this is David Willet who commands us, and here also is Tayoga, whom you remember in the vale of Onondaga."

Father Drouillard saluted them gravely.

"You are the enemies of my country," he said, "but I will not deny that I am glad to see you here. I understand that the savage, Tandakora, means to attack this house to-night, thinking that it holds a British garrison. Well, it seems that he will not be far wrong in his thought."

A ghost of a smile flickered over the priest's pale face.

"A garrison but not the garrison that he expects to destroy," said Willet. "Tandakora fights nominally under the flag of France, but as you know, Father, he fights chiefly to gratify his own cruel desires."

"I know it too well. Come inside. M. de Chatillard wishes to see you."

Willet, Robert, Tayoga and Zeb Crane went in, and were shown into the bedroom where the Seigneur Louis Henri Anatole de Chatillard, past ninety years of age, lay upon his last bed. He was a large, handsome old man, fair like so many of the Northern French, and his dying eyes were full of fire. Two women of middle years, his granddaughters, knelt weeping by each side of his bed, and two servants, tears on their faces, stood at the foot. Willet and his comrades halted respectfully at the door.

"Step closer," said the old man, "that I may see you well."

The four entered and stood within the light shed by two tall candles. The old man gazed at them a long time in silence, but finally he said: "And so the English have come at last."

"We're not English, M. de Chatillard," said Willet, "we're Americans, Bostonnais, as you call us."

"It is the same. You are but the children of the English and you fight together against us. You increase too fast in the south. You thrive in your towns and in the woods, and you send greater and greater numbers against us. But you cannot take Quebec. The capital of New France is inviolate."

Willet said nothing. How could he argue with a man past ninety who lay upon his dying bed?

"You cannot take Quebec," repeated M. de Chatillard, rising, strength showing in his voice. "The Bostonnais have come before. It was in Frontenac's time nearly three-quarters of a century ago, when Phipps and his armada from New England arrived before Quebec. I was but a lad then newly come from France, but the great governor, Frontenac, made ready for them. We had batteries in the Sault-au-Matelot on Palace Hill, on Mount Carmel, before the Jesuits' college, in the Lower Town and everywhere. Three-quarters of a century ago did I say? No, it was yesterday! I remember how we fought. Frontenac was a great man as Montcalm is!"

"Peace, M. de Chatillard," said Father Drouillard soothingly. "You speak of old, old times and old, old things!"

"They were the days of my youth," said the old man, "and they are not old to me. It was a great siege, but the valour of France and Canada were not to be overcome. The armies and ships of the Bostonnais went back whence they came, and the new invasion of the Bostonnais will have no better fate."

Willet was still silent. He saw that the old siege of Quebec was much more in M. de Chatillard's mind than the present one, and if he could pass away in the odour of triumph the hunter would not willingly change it.

"Who is the youth who stands near you?" said M. de Chatillard, looking at Robert.

"He is Robert Lennox of the Province of New York," replied Father Drouillard, speaking for Willet. "One of the Bostonnais, but a good youth."

"One of the Bostonnais! Then I do not know him! I thought for a moment that I saw in him the look of some one else, but maybe I was mistaken. An old man cheats himself with fancies. Lad, come thou farther into the light and let me see thee more clearly."

The tone of command was strong in his voice, and Robert, obeying it, stepped close to the bed. The old man raised his head a little, and looked at him long with hawk's eyes. Robert felt that intent gaze cutting into him, but he did not move. Then the Seigneur Louis Henri Anatole de Chatillard laughed scornfully and said to Father Drouillard:

"Why do you deceive me, Father? Why do you tell me that is one, Robert Lennox, a youth of the Bostonnais, who stands before me, when my own eyes tell me that it is the Chevalier Raymond Louis de St. Luc, come as befits a soldier of France to say farewell to an old man before he dies."

Robert felt an extraordinary thrill of emotion. M. de Chatillard, seeing with the eyes of the past, had taken him for the Chevalier. But why?

"It is not the Chevalier de St. Luc," said Father Drouillard, gently. "It is the lad, Robert Lennox, from the Province of New York."

"But it is St. Luc!" insisted the old man. "The face is the same, the eyes are the same! Should I not know? I have known the Chevalier, and his father and grandfather before him."

The priest signed to Robert, and he withdrew into the shadow of the room. Then Father Drouillard whispered into M. de Chatillard's ear, one of the servants gave him medicine from a glass, and presently he sank into quiet, seeming to be conscious no longer of the presence of the strangers. Willet, Robert and the others withdrew softly. Robert was still influenced by strong emotion. Did he look like St. Luc? And why? What was the tie between them? The question that had agitated him so often stirred him anew.

"Very old men, when they come to their last hours, have many illusions," said Willet.

"It may be so," said Robert, "but it was strange that he should take me for St. Luc."

Willet was silent. Robert saw that as usual the hunter did not wish to make any explanations, but he felt once more that the time for the solution of his problem was not far away. He could afford to wait.

"The Seigneur cannot live to know whether Quebec will fall," said Tayoga.

"No," said Willet, "and it's just as well. His time runs out. His mind at the last will be filled with the old days when Frontenac held the town against the New Englanders."

The rangers were disposed well about the house, and they also watched the landing. Tandakora and his men might come in canoes, stealing along in the shadow of the high cliffs, or they might creep through the fields and forest. Zeb Crane, who could see in the dark like an owl and who had already proved his great qualities as a scout and ranger, watched at the river, and Willet with Robert and Tayoga was on the land side. But they learned there was another château landing less than a quarter of a mile lower down, and Tandakora, coming on the river, might use that, and yet make his immediate approach by land.

Willet stood by a grape arbour with Robert and the Onondaga, and watched with eye and ear.

"Tandakora is sure to come," said the hunter. "It's just such a night as he loves. Little would he care whether he found English or French in the house; if not the English whom he expects, then the French, and dead men have nothing to say, nor dead women either. It may be, Tayoga, that you will have your chance to-night to settle your score with him."

"I do not think so, Great Bear," replied the Onondaga. "The night is so dark that I cannot see Tododaho on his star, but no whisper from him reaches me. I think that when the time comes for the Ojibway and me to see which shall continue to live, Tododaho or the spirits in the air will give warning."

Robert shivered a little. Tayoga's tone was cool and matter of fact, but his comrades knew that he was in deadly earnest. At the appointed time he and Tandakora would fight their quarrel out, fight it to the death. In the last analysis Tayoga was an Indian, strong in Indian customs and beliefs.

"Tandakora will come about an hour before midnight," said the Onondaga, "because it will be very dark then and there will yet be plenty of time for his work. He will expect to find everybody asleep, save perhaps an English sentinel whom he can easily tomahawk in the darkness. He does not know that the old Seigneur lies dying, and that they watch by his bed."

"In that case," said the hunter with his absolute belief in all that Tayoga said, "we can settle ourselves for quite a wait."

They relapsed into silence and Robert began to look at the light that shone from the bedroom of M. de Chatillard, the only light in the house now visible. He was an old, old man between ninety and a hundred, and Willett was right in saying that he might well pass on before the fate of Quebec was decided. Robert was sure that it was going to fall, and M. de Chatillard at the end of a long, long life would be spared a great blow. But what a life! What events had been crowded into his three generations of living! He could remember Le Grand Monarque, The Sun King and the buildings of Versailles. He was approaching middle age when Blenheim was fought. He could remember mighty battles, great changes, and the opening of new worlds, and like Virgil's hero, he had been a great part of them. That was a life to live, and, if Quebec were going to fall, it was well that M. de Chatillard with his more than ninety years should cease to live, before the sun of France set in North America. Yes, Willet was right.

A long time passed and Tayoga, lying down with his ear to the earth, was listening. It was so dark now that hearing, not sight, must tell when Tandakora came.

"I go into the forest," whispered the Onondaga, "but I return soon."

"Don't take any needless risks," said Willet.

Tayoga slipped into the dusk, fading from sight like a wraith, but in five minutes he came back.

"Tandakora is at hand," he whispered. "He lies with his warriors in the belt of pine woods. They are watching the light in the Seigneur's window, but presently they will steal upon the house."

"And find us on watch," said Willet, an exultant tone appearing in his voice. "To the landing, Robert, and tell Zeb they're here on our side."

The lank lad returned with Robert, though he left part of his men at that point to guard against surprise, and the bulk of the force, under Willet, crowded behind the grape arbour awaiting the onslaught of Tandakora who, they knew, would come in caution and silence.

Another period that seemed to Robert interminable, though it was not more than half an hour, passed, and then he saw dimly a gigantic figure, made yet greater by the dusk. He knew that it was Tandakora and his hand slid to the trigger and hammer of his rifle. But he knew also that he would not fire. It was no part of their plan to give an alarm so early. The Ojibway vanished and then he thought he caught the gleam of a uniform. So, a Frenchman, probably an officer, was with the warriors!

"They have scouted about the house somewhat," whispered Tayoga, "and they think the soldiers are inside."

"In that case," Willet whispered back, "they'll break down the front door and rush in for slaughter."

"So they will. It is likely that they are looking now for a big log."

Soon a long, dark shape emerged from the dark, a shape that looked like one of the vast primeval *saurians*. It was a dozen warriors carrying the trunk of a small tree, and all moulded into one by the dusk. They gathered headway, as they advanced, and it was a powerful door that could withstand their blow. One of the ambushed rangers moved a little, and, in doing so, made a noise. Quick as a flash the warriors dropped the log, and another farther back fired at the noise.

"Give it to 'em, lads!" cried Willet.

A score of rifles flashed and the warriors replied instantly, but they were caught at a disadvantage. They had come there for rapine and murder, expecting an easy victory, and while Tandakora rallied them they were no match for the rangers, led by such men as Willet and his lieutenants. The battle, fierce and sanguinary, though it was, lasted a bare five minutes and then the Ojibway and those of his band who survived took to flight. Robert caught a glimpse among the fleeing men of one whom he knew to be the spy, Garay. Stirred by a fierce impulse he fired at him, but missed in the dusk, and then Garay vanished with the others. Robert, however, did not believe that he had been recognized by the spy and he was glad of it. He preferred that Garay should consider him dead, and then he would be free of danger from that source.

The firing was succeeded by a few minutes of intense silence and then the great door of the Château de Chatillard opened again. Once more Father Drouillard stood on the step, holding a lamp in his hand.

"It is over, Father," said Willet. "We've driven off part of 'em and the others lie here."

"I heard the noise of the battle from within," said Father Drouillard calmly, "and for the first time in my life I prayed that the Bostonnais might win."

"If you don't mind, Father, bring the lamp, and let us see the fallen. There must be at least fifteen here."

Father Drouillard, holding the light high, walked out upon the lawn with steady step.

"Here is a Montagnais," said Willet, "and this a St. Regis, and this a St. Francis, and this a Huron, and this an Ojibway from the far west! Ah, and here is a Frenchman, an officer, too, and he isn't quite dead! Hold the lamp a little closer, will you, Father?"

The priest threw the rays of the lamp upon the figure.

"Jumonville!" exclaimed Robert.

It was in truth François de Jumonville, shot through the body and dying, slain in a raid for the sake of robbery and murder. When he saw the faces of white men looking down at him, he raised himself feebly on one elbow and said:

"It is you again, Willet, and you, too, Lennox and Tayoga. Always across my path, but for the last time, because I'm going on a long journey, longer than any I ever undertook before."

Father Drouillard fell on his knees and said a prayer for the dying man. Robert looked down pityingly. He realized then that he hated nobody. Life was much too busy an affair for the cherishing of hate and the plotting of revenge. Jumonville had done him as much injury as he could, but he was sorry for him, and had he been able to stay the ebbing of his life, he would have done so. As the good priest finished his prayer the head of François de Jumonville fell back. He was dead.

"We will take his body into the house," said Father Drouillard, "prepare it for the grave and give him Christian burial. I cannot forget that he was an officer of France."

"And my men shall help you," said Willet.

They carried the body of Jumonville into the château and put it on a bench, while the servants, remarkably composed, used as they were to scenes of violence, began at once to array it for the grave.

"Come into the Seigneur's room," said Father Drouillard, and Robert and Willet followed him into the old man's chamber. M. de Chatillard lay silent and rigid. He, too, had gone on the longest of all journeys.

"His soul fled," said Father Drouillard, "when the battle outside was at its height, but his mind then was not here. It was far back in the past, three-quarters of a century since when Frontenac and Phipps fought before Quebec, and he was little more than a lad in the thick of the combat. I heard him say aloud: 'The Bostonnais are going. Quebec remains ours!' and in that happy moment his soul fled."

"A good ending," said Willet gravely, "and I, one of the Bostonnais, am far from grudging him that felicity. Can my men help you with the burial, Father? We remain here for the rest of the night at least."

"If you will," said Father Drouillard.

Zeb Crane touched Robert on the arm a little later.

"Tayoga has come back," he said.

"I didn't know he'd gone away," said Robert surprised.

"He pursued Tandakora into the dark. Mebbe he thought Todo-daho was wrong and that the time for him to settle score with the Ojibway had re'lly come. Any way he wuz off after him like an arrer from the bow."

Robert went outside and found Tayoga standing quietly by the front door.

"Did you overtake him?" he asked.

"No," replied the Onondaga. "I knew that I could not, because Tododaho had not whispered to me that the time was at hand, but, since I had seen him and he was running away, I felt bound to pursue him. The legs of Tandakora are long, and he fled with incredible speed. I followed him to the landing of the next château, where he ran down the slope, leaped into a canoe, and disappeared into the mists and vapours that hang so heavily over the river. His time is not yet."

"It seems not, but at any rate we inflicted a very thorough defeat upon him to-night. His band is annihilated."

The bodies of all the fallen warriors were buried the next day, and decent burial was also given to Jumonville. But that of the Seigneur de Chatillard was still lying in state when Willet and the rangers left.

"If you wish," said the hunter to Father Drouillard, "I can procure you a pass through our lines, and you can return that way to the city. We don't make war on priests."

"I thank you," said Father Drouillard, "but I do not need it. It is easy for me to go into Quebec, whenever I choose, but, for a day or two, my duty will lie here. To-morrow we bury the Seigneur, and after that must put this household in order. Though one of the Bostonnais, you are a good man, David Willet. Take care of yourself, and of the lad, Robert Lennox."

The hunter promised and, saying farewell to the priest, they went back to Wolfe's camp, east of the Montmorency, across which stream De Levis lay facing them. During their absence a party of skirmishers had been cut off by St. Luc, and the whole British army had been disturbed by the activities of the daring Chevalier. But, on the other hand, Wolfe was recovering from a serious illness. The sound mind was finding for itself a sounder body, and he was full of ideas, all of the boldest kind, to take Quebec. If one plan failed he devised another. He thought of fording the Montmorency several miles above its mouth, and of attacking Montcalm in his Beauport camp while another force made a simultaneous attack upon him in front. He had a second scheme to cross the river, march along the edge of the St. Lawrence, and then scale the rock of Quebec, and a third for a general attack upon Montcalm's army in its Beauport entrenchments. And he had two or three more that were variations of the first three, but his generals, Murray, Monckton and Townshend, would not agree to any one of them, and he searched his fertile mind for still another.

But a brave general, even, might well have despaired. The siege made no apparent progress. Nothing could diminish the tremendous strength that nature had given to the position of Quebec, and the skill of Montcalm, Bougainville, and St. Luc met every emergency. Most ominous of all, the summer was waning. The colours that betoken autumn were deepening. Wolfe realized anew that the time for taking Quebec was shortening fast. The deep red appearing in the leaves spoke a language that could not be denied.

Robert, about this time, received an important letter from Benjamin Hardy. It came by way of Boston, Louisbourg and the St. Lawrence. It told him in the polite phrase of the day how glad he had been to hear from Master Jacobus Huysman that he was not dead, although Robert read easily between the lines and saw how genuine and deep was his joy. Mr. Hardy saw in his escape from so many dangers the hand of providence, a direct interposition in his behalf. He said, from motives of prudence, no mention of Robert's return from the grave had been made to his acquaintances in New York, and Master Jacobus Huysman in Albany had been cautioned to say as little about it as possible. He deemed this wise, for the present, because those who had made the attempts upon his life would know nothing of their failure and so he would have nothing to fear from them. He was glad too, since he was sure to return to some field of the war, that he had joined the expedition against Quebec. The risk of battle there would be great, but it was likely that in so remote a theatre of action he would be safe from his unknown enemies.

Mr. Hardy added that great hopes were centred on Wolfe's daring siege. All the campaigns elsewhere were going well, at last. The full strength of the colonies was being exerted and England was making a mighty effort. Success must come. Everybody had confidence in Mr. Pitt, and in New York they were hopeful that the shadow, hovering so long in the north, would soon be dispelled forever.

In closing he said that when the campaign was over Robert must come to him in New York at once, and that Willet must come with him. His wild life in the woods must cease. Ample provision for his future would be made and he must develop the talents with which he was so obviously endowed.

The water was in Robert's eyes when he finished the letter. Aye, he read between the lines, and he read well. The old thought that he had friends, powerful friends, came to him with renewed strength. It was obvious that the New York merchant had a deep affection for him and was watching over him. It was true of Willet too, and also of Mr. Huysman. His mind, as ever, turned to the problem of himself, and once more he felt that the solution was not far away.

The next day after he had received the letter Zeb Crane returned from Quebec, into which he had stolen as a spy, and he told Robert and Charteris that the people there, though suffering from privation, were now in great spirits. They were confident that Montcalm, the fortifications and the natural strength of the city would hold off the invader until winter, soon to come, should drive him away forever.

August was now gone and Wolfe wrote to the great Pitt a letter destined to be his last official dispatch, a strange mixture of despondency and resolution. He spoke of the help for Montcalm that had been thrown into Quebec, of his own illness, of the decline in his army's strength through the operations already carried out, of the fact that practically the whole force of Canada was now against him, but, in closing, he assured the minister that the little time left to the campaign should be used to the utmost.

While plan after plan presented itself to the mind of Wolfe, to be discarded as futile, Robert saw incessant activity with the rangers and fought in many skirmishes with the French, the Canadians and Indians. Tandakora had gathered a new band and was as great a danger as ever. They came upon his ruthless trail repeatedly, but they were not able to bring him to battle again. Once they revisited the Château de Chatillard, and found the life there going on peacefully within the English lines. Father Drouillard had returned to Quebec.

Another shade of colour was added to the leaves and then Robert saw a great movement in Wolfe's camp before the Montmorency. The whole army seemed to be leaving the position and to be going on board the fleet. At first he thought the siege was to be abandoned utterly and his heart sank. But Charteris, whom he saw just before he went on his ship with the Royal Americans, reassured him.

"I think," he said, "that the die is cast at last. The general has some great plan in his head, I know not what, but I feel in every bone that we're about to attack Quebec."

Robert now felt that way, too. The army merely concentrated its strength on the Heights of Levis and Orleans on the other side, then took ship again, and in the darkness of night, heavily armed and provisioned, ran by the batteries of the city, dropping anchor at Cap Rouge, above Quebec.

Throughout these movements on the water Robert was in a long boat with Willet, Tayoga and a small body of rangers. In the darkness he watched the great St. Lawrence and the lights of the town far above them. What they would do next he did not know, and he no longer asked. He believed that Charteris was right, and that the issue was at hand.

CHAPTER 16

The Reckoning

Robert's belief that the issue was at hand was so strong that it was not shaken at all, while they hovered about the town for a while. He heard through Charteris that Wolfe was again ill, that he had suffered a terrible night, but that day had found him better, and, despite his wasted frame and weakness, he was among the troops, kindling their courage anew, and stimulating them to greater efforts.

"A soul of fire in an invalid's frame," said Charteris, and Robert agreed with him.

Through Zeb Crane's amazing powers as a spy, he heard that the French were in the greatest anxiety over Wolfe's movements. They had thought at first that he was abandoning the siege, and then that he meditated an attack at some new point. Montcalm below the town and Bougainville above it were watching incessantly. Their doubts were increased by the fierce bombardments of the British fleet, which poured heavy shot into the Lower Town and the French camp. The French cannon replied, and the hills echoed with the roar, while great clouds of smoke drifted along the river.

Then an afternoon came when Robert felt that the next night and day would tell a mighty tale. It was in the air. Everybody showed a tense excitement. The army was being stripped for battle. He knew that the troops on the Heights of Levis and at Orleans had been ordered to march along the south shore of the St. Lawrence and join the others. The fleet was ready, as always, and the army was to embark. This concentration could not be for nothing. Before the twilight he saw Charteris and they shook hands, which was both a salute and a farewell.

"We take ship after dark," said Charteris, "and I know as surely as I'm standing here that we make some great attempt to-night. The omens and presages are all about us."

"I feel that way, too," said Robert.

"Tododaho will soon appear on his star," said Tayoga, who was with Robert, "but, though I cannot see him, I hear his whisper already."

"What does it say?" asked Robert.

"The whisper of Tododaho tells me that the time has come. We shall meet the enemy in a great battle, but he does not say who will win."

"I believe that, if we can bring Montcalm to battle, we can gain the victory," said Charteris. "I for one, Tayoga, thank you for the prophecy."

"And I," said Robert. "But we'll be together to the end."

"Aye, Dagaeoga, and together we shall see what happens."

Robert also saw the Philadelphians and the Virginians, and he shook hands with them in turn, every one of them giving a silent toast to victory or death. He found Grosvenor with his own regiment, the Grenadiers.

"We may meet somewhere to-morrow, Grosvenor," he said, "but neither of us knows where, nor under what circumstances."

"Just so we meet after victory, that's enough," said Grosvenor.

"Aye, so it is."

The boom of a cannon came from down the river, it was followed by another and another and then by many, singularly clear in the September twilight. A powerful British fleet ranged up in front of the Beauport shore and opened a fierce fire on the French redoubts. It seemed as if Wolfe were trying to force a landing there, and the French guns replied. In the distance, with the thunder of the cannonade and the flashes of fire, it looked as if a great battle were raging.

"It is nothing," said Willet to Robert, "or rather it is only a feint. It will make Montcalm below the town think he is going to be attacked, and it will make Bougainville above it rest more easily. The French are already worn down by their efforts in racing back and forth to meet us. Our command over the water is a wonderful thing, and it alone makes victory possible."

Robert, Willet and Tayoga with a dozen rangers went into a long boat, whence they looked up at the tall ships that carried the army, and waited as patiently as they could for the order to move. "See the big fellow over there," said Willet, pointing to one of the ships.

Robert nodded.

"That's the *Sutherland*, and she carries General Wolfe. Like the boat of Caesar, she bears our fortunes."

"Truly 'tis so," said Robert.

A good breeze was blowing down the river, and, at that moment, the stars were out.

"I see Tododaho with the wise snakes in his hair," said Tayoga in an awed whisper, "and he looks directly down at me. His eyes speak more plainly than his whisper that I heard in the twilight. Now, I know that some mighty event is going to happen, and that the dawn will be heavy with the fate of men."

The sullen boom of a cannon came from a point far down the river, and then the sullen boom of another replying. Quebec, on its rock, lay dark and silent. Robert was shaken by a kind of shiver, and a thrill of tremendous anticipation shot through him. He too knew instinctively that they were upon the threshold of some mighty event. Whatever happened, he could say, if he lived, that he was there, and, if he fell, he would at least die a glorious death. His was the thrill of youth, and it was wholly true.

It was two hours past midnight and the ebb tide set in. The good wind was still blowing down the river. Two lanterns went aloft in the rigging of the *Sutherland*, and the signal for one of the great adventures of history was given. All the troops had gone into boats earlier in the evening, and now they pulled silently down the stream, Wolfe in one of the foremost.

Robert sat beside Tayoga, and Willet was just in front of them. Some of the stars were still out, but there was no moon and the night was dark. It seemed that all things had agreed finally to favour Wolfe's supreme and last effort. The boats carrying the army were invisible from the lofty cliffs and no spying canoes were on the stream to tell that they were there. Robert gazed up at the black heights, and wondered where were the French.

"Are we going directly against Quebec?" he whispered to Willet. "'Tis impossible to storm it upon its heights."

"Nay, lad, nothing is impossible. As you see, we go toward Quebec and I think we land in the rear of it. 'Tis young men who lead us, the boldest of young men, and they will dare anything. But I tell you, Robert, our coming to Quebec is very different from what it was when we came here with a message from the Governor of the Province of New York."

"And our reception is like to be different, too. What was that? It sounded like the splash of a paddle ahead of us."

"It was only a great fish leaping out of the water and then falling back again," said Tayoga. "There is no enemy on the stream. Truly Manitou tonight has blinded the French and the warriors, their allies. Montcalm is a great leader, and so is St. Luc, but they do not know what is coming. We shall meet them in the morning. Tododaho has said so to me."

The boats passed on in their slow drifting with the tide. Once near to a lofty headland, they were hailed by a French sentinel, who heard the creaking of the boats, and who saw dim outlines in the dark, but a Scotch officer, who spoke good French, made a satisfactory reply. The boats drifted on, and the sentinel went back to his dreams, perhaps of the girl that he had left in France.

"Did I not tell you that Manitou had blinded the French and the warriors, their allies, to-night?" whispered Tayoga to Robert. "Ninety-nine times out of a hundred the sentinel would have asked more, or he would have insisted upon seeing more in the dark, but Manitou dulled his senses. The good spirits are abroad, and they work for us."

"Truly, I believe it is so, Tayoga," said Robert.

"The French don't lack in vigilance, but they must be worn out," said Willet. "It's one thing to sail on ships up and down a river, but it's quite another for an army racing along lofty, rough and curving shores to keep pace with it."

They were challenged from another point of vantage by a sentinel and they saw him running down to the St. Lawrence, pistol in hand, to make good his question. But the same Scotch officer who had answered the first placated him, telling him that theirs were boats loaded with provisions, and not to make a noise or the English would hear him. Again was French vigilance lulled, and they passed on around the headland above Anse du Foulon.

"The omens are ours," whispered Tayoga, with deep conviction. "Now, I know that we shall arrive at the place to which we want to go. Unless Manitou wishes us to go there, he would not have twice dulled the senses of French sentinels who could have brought a French army down upon us while we are yet in the river. And, lo! here where we are going to land there is no sentinel!"

"Under heaven, I believe you're right, Tayoga!" exclaimed Willet, with intense earnestness.

The boats swung in to the narrow beach at the foot of the lofty cliff and the men disembarked rapidly. Then, hanging to rocks and shrubs, they began to climb. There was still no alarm, and Robert held his breath in suspense, and in amazement too. He did not know just where they were, but they could not be very far from Quebec, and General Wolfe was literally putting his head in the lion's mouth. He knew, and every one around him knew, that it was now victory or death. He felt again that tremendous thrill. Whatever happened, he would be in it. He kept repeating that fact to himself and the thought of death was not with him.

"The dawn will soon be at hand," he said; "I feel it coming. If we can have only a half hour more! Only a half hour!"

"It will come with clouds," said Tayoga. "Manitou still favours us. He wills that we shall reach the top."

Robert made another pull and surmounted the crest. Everywhere the soldiers were pouring over the top. A small body of French sentinels was taken by surprise. Some of them were captured, and the others escaped in the dusk to carry the alarm to the city, to Montcalm and to Bougainville. But Wolfe was on the heights before Quebec. From points farther up the river came the crash of cannon. It was the French batteries firing upon the last of the boats, and upon the ships bringing down the rest of the troops. But it was too late to stop the British army, which included Americans, who were then British too.

"The dawn is here," said Tayoga.

The east was breaking slowly into dull light. Heavy clouds were floating up from the west, and the air was damp with the promise of rain. The British army was forming rapidly into line of battle, but no army was in front of it. The daring enterprise of the night was a complete success, and Montcalm had been surprised. He was yet to know that his enemy had scaled the heights and was before Quebec.

"We've gained a field of battle for ourselves," said Willet, "and it's now for us to win the battle itself."

The mind of Wolfe was at its supreme activity. A detachment, sent swiftly, seized the battery at Samos that was firing upon the ships and boats. Another battery, farther away at Sillery, was taken also, and the landing of additional troops was covered. A party of Canadians who came out of the town to see who these intrusive strangers might be, were driven back in a hurry, and then Wolfe and his officers advanced to choose their ground, the rangers hovering on the flanks of the regulars.

Where the plateau was only a mile wide and before Quebec, the general took his stand with the lofty cliffs of the St. Lawrence on the south and the meadows of the St. Charles on the north. The field, the famous Plains of Abraham, was fairly level with corn fields and bushes here and there. A battalion of the Royal Americans was placed to guard the ford of the St. Charles, but Robert saw the others, his friends among them, formed up in the front ranks, where the brunt of the battle would fall. Another regiment was in reserve. The rangers, with Robert, Tayoga and Willet, still hovered on the flanks.

Robert felt intense excitement. He always believed afterward that he understood even at that instant the greatness of the cloudy dawn that had come, and the momentous nature of the approaching conflict, holding in its issue results far greater than those of many a battle in which ten times the numbers were engaged.

"How far away is Quebec?" he asked.

"Over there about a mile," replied Willet. "We can't see it because the ridge that the French call the Buttes-a-Neveu comes in between."

"But look!" exclaimed Robert. "See, what is on the ridge!"

The stretch of broken ground was suddenly covered with white uniforms. They were French soldiers, the battalion of Guienne, aroused in their camp near the St. Charles River by the firing, and come swiftly to see what was the matter. There they stood, staring at the scarlet ranks, drawn up in battle before them, unable to credit their eyes at first, many of them believing for the moment that it was some vision of the cloudy dawn.

"I think that Montcalm's army will soon come," said Willet to Robert. "You see, we're literally between three fires. We're facing the garrison of Quebec, while we have Montcalm on one side of us and Bougainville on the other. The question is which will it be, Bougainville or Montcalm, but I think it will be Montcalm."

"I know it will be Montcalm," said Robert, "and I know too that when he comes St. Luc will be with him."

"Aye, St. Luc will be with him. That's sure."

It was even so. Montcalm was already on his way. The valiant general of France, troubled by the hovering armies and fleets of Britain, uncertain where they intended to strike or whether they meant to strike at all, had passed a sleepless night. At dawn the distant boom of the cannon, firing at the English ships above the town, had come to his ears. An officer sent for news to the headquarters of the Marquis de Vaudreuil, the Governor-General of New France, much nearer to the town, had not returned, and, mounting, he galloped swiftly with one of his aides to learn the cause of the firing. Near the Governor-General's house they caught a distant gleam of the scarlet ranks of Wolfe's army, nearly two miles away.

When Montcalm saw that red flash his agitation and excitement became intense. It is likely that he understood at once the full danger, that he knew the crisis for Canada and France was at hand. But he dispatched immediately the orders that would bring his army upon the scene. The Governor-General, already alarmed, came out of his house and they exchanged a few words. Then Montcalm galloped over the bridge across the St. Charles and toward the British army. It is stated of him that during this ride his face was set and that he never spoke once to his aides.

Behind Montcalm came his army, hurrying to the battle-field, and, taking the quickest course, it passed through Quebec, entering at the Palace Gate and passing out through those of St. Louis and St. John, hastening, always hastening, to join the battalion of Guienne, which already stood in its white uniforms and beneath its banners on the Buttes-a-Neveu.

Montcalm's army included the veterans of many victories. Through long years they had fought valiantly for France in North America. At Ticonderoga they had shown how they could triumph over great odds, over men as brave as themselves, and, as they pressed through the narrow streets of the quaint old town, they did not doubt that they were going to another victory. With them, too, were the swart Canadians fighting for their homes, their flag and, as they believed then, for their religion, animated, too, by confidence in their courage, and belief in the skill of their leaders who had so seldom failed.

Behind the French and the Canadians were the Indians who had been drawn so freely to Montcalm's banner by his success, thinking anew of slaughter and untold spoil, such as they had known at William Henry and such as they might have had at Ticonderoga. The gigantic Tandakora, painted hideously, led them, and in all that motley array there was no soul more eager than his for the battle.

On that eventful morning, which the vast numbers of later wars cannot dim, the councils of France were divided. Vaudreuil, fearing an attack on the Beauport shore, did not give the valiant Montcalm all the help that he could spare, nor did De Ramesay, commanding the garrison of Quebec, send the artillery that the Marquis asked.

But Montcalm was resolute. His soul was full of fire. He looked at the ranks of Wolfe's army drawn up before him on the Plains of Abraham, and he did not hesitate to attack. He would not wait for Bougainville, nor would he hold back for the garrison of Quebec. He saw that the gauge of battle had been flung down to him and he knew that he must march at once upon the British—and the Americans. Mounted on a black horse, he rode up and down the lines, waving or pointing his sword, his dark face alive with energy.

Montcalm now formed his men in three divisions. M. de Senezergues led the left wing made up of the regiments of Guienne and Royal Roussillon, supported by Canadian militia. M. de Saint Ours took the right wing with the battalion of La Sarre and more Canadian militia. Montcalm was in the centre with the regiment of Languedoc and the battalion of Béarn. On both flanks were Canadians and numerous Indians.

Robert from his position on a little knoll with Willet and Tayoga watched all these movements, and he was scarcely conscious of the passage of time. There was a shifting in the British army also, as it perfected its alignment, and the bagpipes of the Scotchmen were already screaming defiance, but his eyes were mainly for the French before him. He recognized Montcalm as he rode up and down the lines, raising his sword, and presently he saw another gallant figure on horseback that he knew. It was St. Luc, and the old thrill shot through him: St. Luc for whom the ancient M. de Chatillard had taken him, St. Luc with whom he must have some blood tie.

Though it was now far beyond the time for the rising of the sun, the day was still dark, heavy with clouds, and now and then a puff of rain was blown in the faces of the waiting men, though few took notice. The wait and the preparations had to Robert all the aspects of a duel, and the incessant shrill screaming of the Scotch bagpipes put a fever in his blood, setting all the little pulses in his head and body to beating. Ever after he maintained that the call of the bagpipes was the most martial music in the world.

The crackle of firing broke out on the flanks. The Canadian and Indian sharpshooters, from the shelter of houses, bushes and knolls, had opened fire. Now and then a man in scarlet fell, but the army of Wolfe neither moved nor replied, though some of the New England rangers, stealing forward, began to send bullets at their targets.

"I see Tandakora," said Tayoga, "and, in an hour, the score between us will be settled. Tododaho told me so last night, but it is still uncertain which shall be the victor."

"Can't you get a shot at him?" asked Robert.

"It is not yet time, Dagaeoga. Tododaho will say when the moment comes for me to pull trigger on the Ojibway."

Then Robert's gaze shifted back to the figure of St. Luc. The chevalier rode a white horse, and he was helping Montcalm to form the lines in the best order for the attack. He too held in his hand a sword, the small sword that Robert had seen before, but he seldom waved it.

"Are they ever coming?" asked Robert, who felt as if he had been standing on the field many hours.

"We've not long to wait now, lad," replied Willet. "Our own army is ready and I think the fate of America will soon be decided here on this cloudy morning."

Another light puff of rain struck Robert in the face, but as before he did not notice it. The crackling fire of the sharpshooters increased. They were stinging the British flanks and more men in scarlet fell, but the army of Wolfe remained immovable, waiting, always waiting. It was for Montcalm now to act. French field pieces added their roar to the crackle of rifles and muskets, and now and then the fierce yell of the Indians rose above both. Robert thought he saw a general movement in the French lines, and his thought was Willet's also.

"The moment has come! Steady, lads! Steady!" said the hunter.

The whole French army suddenly began to advance, the veterans and the militia together, uttering great shouts, while the Indians on the flanks gave forth the war whoop without ceasing. Robert remained motionless. The steadfastness of soul that he had acquired on the island controlled him now. Inwardly he was in a fever, but outwardly he showed no emotion. He glanced at Montcalm on the black horse, and St. Luc on the white, and then at the scarlet and silent ranks of Wolfe's army. But the French were coming fast, and he knew that silence would soon burst into sudden and terrible action.

"The French lines are being thrown into confusion by the unevenness of the ground and the rapidity of their advance," said Willet. "Their surprise at our being here is so great that it has unsteadied them. Now they are about to open fire!"

The front of the charging French burst into flame and the bullets sang in the scarlet ranks. Wolfe's army suddenly began to move forward, but still it did not fire, although the battle of the skirmishers on the flanks was rapidly increasing in ferocity. The rangers were busy now, replying to the Indians and Canadians, but Robert still took rapid glances and he looked oftenest toward the Americans, where his friends stood. The advance of the French became almost a run, and he saw all the muskets and rifles of his own army go up.

A tremendous volley burst from the scarlet ranks, so loud and so close together that it sounded like one vast cannon shot. It was succeeded presently by another, and then by an irregular but fierce fire, which died in its turn to let the smoke lift.

Robert saw a terrible sight. The ground where the French army had stood was literally covered with dead and wounded. The two volleys fired at close range had mowed them down like grain. The French army, smitten unto death, was reeling back, and the British, seizing the moment, rushed forward with bayonet and drawn sword. The Highlanders, as they charged with the broadsword, uttered a tremendous yell, and Robert saw his own Americans in the front of the rush. He caught one glimpse of the tall figure of Charteris and he saw Colden near him. Then they were all lost in the smoke as they attacked.

But Wolfe had fallen. Struck by three bullets, the last time in the breast, he staggered and sat down. Men rushed to his aid, but he lived just long enough to know that he had won the victory. Before the firing died away, he was dead. Montcalm, still on horseback, was shot through the body, but he was taken into the city, where he died the night of the next day. Senezergues, his second in command, was also mortally wounded, and Monckton, who was second to Wolfe, fell badly wounded too.

But Robert did not yet know any of these facts. He was conscious only of victory. He heard the triumphant cheers of Wolfe's army and he saw that the French had stopped, then that they were breaking. He felt again that powerful thrill, but now it was the thrill of victory.

"We win! We win!" he cried.

"Aye, so we do," said Willet, "but here are the Canadians and Indians trying to wipe out us rangers."

The fire in front of them from the knolls and bushes redoubled, but the rangers, adept at such combats, pressed forward, pouring in their bullets. The Canadians and Indians gave ground and the rangers, circling about, attacked them on the flank. Tayoga suddenly uttered a fierce shout and, dropping his rifle, leaped into the open.

"Now, O Tandakora!" he cried. "The time has come and thou hast given me the chance!"

The gigantic figure of Tandakora emerged from the smoke, and the two, tomahawk in hand, faced each other.

"It is you, Tayoga, of the clan of the Bear, of the nation Onondaga, of the league of the Hodenosaunee," said the chief. "So you have come at last that I may spit upon your dead body. I have long sought this moment."

"Not longer than I, Ojibway savage!" replied Tayoga. "Now you shall know what it is to strike an Onondaga in the mouth, when he is bound and helpless."

The huge warrior threw back his head and laughed.

"Look your last at the skies, Onondaga," he said, "because you will soon pass into silence and darkness. It is not for a great chief to be slain by a mere boy."

Tayoga said no more, but gazed steadily into the eyes of the Ojibway. Then the two circled slowly, each intently watching every movement of the other. The great body of Tandakora was poised like that of a panther, the huge muscles rippling under his bronze skin. But the slender figure of Tayoga was instinct also with strength, and with an incomparable grace and lightness. He seemed to move without effort, like a beam of light.

Tandakora crouched as he moved slowly toward the right. Then his arm suddenly shot back and he hurled his tomahawk with incredible force. The Onondaga threw his head to one side and the glittering blade, flying on, clove a ranger to the chin. Then Tayoga threw his own weapon, but Tandakora, with a quick shift evading it, drew his knife and, rushing in, cried:

"Now I have you, dog of an Onondaga!"

Not in vain was Tayoga as swift as a beam of light. Not in vain was that light figure made of wrought steel. Leaping to one side, he drew his own knife and struck with all his might at the heart of that huge, rushing figure. The blade went true, and so tremendous was the blow that Tandakora, falling in a heap, gave up his fierce and savage soul.

"They run! They run!" cried Robert. "The whole French army is running!"

It was true. The entire French force was pouring back toward the gates of the city, their leaders vainly trying to rally the soldiers. The skirmishers fell back with them. A figure, darting from a bush, turned to pull trigger on Robert, and then uttered a cry of terror.

"A ghost! It is a ghost!" he exclaimed in French.

But a second look told Achille Garay that it was no ghost. It may have been a miracle, but it was Robert Lennox come back in the flesh, and his finger returned to the trigger. Another was quicker. The hunter saw him.

"That for you, Garay!" he cried, and sent a bullet through the spy's heart. Then, drawing the two lads with him, he rushed forward in pursuit.

The confusion in the French army was increasing. Its defeat was fast becoming a rout, but some of the officers still strove to stay the panic. Robert saw one on a white horse gallop before a huddle of fleeing men. But the soldiers, swerving, ran on. A bullet struck the horse and he fell. The man leaped clear, but looked around in a dazed manner. Then a bullet struck him too, and he staggered. Robert with a cry rushed forward, and received into his arms the falling figure of St. Luc.

He eased the Chevalier to the ground and rested his head upon his knee.

"He isn't dead!" he exclaimed. "He's only shot through the shoulder!"

"Now, this is in truth the hand of Providence," said Willet gravely, "when you are here in the height of a great battle to break the fall of your own uncle!"

"My uncle!" exclaimed Robert.

The Chevalier Raymond Louis de St. Luc smiled wanly.

"Yes, my nephew," he said, "your own uncle, though wounded

grievously, on this the saddest of all days for France, son of my dear, dead sister, Gabrielle."

Then he fainted dead away from loss of blood, and the Canadian, Dubois, appearing suddenly, helped them to revive him. Robert hung over him with irrepressible anxiety.

"The brother of my mother!" he exclaimed. "I always felt there was a powerful tie, a blood tie, uniting us! That was why he spared me so often! That was why he told me how to escape at Ticonderoga! He will not die, Dave? He will not die?"

"No, he will not die," replied Willet. "The Marquis de Clermont can receive a greater wound than that, and yet live and flourish."

"The Marquis de Clermont!"

"Aye, the Chevalier de St. Luc is head of one of the greatest families of France and you're his next of kin."

"And so I'm half a Frenchman!"

"Aye, half a Frenchman, half an Englishman, and all an American."

"And so I am!" said Robert.

"Truly it is a great morning," said Tayoga gravely. "Tododaho has given to me the triumph, and Tandakora has gone to his hereafter, wherever it may be; the soul of Garay is sped too, France has lost Canada, and Dagaeoga has found the brother of his mother."

"It's true," said Willet in a whimsical tone. "When things begin to happen they happen fast. The battle is almost over."

But the victorious army, as it advanced, was subjected to a severe fire on the flank from ambushed Canadians. Many of the French threw themselves into the thickets on the Coté Ste.-Genevieve, and poured a hail of bullets into the ranks of the advancing Highlanders. Vaudreuil came up from Beauport and was all in terror, but Bougainville and others, arriving, showed a firmer spirit. The gates of Quebec were shut, and it seemed to show defiance, while the English and Americans, still in the presence of forces greater than their own, entrenched on the field where they had won the victory, a victory that remains one of the decisive battles of the world, mighty and far-reaching in its consequences.

A night of mixed triumph and grief came, grief for the loss of Wolfe and so many brave men, triumph that a daring chance had brought such a brilliant success. Robert found Charteris, Grosvenor, Colden and the Virginians unharmed. Wilton was wounded severely, but ultimately recovered his full strength. Carson was wounded also, but was as well as ever in a month, while Robert himself, Tayoga, Willet and Zeb Crane were not touched.

But his greatest interest that night was in the Chevalier de St. Luc,

Marquis de Clermont. They had made him a pallet in a tent and one of the best army surgeons was attending so famous and gallant an enemy. But he seemed easiest when Robert was by.

"My boy," he said, "I always tried to save you. Whenever I looked upon you I saw in your face my sister Gabrielle."

"But why did you not tell me?" asked Robert. "Why did not some one of the others who seemed to know tell me?"

"There were excellent reasons," replied the wounded man. "Gabrielle loved one of the Bostonnais, a young man whom she met in Paris. He was brave, gallant and true, was your father, Richard Lennox. I have nothing to say against him, but our family did not consider it wise for her to marry a foreigner, a member of another race. They eloped and were married in a little hamlet on the wild coast of Brittany. Then they fled to America, where you were born, and when you were a year old they undertook to return to France, seeking forgiveness. But it was only a start. The ship was driven on the rocks of Maine and they were lost, your brave, handsome father and my beautiful sister—but you were saved. Willet came and took you into the wilderness with him. He has stood in the place of your own father."

"But why did not they tell me?" repeated Robert. "Why was I left so long in ignorance?"

"There was a flaw. The priest who performed the marriage was dead. The records were lost. The evil said there had been no marriage, and that you were no rightful member of the great family of De Clermont. We could not prove the marriage then and so you were left for the time with Willet."

"Why did Willet take me?"

Raymond Louis de St. Luc turned to Willet, who sat on the other side of the pallet, and smiled.

"I will answer you, Robert," said the hunter. "I was one of those who loved your mother. How could any one help loving her? As beautiful as a dream, and a soul of pure gold. She married another, but when she was lost at sea something went out of my life that could never be replaced in this world. You have replaced it partly, Robert, but not wholly. It seemed fitting to the others that, being what I was, and loving Gabrielle de Clermont as I had, I should take you. I should have taken you anyhow."

Robert's head swam, and there was a mist before his eyes. He was thinking of the beautiful young mother whom he could not remember.

"Then I am by blood a De Clermont, and yet not a De Clermont," he said.

"You're a De Clermont by blood, by right, and before all the world," said Willet. "I've a letter from Benjamin Hardy in New York, stating that the records have been found in the ruins of the burned church on the coast of Brittany, where the marriage was performed. Their authenticity has been acknowledged by the French government and all the members of the De Clermont family who are in France. Copies of them have been smuggled through from France."

"Thanks to the good God!" murmured St. Luc.

"And Adrian Van Zoon? Why has he made such war against me?" asked Robert.

"Because of money," replied Willet. "Your father was a great owner of shipping, inherited, as Richard Lennox was a young man under thirty when he was lost at sea. At his death the control of it passed into the hands of his father's partner, Adrian Van Zoon. Van Zoon wanted it all, and, since you had no relatives, he probably would have secured it if you had been put out of the way. That is why you were safer with me at Albany and in the woods, until your rightful claims could be established. Benjamin Hardy, who had been a schoolmate and great friend of your father, knew of this and kept watch on Van Zoon. Your estate has not suffered in the man's hands, because, expecting it to be his own, he has made it increase. Jonathan Pillsbury knew your history too. So did Jacobus Huysman, in whose house we placed you when you went to school, and so did your teacher, Master Alexander McLean."

"I had powerful friends. I felt it all the time," said Robert.

"So you had, lad, and it was largely because they saw you grow up worthy of such friendship. You're a very rich man, Robert. There are ships belonging to you on nearly every sea, or at least there would be if we had no war."

"And a Marquis of France—when I die," said St. Luc.

"No! No!" exclaimed Robert. "You'll live as long as I will! Why, you're only a young man!"

"Twenty-nine," said St. Luc. "Gabrielle was twelve years older than I am. You are more a younger brother than a nephew to me, Robert."

"But I will never become a Marquis of France," said Robert. "I am American, English to the core. I have fought against France, though I do not hate her. I cannot go to France, nor even to England. I must stay in the country in which I was born, and in which my father was born."

"Spoken well," said Willet. "It was what I wanted to hear you say. The Chevalier will return to France. He will marry and have children of his own. Haven't we heard him sing often about the girl he left on the bridge of Avignon? The next Marquis of Clermont will be his son and not his nephew."

Which came to pass, as Willet predicted.

Robert stayed long that night by the pallet of his uncle, to whom the English gave the best of attention, respecting the worth of a wounded prisoner so well known for his bravery, skill and lofty character. St. Luc finally fell asleep, and, going outside, Robert found Tayoga awaiting him. When he told him all the strange and wonderful story that he had heard inside the tent, the Onondaga said:

"I suppose that Dagaeoga, being a great man, will go to Europe and forget us here."

"Never!" exclaimed Robert. "My home is in America. All I know is America, and I'd be out of place in any other country."

And then he added whimsically:

"I couldn't go so far away from the Hodenosaunee."

"Dagaeoga might go far and yet never come to a nation greater than the great League," said Tayoga, with deep conviction.

"That's true, Tayoga. How stands the battle? I had almost forgotten it in the amazing tide of my own fortunes."

"General Wolfe is dead, but his spirit lives after him. We are victorious at all points. The French have fled into Quebec, and they yet have an army much more numerous than ours, if they get it all together. But Montcalm was wounded and they say he is dying. The soul has gone out of them. I think Quebec will be yielded very soon."

And surrendered it was a few days later, but the victors soon found that the city they had won with so much daring would have to be defended with the utmost courage and pertinacity. St. Luc, fast recovering from his wound, was sent a prisoner to New York, together with De Galissonnière, who had been taken unhurt, but Robert did not get away as soon as he had expected. Quebec was in peril again, but now from the French. De Levis, who succeeded Montcalm as the military leader of New France, gathering together at Montreal all the fragments of the French power in Canada, swore to retake Quebec.

Robert, Tayoga and Willet, with the rangers, served in the garrison of Quebec throughout the long and bitter winter that followed. In the spring they moved out with the army to meet De Levis, who was advancing from Montreal to keep his oath. Robert received a slight wound in the battle of Ste. Foy that followed, in which the English and Americans were defeated, and were compelled to retreat into Quebec.

This battle of Ste. Foy, in which Robert distinguished himself again with the New England rangers, was long and fierce, one of the most sanguinary ever fought on Canadian soil. De Levis, the French commander, showed all the courage and skill of Montcalm, proving himself a worthy successor to the leader who had fallen with Wolfe, and his men displayed the usual French fire and courage.

Hazen, the chief of the rangers, was badly wounded in the height of the action, but Robert and Willet succeeded in bringing him off the field, while Tayoga protected their retreat. A bullet from the Ononda-ga's rifle here slew Colonel de Courcelles, and Robert, on the whole, was glad that the man's death had been a valiant one. He had learned not to cherish rancour against any one, and the Onondaga and the hunter agreed with him.

"There is some good in everybody," said Willet. "We'll remember that and forget the rest."

But Robert's friends in the Royal Americans had a hard time of it in the battle of Ste. Foy, even harder than in Wolfe's battle on the Plains of Abraham. They were conspicuous for their valour and suffered many casualties. Colden, Cabell and Stuart were wounded, but took no permanent hurt. Charteris also received a slight wound, but he recovered entirely before his marriage in the summer with the lovely Louise de St. Maur, the daughter of the Seigneur Raymond de St. Maur, in whose house he had been a prisoner a long time in Quebec.

It was Robert's own personal contact and his great friendship for Charteris, continuing throughout their long lives in New York, that caused him to take such a strong and permanent interest in this particular regiment which had been raised wholly in the colonies and which fought so valiantly at Duquesne, Louisbourg, Ticonderoga, Quebec, Ste. Foy, and in truth in nearly all the great North American battles of the Seven Years' War.

It was at first the Sixty-Second Regular Regiment of the British Army, "Royal American Provincials," but through the lapsing of two other regiments it soon became the Sixtieth. Its valour and distinction were so high when composed wholly of Americans, except the superior officers, that nearly seventy years subsequent to the fall of Quebec the Englishmen, who after the great quarrel had replaced the Americans in it, asked that they be allowed to use as their motto the Latin phrase, *Celer et audax*, "Swift and Bold," "Quick and Ready," which Wolfe himself was said to have conferred upon it shortly before his fall upon the Plains of Abraham. And in memory of the great deeds of their American predecessors, the gallant Englishmen who succeeded them were permitted by the British government to use that motto.

Despite their defeat at Ste. Foy, the English and Americans held the capital against De Levis until another British fleet arrived and compelled the retreat of the brave Frenchmen. More reinforcements came from England, the powerful army of Amherst advanced from the south, Montreal was taken, and it was soon all over with New France.

Canada passed to England, and after its fall English and American troops, men of the same blood, language and institutions, did not stand together again in a great battle for more than a century and a half, and then, strangely enough, it was in defence of that France which under one flag they had fought at Duquesne and Ticonderoga, at Quebec and Ste. Foy.

Robert, Tayoga and Willet went back to the colonies by land, and after a long journey stopped at Albany, where they received the warmest of welcomes from Master Jacobus Huysman, Master Alexander McLean and Caterina.

"I knew Robert that some time you would come into your own. I hold some of the papers about you in my great chest here," said Jacobus Huysman. "Now it iss for you to show that you understand how to use great fortune well."

"And never forget your dates," said Master Alexander. "It is well to know history. All the more so, because you have had a part in the making of it."

Warm as was their welcome in Albany, it was no warmer than that given them in New York by Benjamin Hardy and Jonathan Pillsbury. The very next day they went to the house of Adrian Van Zoon for a reckoning, only to find him dead in his bed. He had heard the night before of Robert's arrival; in truth, it was his first intimation that young Lennox was alive, and that all his wicked schemes against him had failed.

"It may have been a stroke of heart disease," said Benjamin Hardy, as they turned away, "or——"

"He has gone and his crimes have gone with him," said Robert. "I don't wish ever to know how he went."

A little later the Chevalier Raymond Louis de St. Luc, Marquis de Clermont, the war now being over, sailed with his faithful Canadian attendant, Dubois, from New York for France. The parting between him and his nephew was not demonstrative, but it was marked by the deepest affection on either side.

"France has been defeated, but she is the eternal nation," said St. Luc. "She will be greater than ever. She will be more splendid than before."

The De Clermonts were a powerful stock, with their roots deep in the soil. A son of St. Luc's became a famous general under Napoleon, a great cavalry leader of singular courage and capacity, and a lineal descendant of his, a general also, fought with the same courage and ability under Joffre and Foch in the World War, being especially conspicuous for his services at both the First and Second Marne. At the Second Marne he gave a heartfelt greeting to two young American officers named Lennox, calling them his cousins and brothers-in-arms, in blood as well as in spirit. They were together in the immortal counter-stroke on the morning of July 18, 1918, when Americans and French turned the tide of the World War, and sealed anew an old friendship. They were also together throughout those blazing one hundred and nineteen days when British, French and Americans together, old enemies and old friends who had mingled their blood on innumerable battle-fields, destroyed the greatest menace of modern times and hurled the pretender to divine honours from his throne.

Robert found his fortune to be one of the largest in the New World, but he kept it in the hands of Benjamin Hardy and David Willet, who increased it, and he became the lawyer, orator and statesman for which his talents fitted him so eminently. A marked characteristic in the life of Robert Lennox, noted by all who knew him, was his liberality of opinion. He had his share in public life, but the bitterness of politics, then so common in this country as well as others, seemed never to touch him. He was always willing to give his opponent credit for sincerity, and even to admit that his cause had justice. In his opinion the other man's point of view could always be considered.

This broadness of mind often caused him to incur criticism, but it had become so much his nature, and his courage was so great, that he would not depart from it. He had been through the terrible war with the French, and, even before he knew that he was half a Frenchman by blood, he had gladly acknowledged the splendid qualities of the French, their bravery and patience, and their logical minds. He always said during the worst throes of their revolution that the French would emerge from it greater than ever.

His position was similar in the Revolutionary War with the English. While he cast in his lot with his own people, and suffered with them, he invariably maintained that the English nation was sound at the core. He had fought beside them in a great struggle and he knew how strong and true they were, and when our own strife was over he was most eager for a renewal of good relations with the English, always saying that the fact that they had quarrelled and parted did not keep them from being of the same blood and family, and hence natural allies.

He consistently refused to hate an individual. He always insisted that life was too busy to cherish a grudge or seek revenge. Bad acts invariably punished themselves in the course of time. He was able to see some good, a little at least, in everybody. Searching his mind in after years, he could even find excuses for Adrian Van Zoon. He would say to Willet that the man loved nothing but money, that perhaps he had been born that way and could not help it, that he had made his attempts upon him under the influence of what was the greatest of all temptations to him, and that while he paid the slaver to carry him away he had not paid him to kill him. As for Garay, he would say that he might have exceeded orders. He would say the same about the shots the slaver had fired at him at Albany.

This tolerance came partly from his own character, and partly from an enormous experience of life in the raw in his young and formative years. He knew how men were to a large extent the creatures of circumstances, and on the individual in particular his judgments were always mild. He had two favourite sayings:

"No man is as bad as he seems to his worst enemy."

"No man is as good as he seems to his best friend."

His own faults he knew perfectly well to be quickness of temper and a proneness to hasty action. Throughout his life he fought against them and he took as his models Willet and Tayoga, who always appeared to him to have a more thorough command over their own minds and impulses than any other men he ever knew.

Aside from his brilliancy and power in public life, Lennox had other qualities that distinguished him as a man. He was noted for his cosmopolitan views concerning human affairs. He had an uncommon largeness and breadth of vision, all the more notable then, as America was, in many respects, outside the greater world of Europe. People in speaking of him, however, recalled the extraordinary variety and intensity of his experiences. Much of his story was known and it was not diminished in the telling. He was always at home in the woods. He had an uncommon sympathy for hunters, borderers, pathfinders and all kinds of wilderness rovers. He understood them and they instinctively understood him, invariably finding in him a redoubtable champion. He was also closely in touch with the Indian soul, and his friends used to say laughingly that he had something of the Indian in his own nature. At all events, the Great League of the Hodenosaunee found in him a defender and he was more than once an honoured guest in the Vale of Onondaga.

On the other hand, his interest in European affairs was always keen and intelligent, especially in those of England and France, with whose sons he had come into contact so much during the great war. He maintained a lifelong correspondence with his friend, Alfred Grosvenor, who ultimately became a nobleman and who sat for more than forty years in the House of Lords. Lennox visited him several times in England, both before and after the quarrel between the colonies and the mother country, which, however, did not diminish their friendship a particle. In truth, during those troubled times Grosvenor, who was noted for the liberality of his sentiments and for an affection for Americans, conceived during his service as a soldier on their continent in the Seven Years' War, often defended them against the criticism of his countrymen, while Lennox, on his side, very boldly told the people that nothing could alter the fact that England was their mother country, and that no one should even wish to alter it.

But his correspondence with his uncle, Raymond Louis de St. Luc, Marquis de Clermont, not so many years older than himself, covered a period of nearly sixty years filled with world-shaking events, and, though it has been printed for private circulation only, it is a perfect mine of fact, comment and illumination. St. Luc was one of the few French noblemen to foresee the great Revolution in his country, and, while he mourned its excesses, he knew that much of it was justified. His patriotism and courage were so high and so obvious that neither Danton, Marat nor Robespierre dared to attack him. As an old man he supported Napoleon ardently until the empire and the ambitions of the emperor became too swollen, and, while he mourned Waterloo, he told his son, General Robert Lennox de St. Luc, who distinguished himself so greatly there and who almost took the château of Hougoumont from the English, that it was for the best, and that it was inevitable. It was the comment of St. Luc, then eighty-five years old and full of experience and wisdom, that a very great man may become too great.

Lennox was noted for his great geniality and his extraordinary capacity for making friends. Yet there was a strain of remarkable gravity, even austerity, in his character. There came times when he wished to be alone, to hear no human voices about him. It was then perhaps that he thought his best thoughts and took, too, his best resolutions. In the great silences he seemed to see more clearly, and the path lay straight before him. Many of his friends thought it an eccentricity, but he knew it was an inheritance from his long stay alone upon the island, a period in his life that had so much effect in moulding his character.

It was this ripeness of mind, based upon fullness of information and deep meditation, that made him such a great man in the true

LEONAUR

ALSO FROM LEONAUR
AVAILABLE IN SOFTCOVER OR HARDCOVER WITH DUST JACKET

TROS OF SAMOTHRACE 1: WOLVES OF THE TIBER *by Talbot Mundy*—When his ship is taken and his crew slaughtered Tros of Samothrace is captured by Imperial Rome.

TROS OF SAMOTHRACE 2: DRAGONS OF THE NORTH *by Talbot Mundy*—Tros of Samothrace burns for vengeance and has declared himself the implacable enemy of Rome.

TROS OF SAMOTHRACE 3: SERPENT OF THE WAVES *by Talbot Mundy*—Tros, his allies and the forces of Rome have drawn apart to prepare for the conflict to come.

TROS OF SAMOTHRACE 4: CITY OF THE EAGLES *by Talbot Mundy*—As Tros of Samothrace continues in his attempts to confound Caesar's plans for the invasion of Britain, he journeys to the Eternal City to seek the aid of its great leaders—and Caesar's opponents—Cato, Pompey and the Vestal Virgins themselves!

TROS OF SAMOTHRACE 5: CLEOPATRA *by Talbot Mundy*—Cleopatra—Queen of Egypt—is a formidable character ever ready to play the game of intrigue, betrayal and shifting loyalties to suit her own objectives. Blood will surely be spilt and once again Tros finds himself inexorably caught up in monumental events that threaten his life and those he loves.

TROS OF SAMOTHRACE 6: THE PURPLE PIRATE *by Talbot Mundy*—The epic saga of the ancient world—Tros of Samothrace—draws to a conclusion in this sixth—and final—volume. Julius Caesar has been assassinated and Queen Cleopatra of Egypt finds herself in a perilous position and desperate for allies to secure her power.

THE ILLUSTRATED & COMPLETE BRIGADIER GERARD *by Sir Arthur Conan Doyle*—These are the adventures of Conan Doyle's incomparable French hero-the finest swordsman in the Light Cavalry-Etienne Gerard. Arranged for the first time in historical chronological order, his many enthusiasts can now properly appreciate his colourful career as he fights, loves and blunders his way through the Napoleonic epoch-from his earliest adventure as a young blade determined to reach his lady love despite the unwelcome attention of her fathers bull-through many campaigns and special missions-to the bloody field of Waterloo, the downfall of his beloved Emperor and beyond. This is the complete collection of these classic stories. What makes this edition exceptional is the inclusion of nearly 140 illustrations-mostly by the famed military artist William Barnes Wollen-which accurately portray the spirit of the stories and the uniforms and scenes of the events they portray.

LEONAUR

ALSO FROM LEONAUR
AVAILABLE IN SOFTCOVER OR HARDCOVER WITH DUST JACKET

CHARLIE CHAN VOLUME 1: THE HOUSE WITHOUT A KEY & THE CHINESE PARROT *by Earl Derr Biggers*—Two Complete Novels Featuring the Legendary Chinese-Hawaiian Detective.

CHARLIE CHAN VOLUME 2: BEHIND THAT CURTAIN & THE BLACK CAMEL *by Earl Derr Biggers*—Two Complete Novels Featuring the Legendary Chinese-Hawaiian Detective.

CHARLIE CHAN VOLUME 3: CHARLIE CHAN CARRIES ON & KEEPER OF THE KEYS *by Earl Derr Biggers*—Two Complete Novels Featuring the Legendary Chinese-Hawaiian Detective.

THE PHILO VANCE MURDER CASES: 1—THE BENSON MURDER CASE & THE 'CANARY' MURDER CASE *by S. S. Van Dine*—Two complete cases featuring the great fictional detective.

THE PHILO VANCE MURDER CASES: 2—THE GREENE MURDER CASE & THE BISHOP MURDER CASE *by S. S. Van Dine*—Two complete cases featuring the great fictional detective.

THE PHILO VANCE MURDER CASES: 3—THE SCARAB MURDER CASE & THE KENNEL MURDER CASE *by S. S. Van Dine*—Two complete cases featuring the great fictional detective.

THE PHILO VANCE MURDER CASES: 4—THE DRAGON MURDER CASE & THE CASINO MURDER CASE *by S. S. Van Dine*—Two complete cases featuring the great fictional detective.

THE PHILO VANCE MURDER CASES: 5—THE GARDEN MURDER CASE & THE KIDNAP MURDER CASE *by S. S. Van Dine*—Two complete cases featuring the great fictional detective.

THE PHILO VANCE MURDER CASES: 6—THE GRACIE ALLEN MURDER CASE & THE WINTER MURDER CASE *by S. S. Van Dine*—Two complete cases featuring the great fictional detective.

THE COMPLETE RAFFLES: 1—THE AMATEUR CRACKSMAN & THE BLACK MASK *by E. W. Hornung*—The classic tales of the gentleman thief.

THE COMPLETE RAFFLES: 2—A THIEF IN THE NIGHT & MR JUSTICE RAFFLES *by E. W. Hornung*—The classic tales of the gentleman thief..

CPSIA information can be obtained at www.ICGtesting.com
Printed in the USA
BVOW04s1827170813

328662BV00001B/127/P